FLEET LANDING

WENDY GEE

ISBN: 978-1-953865-87-8 (Paperback)

ISBN: 978-1-953865-88-5 (eBook)

Library of Congress Control Number: 2025902739

Any references to historical events, real people, or real places are used fictitiously. All characters, incidents, and dialogue are drawn from the author's imagination and are not to be construed as real.

Books Fluent

3014 Dauphine Street

New Orleans, LA

70117

For Chief Mike

1

A sea of white college chumps jammed Marion Square like they owned the place. Trust-fund babies, offspring of trust-funded parents, sprawled next to other well-heeled students under the park's spreading oaks. Lamar could almost feel waves of entitlement rolling off them and resented their haughty attitude. After a moment of loathing, he shifted his attention to the street.

Seven anxious minutes passed before a Mercedes finally crawled to the curb. The passenger flagged Lamar and pushed out a paper sack.

Lamar emerged from the shadow of a downtown Charleston office building and poked his head near the sleek four-door's front window with forced nonchalance. "Can't believe you're running late for my last one."

Then, he caught the glint from a SIG Sauer pistol resting on the stranger's lap. Lamar raised his hands in a show of surrender, and a wobbly smile flicked the corners of his mouth. "Uh, sorry. You aren't who I expected."

The passenger snarled, his upper lip curling into a menacing scar running the length of his cheek. Tattoos coated dark, thick arm muscles like a painted sleeve. "Just do your thing, dumbass."

Once the Mercedes disappeared into traffic, Lamar thumbed a block of cash in the bag before fishing out the prepaid cell phone. A text message spelled out his final target's address. He crammed the bag into his backpack, hiked his jeans, then jogged past the knot of curvy coeds huddled around a food truck. The view would've been right nice if he wasn't so amped.

At East Bay Street, Lamar zigged left for eight blocks through a tidy working-class district running alongside the Cooper River. He spotted a container ship, the length of four football fields, gliding over gray and black undulations while making its way to one of the huge container terminals upriver. Once the road forked onto Nimitz Avenue, the city's northeast side lapsed into a ten-by-ten-block grid of pockmarked streets and desolate sidewalks. Scarcely two miles from the opulent Battery promenade, Fleet Landing was home to so many subsidized apartments and dilapidated row houses it seemed more or less dead—close enough to call the coroner.

Lamar veered off near an abandoned port authority building to catch his breath. He levered himself under the chain-link fence surrounding an ancient playground. Spikes of wild onions had replaced chalk lines that once defined the first and third baselines. A pile of used condoms stood in for home plate, and a bald tire approximated second. Lamar yanked a handful of weeds from an old on-deck circle, then toed the dirt with his boot.

He spread a leafy veil shrouding the termite-infested dugout, plopped on a rotted bench, and lost himself in a stew of sweltering summer nights. He was twelve again. Shagging balls on the crappy infield. Flinging darts to the shortstop covering second. The kid tapped the bag and tossed to first in one fluid motion.

Two outs. Four-six-three in the scorebook.

Lamar could summon happy thoughts about the hood no matter how far it sank. And baseball was in his blood. He'd parlayed a knack for turning the double play into an athletic scholarship. Come fall, he was headed to Clemson University, determined to forge his future through hard work. Something those chumps lolling at Marion Square could never imagine.

He raked his fingers through tight curls before spotting the seagull colony perched along uneven rooftops. Their beady eyes sent a sickening shiver of shame that prickled his neck. Lamar had never signed up for a daylight job and longed for his trusted accomplice, the inky darkness that'd made him invisible on all of his previous assignments. His gut flushed with acid and he hoped he didn't puke.

Storm clouds gathered into an ominous formation.

Better get going, he told himself.

Until the final job was finished, Falcon still had his stones in a wringer.

2

Sydney tucked a strand of chestnut-colored hair behind one ear, then poked her head through an open door.

"Action 7 News at your service. What's the hot lead you called about?" She laughed when she spotted her pal autographing baseballs. "I'm thinking that refreshing your collection of client swag is hardly worthy of scrambling the station van."

The modest law firm on the third floor of a converted four-story sail factory reminded Sydney of her newsroom cubby: crammed with stacks of never-ending business. She removed a folder from the guest chair and searched for a place to lay the darn thing without disturbing the guy's elaborate piling system.

Rob Noble, the Black community's most famous scion, tossed her a signed baseball. "That ball and file are for you."

"Will your souvenirs generate any bacon if I can hawk 'em online?"

"Doubt it." Rob grinned. "But the RiverDogs are retiring my jersey in a few weeks. I sign a couple dozen balls every morning so they'll have plenty to give away on Rob Noble Night."

Sydney slid onto the chair and dropped the signed memento in her purse. "Is that your big story? If so, I'm all in. But you could've told me over the phone. Now, you'll need to slip me a pair of box seats for my troubles."

As a former catcher for Charleston's minor league franchise, Rob had been a cinch for the majors until bum knees destroyed his chance at the show. Though, in Sydney's view, the guy couldn't hit a major league slider to save his Aunt Agatha. To everyone's good fortune, neither sore joints nor his inability to tag the crafty breaking pitch hampered his legal prowess. These days, he could've been a partner in any law firm in the city. Instead, he'd founded the Innocence Network, which served mostly low-wealth clients of color.

"I can talk baseball all day, but it's not why I invited you." Rob pushed the cap on his Sharpie, then placed the case of baseballs atop a cluttered credenza. He lumbered around the desk. "After striking out with dozens of petitions, peppered with a whole mess of motions that never made it out of the infield, I finally homered and wrangled a retrial for a good man holed up in Lieber."

Sydney raised a palm. "Let me guess. The guy serving time in our finest correctional institution didn't do what the state said he did. Frankly, I'm shocked." Her voice was saturated with mock exasperation.

"True, 'cept you didn't ask about his crime. I figured it'd spark your interest."

"Potential passion project?"

"Local history. With a side of moral indignation. And a villain you'll want to sink your manicured nails into—and shred."

"Ooh, I do love a promising trifecta." Sydney opened the folder. Clipped inside, a police booking photo showed a Black teenager with an old-style hi-top fade haircut, shaved on the sides and about three inches long on top. His features were arranged in a semi-tough-guy mask, but his eyes were wide and frightened. Her eyebrows shot up when she read the kid's charge. "Arson? Which one? I thought our rash of fires in Fleet Landing remain unsolved."

"The young man you are looking at is from a different era. But at least the current fire-setter is taking a break."

"Think he's done?" She knew too many months had slipped by with no arrests. That perceived lack of law enforcement response didn't sit well with the locals.

"More like a seventh-inning stretch." Rob worked his jaw. "We're bombarded with requests for claims assistance. One insurance company with a big stake in the neighborhood is stonewalling beneficiaries. Get this: they believe homeowners are responsible for the fires."

"Ridiculous," Sydney scoffed. "The amount of those claims wouldn't be worth burning their own homes. Besides, the fire department thinks some rando homeless guy is their best suspect."

Rob nodded. "But we're way off in left field." He pointed to the folder on Sydney's lap. "Nathan Sharpe was wrongly convicted of the big train station fire back in 1985. Steamrolled due to ineffective counsel."

Sydney was unfamiliar with the event since she'd only lived in the city for seven years. "Save it for the jury. I hoped you'd offer me a story with a sensational capital murder."

"You want sensational? Thirty-nine souls perished in the blaze. Nate was sentenced to as many consecutive life sentences. But I swear to you, the guy is innocent." Rob blew out a jet of air and brought his palms together. "This is Nate's last chance. No more appeals. No additional bunnies in the proverbial fedora. If I fail, the entire weight of our justice system will have crashed onto a blameless man who'll rot in prison. But my case is in the crapper. I really need your help."

Thirty-nine victims.

Sydney clenched her fist. She understood firsthand the toll that grisly memories carved into survivors. She lived with the ghosts from five marines who'd died during a firefight while she embedded with a rifle company in Iraq more than a decade earlier. That ambush sent her careening down a path of risky behavior, doubt, and pain from which she'd never recovered. Their names became her mantra: *Crandall. Reed. Slater. Townsend. Walters.*

Had this Nate fellow lost friends in the fire? Heard any screams as they burned? She skimmed the file without finding answers. Perhaps he'd been spared such awful recollections.

Rob seemed to understand her silence and poured a Diet Mountain Dew.

She reached for the glass, then brushed past the moment. "Must be a big ask if you're plying me with my favorite elixir."

"South Carolina's Appeals Court ordered our 9th Circuit to only reconsider the technical facts. Means I need a fire whiz with impeccable credentials to reinterpret the original case and testify on Nate's behalf." He pointed toward the folder again. "Had to scratch the city fire marshal from the lineup when I discovered the chief canned him. I've called around. Those experts are a rare breed."

"Arson investigation isn't something they teach in J-School, but I'm willing to fake it for you."

"You crack me up, Syd. Seriously, anyone legit come to mind?"

She drummed her polished nails on the folder. "I know a guy in Myrtle Beach who might fit the bill. Or he'll know someone who will. What's your timeline?"

"Thursday."

Sydney thumbed through the contacts in her cell phone. "Next week? Seems quick."

Rob shook his head. "This Thursday. Day after the day after tomorrow."

Sydney dropped the phone into her purse and attempted to pass the file back.

He edged behind the desk, waving his hands. "Oh no you don't. It's yours now; you've touched it."

"Then you better ask for a continuance until you find someone."

The corners of Rob's mouth sagged, a departure from his normal upbeat nature. "Trouble is, I have another case before the same judge assigned to the Sharpe trial. The solicitor has dragged her feet for weeks. I argued speedy trial and begged the judge to force the prosecution's hand. His Honor said he hoped I felt the same way 'bout all my cases, and placed Nate on the rocket docket."

"But you aren't ready for trial."

"Just need that darned expert and I'm good to go. Help me and I'll owe you double. I'll even pay off your ginormous french fry tab at the Blue Pelican Grill." Rob placed his palms together again to drive home the point. "Pa-leeze."

Sydney ran a thumb over the file's edge. Part of her wanted to leap from the chair and say "yes" in three languages. Rob had never steered her wrong, and the prospect of a deep dive into a decades-old murder-arson intrigued her. As for Nathan Sharpe . . .

The young man's frightened expression floated in her mind.

If he was innocent, and Rob was rarely wrong, that would be one helluva story. A potential forty-share—journalistic magic.

"Manage this right," Rob said, with a seemingly uncanny ability to read her mind, "and it'll add another Lowcountry Emmy to your scrapbook career."

"No need to oversell. I'm hooked. Besides . . ." She winked at the shelf behind Rob's desk loaded with trophies and plaques. "Look who's joking about naked displays of self-aggrandizement."

"One can never collect too much hardware. But seriously, Syd. If anyone can find an expert arson investigator, it's you. And if anyone can air a report convincing the public Nate is innocent, well, that's you too."

Sydney slid the file into her purse. "Challenge accepted. But no promises. Plus, I'm gonna take a hard look at Nate's story and decide for myself whether he's innocent. One of my superpowers is unraveling truth from lies and secrets."

"Read the file," Rob said. "It'll stoke your anger. And I'm confident you'll reach the same conclusion I did."

"Three days isn't much time. Let's hope this is a slow news week."

3

Lamar sprinted the rest of the way, slowing when he neared the shabby street north of Spruance.

He unzipped his backpack to inspect the pickle jar he'd filled with homemade napalm—a blistering concoction of toilet bowl cleaner and gasoline. Perspiration snaked down his spine as he zeroed in on his target, the respectable corner house at 1389 Kinkaid.

He clenched his eyes and felt his hands tremble as he mulled his options.

Like most janky deals forged in coercion and secrecy, nothing had been put in writing. Even so, Lamar had given his word—set ten fires for Falcon and nothing would happen to Mama. Nine fires into the pact and everyone had made good on their promises.

Lamar forced himself to take a breath. Then another. He'd invested too much to bail—with only one job until he and Mama were home free.

From across the street, he studied his target along with the ragged shack to its left. Lamar had always held a ridiculous optimism no one would ever be physically hurt from his fires. He'd been lucky so far and didn't want to jinx his streak. Despite feeling exposed and vulnerable, he pushed up his sleeves and knocked on both front doors—something he'd never had to do before. When nobody emerged from either place, Lamar accepted that as a good sign. Nevertheless, he emptied more than half of his flammable blend at the curb.

The two houses crunched together with barely enough room to wedge between. At the rear of the corner house, Lamar stuffed wads of stray newspapers under old chair cushions, lighting each wad with his Zippo. He lit the pickle jar fuse and tossed the container at the house. Glass shattered and a burst of fiery chemicals clung to flaky siding.

Lamar leapt from the back porch. He darted through an alley and zipped across the street. He skidded around the next corner, cut left, then raced past a half dozen scorched houses. Withered vines spindled their blackened timbers—indelible scars he'd seared into the neighborhood. One block later, he hurdled a beagle chained to a post, then slid behind an overgrown oleander hedge.

A geyser of orange flames speared above the rooftops. Lamar's nostrils filled with fetid smoke and his mouth went dry as the inferno intensified.

Damn, this is messed up, Lamar thought as he identified secondary and tertiary fires erupting from new sources along Spruance.

Fires he hadn't set.

Each more volatile than his blaze. His mind raced with concern. Why was somebody else torching this location? Competition? Copycat?

Lamar crammed his hoodie into the backpack and joined onlookers as the fires swallowed four homes and seemed eager to consume more. He winced as vinyl cladding melted off a three-story house with a portentous hiss moments before second-floor timbers gave way. Nearby, a two-hundred-year-old live oak sparked, then burst into flames, launching embers in every direction. A single glowing leaf wafted onto the trunk of an abandoned Chevy.

He plucked the disposable phone from his bag and jabbed in 911. Lamar's adrenaline spiked when he provided an address to the emergency services operator, hoping the burner phone was untraceable. He disconnected, then leapt into action. Pounding on doors. Helping neighbors flee their vulnerable residences. In those precious moments, Lamar didn't feel like the pariah he'd become.

Once the first fire truck arrived on scene, Lamar dropped back and ran west, negotiating familiar cracks in the buckled sidewalk. No need to avoid doorbell security cameras or weave a convoluted path.

Drug dealers and pimps in this part of town protected themselves with angry pit bulls and loaded Glocks rather than technology.

He rammed his key in the house door. A *ka-thump* from his pulse pounded in his ears when he caught sight of the woman in his kitchen. "Mama—" Lamar's voice cracked. Sweat dripped from his face and soaked his T-shirt at the neck and armpits.

Lorraine Gallivant parked a steaming iron on the counter near the sink. Tiny lines creased her forehead. "Why aren't you in school?" Her nose wrinkled. "And what stinks?" The blue-and-white apron she'd pressed cascaded onto the floor.

"Spilled some gunk. Chemistry class." Elaborate excuses ping-ponged in his brain. "Came home to rinse my backpack."

Mama skirted the kitchen table littered with Lamar's high school lab reports and huge textbooks. She reached for his bag. "I'll do it. You go clean up."

"No, Mama." Lamar squeezed the backpack under his arm and tried to ignore the hollow thud in the pit of his stomach. "It's my bad. Besides, I thought you'd already be at work."

"You're a stubborn young man, but I love you to the moon." Mama fluffed the apron as a trill of sirens flared through an open window. "Any idea what all the commotion is about?"

Lamar cleared his throat. "Probably some fool burning the hood again."

Mama draped the apron over her purse. "Same fool will do me a favor if those fires drive out the gang. We may be poor—"

"But we ain't trash," Lamar snorted.

She wadded a dish towel and threw it at him. "Don't mock me, child."

Lamar spotted a letter on the counter from another real estate agent itching to acquire their house. He'd seen dozens before and knew Mama was the last one on the block who refused to sell. He kissed her cheek and frowned at the envelope, regretting his contribution to the exodus.

"You ever gonna pocket the money?" Lamar held the unopened envelope for her benefit. "Escape Fleet Landing?"

"We're staying on principle. Besides, what darned fool is filling your precious head with nonsense? No one has offered half what our place is worth."

Lamar had heard rumors of big money if you sold out. A bolt of nervous energy made him tense up. "Hey, why don't I swing by the restaurant and walk you home this afternoon? After baseball practice. Around five?"

Mama shook her head. "Ten-thirty, please. I'm pulling a double."

"Aw, you work too hard."

Mama rested a hand on his shoulder. "You know how proud I am? Honor roll. Varsity baseball team captain. Full ride to Clemson. So proud." She blew him a kiss and left.

Their tribe was small, just the two of them. Mama was the undisputed Alpha, and Lamar admired the brute force of her idealism. He knew if he kept Mama safe, the pack was safe.

He was also aware that his illicit endeavors earned more money than her waiting tables brought in, so he helped ease the family's financial burden by handing over all the legitimate money he made mowing the school's ball fields. And he secretly slipped some cash he received from lighting the fires into Mama's cookie jar where she kept her tip money.

Even so, Lamar would rather return the dirty stash of unopened money he'd hidden in the hall closet and rewind the calendar. But since he could do neither, he vowed to put the cash to good use one day. Maybe pay for graduate school or a new car for Mama.

Lamar shoved his jeans and favorite hoodie into a trash bag. He stripped off his T-shirt, then jumped in the shower and did his best to scrub away any traces of his gasoline mixture. As he dried off, he imagined he could still smell accelerant on his skin. He dropped the towel, his shoulders wilting from exhaustion.

"This one was for you, Mama," he muttered. "I did 'em all to protect you."

4

Hot, hungry flames gobbled aged lumber despite dozens of Charleston's Bravest conducting a furious full-court press to contain the wind-whipped inferno's assault on beleaguered Fleet Landing.

Attack lines from first-due units snaked into multiple front and rear doors from hydrants blocks away. Second-due units mounted defensive efforts while crews from additional pumpers kicked in front doors and shouted for occupants to escape the blaze.

Special Agent Cooper "Coop" Bellamy nosed his Jeep behind two ladder trucks straddling Kinkaid Street and instinctively switched into arson investigator mode—sizing up conditions, assessing hazards, and estimating the debris field. To his horror, the tightly packed, century-old, wooden houses lining the narrow block formed a perfect crucible.

Coop ignored the blur of sirens and crush of hoses.

He sprinted over to a burgundy truck parked halfway down the curb and located a familiar battalion chief. "Hot damn, Paul. Glad you're the one in charge of this mess."

The ruddy-faced firefighter glanced between the conflagration, Coop, and a dry-erase board in rapid succession. "Chief Sinclair said she put the bite on ATF. Never imagined they'd send a hotshot like you."

"The chief is an old friend." The invitation also offered Coop an opportunity to address mounting problems with his estranged eleven-year-old daughter, who lived with his ex-wife in nearby I'On. Though, reconciliation stretched his imagination, since Haley wouldn't even speak to him.

"How'd you get here so fast?" Paul asked.

"I was visiting the King Street station when the callout came. A probie gave me a radio and directions. Said if I got lost, I should follow the smoke." Coop pointed toward the sky where the fire's murky discharge had coalesced into a thick black stain.

Paul signaled his assistant and tapped a vacant space on the tactical Assignment and Accountability board.

The assistant responded by shouting into his radio. "Dispatch, request all available units. And call the off-duty guys. At least twenty structures fully engulfed."

Paul straightened. "Damn probie didn't know you used to be a helluva firefighter back in the day. Before you crossed to the dark side."

Coop clutched his chest. "Back in the day. Dark side."

Radios echoed as an emergency services operator dispatched more apparatuses to the scene. "Ladder 101, Battalion 106, Engines 118, 202, 219, 303. Respond to Kinkaid fireground. Be advised, heavy traffic on the bridges."

"Enough about me," Coop said. "You have a real brouhaha on your hands. I don't usually arrive until the ashes are cold, but I'm still a helluva firefighter. What can I do?"

"Have the police seal the street. Expand the perimeter. And suit up."

"I'm on it." Coop flagged a rangy apple-cheeked cop, placed a hand on the guy's shoulder, then flashed the badge he'd tugged from his pocket. "Back these spectators away. Move the cars out of the street and off supply lines. Fire command needs a clean five-block perimeter to maneuver. And place extra cruisers on bridge ramps to clear a path for trucks coming from East Cooper and West Ashley."

The young cop lifted a defiant chin. "I don't work for you."

Coop acknowledged the longstanding cop-firefighter rivalry with the thread of a smile. "Son, now isn't a good time to be a jackass. Besides, interfering with a firefighter in the performance of his duty is a felony."

"Roger." The cop grabbed his radio.

Coop ditched the smile. In fact, now seemed like a really bad time for any funny business because this fire broke the mold. The inexhaustible Fleet Landing arsonist had tossed out his playbook with a brazen daylight number.

•

Lamar returned to school in time for fourth period integrated calculus taught by a woman he had high hopes of marrying one day. As the smoking-hot graduate student from College of Charleston dealt out last week's homework, he plopped at his desk and jiggled his leg so hard, he thought it might fall off.

Every fire stole something from him. This one claimed all he had left.

Setting a daylight fire had felt like tight-roping across a river of pointy knives—on a windy day. And Lamar knew for damn-sure positive other fools were to blame for the additional fires that engineered the blaze's monstrous size.

He worked the problem over in his head like a complex quadratic equation with several unknowns. Then, a stone-cold solution flattened him like a brushback pitch. Falcon wasn't about to let him walk away, and undoubtedly had hired the Mercedes bag men to set those extra fires. That made Lamar damn-sure positive of something else. He'd become an expendable pawn in Falcon's war on Fleet Landing.

He chewed on that emerging reality while mouthing an expression he'd heard Mama say a million times. "The trouble with trouble . . . is you don't know it's trouble—until you're in deep-shit trouble." He sucked in a gulp, then cracked open his textbook to the chapter on calculating the area under a curve and buried himself in theorems.

5

Strobing red and blue lights caromed off trees and buildings lining Kinkaid Street. Sydney's cameraman, Reggie, ignored the crude barrier formed by a phalanx of police cruisers and fire trucks as he bullied his way toward the massive fire. Wisps of jasmine and oleander emanated from soggy clumps bordering charred buildings. The aroma offered a respite from the pungent stench smothering the block.

Sydney prowled the jam-packed street while phoning her TV station. "We need to go live. This is an out-of-control hellfire."

"No way to hitch an uplink," said Olivia Hampton, Action 7's senior producer. "The Osprey is stuck in traffic."

"So, send another satellite truck."

"Y'all 'bout as helpful as—"

"Yeah, yeah." Sydney lowered the phone without disconnecting, distracted by two firefighters in yellow turnout gear hacking a roof with pick-head axes and a chain saw. Sparks fountained, then plumes of soot spit through yawning holes. She gagged when a sour taste slapped the back of her tongue. A heartbeat later, the house flooded with a ghastly orange glow and the fire inside went rogue.

Flashover.

Blistering heat had breached the attic. Sydney knew the temperature inside could go as high as eight hundred degrees. Maybe more. Enough to sear a man's throat closed with his last breath.

"Jump," Sydney screamed. "Get off the roof."

A ferocious whirlwind shot into the sky. Firefighters bolted from inside the house, jerking their hoses behind them. A flurry of flames raced along tinder-dry rooftops as an aerial ladder truck maneuvered its articulated boom over the burning house like a monkey reaching into a campfire to pluck roasting bananas from the coals. The stranded pair flailed beyond the boom's reach, then the telescoping arm vanished in a curtain of billowing smoke.

Sydney spiraled back to her worst day. Fleet Landing disappeared, replaced by images of rocket-propelled grenades hissing overhead, forcing her to cower into the pavement. She swallowed a scream.

Stray pebbles pressed into her flesh, and pinpricks of pain brought Sydney back. She shielded her face as super-charged hot air slammed into her. When she refocused on the house, she spotted the two firefighters clinging to the boom. Sydney fluttered her silk blouse to shake off hot embers and a mantle of ash, thereby erasing her brief foray into that other world.

"Sheesh, that's close," she said.

"Syd? You okay?" Olivia pleaded, still connected on the open phone line.

Sydney rubbed grime and sweat from her face before putting the phone to an ear. Her fingers flexed open and closed on the cell. "Wind is fanning flames along Kinkaid and Spruance. It's a real cluster."

She disconnected and hurried over to a man with sandy blond locks and a golden mustache. Despite boyish good looks, she guessed he was mid-thirties, same as her. "Sydney Quinn, Action 7 News. What's your name? Tell me what's happening."

The guy ignored her, preoccupied with adjusting the suspenders attached to his black Nomex pants. Reflective silver stripes circled his ankles. When his eyes finally met hers, they exchanged an unexpected spark. "Coop Bellamy. Stay back five hundred feet. This isn't a drill."

"Tuck me in your hip pocket. I know what I'm doing," she said.

"You're kidding, right?" Coop spoke with a swagger that signaled he was accustomed to being in control.

Sydney echoed his determination. "C'mon, you're only saying

that because you may be unaware I'm kind of a big deal around here. I've toured the fire academy. I'm familiar with PASS." She pointed at his Personal Alert Safety System device—a specialized distress alarm, relishing the chance to flaunt her technical acumen and impress the stubborn firefighter. "It's in your best interest to have a seasoned journalist by your side to keep all the facts straight. Imagine the possibilities."

Coop barked a laugh as he fastened a walkie-talkie and air monitor onto his flame-resistant gear. "We have a slew of rules prohibiting unofficial civilian involvement. And in my business, rules save lives."

Go ahead, underestimate me. It'll be fun, Sydney thought.

She planted her feet. "In my business, we value truthful information."

Their shared gaze lingered, and a silent understanding passed between them. They were venturing forward bound by a force stronger than rules—a budding bond neither had anticipated.

Once they arrived at the command post, Sydney tried to offer an olive branch. "Look, no time for semantics. I have a press pass." Then she pointed at the whiteboard where Engines 15 and 7 were labeled RIT in red letters. "What's this?" She pursed her lips, peeved for needing him to decipher the initials. So much for impressing the hunky firefighter.

Coop motioned for the Engine 15 captain huddled with his team near the front bumper. "This gal likes information. Give her a speedy tutorial on RIT. Then find someplace safe for her to report from."

The captain nudged Sydney by the elbow and escorted her across the street. "Rapid Intervention Team. Specially trained firefighters. Poised to rescue our guys if they need help."

The roar of fire nearly drowned out his staccato.

"How?" Sydney shouted.

"We monitor radio communications. And for this fire, command staged a second RIT. On Spruance. Because so many crews are deployed."

Radios snapped as the captain scrambled to rejoin his team.

Sydney crabbed back to the command post and slid behind a tree. Intense heat from the conflagration singed overhead power and phone lines. Smoke, thick as dryer lint, caked the air with defeat.

Reggie sidled alongside her. "I managed to grab the full buffet—guys cutting holes in the roof, sprinting into the fire, toting an old woman from her house. Your script gonna sync?"

Exactly what she'd expected.

A warm gush of admiration and relief swamped her since she suspected Reggie had gambled his personal safety for their story. She offered a wonky smile. "Never do that again."

"What?"

"Take unnecessary risks."

Reggie shrugged, then hoisted the video camera onto his shoulder. He filmed a firefighter drawing a crude representation of the blazing block, labeling Kinkaid Street on the north side as Alpha and the other sides as Bravo, Charlie, and Delta in a clockwise fashion. Command post activity offered great visuals for a supplemental B-roll. Sydney could add voiceover later, if needed, once Reggie edited the package for broadcast.

Coop caught her eye again and the edges of his mouth curled. He gestured to the rangy cop. "Handcuff those two reporters to a tree."

"Bad protocol, sir," the officer said. "Much as I'd enjoy it."

"Fatalities? Arson?" Sydney moved in, firing questions, without letting Coop's handsome features throw her for a curve.

He shook his head. "Command is focused on evacuating citizens. Containing the blaze. Don't you have a producer you can annoy?"

She enjoyed his warm grin.

He continued. "By the way, we're relocating in case this thing jumps Nimitz."

"If that happens, Tipton Terrace will be in the crosshairs," Sydney said.

Coop flipped his palms. "What's Tipton Terrace?"

"An ancient public housing high-rise. Hundreds live there. You have to help them."

"You bet. Lifesaving is kinda my thing." Coop spoke with unbridled assurance. "Now, please back away. And take your camera guy too."

"Oh, all right. You said 'please.'"

But before Sydney had a chance to retreat, spit from an automatic weapon pinged overhead. She dove onto the ground. "Shots fired! Shots fired!" She scanned the screaming crowd scurrying in every direction. "Where's it coming from?"

Bullets fragged into shrapnel as they splintered the pavement. The metallic odor of exploded ordinance jangled Sydney's nerves. Her brain began to nibble at the edges of her personal darkness again, so she massaged her temples with the heels of her palms.

More bullets zinged overhead.

A taillight on the command truck shattered and someone yelped.

Radio crackle cut through the gunfire, skittering the frenzied situation even more sideways. "MAYDAY. MAYDAY. MAYDAY. Three in the soup."

6

Sydney crawled to the battalion chief's side. "You're hit," she said, yanking off her scarf and wrapping it above a hole in his pant leg to slow the bleeding.

The chief collapsed onto his good knee behind the truck's wheel well, clutching his outstretched left thigh as he spoke into his hand-held radio. "All units on scene, standby for Mayday."

The radio squawked. "Command, this is Engine 8." A firefighter on the other end labored to provide his team's location. "Making a second pass. Bottom dropped out. Two men hung up in rebar. I'm pinned under a pile of floor joists. Send a Stokes. The K-12. More oxygen—"

The radio fell quiet.

"Eight, come in," the battalion chief shouted.

The Engine 15 rescue crew sprinted toward the apartment building where the firefighters were trapped. Sydney's eyes burned and she forgot to breathe.

After another long minute, a transmission broke the agonizing silence. "Oh, hell, Chief. Better call my wife. We aren't gonna make it . . ." The firefighter's voice trailed off. "No way—"

"Stay with me, Eight. My best darn RIT team is on the way. Everybody goes home tonight." The battalion chief pivoted to face Coop. "Evacuate everyone from the Tip. Send two crews."

Coop made a flurry of calls before pocketing his cell phone. He carried the wounded man to his Jeep and they sped off.

Sydney watched them go, then found Reggie crouched behind a fire engine, water sloshing in the curb behind him. She rinsed blood from her hands while he pointed at a teenage girl hoisting a semiautomatic above her waist.

"Who is she?" Sydney asked.

Reggie ducked as the girl flared her weapon in their direction. "No idea, but she's sporting an anchor tattoo without a rope. All the Fleet Landing bangers wear that ink."

"Why the warrior-killing bullshit? Who shoots at emergency personnel?"

Reggie popped with excitement, not his typical Zen calm. "Flashpoint. The fire's a catalyst for bad crap happening here. Like heavy-handed police tactics. Condescending politics. Unsolved serial arsons. Persistent injustice. I'm just rattling off the top of my head. Because—" He tipped the camera toward the kid. "She's kinda shooting at us, too."

The girl lowered the compact submachine gun to her side as uniformed officers assumed menacing firing stances, ready to take her down.

"Drop the weapon," a burly cop growled.

The rail-thin girl, maybe fifteen, reminded Sydney of the Iraqi kids hanging outside their base camp. Lawlessness had sprouted everywhere until marines plied them with sweets and trinkets in exchange for their guns. This time, cops weren't offering candy.

Shadows covered the girl like a murky tide. Sydney's heart sank with an inward shudder as the girl glared at officers, seeming to dare them to shoot.

"Damn you, drop the weapon," the cop repeated. "On the ground. Do it. NOW.

Another cop interrupted, forcing the girl to turn his way. "You haven't killed anybody yet. I'll help you."

The girl deliberated a beat. "What you gonna do for me? I lit this fire. Now, fireflies letting my house burn."

The cop frowned. "You started the fire? Why?"

The girl cut her head left and right before landing on Reggie and his camera. Her eyes ringed with desperation before popping off the MAC-10.

"GUN," several cops shouted in unison as they opened fire.

Blood mushroomed from the teen's chest, and she crumpled. Bystanders needed only a few heartbeats to calibrate what'd happened. Another cop shooting. In a poor neighborhood teeming with frustration and mistrust. The crowd surged, punching and taunting first responders. Knocking over street signs. Lobbing rocks. Uniformed officers retreated into squad cars.

Reggie caught a brick on his right temple and collapsed on the sidewalk. A chunk of flesh dangled from his scalp, and blood puddled on broken concrete. Sydney dropped to his side, then tore off a patch of blouse and gently dabbed it near Reggie's gash. From her experience, the problem wasn't the bleeding so much as the possibility of traumatic brain injury from the blow. "Stay with me, Reg. I'll get us out of this mess."

Sydney had no way to move him while the violent riptide spread around them. So, she did her best to shield him from further damage.

An engineer from a nearby fire truck shouted on the rig's public-address system. "Keep it together, people."

The crowd responded by hurling bottles, prompting him to launch a stream of water from the deck gun, slamming them onto their butts.

Sydney sensed a presence beside her and spun, hands raised, ready to punch or block. Then she recognized Cal Hampton, her producer's brother.

Cal, a fair-skinned African American, knelt beside her. "Come on. I know a way out."

"I won't leave Reggie," she said.

With a curt nod, Cal hefted the cameraman's limp body over his shoulder with surprising strength. "Follow me."

•

Coop thumbed the Jeep's radio. "Dispatch, I need a location for the nearest EMS."

An emergency operator responded, "Straight ahead, ETA less than a minute."

"Roger." Coop returned the mic to the dash and patted his wounded friend's arm. "Happy to say, it's only a flesh wound, Paul."

The battalion chief's face contorted. "Hurts like a sonovabitch. But I'm more concerned about the Engine 8 boys. And I need to pass command—"

"I phoned your assistant chief. He told me RIT reached 'em and hooked up comms to reassure their families. He also took command when the shooting pinned us down."

Paul drew in a gulp before switching the discussion from tactical to personal. "I know this isn't the time, but I'm sorry to hear about your breakup. Same thing happened to me a year back." His face pinched with pain as he rearranged his injured leg. "Remarried now, wife number three. This job sure takes a toll. Especially on the kids."

Coop gripped the wheel, uncomfortable talking about his family. "I hate being a part-time father. Haley and I didn't leave it too good last weekend." He reached for his lopsided BEST DAD EVER coffee mug. "I want to fix matters with her."

"Hope it works out," Paul said.

Three blocks later, Coop maneuvered behind an ambulance blocking the street. "I'll find you after we wrap. And I'll call your wife soonest." He raced around the Jeep to assist the paramedics. "Valuable cargo, gents."

Medical technicians lifted Paul onto a stretcher and slid him into their rig. One tech hooked Paul to a jumble of monitors and electronic gadgets. Another applied compression bandages and opened an IV drip line. Coop slammed the door closed and slapped the truck's rear window. The driver flicked on the vehicle's lights and sirens, then headed for Medical University Hospital.

Coop's cell phone vibrated as he dashed back to the Jeep. His ex-wife's image flashed on the screen. He reflexively slammed both palms against the steering wheel before answering.

"Are you crazy?" Cassie Bellamy's icy tone landed like an uppercut.

"Absolutely not. But I suppose you have evidence to the contrary," Coop said.

"Did you tell Haley she could opt out of visitation?"

"She said she wanted—"

"She's only a kid. She doesn't know what she wants. Dammit, you and I are the adults, and we can hardly find our way through this mess."

Coop prepared to tightrope their typical argument about how he never tackled his responsibilities as a parent. "I wanted to give her some space." He squeezed his lips tight. "Anything else? I'm kinda busy here."

Cassie exploded. "Your job always interferes."

Coop interrupted her tirade. "I won't let people down because it's inconvenient for you. You married a firefighter. Haley didn't have a choice." He paused to recalibrate his caustic tone. "Let me win her back, my way. I'm in town, so I'll swing by tonight and surprise her. We can sort it out over ice cream."

The line went dead.

Coop thumbed the radio. "Dispatch, where's Kinkaid Fire Command's new location?"

The radio crackled. "Nimitz and Knox."

"Roger, Dispatch. ATF One, out." He flicked a dashboard toggle for his light bar, checked the rearview, then U-turned using the entire intersection.

7

Back at the massive fire, the line between order and chaos blurred with dizzying speed. The surging crowd laid waste to things the fire hadn't already taken. Sydney hefted the camera, then buried her head in the small of Cal's back as they wormed their way ahead, elbows out.

But Sydney wasn't the type to keep her head down for long.

She fished a cell phone from her purse to call Olivia. "A mob of lunatics hit Reggie in the head with a rock. Cops shot a Black girl. And they're rioting."

"Is the fire out?" Olivia asked.

"There's a rescue operation somewhere too. At least three firemen are stranded. I lost contact with my new fire guy."

"Where are you?"

"Cal's lugging Reggie."

"My Cal? What's my Cal doing at a riot?"

"Olivia, focus," Sydney protested. "I have no cameraman, no feed—"

Without warning, a gut-rumbling explosion rocked the peninsula, setting off car alarms and unleashing a torrent of debris. Sydney pitched sideways and tumbled onto her haunches. Cal dropped to his knees, barely keeping Reggie from crashing onto the ground. Broken glass carpeted the sidewalk and tree limbs hung at odd angles.

Cal tugged her sleeve. "Dammit, that felt like a bomb."

Everything sounded fuzzy and her head numbed. Gingerly, Sydney fingered jagged shards spiking into her shoulder. Rivulets of blood trickled down her arm. She glanced east toward the river as giant plumes of coal-colored smoke arced into the sky. "I think it came from Tipton Terrace."

She wondered whether Coop and the other firefighters had managed to evacuate Tip's residents before the explosion. And what about the stranded Engine 8 team? Had the department's best RIT team saved them as well?

Sydney eyed Reggie with concern. The man had once been fit as a racehorse. Now, his damaged body hung limp.

Her mind regressed to their initial encounter. He'd sought her out while she prepped for her first live broadcast from Augusta National. Walked right up to her in the clubhouse and offered unsolicited advice. "Golf is a mental game as much as a physical one," he'd said. "Ask these guys about their pre-shot rituals, superstitions, and so forth. Get into their heads, and you'll establish your mark at this network."

"Oh? Is that all?" Sydney said.

Reggie shook his head. "Lose the lipstick and eyeliner. This isn't community theater." He smiled as if to soften his words, then handed her a tube of Jazz Spice lip gloss. "This complements your brunette locks and will play better during close-ups."

Next day, she found him in the production trailer as he was gearing up to walk the course. "You're with me, Mr. Baker."

Both skilled and ambitious, they hitched onto each other and never looked back. They moved from the Golf Network to Charleston's midsize market, hoping to one day be snatched by a major network or first-rate cable news team.

Reggie was married now—Regina. One kid—Rose. Everyone called them R-cubed.

Sydney forced herself to stretch. Her muscles were tight and throbbing. She quit testing her shoulder because it made the bleeding worse. Cal mouthed something she couldn't decipher. Her thoughts continued to wander through gauzy noise.

Reggie often spoke of hunting the perfect wave or framing an ideal picture. His description of the rush made Sydney want to grab a longboard or camera and join him. Hopefully, she'd have the chance one day soon. When Reggie was back on his feet.

Right now, though, she needed to compartmentalize.

Sydney helped rearrange her cameraman across Cal's shoulders, then signaled toward flashing lights a few hundred yards away. Her pulse jackhammered. "Let's move."

•

A shock wave from the blast caused Coop to jerk the wheel, nearly clipping a parked car. "Whoa," he groaned and grabbed the dash mic. "Dispatch, this is ATF One. What the hell was that?"

"Uh, I'll check—"

"Cancel my last. Patch me to the fire chief." Coop snaked his way through downtown streets choked with pandemonium. Four blocks from the new command post, he was forced to abandon his Jeep in a narrow alley. He tuned the radio on his belt and wrenched a helmet from the back seat. Coop slung an investigator's kit and one loaded with evidence collection materials over each shoulder. He moved through the alley onto Nimitz, laboring to find a coordinated stride in the bulky turnout gear.

"Coop, what's your twenty?" asked Chief Mackenzie Sinclair, Charleston Fire Department's top dog.

Coop stumbled as he reached for his radio. He leaned against a stalled city bus and keyed the mic. "Three blocks south of new Kinkaid command." He sucked in a noisy gulp. "On foot. You there, Chief?"

"Roger. Also, establishing second command post at Tip Tower." She paused. "Coop, it's bad."

He lumbered upstream, eventually gaining momentum, though the hard equipment case thumped against his back. On the next downbeat, he cradled the kit under his arm like a running back. Coop keyed the mic clipped to his shoulder. "That blast. A gas leak, right?"

"Hurry, Coop."

8

EMTs glided Reggie's stretcher into the ambulance and strapped him next to another bloodied casualty. He hadn't regained consciousness yet—a bad sign. But he was in good hands now. Sirens blared as the rig weaved up the sidewalk, skirting lookie-loos and other emergency vehicles.

Sydney and Cal crouched behind a fence to dodge the raucous crowd. "You saved us back there." She offered a polite smile despite pain vibrating through her shoulder. A paramedic had removed the jagged glass and draped her in bandages. "Bravery must run in your family. I know Olivia would fall on a grenade for me."

Cal grinned. "I'm *boss* on my console playing Triple A death-match PvP games. I guess any courage I muster online just sorta spilled out."

"I have no idea what you're saying, but it worked." She gave him a peck on the cheek. "Where did you come from?"

Cal wiped his hands on a pant leg. "My office is on Calhoun. I caught the alarm on my scanner and scooted over for a peek."

"Didn't know you took such an interest in fire." Sydney grabbed the camera and moaned.

"Nothing like that." Cal removed his expensive charcoal suit coat, yanked the knot on his necktie from side to side, then flicked open the top button of his shirt. "My company holds policies on loads of properties in Fleet Landing. One of only two local firms to offer affordable insurance for those with modest incomes."

Even a riot couldn't ruffle Cal. Capped teeth. Perfect hair. More *Ebony* model than insurance representative.

He bunched his shirt sleeves at his elbow. "Kinkaid, Spruance, Farragut, Nimitz, Knox—the whole of Fleet Landing's suspicious fire trail. See, I'm on a short leash with corporate, since insuring them was my idea. You know, the Black guy peddling policies to Black clients."

"I heard one firm blames policyholders for their fires. Yours?" Sydney asked.

He nodded. "My executives enjoy taking extreme measures to roadblock settlements. Today's mess is sure to cost me my job."

"Your company doesn't think—"

"It's simply about money. Corporate greed trumps altruism every time." Cal tossed his coat over his shoulder. "Want to grab lunch?"

"Rain check. I better film the explosion site. While I'm at it, I want to check on the stranded firemen. Cross your fingers we haven't sustained mass casualties."

Cal took the camera from Sydney and flicked open the viewfinder. "Olivia will have a conniption if I don't assist you."

They made a beeline toward Tipton Terrace.

Three blocks later, Sydney couldn't pull her gaze away from the apocalyptic dreamscape. The blast had sheared off the once-towering eyesore's face, leaving smoke to drift across a canvas of ruptured bricks and exposed steel girders. A massive portion of the roof had caved in, pancaking several floors on the northwest side. Pink insulation, vomited from the blast, dangled like tinsel from tree limbs.

Scores of screaming tenants filled the parking lot, too stunned to witness the unfolding destruction. A few marooned residents climbed onto balconies as tendrils of flame licked close by.

A teen next to Sydney shrieked, "Holy shit, a woman dropped her baby out the window."

Sydney followed the kid's gaze to a second-story apartment. Heat shimmer distorted the image.

"Nope," cried someone else. "She tossed a suitcase, but she's gonna jump."

A big guy jerked Sydney's arm. "Let's go catch her. At least break her fall."

"Yeah, TV stud-ette," said another, using the nickname media outlets had saddled on her following one big lie from the past, told so often, it'd become calcified as fact. "Just like you saved those marines during the war."

Sydney's heart thumped as loud as a drum line, but she couldn't will herself to act. An unbearable pressure built behind her eyeballs. She scrunched her lids tight, hoping to prevent them from blowing their sockets.

Another person tugged her blouse.

"Wait!" Sydney shouted an instant before a chunk of building crashed to the ground, narrowly missing the collection of would-be rescuers.

"Holy crap, you protected us," someone yelled.

"Saved our lives," shrieked another.

More lies. Cowardice mistaken for heroic wisdom. Soon, unwarranted applause replaced high-pitched keening. Sydney desperately needed to undertake something more constructive than holding hands in a prayer circle.

She crisscrossed through a broken chain of puddles and found a seared mattress slammed against the fence. She tugged it back to the building and positioned the thing to create a makeshift landing area. Cal tossed a second mattress atop the first.

Next, Sydney windmilled her arms in an exaggerated gesture to encourage the lady on the ledge to leap from her precarious post. She squealed as the fire inched closer, then shook her head.

Made sense.

Who'd want to dive onto a tiny pincushion without any safety guarantees? The woman's prospects were dicey, at best.

"You can do this. Jump," Sydney shouted.

A split second later, the woman hurled herself off the precipice and landed on the lumpy pile. She scrambled to her feet without injury, then threw her arms around Cal and sobbed. That small showing of appreciation propelled Sydney and Cal to repeat the effort several more times.

•

Coop arrived at the relocated Kinkaid command post, sucking wind. His lungs were as hot as a blowtorch. After a few noisy breaths, he peeled an ID label from a strip attached to his helmet and fastened it to the accountability board. He edged beside the fire chief, who was locked in conversation with a gaggle of anxious suits. Coop recognized Charleston's mayor, Boyd Wallace, from photos.

Chief Sinclair, a former All-American basketball star, towered over the six-foot-two special agent. "Coop, you did a great service moving my battalion chief to cover. Notify his wife?" she asked.

"No, ma'am," Coop said. "But I want to make the call. Paul and I served together in the Columbia Fire Department."

She signaled a pair of firefighters to help with his gear. "Tell her I'm sorry we can't be there in person for her, yet. I'll head to the hospital once we catch a break."

"She married a firefighter, so she knows the score, Chief." Coop eyed Mayor Wallace jiggling coins in his pocket. "It can wait until—"

"Make the call, Coop." Chief Sinclair smiled at the dignitaries. "Then we'll solidify your reputation with city leadership."

Coop shaded a few steps away and hit speed dial. Injury and death were constant companions for firefighters and their families. Even so, he hated sharing news a loved one had been hurt in the line of duty. He provided Paul's third wife with a quick rundown, then finished by saying, "He should enjoy a full recovery. I'll phone my ex. She's an orthopedic resident at the trauma center and can help you translate medical details."

After he disconnected, a radio squawked with the RIT captain's voice, announcing his team had safely secured the Engine 8 fire-fighters from their Mayday call. Coop forcibly exhaled, relieved Chief Sinclair wouldn't have to conduct any heart-wrenching death notifications. "Wow, that's good news." He faced the suits. "Now, what are your questions?"

Mayor Wallace erupted. "Tell me how this happened. In my city."

Coop said, "I'm here to assist Chief Sinclair with a thorough investigation of this fire and explosion. I strongly recommend you increase the threat level to activate state and federal resources. And impose a mandatory, citywide curfew to remove citizens from the streets."

Wallace bristled. "I came here for a briefing. Not be told what to do."

Chief Sinclair rested a hand on Wallace's arm. "Perhaps a voluntary curfew might give people the proper incentive to return home."

Coop intended to offer another strategic point. Instead, he chose an item that might rouse the politician's interest. He hated having to stroke fragile egos. "Hold a press conference. Show people you're in command. Encourage them to go home until first responders finish their lifesaving efforts."

Chief Sinclair said, "If we're going to nab the bastard who did this, do the press conference. Tell the public to send videos to my fire marshal division. FMD will help the arson task force."

Mayor Wallace glued on a smirk, seemingly fond of the presser idea. He scribbled a few notes on the back of an envelope before wandering away in search of a spotlight.

Chief Sinclair motioned one of her assistants to trail Wallace. She turned to another. "Phone tech support. I want a dedicated website, social media page. Anything our geeks want to corral all the incoming vid." She spun back to Coop. "What else?"

"How do you tolerate him, Chief?"

She rolled her eyes. "He's predictable."

Coop shook his head, then fired off an action list for the assistant. "Execute every mutual aid agreement to ensure full coverage. Secure nonessential utilities on the peninsula and call the water authority to increase their pressure to keep your lines charged." He ticked off a number of other items before eyeing Chief Sinclair. He wanted to ensure he was helping without overstepping. "Need me to call the governor?"

She waved him off. "The Tip scene isn't secure, but I'll drive Wallace over so he can be on TV. Who knows, maybe we'll get lucky." She winked. "One last thing. Still a hard-ass? Everything by the book?"

"Sure," Coop said. "Rules save lives."

"Except?"

"No exceptions."

"Good, because I'm putting you in charge of my fire investigation teams. And I want you to lead the task force. Start here at Kinkaid, then check in with Tip's command."

Coop never expected he'd find himself bogged down heading her joint team. "I think ATF planned for me to serve in strictly an advisory capacity. This is *your* investigation. I'll work with your fire marshal."

"Fired him two weeks ago."

"What about—"

"Already cleared it with your boss. He's delighted you accepted a leadership role." Chief Sinclair rubbed the nape of her neck. "I've scraped together five teams. North Charleston and Summerville Fire Departments will kick in more if needed. Keep me in the loop."

Further protest was useless.

•

Coop phoned Cassie to enlist her help with Paul's wife. After a handful of terse replies from the former Mrs. Bellamy, he pocketed his cell phone.

One of the firefighters who'd helped Coop with his gear emerged from the command tent flanked by four others. He stuck out his hand. "Captain Larry Bosco, deputy fire marshal. We're all yours."

Coop squared off in front of the city's assistant fire marshals. "Anybody have a problem with that?"

Bosco scanned his colleagues. "We're good to go. What's next?"

Coop wiped his brow with the back of his hand. Despite the scene's enormity, he was confident they'd draw on procedures ingrained from experience and countless training exercises. His mind ticked through a tentative inventory of supplies and people required for the immense task at hand. "We're going to need a lot more help. Any idea where to find bodies for reviewing video while we're working out here?"

"I can call up our student interns," Bosco said. "We've got a pool of college kids who'd love that sort of thing."

"Great." Coop smoothed his mustache. "If this fire is the Fleet Landing arsonist's work, we'll need a lot of luck, too. Every engine is pumping eighteen hundred gallons of water per minute. Multiply by two dozen or more trucks."

"You think the aerials blew away evidence?" Bosco asked.

Coop crossed his arms. "When it starts bad, it ends bad."

9

Coop assigned each assisstant fire marshal to lead an investigation team composed of four other firefighters and deployed them to the Kinkaid fireground.

Bloated raindrops fell as he rounded the corner of an abandoned port services building fronting a vast prairie of deserted riverfront acreage. From this angle, he spotted the carcass of Tipton Terrace and jerked the phone from his pocket to call his boss, the Charlotte Field Office's special agent in charge. "Hey, Dan. You tell Chief Sinclair I'd lead their whole investigation?" He winced at the edge in his voice. He'd meant to keep it light, since he respected the SAC's authority.

"We haven't spoken," Dan said. "How long does she need you? Our team caught a fresh case in Greensboro."

"You want to work out the schedule with her?" Coop asked.

"Nah, I'll put Kennedy on the Greensboro thing. A chance for him to earn his bones without you lurking over his shoulder."

Papers shuffled on Dan's end, and Coop didn't know if he should interrupt.

"Sinclair put you in charge, huh?" Dan laughed. "Mac sure has lady balls."

Coop thought his boss understood that field agents preferred the latitude of assisting rather than supervising. "Might be here more than a week."

"Don't screw up." Dan disconnected.

Coop pocketed the phone, then located the police department's gray-and-black mobile command post parked near Tip's fence line.

A grim-faced guy pushed open the trailer's door before Coop had a chance to rattle up the steps. Coop pegged him as a plainclothes detective, maybe six-three, with ropy muscles, dark skin, and curly black hair graying at the temples. Guys like him tended to act like real pricks around firefighters. Former rock-star quarterback who'd dated the head cheerleader. King of the squad room. The whole shebang.

The man surveyed Coop, seemingly calculating the threat the way veteran cops did. "Who are you?" the cop asked.

"ATF," Coop said.

"Prove it."

Coop smoothed his mustache. Nothing said badass firefighter like an awesome 'stache. "Show me yours, and I'll show you mine."

The detective worked his jaw, then flipped open his wallet, producing a gold shield. When he eyed Coop's gold-and-blue federal shield, he forced the world's faintest smile. The guy stuck out his hand. "Draymond Bernadino. Friends call me Dino. A few colleagues call me Lieutenant Dino when they're being cute. Or stupid. You decide."

Coop removed his jacket, then slid his badge onto a lanyard. Had to admit, he was proud of the impression the darn thing made. "Bernadino, huh?"

"Wasn't one of your choices," the cop said.

"Sounds kinda Italian," Coop mumbled.

Dino smacked a palm on his thigh as though he'd driven down this road before. "You saying a Black cop can't be Italian?"

Coop threw his hands in the air and shot a capitulating glance. "Okay, okay. Dino it is." He shoved his hand out. "Special Agent Cooper Bellamy. *Everyone* calls me Coop."

"Messing with your head." Dino grinned. "I know who you are. Lots of people counting on you. You as good as they say?"

"Not sure who *they* are. But if you want the guy the *New York Times* calls the foremost arson authority on the East Coast, then yeah. I'm your guy."

Dino tossed his head back and hooted. "The modest thing works for you. C'mon, I'll show you around." He propped the door open with his foot.

"Thanks, but I'll handle it from here." Coop climbed aboard, then spun back to Dino. "Free for a beer later?"

Dino flicked rain from his forehead and pushed sunglasses into a shirt pocket. "I'm partial to bourbon. Guys inside can give you my contact info."

Coop stepped into the command post thinking he'd made a new friend.

Inside, eleven uniformed officers worked computers lining the forty-foot van. City cops were clearly rewarded with better HQ gear than the fire department.

The captain in charge of the command post demanded to see Coop's creds. "ATF, huh?" The captain nodded approval. "How come you guys always drop the E?"

Coop knew what he meant. The actual name of his organization was the Bureau of Alcohol, Tobacco, Firearms, and Explosives though everyone called them ATF. The latter longstanding area of expertise had been formally added when they transferred from Treasury to Justice as part of the Homeland Security shakeup following the Twin Towers attack.

Coop shrugged his shoulders. "Dunno. You should ask the director."

The captain lost interest, so Coop persuaded an officer from CPD's technical division to launch their drone to capture fire scene and explosion site reconnaissance pictures. Images quickly filled the massive screen at their console. Another tech cop adjusted the contrast dial, resulting in enough clarity to read each firefighter's name embossed in reflective letters on their turnout coat's tail.

"Please record this," Coop said.

The tech supervisor flicked a toggle. "No prob. Besides, everything is captured on our secure server."

Coop dropped into a chair between the two technical cops.

He'd tackled plenty of scenes and enjoyed the challenge of determining the origin and cause of every suspicious fire. Yet, the Kinkaid fireground involved so much destruction, he expected investigators would find scores of dead bodies. And fatalities ratcheted sky-high stakes.

Coop cued the city's geographic information system on a laptop and typed in "1389 Kinkaid," the original 911 call's address. "Circle over the corner of Kinkaid and Farragut," he said, then examined the GIS's street view taken long before the fire. He compared it to the drone view of charred brick footings and a crumbling stone fireplace—all that remained of the structure built in 1915.

"Whoa Nelly," the drone pilot said. "At least two whole blocks are wiped out."

Coop searched the TV screen and developed a game plan. He keyed the radio to communicate with his investigation units. "All teams, 1389 Kinkaid is ground zero. Team One, interview first due firefighters for roll-up details. Team Two, document the scene. If you find anything unusual, mark it and collect it. Then gather samples. Basic forensics work. Team Three, talk to Detective Tate." Coop pointed at two other zones on the large monitor and the tech operator centered the drone directly overhead. "Team Four, poke around Spruance, about halfway down the block. There's a multiunit brick structure with unusual rear damage. Might find additional points of origin."

"Team Four, boss," the leader said. "Working our way to Spruance."

"Good to go. Team Five, coordinate with CPD officers. Ensure a tight perimeter for evidence preservation and safety. Then report to Captain Bosco, Team Two Leader, for further assignment. Plenty of time before sunset to complete an initial assessment."

"Roger, Team Five with the police," the team leader said. "Will we need to strong-arm them?"

Coop didn't try to hide a lazy grin aimed at the tech officers flanking him. "Cops always come around when things get exciting. I think this situation qualifies. ATF One, out."

"Want me to fly over Tip Towers now?" the drone operator asked, unfazed by Coop's sweeping rebuke.

Coop smoothed his mustache. "First, zoom in at Kinkaid. I want to capture people in the streets around the entire scene."

The drone operator dipped his device and refocused the magnification. "Anything specific?"

"Just collecting who's here and what they're doing. May give us squat. Or—"

"We might catch a hydrant-humping weenie-whacker whose mug we can submit for facial recognition. Then apprehend." The drone operator bowed with satisfaction. "You know—Exciting cop stuff."

Coop pushed himself up from the chair to stretch. "Something like that."

<h1 style="text-align:center">10</h1>

Sydney stuck her face in cool spray coming off a hydrant.

Hoses stretched for blocks as firefighters connected to every available plug and pumper so they could knock down the powerful blaze generated by a mystery explosion. Hot glass continued to blow, and a nasty brew of toxic soot funneled away.

Cal hit speed dial for the newsroom and handed Sydney his cell phone.

Olivia answered on the first ring. "Y'all safe? Where are you? What's happening?"

Sydney dabbed at bloodstains on her blouse. "The Tip blew up. It's a friggin' nightmare. Any news on what caused the blast?"

Olivia hesitated. "I sorta hoped you'd tell me."

Cal pointed over Sydney's shoulder at Mayor Wallace and an entourage. "Wonder what they want?"

Sydney crafted a sly grin. "Keep the camera handy in case he gets his shoes dirty."

"Who's getting dirty? And you haven't told me if you and Cal are okey-dokey."

"The mayor, fire chief, and a scrum of straphangers just arrived. It's way too early for a presser here." Sydney rubbed her sore shoulder. "Oh, we're fine." She disconnected and returned Cal's phone.

Menacing clouds swirled overhead as fat drops continued to fall. Sydney wondered whether rain helped or hindered firefighting efforts. She signaled a guy with an ABC camera, and they knifed toward the politician.

Mayor Wallace eyed the cameras and adopted a somber expression as residents swarmed around him. "This is an active fire and rescue operation. We're doing everything possible."

The mob booed his toady bromide.

He continued. "The situation is serious. I need you to heed the advice of our first responders."

The crowd hurled questions. "Did a terrorist blow up Tip Towers?"

"Why did cops shoot the girl?"

"Is it true that gangs are looting Meeting Street?"

"Where am I going to sleep tonight?"

Mayor Wallace patted the air with both palms. "Answers to all your questions in due time. Once we sort out what happened."

The ABC reporter shouted, "Can you provide the cops' names who were involved in the shooting?"

Sydney shook her head at the rookie mistake. Wallace would never throw any of his public servants under the steamroller without due process.

"This isn't Ferguson or Kenosha or Portland." Wallace's face flushed. "Taking a life is heartbreaking. Even the life of a citizen who demonstrated careless disregard for our police and firefighters. Nothing is gained by calling out officers who acted with courage and speed to quell the rising tide of disobedience."

Great speech, though Sydney worried the disaster and shooting placed an obvious strain on careworn residents. Chief Sinclair must have registered the same concern since she whispered in Wallace's ear.

He shooed her away with theatrical brio. "Several tragic events occurred on the peninsula today. Officers from police and sheriff's departments are canvassing, asking for help. I beg you to assist them by sending your videos to a tip line established for this express purpose."

"Any reward?" someone shouted.

Others lashed out. "You can't protect us."

"What are you covering up?"

"No cover-up," Mayor Wallace insisted.

The crowd chanted, "LIAR. LIAR."

Wallace clenched his fists and appeared ready to tee off on the next person who pushed him. "I'll ensure our task force maintains transparency. I appoint—" He snapped his head toward the tiny press pool. "Sydney Quinn as a civilian observer."

Sydney's jaw dropped, yet she didn't object. Any reporter would jump at the insider access she'd just obtained. She only hoped the additional work wouldn't interfere with her promise to assist Rob Noble.

The fire chief quieted the crowd. "My teams are aggressively fighting every fire. But we'll retreat if we aren't safe. Please let them do their job."

"And I'm asking everyone to clear the streets." Mayor Wallace spun on a heel and zipped to the safety of his chauffeured city ride.

Cal tapped Sydney on the arm. "Did you know he was gonna choose you?"

She shook her head. "Hope you managed to keep him in frame."

Cal rested the camera on the ground. "How does Reggie do it without a tripod?"

Sydney smoothed wet hair from her neck and turned away with leaky eyes at the mere mention of her injured photojournalist.

"Aw, c'mon," Cal said. "I didn't mean for you to cry."

"Releasing anxiety." She mopped her cheek with the back of her hand. "Every so often, it shows in liquid form."

Cal arched an eyebrow but became distracted by a drone whirring overhead. "Who does that belong to?"

Sydney reached for the TV camera and zoomed in on the ugly six-legged spider with rotors on each leg. "CPD. Wonder what they're searching for?"

"Or who?"

•

Lamar drifted through seventh period and nearly fell out of his chair when his personal cell phone vibrated with an incoming text from the Fire Marshal's Office: *Report to Moultrie Building when safely possible for intern assignment.*

He slapped his forehead with both palms.

Falcon had forced him to volunteer for the internship a few weeks back. At the time, it seemed like a good way to keep tabs on the evolving arson inquiry. Now, it felt like a net cinching around him. He didn't want to tread so close to the dragon slayers, and it would take every ounce of his wit to keep them from realizing he was the dragon.

When the bell rang, Lamar scribbled a note for his baseball coach before heading to the Moultrie Building.

•

By two o'clock, overhaul operations were underway at Kinkaid's enormous fireground.

Crews were tearing out walls and ceilings to ensure hot spots didn't reignite. Noxious gases, mangled rebar, and falling debris continued to pose real threats to firefighter safety. Coop was quite aware he'd sent his teams in too early, but he'd calculated the risk.

Meanwhile, he turned his attention to Tip's explosion site while working from the drone images. Since explosions followed the immutable laws of physics, Coop was confident he could pinpoint the seat of Tip's blast. His ability to prove it, for criminal prosecution purposes, would be difficult because ongoing defensive tactics compromised evidence recovery. Even so, every fire left something behind.

When he'd seen enough, Coop pocketed a flash drive, then hopped in the back seat of a patrol unit parked outside the command post to phone the fire chief. "How'd the presser go?"

"People want money from the situation," Chief Sinclair said. "Where do we stand?"

"Processing the scene at Kinkaid. Our focus is 1389. I'm hoping first-due crews shed valuable information."

"Such as smoke color? Anything strange? Multiple points? Familiar faces—"

"You are good at this." Coop hoped the chief would properly interpret his sarcasm.

"I'm giving you the finger right now."

"Happens a lot."

"What about Tippy Towers?"

"I'm thinking gas leak," Coop said. "But I'm contractually obligated to avoid guessing."

"Flipping you the bird again. Go on."

Coop trusted Chief Sinclair so he quit couching his words. "Easy to conclude the Tip's thing is accidental, but not how I see it. Gas leak explains the volume of damage to the ground floor. Liquefied petroleum being heavier than air. Though a single leak, intentional or unintentional, didn't rip the building's face off. And, if a bad line ruptured, it'd trigger multiple explosions as vapors ignited down the line. Doesn't match what I heard, felt, or saw."

"Can you think of any scenario where Tip's is intentional?"

"I've envisioned enough to fill dozens of crime novels. I figure, if I can dream it, then I have a good shot at protecting citizens from nut jobs. But I'd better save my theory until we're on a secure line."

Chief Sinclair agreed. "And Kinkaid?"

"Despite contrasting styles, I feel the Tip and Kinkaid are related."

"My former fire marshal never shared your unique imagination. He fixated on an unknown homeless transient. I never bought it." Chief Sinclair sighed. "We're missing something linking these fires. I want you to find it. Oh, Wallace assigned a TV reporter from Channel 7 to observe the task force. Be sure she doesn't do or say anything spoiling your case."

Coop wondered whether the reporter was the brunette he'd met earlier. If so, maybe working closely with a member of the dreaded Fourth Estate wouldn't be so bad. He cleared his throat. "Chief, I'm concerned that neither of today's callouts match the arson profile we were working from. I'll ask the police to lean on their favorite informants. Maybe we can jump ahead before the reporter gets in our way."

11

Action 7 News was located east of the Cooper River on a sliver of land cleverly called East Cooper. Actually, the TV station resided in Mount Pleasant, but the suburban community required further definition. A wall of rainwater splashed against four giant satellite dishes surrounding the peeling, green brick, two-story building.

A little after 2 p.m., Sydney tossed a wad of gum at an abandoned equipment shed that served as a haven for squatting spiders and flung open the station's back door. The stale odor of fried onions permeated the newsroom, a labyrinth of burlap-covered partitioned workspaces with more nooks and crannies than an English muffin. Sydney limped to her cubicle and rolled a suitcase under the desk.

She'd called Reggie's wife earlier, then spent the next hour at her house aimlessly collecting wardrobe items. She was prodded into more constructive action when she received a text from her Myrtle Beach contact that he was on vacation. That prompted a flurry of calls to ten statewide fire marshals hoping to secure an expert for Rob's team.

Then Sydney side-tracked for an internet search of the old train station fire's high points. Rob hadn't oversold. News accounts revealed the case was riddled with racially charged innuendo and supposition, though the verdict hinged on Nathan Sharpe's so-called confession. She wondered how Rob would dispose of such a pesky detail at a new trial, which was bound to open old wounds, reignite rumors, and frustrate area residents who'd moved on with their lives.

Sydney worked her way to the senior producer's desk, located on a raised platform jokingly dubbed the altar.

Olivia chucked a pen on her run sheets. "I sense a disturbance in the force. What gives, Sugar Booger?"

Sydney flopped onto the chair beside Olivia. "I promised Rob Noble I'd find him a fire expert."

Olivia's face knotted in confusion.

"You know, the Innocence Network guy," Sydney said.

"Oh, that Rob Noble." Olivia appeared still muddled.

"He's Nathan Sharpe's attorney. Rob's been assigned a court date this Thursday."

The producer and former beauty pageant winner examined her nails. "What's in it for me?"

"If Rob performs his usual magic at the retrial, Nate will be exonerated. Can you imagine? The guy's been locked away for nearly four decades."

"Suppose I'd grin like a possum eating a sweet potato. But you already have plenty to do with what's happening in Fleet Landing. And you know I hate feasting on the carcass of ancient news. Especially a story older than both of us."

Sydney ticked off pertinent points on outstretched fingers. "The train station disaster will be an unsolved crime when Rob proves Nate didn't do it. Besides, it's the kind of juicy human-interest story the public devours."

"Sounds like you made up your mind. What about editorial impartiality?"

Sydney grinned. "I'm famous for my verisimilitude."

Olivia shook her head. "I only allow your highfalutin vocabulary because you are number one in our timeslot."

"And I pursue stories that keep me on top. According to Rob, the entire prosecution was a fabrication that resulted in a faulty conviction."

"Fairness, huh? That's your motivation?"

Sydney jumped to her feet and braced her hands on her hips. "Ratings. Fairness. Ratings."

"Don't be redundant. Those Broadcaster Barbie pearly whites

only move the needle so far."

"How about this? No loose ends. The hero shines. Justice prevails." Sydney punched a fist in the air. "Friggin' refreshing."

"What's this Nate fellow got planned if he's released?"

"Haven't met him yet." Sydney made a mental note to have her name added to his visitor list. "If I were him, I wouldn't stick around. This city must be a painful reminder of all that he lost."

"He's lucky to have Ms. Verisimilitude on his side."

"My presence is mostly ornamental." Sydney cocked an eyebrow. "As I mentioned, I promised Rob I'd locate a fire investigator. Nate's screwed if I foul up. Know anyone with the proper credentials?"

"You gnawed the apple, so this one's on you."

"Any word on Reggie?"

"Still in surgery."

Sydney bit her lip. "I spoke with his wife. She cried for twenty minutes."

"I've assigned Eric to you. He's editing Reggie's video as we speak and will join you at your Tip's remote shoot at six." Olivia sent Sydney away with a kind yet dismissive finger flutter.

•

Sydney returned to her cubicle, anxious to dig deeper into Nathan Sharpe's story and take her mind off Reggie's predicament.

She came at field reporting with the sleek cool of a panther on the prowl. But Sydney approached factfinding with the frothing enthusiasm of a deranged tigress. She believed she held a duty to tell an honest and complete story. In doing so, she focused on the salient, rather than sensational, to maintain her unique covenant with the public.

Especially crime victims.

And the train station arson was a serious crime.

Sydney cleared space atop her desk and dumped three bags filled with a collection of clippings, videotapes, and photos Mandy

Reynolds, the station researcher, and her best friend, had retrieved from archives. She sorted the materials chronologically. The fire came first, followed by the investigation's public record including false leads, Nate's trial, and anniversary tributes. She also set aside any article mentioning the former solicitor, Boyd Wallace—the current city mayor.

Sydney subdivided the fire stack into initial reports and witness accounts. Once loose papers were organized, she arched her back, stretching sore muscles that had become angry from hunching over the desk. She let out a groan as she bent for her toes, shook out her arms, and then rolled her shoulders.

Sydney figured those newspaper articles served as the most expedient, albeit unofficial, version of an old story. She took pains to create a summary from the sanitized hodgepodge. Headlines sometimes ran with side matters, superfluous or of little investigatory value, yet titillating with morbid curiosity. The motherload of detailed facts would be in official police records, which she couldn't access without filing a Freedom of Information request that could take weeks to process. Undaunted, she possessed unique skills to read between the lines of news accounts.

Sydney made dozens of entries on a timeline including emergency response, fire containment, rescue operations, and the grim discovery of fatalities. As she studied the details, Sydney grew both fascinated and saddened by the train station fire's scale. Exactly like what she'd experienced with the day's fire and explosion.

She clamped her eyes and imagined the horror of being trapped in a burning building. No way out. Smoke filling nicotine-stained lungs. Searing heat overcoming tender skin.

A prayer. A last gasp.

Sydney reached into her bottom drawer and retrieved a battered shoebox tied with a yellow ribbon. The box contained wrenching reminders from her days as a reporter in Iraq. A marine from her home state of Michigan, for reasons she no longer recalled, suggested she fill the box with souvenirs before returning home.

She thumbed through snapshots of happy marines brandishing rifles, playing video games, celebrating birthdays. She gripped a pack of peppermint chewing gum, rock-hard and stale with age, as though it possessed magical properties. Then hugged an autographed Hershey bar wrapper and collection of letters from home.

Sydney ran a trembling finger across the heart-shaped military medal, with purple ribbon edged in white stripes. A shiny gold profile of George Washington was tacked in the heart's center. Her shoulders heaved. Then a dry sob racked her so hard, she doubled over. Same thing happened every time she held the medal, privately bestowed by her marines after being shot by a Taliban sniper.

She wet her lips and continued rummaging through the box until she found the platoon photo. A team picture taken before . . .

"Trouble in River City. We have five angels."

Navy medical staff referred to dead marines as angels. "River City," a phrase that made everyone's bowels curdle, was code to cut off communications until family members back home received notification through official channels. More than forty-four hundred American military personnel gave their lives in the Iraq War. Sydney knew only five.

Crandall. Reed. Slater. Townsend. Walters.

She reached for the platoon gunny sergeant's photo. Sydney had always suggested people imagine him as an Armani model in cammies, with a high-and-tight haircut—and a much lower income.

She blotted her cheeks using the back of her hand, then retied the bow on her shoebox and slipped it back into the drawer. Sydney scooped a collection of ancient VHS tapes under one arm and marched to Editing Bay 5, her inner sanctum, emboldened with a renewed sense of purpose. Latching the soundproof door, she covered the side window with its withered paper sash to avoid interruption and tuned out the buzz from a hectic newsroom. After feeding the first cassette into an equally ancient tape deck, she cracked open a fresh Diet Mountain Dew.

Date and time stamps were imprinted along the video frame's bottom edge. Bill Boerne, an Action 7 legend who'd passed away last year from a long-running battle with lung cancer, appeared on camera as the senior reporter. Sydney admired the classic filming and editing technique he and his photojournalist employed for their packages. Traditional long-range establishing shots showed the environment, panning to reveal the train station's exterior, then zooming for close-ups. Next came a jump cut to witnesses and survivors.

Sydney also fed tapes from local Channels 2 and 5. Duplication and innuendo ran rampant, and initial reporting consistently lacked detail. Facts were likely withheld by police on scene.

In the next series of tapes, the timeline advanced about an hour. Channels 7 and 13 used similar shots and talked to the same people. Their reporters probably worked side-by-side. Women wearing plaid skirts, high-waisted slacks, and frilly blouses wept as they fled the massive train depot. Men in stonewashed jeans and preppy tennis sweaters toted small suitcases as they jogged from the smoky building. Big hair, the result of over-processed perms, filled the screen. And the ladies wore funny coifs too.

Ah, 1985.

Add a boyfriend rocking a mullet wig, and that'd be the stuff of a Sydney Quinn retro party legend.

Fast forward.

A bevy of uniformed cops flanked the train station's main entrance, cordoning off the public and press. Inside, Sydney imagined police evidence collection procedures well underway. Employing tape measures and crime scene barrier tape. Sealing ash and residue collection containers for future scientific analysis. Filling body bags.

She straightened when a young Nathan Sharpe appeared on camera talking to cops. She recognized him from the police booking photo in Rob's file.

Nate led two cops to a shoeshine stand. Bill Boerne and his film crew followed them inside the train station. Nate pointed to where he'd first spotted smoke and flames. He said he bolted into action, clearing the waiting area and food court, helping people navigate to safety through blinding smoke.

In Sydney's opinion, Nate was short and scrawny as compared to the beefy cops sandwiching him. And to her trained eye, he appeared jacked, perhaps from the harrowing experience and frustrated by the cop's repetition. On camera, Nate recounted several unsuccessful attempts to pry open the smoking lounge, moving instead to a neighboring newsstand until he almost suffocated.

The police seemed eager to search his responses for inconsistencies and grilled Nate again.

"Anything unusual?" a bald cop asked.

"Anyone acting squirrely?" the second cop added.

Nate frowned. "Yeah, a guy—"

"What guy?" Deuce asked.

"Probably a firefighter. Maybe? I don't want any trouble."

"Can you describe him?" Baldy pressed forward, leaving little space between him and Nate.

"White guy."

Baldy rolled his eyes. "Sure. Lots of white guys in the depot."

The second cop spotted Action 7's camera and waved Bill Boerne off. "Hey, get outta here. This is a crime scene, not a sideshow." Deuce swung back to Nate while Bill let the camera roll. "Why'd that particular white guy catch your attention?"

"It happened so quick," Nate said. "One minute, I'm busy at my stand. Then, smoke and flames . . . Got sorta crazy real fast. I just clicked into action."

"Anything else?"

"I was scared."

"Thanks," Baldy said.

Sydney supposed Baldy hadn't meant it.

Baldy continued. "This is helpful. I'll need a formal statement. And my detectives need to talk with you."

"I want to help," Nate said.

Sydney read genuine sincerity in Nate's voice and demeanor. He'd cooperated the whole stretch. Nothing about him spelled perpetrator.

"Anything you need," Nate continued.

Baldy pointed at Deuce. "This officer is going to drive you to the station."

"Well, I guess. How long does it take? I gotta tell everyone I'm fine. They'll be worried 'bout me."

"A few minutes," Deuce said. "I'll radio ahead so they know you're coming. No waiting. First-class service."

Baldy gave a knowing glance to Deuce, who placed a firm hand on Nate's shoulder and guided him to a patrol car.

The tape ended there.

Sydney duped the clip onto a flash drive. The segment was shaky, with muffled sound and video blurred by lingering smoke. But Nate's lengthy questioning and frame-up, as Rob suspected, commenced only minutes later.

For Sydney, every great story started with its own magnetic pull. A force field so strong it glommed onto her with unrelenting force. Nathan Sharpe's story generated that reaction.

By all accounts, he was a man punished for something he claimed he didn't do. Nate's only crime seemed to have been *wrong place, wrong time*.

What if he hadn't saved people? What if he hadn't offered to assist those two cops? Would they have even focused on him? Sydney was free-associating an explanation that might not have been factual, yet the end result never wavered—Nate had been convicted.

She returned to her desk and uploaded the digital file to Rob Noble's email. Next, Sydney folded her notepad to a clean sheet and scribbled questions and tasks. She was bothered by missing information, discrepancies, and downright impossibilities. Reporters should have run those incongruities to ground while they were still fresh.

Sydney outlined her notes into thirty-second, sixty-second, two-minute, and four-minute script and video packages for future use. Compressing volumes of information into tight storylines was another valuable superpower for the hotshot TV reporter.

12

Coop arranged delivery of a rental truck for his teams to store gear and any evidence they collected. He also procured an assortment of floodlights and generators in case they worked past sunset. Once those details were settled, he hoofed west two blocks, weaving through a fleet of command vehicles, patrol cars, and fire engines still on scene. He checked his watch—three o'clock.

When he reached 1389 Kinkaid, Coop radioed his location to the Kinkaid Incident Commander, then removed his turnout jacket and pants. A gust slapped his sweat-soaked underwear, bringing relief. He slipped into Tyvek coveralls, and brought a breathing mask and helmet when he joined the deputy fire marshal squatting near the debris field.

Captain Bosco bounced with excitement. "Smell the gasoline?"

The faint odor of oxidized hydrocarbons was obvious to both skilled investigators.

"What about rubble?" Coop asked.

"Collected samples from here and over there." Bosco pointed to several numbered placards denoting evidence and comparative sample collection sites that dotted the place like a gnome campground. "Need more airtight containers."

"You've been taught well, Grasshopper. I have extra cans in my Pelican case."

"Want to act as my sous-sifter?"

"How long have you been sitting on that one?" Coop asked.

"Forever." Bosco heaved a tote to Coop. "Help me with the tent. The rain is relentless and our scene's a real mess."

They fit four aluminum poles into the canvas top's corners and jammed the poles into the ground over a specific site Coop chose to excavate.

Bosco said, "Megan interviewed the first due boys. They told her the flame was white-hot when they rolled up. Squirrely towers of black smoke. The entire crew thinks it started cooking on the back porch. Around here, based on the cement footings." He pointed at cones he'd placed to mark locations of probable walls and doors. "Fire jumped from one house to the next ahead of suppression teams."

Coop knew their investigative photos and drawings would be confirmed with the owner or former residents later. "Nothing burns hotter than a house fire." He thumbed his radio. "Sheila, this is Coop. Did you pull the deed for 1389 Kinkaid?"

"I did." The admin assistant forgot to release the mic key while shuffling papers. "Here we go. Owned by Magnolia Investment Group of Florence."

"And?" Coop asked.

"They're a subsidiary of Hilton Head's Atlantic Realty, LLC, operating under the umbrella of Peachtree Properties from Atlanta. The paper trail grows cold from there."

"Any humans involved?"

"Only holding companies. Further research will likely lead to offshore shell corporations. All in all, that level of deception is pretty unusual for Fleet Landing addresses." Sheila paused. "One more thing. School's out. Your wife dropped Haley off here. Said you'd understand."

"Ex-wife," Coop said with a tinge of wounded pride.

"Any suggestions for entertaining her?"

Coop scratched his head. "Get her to do her homework. I owe you." He disconnected and turned to Bosco. "Let's rock and roll."

Coop moved with quiet efficiency erecting a sifting station by laying the drop cloth on the ground and placing Bosco's five-gallon plastic drum on the vinyl sheet. Next, he inspected the sieve and tweezers from his kit, fresh gloves, and an array of tin cans, small bottles, and plastic bags. He placed a business card near the gear for basic identification reference and snapped several photos.

Typically, Coop hunted for telltale points of origin by finding burn patterns: U- or V-shaped scorch marks outside the fire's burn path. Then he'd work backward, examining every charred item in the path. However, when an entire building burned to the ground, determining where the fire originated became extremely difficult and he often relied on witness accounts such as first responders.

Coop lowered onto his knees to scrutinize 1389 Kinkaid's debris field. He pointed at the scorched footing blocks. "If the fire started in this area and burned as hot as we think, it consumed everything before crews could hit it with water."

"Squirting the wet stuff on the red stuff," Bosco said with a grin. "Days like this, I sort of miss being at the firehouse." He dipped a hand trowel into the soot and emptied it into the sieve mounted atop the drum.

Coop carefully moved the ash in the sieve from side to side with his tweezers, scavenging for a golden needle in the soggy haystack. "Working the front line is great. But I think this is more fun."

The two men settled into a rhythm, and after an hour of painstaking sifting and cataloging, Coop recovered two chunks of clear glass, each no larger than a quarter. He cracked open the hardened case where he stored technical gear, then removed a portable gas chromatograph from its foam-fitted nest.

"Wow, a portable GC," Bosco said, wide-eyed.

"Standard ATF equipment. Not as fancy as what the lab rats use, but it's great in the field. Play your cards right, and I'll leave it with you once we clear this investigation."

The GC was one piece of specialized high-tech do-da in a fire investigator's arsenal of professional paraphernalia. Investigators like Coop depended mostly on science to determine the origin and cause of fires, yet benefited from intuition and luck to solve complex puzzles. High-tech do-das improved his luck.

Coop swiped the GC's wand over the glass chunks until blips and peaks emerged on the device's screen. He pulled a short stack of plastic cards from the case depicting common element exemplars and compared the results. "Chemical signature indicates gasoline. Along with lots of trace elements in the mix. Accelerant use is highly probable and matches what we smelled and what the first-due crew spotted."

"Glad we can offer the crime lab something besides ash," Bosco said.

Radios squelched. "Fire units, be advised. Reports of continued looting on King and Market Streets. Avoid area if practical."

"Man, this day keeps getting interesting," Bosco said.

Processing the scene was exhausting work. Coop stood and pain stabbed his lower back from being hunched over. He was hungry and wished he could join his daughter for ice cream. He glanced at his watch. He'd opened his official investigation four hours ago.

•

Sydney left the editing bay and reconnected with her colleagues in the newsroom.

Olivia arranged a turkey sandwich and cold Dew on her desk. "Fowler Jenkins called."

"He's one of the fire marshals I phoned for Rob. Any message?" Sydney wolfed into the sandwich.

"Want me to omit his obscenities?" Olivia asked.

Sydney nodded, mouth full.

"Then, no message."

"Any other callbacks?"

"Everyone on your list." Olivia riffled the message slips. "Most declined your request. Some laughed. Two wanted the work but couldn't spare the time."

"That blows." Sydney finished the sandwich and drained the Dew. "What about Reggie?"

Olivia manufactured a smile. "Nothing new."

Sydney absently juggled apples from Olivia's bowl.

When she bobbled the fruit, her producer didn't flinch. "See, you aren't as badass as you think you are."

Mandy bounded over, wearing a skirt and blouse dyed in a riot of colors. "Olivia said you were looking for an arson expert. Think I found one."

Sydney adored her pal's peculiar tastes despite the obvious fashion risk. "From your never-ending family tree?"

Mandy tilted her head. "I phoned the fire chief's office. Asked who was investigating today's arson since the fire marshal is gone. The information officer told me they have an ATF agent on-site. Special Agent Cooper Bellamy. Tops in his field. And handsome, too." Mandy handed Sydney a photo.

She recognized the man from the Kinkaid Street inferno and churned with excitement.

"He's also heading the task force," Mandy added. "Since you're in that group, you play nice. Bat an eyelash. Presto. He's on your team."

Sydney pushed her lips in and out. It'd be fun working with him since he'd given her the once-over—twice. "When have I ever had to bat an eyelash?" Without waiting for a response, she asked, "Any idea where to find him?"

Before Mandy answered, Sydney's cell phone vibrated with a text from the very Special Agent Bellamy: *I'm told you are assigned to the task force. Meet at Moultrie Building, 7 p.m.*

•

Coop departed the Kinkaid fireground, leaving further evidence collection in his team's capable hands. He spent the next hour at the fire chief's office scanning old files from which he crafted a solid circumstantial case against two local gangs called the 843Z and Rivertown Academy. He hoped to tie either or both of them to a torch-and-repair rip-off similar to schemes he'd worked in the

Mid-Atlantic region.

Coop concluded the former fire marshal had clearly misread the gang's connection to the spate of nuisance fires hounding Fleet Landing. Instead, he'd targeted nearly twenty homeless people.

When that strategy didn't pan out, the former fire marshal shifted focus to who he deemed were disgruntled city employees. He'd cast aspersions on dozens of men and women from public works, parks and rec, and school bus drivers. After those accusations fizzled, the employees became disgruntled, all right.

Coop phoned Detective Tate, of the Charleston Police Department, to discuss his scam theory. The detective agreed the theory had merit since Fleet Landing attracted con artists like fly-paper. Police would start rounding up as many gangbangers for interrogation as possible. Coop knew he lacked the patented federal law enforcement smugness to pretend he'd solved everything so quickly. But nabbing bangers served as a good first move in his effort to stop the fires.

Next, he phoned his ATF boss. "What does the Bureau have on gangs and guns in this area?"

"Any names for me?" Dan asked.

"Try eight-four-three-zee. Local street gang named after the area code."

The special agent-in-charge keyed into his computer. "Oh yeah, they're bad to the bone with a laundry list of prior felonics. Also have plenty of warrants on some affiliates. I'll email the docs in case you can serve them."

"What about Rivertown Academy?" Coop asked.

After a quick file search, Dan responded, "They're clean."

13

The Fire Marshal Division's student interns commandeered the Moultrie Building's second-floor conference area so they'd have a large enough place to work. Didn't take long for the room to fill with empty coffee cups, soda cans, and pizza boxes. A musty odor of pepperoni collided with Axe deodorant, while a song by the Chainsmokers pulsated from somewhere amid the throng.

Lamar watched four college chumps argue over protocols for culling a tsunami of citizen videos. Two other teams, assigned to organize and analyze photographs from the same host of sources, operated without hang-ups.

Knob, a freshman from the Citadel, asserted himself. "Before we slice and dice, did techs back up the files?"

"Hope so," said a redheaded marketing major wearing a Charleston Southern University T-shirt. "I don't want to go to jail for tampering with evidence."

Lamar's gut churned thinking of potential incriminating videos of him. If so, he'd be the one tampering with evidence.

Knob seemed prepared to take charge when the firefighter supervising Lamar's team intervened. "Chill, fellas. Our files are secure on multiple servers. You're working with dupes. Sort the files into two main areas—"

"Kinkaid and Tipton Terrace," Knob stated as though he was the only intern with that obvious information.

"Tip," Lamar offered, lathered with a huge dose of arrogance.

"Is there a difference?" Red asked.

"Depends."

Knob puffed out his chest. "On what?"

Lamar drew himself up to his full six-feet-two. Though initiating a fight with Knob, a chubby excuse for a chump, was the last thing he wanted. "Simply telling you what the locals call the place. Hoping to give y'all a little cred."

The firefighter said, "Kinkaid and the Tip are a good start. Footage may overlap. But once the files are organized by those two firegrounds, we'll parse them with additional filters. Stay hydrated and tell Sheila when you need to leave. She'll keep an eye on the clock for you." The firefighter turned away, then spun back. "Lamar, your neighborhood knowledge is exceptionally valuable. Come with me."

"Looks like homie is teacher's pet," Knob muttered.

Lamar pretended he hadn't heard the wisecrack. He slung his backpack over a shoulder and scaled the stairs two at a time to the third floor, where Charleston Fire Department's Fire Marshal Division comingled with other city agencies.

The firefighter slid a keycard across the RFID reader to unlock the corridor door. He pointed to an empty cubicle crammed full of blueprints, fire code manuals, and crumpled Post-it notes. "Cue up the computer while I find our detective."

Lamar cracked his knuckles and forced himself to act casual, though he was amped from the verbal sparring match with Knob. He hoped gaining access to the third floor afforded him keys to the online kingdom.

Lamar pressed the power button on the computer and slid a stack of blueprints to the credenza while waiting for the old system to show signs of life. He swept the Post-its into a trash receptacle, then pawed through desk drawers until he found a clean pad of paper and a working pen.

A police detective, wearing the inscrutable expression of a veteran cop with his prey in the crosshairs, emerged from the conference room. Heat rose in Lamar's cheeks and he shot off the chair like a bottle rocket.

The detective cleared his throat. "You the intern who's gonna solve my case?"

Lamar reflexively nodded as he shook the detective's out-stretched hand.

"Good, because the people who've worked on this for months are relying on you." The cop turned to the firefighter and grinned. Nothing jovial. More of a fingers-in-your-chest sort of grin.

"What's next?" Lamar's voice cracked.

The detective eyed Lamar from head to toe. "I'm Detective Brody Tate, Charleston Police Department. What I'm about to tell you can never be repeated. We clear?" The cop hiked his foot and rested it on the desk to retie his boot. A heavy-duty Velcro band held a leather ankle holster for his backup weapon. The Ruger pistol fit snugly against the cop's leg.

If the action was meant to intimidate, it worked.

Detective Tate said, "We have reason to conclude the 843Z are involved in Fleet Landing's fires. Familiar with any 843Z?"

"You asking if I'm in a gang?" Lamar said. "Because my jam is second base for Burke High School's baseball team. My mama waits tables at Tyrell's. I'm what some might call an upstanding member of my community."

Detective Tate clapped his hands. "Nice resume. But you didn't answer my question."

Lamar spoke with unadulterated exasperation. "I ain't in no gang. Everyone from the hood isn't ganged up." He crammed his hands in his front pants pockets. "If I'm a bad fit for your project, I'll go back downstairs and sort videos with the college chumps."

Detective Tate rubbed his chin. "Let me reword it to soothe your delicate sensibilities. Do you know about the 843Z?"

Lamar bobbed his head. "They're into drugs and hookers. Real badass. Rather shoot first." A flash of concern crossed Lamar. "Don't ask me to wear a wire."

The cop chuckled. This time for real. Genuine amusement. "A

wire? This isn't reality TV, kid. Relax. I only hoped to avoid a lengthy explanation." Detective Tate signaled the firefighter, who dropped two humongous notebooks on the desk. "These are old-school mug-shot books. I want you to tag anyone you recognize."

Lamar peeled back the first binder's cover. "What'd they do?"

"Don't worry about their bad behavior. Page through and stick a Post-it on the faces you're familiar with." Detective Tate turned to the firefighter. "Shout when he's finished."

Lamar sank into the chair and flipped a few pages in the first binder. He quickly calculated the extent of his assignment, four faces per page, each face shown from the front and side, about fifty to a hundred pages in each notebook. He figured the books had to include punks from Colleton and Dorchester counties, or even from out of state. He wondered how many of those fools were connected to Falcon.

Halfway through the first binder, Lamar spotted the pencil-mustached mug of D'Angelo Hines. D-Jazz, as the gang called him, went to prison a while back for food stamp fraud. After doing a nickel at Lieber Correctional, he'd fallen off the grid. Then he came out of hiding about the time Lamar hooked up with Falcon. Lamar slapped a yellow sticky over D-Jazz's face without regret. Everyone in Fleet Landing was familiar with his misdeeds.

A few pages later, the mugshot of a banger named Robert Moses, also known as Ice, sneered back at him. Lamar recognized Ice as the Mercedes passenger who'd called him a dumbass earlier that day. And he probably lit the extra fires on Spruance too. Maybe even caused the Tip explosion.

Who's the dumbass now? Lamar thought.

Lamar poked the photo, though he opted not to tag him. Instead, he'd hold a little in reserve.

After he finished the first binder, Lamar stretched his arms and his stomach growled. He waved for the firefighter. "I missed out on pizza downstairs. Any chance I can grab a slice?"

"No problem, kid."

Lamar raced down one flight to the intern area. He piled three slices with mushrooms on a napkin, grabbed a cold soda from the ice chest, and slipped the can into his pants pocket. He spun to return upstairs, but the flabby snowflake, Knob, blocked his path.

"What's up, bro?" Knob puffed his chest. "You slumming? I thought they served filet mignon on the third floor."

"You thought wrong." Lamar kept his cool even though the pugnacious twit had a punchable face. "And I ain't your bro. Why you gotta mess with me?"

Knob stepped back and threw his hands in the air. "Didn't mean to hurt your feelings. Black lives matter and all."

Red stepped between the two. "You're such a douche, Dwayne. Lamar's doing his civic duty. Same as us."

Knob brushed past. "Whatever."

Red offered a sympathetic smile. "If it's any consolation, the guy's a jerk to everyone. Sorry—"

"Don't apologize for him." Lamar took a step back and dialed down the testosterone buzz.

Red eyed the pizza in Lamar's hand. "Seriously, no filet?"

Lamar shook his head. "How's the vid scrub going?"

"Lots of shaky footage. We created a storyline mashup syncing time stamps from both fire sites. What about you?" Red pointed upstairs.

"This'll sound kinda lame, but I'm not allowed to say. But thanks for having my back, bro." Lamar stuck out his fist to dap. In the hood, knocking fists was a genuine form of respect.

Red returned the fist bump with a grin that spread across his entire face.

The firefighter was waiting at the third-floor security door. Lamar hurried to his workstation and flicked the tab on the Pepsi can a couple of times, thankful it didn't fizz over when he popped the top. He gobbled the pizza and wished he'd grabbed a whole pie.

Lamar opened the second government-issue, three-ring binder and froze. Right there on the first page—a photo of Falcon standing in the mayor's office with a few other dudes Lamar didn't recognize. Was the task force surveilling Falcon or someone else in the picture?

Lamar breathlessly scanned the rest of the binder eyeing laminated photos and lab analyses of fires—ten of which he'd set. His vision blurred from a rush of blood. He slammed the notebook closed and contemplated whether he'd be able to drop a dime on Falcon without becoming collateral damage. He considered whether to put a Post-it on Falcon's face; then he realized this wasn't a mugshot book.

He signaled the firefighter and passed him the toxic notebook. "This binder contains evidence stuff."

The firefighter frowned. "Let me check with Detective Tate."

Lamar jammed his hands in his front pockets. "I'll hang here."

14

A little before six o'clock, Sydney and Cal squatted on the wet curb in Tip's parking lot, leaning their backs against each other. The air reeked of angry charcoal as white wisps of lingering smoke spiraled overhead.

The blaze had ripped through three dozen homes along Kinkaid and Spruance streets, while chewing roofs and gutting apartments on Nimitz. Melted vinyl siding draped like wet noodles over blackened air conditioning units dangling from broken windows. Troublemakers, hoping to inflict further damage on the shattered neighborhood, mingled with shell-shocked onlookers and displaced residents.

Mandy rounded the satellite truck everyone called The Osprey, an E-350 panel van emblazoned with Action 7 News and stylized eagle logos on all sides. She surveyed Sydney with concern. "You ready for your stand-up?"

Sydney stared at the notebook crushed in her palm. "How's Reggie doing?"

"Out of surgery and in intensive care. Doctors drilled a hole in his head . . ." Mandy started to giggle. More of a nervous little chortle.

Sydney threw an arm around her bestie. "I know what you're thinking. Reggie doesn't need another hole in his noggin."

Mandy pinched her top lip. "I'm sorry I laughed. It's unimaginable what you've been through."

Sydney deflected. "Cal saved Reggie's life. Matter of fact, he saved several lives today."

Mandy spun Cal by the shoulders and enveloped him in a hug.

Cal dug a line in the mud with the heel of his loafer. "Only keeping pace with Sydney. She caught a woman who jumped from the second story."

Mandy's lips parted in shock. "No biggie. She does card tricks, too. I'm surprised your sister didn't mention it." She blotted her puffy cheeks with a sleeve. "Syd, you're live in less than ten minutes."

Julia Mayfair, the senior reporter from Eyewitness 13, moseyed over. "Oh, Syd. What have you uncovered? I'm coming up empty."

"Just another day on location."

"C'mon, I need your help."

Sydney pointed toward the Tip. "Bad juju."

Julia stomped a foot. "You are going about this wrong. It's not a sin to covet thy competition's notes. How do you think I made it through J-school? You probably did all the homework."

"Your point?" Sydney asked.

"Think of the spare time you'll have if we team up. You won't be bogged down prepping for interviews. Watching video."

"Time I could spend on hair and nails. Like you?"

Julia handed her a mirror. "Couldn't hurt."

Sydney gagged at her reflection. Tiny red marks scarred her face and arms. Her silk blouse was speckled with burn holes and stained with sweat and blood. Dingy gauze hugged her right shoulder. And the ratty hair bundled atop her head sprouted wisps in every direction.

Sydney eyed Julia, her friend and nemesis. The woman enjoyed cover-ready makeup and a perfectly coifed mane of strawberry blonde hair folded over one shoulder. "Give me a sec."

Sydney ducked into the Osprey, changed her blouse, then sponged her face and hands with a wad of moist disinfectant wipes. She dabbed on her trademark Jazz Spice lip gloss before running a comb through tangles of long hair.

She turned to Eric. "Spool the first two video clips for my voiceover. How long are they and how much time is allotted for the piece?"

Eric plopped at the engineer's console. "Three whole minutes.

The first video is the gun victim. Run time is forty seconds. I created thirty-five seconds of fire scene stuff for your second VO. I'll loop the feed if you need more film." He fast-forwarded through the two clips while Sydney strummed her fingertips along the spiral of her reporter's pad.

"No loops. I'll give you a cue to shoot live. Reggie likes to start wide, then push in for my close-up. Good for you?"

"Whatever you say. Let me send these to Olivia. You prefer a lapel or stick mic?" Eric typed as he spoke, his hands streaking across the keyboard, transmitting edited video footage to the TV station's control room.

Sydney pushed a wireless interruptible fold-back earpiece, or IFB, into her right ear and pulled a strand of hair forward to cover the communications bud. "Lapel inside, stick outside. Mandy is nabbing a firefighter for our live close."

They moved outside to where Eric had positioned the camera. Sydney glanced at her notes from an interview with the task force's hunky lead detective, certain her information scooped other stations. Sydney eyed Julia, who'd folded her hands into a prayer position, the closest she'd ever come to begging.

Sydney tossed Julia a less than juicy bone. "Some people think the fire led to the Tip explosion. But a law enforcement official indicated that's not true."

Julia snorted, "Duh—"

"Okay, feast on this." Sydney jotted something on her pad and handed the note to Julia. "It's the name of the girl shooter responsible for the riot. You owe me."

"Of course, Sugar. Why else would you keep me around?" Julia took off running toward her camera operator.

Sydney took her mark.

"Glad you could make it," Olivia said. Her voice transmitted from her seat in the control room via the earbud. "I didn't think y'all were gonna be on time. Let's roll title sequence and logo."

After the anchor offered a tease line, Sydney received her cue. She recapped the day's highlights. Fast-moving fire. Riot. Shooting. Explosion. She concluded her first segment by saying, "Police charged forty rioters with disorderly conduct and are holding them at the detention center. Back to you." She signaled Mandy off camera to toss a Diet Mountain Dew, which she chugged like rocket fuel, then lobbed the empty back to her pal.

The anchor read from a script. "A department spokesperson said the officer's training and quick reaction prevented Destiny Hines from killing any bystanders. The shooting victim had a history of mental illness according to a police affidavit. And with thirty rounds in the magazine, she was capable of doing extreme damage. More from our correspondent after we return."

"Dissolve," Olivia said. "We're in commercial. Syd, you there?"

Sydney tapped her earpiece. "Loud and clear. How do we look?"

"Like a roasted Barbie with lip gloss. But it's working for you. Cal around?"

Sydney motioned Cal to stand next to her. "Give your sister a wave."

Cal fluttered his fingers.

"You want to say hi?" Sydney asked.

He waved again, then moved off camera. "Tell her to quit bugging me."

"Cal says hey," Sydney said.

"I'll bet," Olivia said. "He can't drive me crazy if I don't give him my keys. We're live in ten, nine, eight . . ."

A few ticks later, the anchor said, "Sydney, what about a dramatic rescue that took place around the time of the explosion?"

"Nick, first responders weren't the only heroes today." Sydney caught Cal's sheepish grin off camera. "But the team I'd want saving me, if I ever need it, performed one such rescue. Engine 15's Rapid Intervention Team responded to a scary Mayday call."

She made a swirling motion off camera for Eric's fire clip. In a voice-over, she said, "Searching for residents inside an apartment building on Spruance Street resulted in serious injuries for three firefighters. They became ensnared after the fourth floor tilted and eventually collapsed. I'm told one held onto a windowsill while another grabbed a floor joist. The third firefighter was pinned under debris and needed extrication by the RIT team—firefighters specially trained to find and free fellow firefighters."

Sydney signaled Eric to go live and his camera's red light blinked on. "Rescuers cut through rebar, wood, and concrete to free the pinned captain while firefighters aimed their nozzles on adjacent structures to keep the fire from coming too dangerously close. The three firefighters are reported in serious, but stable condition at Medical University Hospital."

The anchor said, "In a related story, Action 7 News senior editor Reginald Baker suffered severe head trauma this morning. On behalf of the entire crew, our prayers are with him and his family. Following the commercial break, we'll return to Tipton Terrace."

"Dissolve," Olivia said. "After Syd's next segment, y'all can scoot."

Sydney believed this day might never end. "I only need a soft cue from Nick."

"And a shower. But I sense you are going for fire-chic. We're live in five, four, three . . ." Her voice trailed off.

•

Lamar toughened when Detective Tate strutted over to the third-floor office cubicle to deconflict problems with the second mugshot binder.

"Couple of questions," the detective said.

Lamar grabbed the pen and steno pad. "Shoot."

The detective doubled over.

Lamar lost his footing. "I mean . . . What I meant . . ."

"That expression cracks me up every time." The detective placed a hand on Lamar's shoulder and poked the tagged page from binder one with his index finger. "Tell me about this guy?"

"D-Jazz. Rather, D'Angelo Hines," Lamar stammered. "Punks call him D-Jazz."

"And?"

"He's in the 843Z." Lamar eyed the firefighter. "May I have another Pepsi?"

"Sure, kid. Sure." He jerked the walkie-talkie from his belt and moved away.

Lamar played it cool. "D-Jazz used to live somewhere over on Kinkaid. In the projects. Wasn't he in prison?"

"Released about a year ago," Detective Tate said.

Lamar shook his head. "Damn."

"Paroled for good behavior. You believe that?"

Lamar crossed his arms. "He come home?"

"Yeah, but we caught him again. About six weeks back. Flung him in jail for thirty days before bouncing him. He hasn't checked in with his parole officer yet. Judge issued a bench warrant." Detective Tate clipped his words like a machine gun. "Any contact with him recently?"

"Hell no." Lamar pushed the notebook away. "Let me break it down for you. One. More. Time. I'm not ganged up. Those dudes scare the crap out of me."

Lamar waited out the detective as though he was ahead with a 3-0 count.

Detective Tate double-tapped D-Jazz's mug shot with his finger. "Is he the only person in this whole binder you know?"

The firefighter returned with a soda and Lamar swallowed a sip before responding. "I don't know D-Jazz." He emphasized each word. "His picture has been on TV and in the paper."

"No one else?"

Lamar shook his head. His throat felt raw. He wanted to gulp the Pepsi but needed the prop to last as long as possible.

Detective Tate pointed at a new book for review in place of the one with lab reports and photos. "Thumb through the remaining mugs jiffy-quick before Special Agent Bellamy arrives." He disappeared into the conference room.

Lamar finished the review in about fifteen minutes without spotting anyone else he recognized. He loped downstairs itching to see if he'd been caught on video. The room was crawling with interns like someone had kicked an ant bed. He spotted Red at the food table.

Lamar's chest heaved with anticipation. "Please show me your Kinkaid mash."

"No prob, bro," Red said.

They moved to a computer, and a few keystrokes later, Red played an edited montage. Plenty of choppy clips of flames clawing at a porch column. Lamar stiffened when two firefighters got stuck on a roof and the place burst into flames.

Red chucked Lamar on the shoulder. "Never seen anything like it. Have you?"

The footage took Lamar's breath away. "Damn. They dead?"

"Nah, a ladder truck grabbed them. But check this out."

Lamar forced himself to focus on Red's next clip with a highlight ring superimposed over a person running away from the scene. The guy wore dark jeans, brown boots, and a hoodie.

Red replayed the clip in slow motion. "Gotta be the bad guy. Right?"

Lamar, the dude in the video, never turned, making facial recognition impossible.

Lamar, the one working as an intern, snuck a quick peek at his Timberlands and immediately regretted it. He became as rigid as a statue expecting Red to call him out for the stupid move. Instead, Red's attention remained riveted on the video. Lamar made a mental note to trash his boots the minute he returned home.

Red fast-forwarded through the montage, stopping when he spotted Lamar's face on screen. "Is that you, bro? Yikes. Didn't know you were there."

White T-shirt, jeans—and those stupid Timberlands.

Lamar ignored the question. "Any more sodas?"

"What flavor?"

"You pick."

Red bounded to the snack table.

Lamar moved the cursor over the clip of him wearing those damn boots and pressed the delete button.

Red returned and handed Lamar a Coke.

Lamar popped open the can, then threw it back like a cowpoke in a spaghetti western. He let out a long, low belch.

Red laughed so hard, bubbles foamed out his nose.

Lamar crushed the can on his forehead and tossed it in the trash.

"Whoa, bro. Recycling bin by the door," Red said. "Fire guys sell the aluminum. Money goes to the kid's burn unit."

Lamar fished the can from the trash. "Cool."

"Wait 'til I show Dwayne you were there."

"Please don't tell our resident douche," Lamar said.

Red held a finger to his lips. "Play your clip again."

Lamar panicked, yet managed to subtly move the cursor over the undo arrow. "What are you working on now?" He tapped the mouse, restoring the erased video clip.

"Enhancing faces in the crowd."

Lamar played the video of him in his T-shirt. "Cops gonna run facial recognition software?"

"Suppose so. I'm cleaning pictures with an algorithm the feds loaned CFD. Fun, but tedious."

"I'll help you after I finish upstairs."

Lamar needed a revised plan to eliminate his evidentiary ties to the fire.

15

Just before 7 p.m., Coop arrived at the Moultrie Building for his first meeting leading the task force.

He surveyed his temporary office on the third floor next to a secure conference room. He placed a couple of personal items on the desk—a picture of his daughter, Haley, and a jar of scorched baseball cards he carried with him.

Haley stood in the doorway wearing an attitude. She stomped around the office, frowned at the baseball cards, then flung her backpack on the sofa.

Coop tried to sweep her into his arms.

She pushed back.

He managed to smooch her on the forehead anyway.

Haley rubbed away his kiss. "I know someone set another fire. Mombo says you'll be busy for weeks."

"But I came to spend time with you."

"How long do I have to stay here? I didn't finish my math home-work." She raised her book as if proffering evidence. "Assignment is due tomorrow."

Coop folded his arms across his chest. "What were you doing all afternoon?"

"I tried—"

"Why is everything a wrestling match with you?"

"Are you serious?" Haley slumped on the couch, hung her head, then drew her shoulders in tight.

Coop turned away, tired of riding her. Parenting was such hard work, and he found himself flailing in a turbulent slipstream.

Haley conjured a defiant silence.

Coop knelt beside her. "Help me patch things with you."

Her eyes ringed with tears. "You have too many rules."

"Rules save lives."

Her lower lip dipped into a pout. "Why?"

Coop eyed the jar of blackened baseball cards. "Because it's my truth. Rules are simple and direct. If things become too complex, people screw up. And when people screw up, other people get injured. Or killed."

Haley rolled her eyes. "Whatever."

Coop started to explode, then reconsidered when his cell buzzed with a text from Dino: *On the way with your newest task force team member.*

"Go ahead," Haley groaned. "I'll work in Sheila's office."

Coop wanted to offer something profound. But he couldn't put any words together without sounding like a louse. "Thanks, Twink."

Haley filed to the rear office while Coop met his guests at the hall door.

Dino said, "Special Agent Bellamy, meet Sydney Quinn, our fair city's most kick-ass reporter. And her new sidekick, Cal Hampton."

Coop's eyes locked on Sydney. She exuded confidence and an energy he'd found appealing from the instant she barreled him over at the Kinkaid fire. "How nice. We've met."

"FBI?" Sydney asked coyly.

Coop shook his head. "ATF."

A tangle of hair toppled from the pile on Sydney's head. She tucked the stray lock behind one ear. "How nice."

"So, you can tell she's annoying." Dino winked. "On the other hand, she's also irritatingly relentless."

"Sheesh, fellas. I'm blushing." Sydney fanned her cheeks with mock exasperation. "Special Agent Bellamy—"

Dino raised a hand. "Call him Coop, Ladybug. You two play nice; I gotta run. Raincheck on the Maker's." He spun toward the stairs.

Coop tweaked an earlobe. "You have a real talent for first and second impressions."

"It's one of my superpowers," Sydney said. "I try not to brag."

"Even though you're kick-ass, I suppose you should expect a tepid reception from the rest of the task force. They aren't inclined to trust the media scrutinizing their every move. Ready?"

"C'mon, you have to ask?"

"You sure you want to meet the group wearing . . .?" He eyed Sydney and Cal, both filthy from their encounter with the fires. "I can offer showers and clean ATF T-shirts if either of you want."

"Ouch." Sarcasm dripped from Sydney. "First, you don't think I'll fit in. Now, you aren't partial to the way I'm dressed."

Cal bit. "You had me at shower."

Coop signaled an assistant to guide Cal to the locker room.

Sydney dropped her purse in Coop's office. "We may have gotten off to a rocky start this morning. Any chance you'd settle up by contributing a little expert testimony for a friend of mine? I'm working with the Innocence Network on the Nathan Sharpe case."

Coop crinkled his eyebrows. "The old train station fire? That was like thirty-five years ago."

Sydney clasped her hands. "The defense needs someone like you to convince a new jury the guy in prison is the wrong guy. Will you help?"

The endeavor sounded interesting and smack dab in Coop's wheelhouse. Plus, it came with the added perk of getting to spend more time with her. "When?"

"This Thursday."

Coop's stomach knotted with disappointment. "No time to prepare. And I have an arsonist to catch. But I'll recommend someone."

Sydney made a teeny shrug, and Coop thought she looked disappointed, too. "Heard you're the best. Needed to ask."

They moved toward the conference room but stopped at a work cubby.

"Who are you?" Coop asked a kid he suspected wasn't on the fire department's payroll.

"Lamar Gallivant, student intern."

Sydney shoehorned into the cubicle and opened the notebook on Lamar's desk.

Lamar snatched the binder and clutched it to his chest. "Sorry, you need permission from Detective Tate or him." He pointed at Coop.

"What's in the notebook?" Coop asked.

Lamar whispered. "Case files."

The wiry kid seemed as strong as a rod of rebar, and Coop admired his diligence. "She can browse."

Lamar handed the notebook to Sydney, then measured his words before speaking. "I live sort of near Kinkaid Street and went over this morning because of the sirens. Spotted two firemen on a burning roof. They fall in?"

Sydney stopped skimming the files. "A huge red truck with one of those long ladder thingies swung over and plucked them before the building became a friggin' fireball."

Coop scratched his chin. "We need to work on your firefighting vocabulary."

"They alive?" Lamar asked again.

Coop said, "Short version, yes."

"Man, I'm glad."

Sydney asked, "What's wrong with my vocab? Huge red truck? Long ladder?"

Coop blurted a laugh. "A genuine firefighter never says friggin'."

Lamar said, "Damn straight. The fire was a real motherfu—"

Sydney held up a hand. "Agreed."

Lamar jammed his hands deep in his pockets. "Sorry."

Sydney sighed. "Don't sweat it. I try to abstain from cursing at least five hours before I go on air."

"I knew it," Lamar extended his hand. "You're the babe on Channel 7. Nice to meet you. The anchor dude said you were at the fire." He stepped back and eyed Sydney with unease. "Holy shit—" He flung his hands to his mouth. "I mean, holy smokes."

He pushed the chair toward her.

"I know, the clothes are trashed." Sydney tapped the notebook. "What are you working on?"

Lamar divided his glance between Sydney and Coop.

Coop noticed an unmistakable odor of gasoline permeating around the teen's backpack. He sliced into the crowded cubical and made a pretense of bending for something on the floor. His internal alarm pegged in the red despite plenty of possible innocent explanations. Perhaps the kid wiped his hands on the pack after he filled a gas tank. Or he may have contacted something in the FMD office. But the presence of gasoline in or on a student's book bag was abnormal.

Lamar scooted aside to give Coop extra space before addressing Sydney. "I'm supposed to ensure the addresses and stuff match."

Coop covertly peeled a treated cotton swab used to collect a residue sample for testing. Maybe he was overreacting. Still, he intended to take every precaution in hopes of catching the elusive arsonist. After he received the lab analysis in a day or two, he'd interview Lamar, if necessary. And if he was wrong about the kid, no harm, no foul. Coop tossed the swab's wrapper in the trash receptacle.

Lamar asked, "Help you with anything?"

"A palmetto bug ran under the credenza. I hate those darn insects. Gives me the willies." Coop shook his upper body with great exaggeration. "Excuse us. We all have work to do."

<h1 style="text-align:center">16</h1>

Coop punched the cipher code, then held the door for Sydney as they entered the Arson Task Force's conference room.

Windows lined the wall opposite the door. City and tri-county maps, clotted with colored push pins to denote which fire department had responded to various callouts, covered another wall next to a large TV monitor. A whiteboard, scrawled with numbers for the group's favorite take-out establishments, lined the door wall.

Coop had worked in scores of war rooms, and this one seemed decent enough. He eyed the group of about twenty professionals assembled from the sheriff's office, South Carolina State Law Enforcement Division, and city police and fire departments. Principals crowded the table while assistants found seats atop a credenza, windowsills, or side chairs. He squeezed around the room, introducing himself to those he didn't know firsthand.

Coop said, "It's great to visit old friends and meet new ones. Let me introduce Sydney Quinn from the local Action News affiliate. Mayor Wallace appointed her to our group. She's also promoting Nathan Sharpe's case for the Innocence Network."

"I caught wind that was coming back around. What's the status?" asked Captain Burton, CPD Crime Lab chief.

Coop was well acquainted with the willowy, no-nonsense cop who held advanced degrees in forensic science. The woman had earned enormous respect beyond the city limits.

"Court convenes Thursday," Sydney said. "I've asked Coop for help. Still twisting his arm."

Coop shook his head hoping to stave off further discussion. "Enough preamble. Who wants to talk about the dead girl?"

Detective Tate spoke first. "Gang Intel identified Destiny Hines, age fifteen. The Medical University is performing forensic ballistics recovery."

"I have her weapon," Captain Burton added. "Someone attempted to file off the serial number from the MAC-10. We raised it and your pals at ATF connected the assault rifle to a couple of unsolved cases in our area. Bolstered the warrant for D-Jazz and others."

"D-Jazz?" Sydney asked.

"D'Angelo Hines. Street name D-Jazz. He's the dead girl's cousin."

Deputy Kane, a buff county sheriff, tossed his pen on a notepad. "Leader of the 843Z. An all-around scumbag with questionable management skills."

Coop snickered. He liked this guy. From his experience, sheriffs and ATF agents were most simpatico.

"D-Jazz did a stretch at Lieber," Detective Tate said. "He's habitual. Released from jail six weeks ago and never checked back with his PO." He tipped his head toward Deputy Kane. "The sheriff sent SWAT to serve a bench warrant for his arrest."

Deputy Kane said, "We also nabbed as many 843Z as we could find. I'm told they are Agent Bellamy's alleged culprits in a repair scam. And CPD rousted another ten lowlifes from North Morrison and West Ashley for good measure. They're in a holding tank at Lockwood."

"Standing by to interrogate," Detective Tate said. "Waiting until you tell us what pot you want stirred. We can sweat them for forty-eight hours if we need to."

Coop folded his hands. "I won't waste time recapping what you can read for yourself. Rather, I want to start by ditching old theories and changing course since our offender has changed up too. His first daylight fire, correct?"

Detective Tate nodded. "And the Tip explosion is a real escalation we didn't expect. What are you thinking?"

"Great question." Coop was happy to transition the focus away from the former fire marshal's approach without stepping on too many toes. "Let's establish attack lines on three fronts, though they aren't mutually exclusive. One, the string of Fleet Landing's nuisance fires employs a distinct M.O. Why? Could it be Black-on-Black crime where the gang is intimidating folks and making money off fear?" Coop tossed his palms up to signal he didn't have an answer or an opinion. "Two, today's Kinkaid fire is distinctly out of character. New variables include daylight, size, and multiple points of origin. Could mean several torches were in play. Three, the Tip explosion. We need to methodically rule out accidental ignition sources, like electrical and gas." Coop smoothed his mustache. "Continue to accumulate evidence. To that end, don't take shortcuts. And let me know if you have any agency-specific concerns."

"What about Falcon?" Sydney asked. "Any idea who he is?"

Detective Tate said, "He takes credit for most Fleet Landing fires. His PR is entirely by word of mouth."

Coop frowned. "Pretty odd that he doesn't grab attention via social media like the cool kids. That way, we'd be able to track him electronically. What else?"

Detective Tate said, "My guys tell me the witness accounts are crap, but we'll lock down gang member alibis."

Captain Burton raised her hand. "Coop, give us your theory on today's events."

Working with this top-notch group is a breeze, Coop thought.

He surmised the former fire marshal had held them back, a mistake he wouldn't repeat. Coop said, "The usual caveats apply. Preliminary analysis. Not for public release." He dove into lecture mode. "Today's Kinkaid fire is most certainly intentional. At Tipton Terrace, I'm leaning toward gas explosion, which is likely intentional, too. Kinda approximates an experiment Chanita and I ran at SLED a couple of years back."

Chanita Proctor, a South Carolina State Law Enforcement Division agent, grinned. "The old Italian restaurant on Gervais Street."

Coop adored Chanita and had worked closely with her when he served in the state fire marshal's office.

Chanita continued, "I remember we shut off the oven's pilot light. Let the gas cook about a half hour. Darn explosion collapsed the whole building faster than a wrecking ball. Rattled windows in a few dormitories on campus too. Thankfully, the governor was out of town and the General Assembly wasn't in session. Helluva sight."

The group chortled in unison.

Coop ticked off the rest of his agenda on outstretched fingers. Then he rubbed his forehead. "Last thing. Brody, do you have an intern working on case histories?"

Detective Tate replied, "He lives in Fleet Landing. Knows the streets better than me, and I worked undercover three times." The detective jerked his cell phone from a belt clip and let out a low whistle. "Crews just pulled five bodies from Tip's rubble, presumably residents."

Sydney shook her head. "Five new angels. I feared worse."

Detective Tate reattached his phone. "Search continues. More fatalities possible. My sources also say Falcon and the 843Z are both taking credit for today's fire and explosion."

"No way," Coop said, not buying the claim. "Another twist."

Since the latest disaster broke with both the gang and Falcon's *modus operandi*, it increased the likelihood that someone completely off Coop's radar had elevated arson to a new and deadly art form.

•

Sydney listened with curiosity as Coop outlined his investigation strategy and plausible persons of interest.

Must've been some basis to his supposition because no one protested. Instead, task force members added layers and new angles to pursue. But Sydney dealt in facts, not hypotheses.

Moreover, she was accustomed to being in the know. Ahead of the curve. The first one picked when choosing sides. But these people were smart, too. And they offered technical details she couldn't report.

Sydney said, "If this D-Jazz character is the 843Z kingpin, and the gang is claiming responsibility for Fleet Landing fires, then D-Jazz must be Falcon. Simple enough, right? Why hide behind an idiotic alias?"

Detective Tate swallowed hard before answering. "We still have a lot of unanswered questions about an unusual repair scam Coop brought to our attention."

Sydney asked, "Would the gang go scorched-earth on the place they control? If it's about intimidation, how do you scare ruins? And why claim credit for destroying your own neighborhood?"

Coop said, "Let's focus on corralling D-Jazz and his associates. Also, ID the Franks. Dive into their last knowns, social media, next of kin. Find out if any connect to the 843Z. I want suspects with solid means, motive, and opportunity."

"Franks?" Sydney asked.

"Victims," Captain Burton said. "It's crude, but not disrespectful. Nicknames protect us from a cruel world."

Sydney narrowed her eyes, rejecting Coop's singular focus on gang involvement. "What about other known arsonists residing in the coastal area? Since today's mess is out of character from the serial string, maybe your pyro isn't in the gang. Could be hiding in plain view."

"Technically, the arsonist isn't a pyromaniac," Coop said.

Detective Tate braced his hands on his hips. "I don't like being told who to round up."

"In fairness, Brody, it's a solid suggestion," Deputy Kane said.

Agent Proctor offered her two cents. "We need to avoid tunnel vision with the gang."

"Am I the only one here who hates a reporter on the team?" Detective Tate snarled.

"Hey." Sydney banged the table with her fist. "I'm right here."

•

Coop waved his arms.

"Folks, let me remind you," he said. "We have dead citizens. Indescribable destruction of personal property. Let's act professionally. Be professionals." He spun toward Detective Tate. "Since we recorded fatalities, presumably as a direct result of arson, is your department assigning a homicide detective to join us?"

Detective Tate tweaked his earlobe. "Dino ordered me to join him at Tip's command when we're finished."

Coop nodded. "I met Lieutenant Bernadino."

Deputy Kane stood to leave. "Hey, Chanita. About that Italian restaurant. How did you detonate the gas?"

"Cell phone. Coop and I weren't sure if we could even spark an explosion. We got jittery at the thirty-minute mark. But that darn thing blew like we'd calculated."

Detective Tate asked, "You think gang chuckleheads tripped pilot lights in every apartment?"

Coop sighed. "Even if they only did half, they took a huge risk because the whole thing might've detonated from another source."

As people exited, Coop flagged Chanita. "I need SLED to work up backgrounds on the entire task force, including the interns. And I loved your comment on tunnel vision. I suppose there's a fine line between being laser-focused at the expense of missing other possibilities. Started me cogitating about how many long-running deals become hijacked by an insider who botches things for the good guys. Your review will stop anyone involved in our joint operation from kicking the can ahead of us—out of reach."

"Smart," Chanita said. "Hey, I forgot to tell you. I gave Captain Bosco three portable photoionization detectors. Count it as a gift for keeping the reporter out of our way. Deep down, my agency isn't a big fan of transparency. Your hands are full with her."

Coop latched the conference room door. "You have no idea."

Sydney's cell phone vibrated after she finished recording an interview with Coop for airing during the late broadcast.

She checked the screen for Caller ID: *Private Number*. She hesitated a beat before answering. "Sydney Quinn."

A grainy voice croaked on the other end. "Channel 7 reporter?"

"Who's this?"

"I'm going to burn it all. The Battery, Market, Upper King. Everything. The South shall rise again—this time in a different color."

Sydney seethed at the caller's temerity. "Is this Falcon?"

"I burnt Kinkaid and blew up Tip Towers. Easy peasy. Check your messages in case you don't think I'm serious." The caller disconnected.

"Who was it?" Coop asked.

She waved him off, then scribbled on her pad, occasionally glancing skyward to conjure the quote. She jammed the notebook into a side pocket. "This lugnut said he's responsible for today's chaos."

Coop moved beside her. "You sure the caller was male?"

Sydney clamped her eyes and moved her lips in and out for several seconds. "Obviously muffled, but definitely adult male. The voice was coarse, with full local twang. Probably fake."

"Go on." Coop jerked a cell phone from his pocket.

"He's prepared to burn more than Fleet Landing. Says he'll target the city's best sections, too." Sydney tapped her phone screen to retrieve the message the caller had mentioned.

Sydney viewed a close-up video of a blaze, trying to ascertain clues regarding its location and relevance. As the fire grew, the videographer retracted the lens, revealing a one-story house with a brick façade. Then the gabled front porch erupted in flames. Sydney let out a shriek when she recognized the blue-and-red-striped pillows on a bench near her front door seconds before they ignited.

"My house," Sydney mumbled.

Fully engulfed.

And belching sparks from the eaves.

Jelly-legged, Sydney slumped to her knees. A fist-sized lump caught in her throat, and she inhaled shaky gulps like a newborn. Her vision narrowed until she only saw flames.

Coop helped Sydney to her feet. Captain Bosco radioed dispatch to send three units to her address.

She bit off a hysterical laugh.

A simple one-alarm fire—that's what Bosco had called it.

Over the years, she'd dealt with unfair reviews, enraged calls from viewers, and assaults on her talent.

But Sydney couldn't process the unfolding horror. Leaping flames on the phone's tiny screen held her gaze.

She naively believed her sizable bank balance protected her from Falcon's destructive reach. Everything she owned, from the necessary to the frivolous. The sentimental. The irreplaceable. All gone.

Along with her prized sense of safety.

Beside her, Coop eyed the video, then snatched her phone. He tapped the screen to open an attached file listing dozens of addresses. Sydney leaned closer, peering over his shoulder as he scrolled the list. Blurry-eyed, she couldn't tell if they were previous targets or future ones.

Coop scowled as he poked in a number on his cell. "Chief, the Channel 7 reporter's house has been attacked. Evidence came to her phone. I'll use my tech sources to narrow down a cell tower the call pinged off." He turned to Detective Tate and Deputy Kane. "D-Jazz moves to the top of our suspect list. Find him. Now. And bring him in."

The largest fire investigation in state history had been underway for about seven hours. And Sydney was the latest victim.

17

Sydney and Cal flew north on Spruill Avenue, ignoring the speed limit, snubbing stop signs, and dodging a gauntlet of parked cars.

Cal pushed the Volkswagen with a heavy foot on the gas. The car crested a small hill, then careened onto McMillan Avenue, spraying a cloud of rocks. Two blocks later, they zipped into the old shipyard and shot right on Hobson, a quiet residential road a stone's throw from the Cooper River. Fat, lazy raindrops thudded the windshield as wipers fanned the glass.

Sydney's stoic face masked her fury as she caught sight of three pumpers from North Charleston's fire department streaming a soft spray onto the smoldering remains of her home. A trickle of gray smoke swirled over singed cinderblock. Her chest tightened, and her hands trembled—red flags she wouldn't be able to fend off an oncoming, full-blown panic attack by sheer force of will.

She'd held it together through the day's gunfire, chaos, and suffocating smoke. Now, the part of her brain holding back an untamed darkness spilled open. Her breathing grew ragged: short, shallow breaths. An undertow pinned her and forced her mind to watch clips from a full-length feature film—the Taliban ambush.

The lead vehicle in our convoy detonated an improvised explosive device.

Cal skidded to a stop, scattering loose gravel and grass chunks into a neighbor's yard. He grabbed the Action 7 video camera and his own thirty-five-millimeter Nikon from the back seat. Sydney kicked open her door and raced up the sidewalk.

Then things snowballed. More like an avalanche.

Her memory flicked from room to room as she recalled every-thing in her house. Dishes in the sink. College sweatshirt folded on a bedroom trunk. Dirty jeans in the hamper. Granite countertops. A leaning tower of plastic take-out containers in her pantry.

Flames licked the soft-skinned Humvee before it burst into a fireball.

Sydney sprinted over to a torched panel van parked in her drive-way. The smell was suffocating.

Burned flesh.

She gaped at the horror of two dead bodies in a scorched utility van. She unleashed a primal scream.

Coop clawed her back from the brink. "Sydney."

She blinked at him; another shriek lodged in her throat.

When did he arrive?

With surprising gentleness, he said, "I'll call the coroner. Any idea who they are?"

Time snapped back into rhythm with a vulgar cadence. Sydney's lips quivered between desperate gasps. She pointed at blackened anchor tattoos on their forearms, then glanced away.

The implication of inked allegiance created static in her muddled brain. She presumed Falcon had sent a very special message—he was willing to kill.

The crippling anxiety waned, leaving her cheeks hot. Then she became defiant. How dare Falcon victimize her. She wasn't a victim. She'd become an enemy combatant in the gang's war on Fleet Landing.

Coop flashed his badge while firefighters rolled hoses to stow on their rigs. "Bellamy, ATF. What can you tell me?"

"We had to let it go. Rolling hot over eighty percent by the time we arrived." The captain had the youthful appearance of a college kid, his voice impossibly bright. Then he eyed Sydney. "Sorry, ma'am. This your house?"

Ma'am?

She folded her arms across her chest and found her voice. "My kitchen was clean yesterday. Sorry you missed it."

Neighbors inched into the street and offered tidy waves of concern.

Sydney glared at Coop. "After you arrest this dipstick, I'm gonna—"

"Sit. Head between your knees so you don't pass out." Coop rested a hand on her back until she ran out of steam.

His gentleness made her ache. Maybe, just this once, she'd do as she was told.

Sydney sat motionless for a full minute until her cell phone vibrated. Leaden with sorrow, she reluctantly answered the call.

"You can stay with me," Mandy said without preamble. "Long as you need."

"You're my rock," Sydney mumbled.

"Uh, not sure how to say this."

"Go ahead. Blurt it out."

"I'm kind of afraid for you. You know, your traumatic stress."

"According to my ATF source, I was about to drop. But I'm good."

Mandy drove her crazy when she went super-friendly on her. Caring about her health. Worrying about her state of mind. Sydney preferred to downplay everything. Her emotions. The situation.

Forgetting about the past. Wrapping in a warm cocoon of epic denial. Those were essential elements in her healing process.

"You caught a raw deal," Mandy said. "But you're surrounded by handsome firefighters. Lots of mustaches, right?"

"Uh-huh." Sydney disconnected and cradled her head in her hands.

Coop's cell chirped. "Yeah, Chief. I'm at Ms. Quinn's now. Appreciate the call. Meet you there." He clicked off and tapped Sydney on the shoulder. "More news for you."

She rubbed blur from her face.

"Mayor Wallace is demanding an update," Coop said with open indignation. "Chief Sinclair wants you there. If you're up to it—"

"Oh, yeah. I'm up to here . . ." She signaled an artificial point over her head.

18

Darkness hugged the city as Sydney and Cal plodded along Broad Street.

Churches, government buildings, and high-end shops afforded the peninsula's primary east-west artery an air of propriety. Outside City Hall, they weaved through hundreds of demonstrators disregarding Mayor Wallace's voluntary curfew. Uniformed officers clad in riot gear—helmets, masks, and batons—saturated the key intersection of Broad and King, where limestone and granite fortresses buttressed all four corners.

Only hours earlier, Sydney had been making plans with Rob Noble for his big night at RiverDogs Stadium and Nathan Sharpe's retrial. Now, her own world had unraveled.

She snorted at the thought. Unraveled? Melodramatic much?

Cal tapped her shoulder. "The camera battery is roadkill. Sorry I didn't notice."

Sydney inventoried the press corps and spotted Julia Mayfair. She popped the battery from the Action 7 camera and held it out toward Julia. The blonde nightmare acknowledged the issue with a frothy wave, then passed a fresh power pack to Sydney like a hot dog vendor at a baseball game. Sydney motioned with a flourish to seal the unspoken deal. Their slate was even again.

With the camera locked and loaded, Sydney found herself searching for Coop, surprised by the bubble of relief she experienced when she spotted him parting the mob. He'd changed into a fresh working uniform: black tactical pants with a zillion stuffed pockets and a gray polo shirt with ATF embroidered on the sleeve. He was dressed like a professional. She looked like the homeless bum she'd become, and hoped he didn't notice.

Coop grabbed Sydney by the arm and tugged her and Cal with him. Boos and whistles erupted from her cronies barred from entry. The stark reality of why she'd been summoned tempered her impulse to gloat. The three passed through a metal detector before hiking to the historic City Hall's second floor. They spilled out in an ornate alcove lined with expensive oil portraits.

Lantana Hardwick, who held the dubious distinction as Nathan Sharpe's sister and the city council member representing Fleet Landing, brushed past lush black walnut desks and threw her arms around Sydney. "Your house. I'm sorry."

"No worries." Lantana's unexpected embrace surprised Sydney. "I only lost a priceless stack of Sheryl Crow CDs and a lifetime of irreplaceable memories. But I'm grateful for what I have left."

"Look, I know we've enjoyed our professional differences, but Rob tells me you're helping Nate. I'm truly grateful—"

Sydney held up a palm. "Haven't done anything yet."

Their conversation was interrupted by Hart Anson, a prominent area real estate developer. He greeted Lantana with a stroke on her cheek that made her flinch.

Anson was a fireplug in railroad-striped seersucker pants and a white golf polo, the traditional warm-weather uniform of wealthy Lowcountry businessmen. Gray wisps overran wavy dark hair on the sides.

Lantana forced a smile. "Where are my manners? This is—"

"Hart Anson," Sydney said. "Your company is responsible for the swanky new student housing at the College of Charleston."

"Among other major projects," Lantana said.

Anson rearranged several files under his arm and shoved out his mitt. "Thanks for the fanfare, ladies." He spoke with the raspy voice of a two-pack-a-day smoker. "And you are Sydney Quinn, reporter extraordinaire, I presume."

Sydney suppressed a chortle. "That's an understatement."

On paper, Anson was a major player in commercial development despite clashing with Mayor Wallace's responsible growth agenda. He also publicly invested in a passel of Fleet Landing residential properties, with an eye toward giving people jobs by rejuvenating dingy—albeit historic—architectures and establishing better services for the downtrodden community. In short, one of the good guys, in Sydney's opinion.

Even so, the city's notable buildings were treasured commodities during hot real estate markets. Mayor Wallace had successfully fought demolition, thereby curtailing construction of bright and shiny buildings. But during the lean years, the mayor and city council had allowed the same endangered treasures to lie fallow—abandoned without interest. The result, an unnecessary blight for the Lowcountry's most jeweled locale.

Sydney continued. "I support your ambitious revitalization efforts."

"We need all the assistance we can muster," Anson said.

Coop signaled everyone into the mayor's office. He claimed a chair between Lantana and Anson. Cal stood to catch a better camera angle.

Mayor Wallace peeked over the top of wire-rimmed glasses. "We're under siege by thugs who think they have a right to set fire to my city." He glanced at Sydney. "Tell everyone about the ultimatum you received."

Sydney glanced at her notepad. "A man called to say, and I quote, 'I'm going to burn the Battery, Market, Upper King. Everything. The South shall rise again. This time in a different color.' Unquote."

Anson said, "My family's beautiful home on the Battery survived the damn Yankee bombings. I sure as hell won't let a lunatic with a Zippo and a bottle of gas chase me out."

Sydney continued. "What did he mean—the South shall rise again . . . in a different color?"

No one spoke.

Sydney restated the obvious, hoping to generate discussion. "So far, he's confined his malice to Fleet Landing. If Falcon heads for the Battery, will it increase the urgency to stop him?"

Wallace glared. "What are you implying?"

Sydney wanted to trust her assessment of the mayor as smart, deliberate, and passionate about the city he headed. She nudged fallen ringlets from her face, a tad perturbed she'd bubbled up. "Falcon has terrorized my neighborhood long enough. The gangs have forced many to abandon our city in droves. They are descendants of slaves and sharecroppers who deserve better."

Lantana eyed Sydney with appreciation.

Anson said, "That's why I'm offering the Tobacco Mill as temporary refuge for Lantana's people displaced by today's fires."

Coop made a confused frown. "Chief Sinclair says you haven't received a certificate of occupancy for that building."

"But these people are in desperate need of shelter," Anson said. "Those are the rules."

Anson met Coop with the suppliant expression of a drowning man.

Coop folded his arms across his chest, signaling a kibosh to the exchange.

Realizing Anson was in an advantageous position to help, Sydney weighed in. "Coop, what's the certificate's importance?"

Coop smoothed his mustache between his fingers, a peculiar habit she recognized as his tell. "As Mr. Anson undoubtedly knows, inspections determine whether premises are safe and in compliance with local building codes."

Anson crossed, then uncrossed his legs before proffering a bulging file. "Well then, here's another idea to offset the city's woes. I've been contacted by a group of investors who want to purchase Tipton Terrace. Right this minute. As is." He dropped the folder onto the mayor's desk, then tapped a finger on the file for emphasis.

Mayor Wallace loosened his tie. "Thank you for your interesting, yet thoroughly inappropriate, suggestion. Timing and finesse have never been among your assets." His voice sounded frazzled. "This is an unimaginably sad day. But we'll move through it."

Lantana jumped to her feet. "I'm not interested in platitudes for *hope* and *tomorrow*. Why have the fires gone on this long without an arrest?"

Wallace narrowed his eyebrows so tight they formed a single fuzzy layer. "If you're unhappy here, maybe you should leave Fleet Landing."

She blurted a bitter laugh. "Seriously? My family's been here over two hundred years. First, working the rice fields. Later, at the shipyard. Plenty of folks from Fleet Landing are all-fired proud, claiming the same heritage."

Nice response. Sydney felt more than a little off-put by Wallace's callousness, and he reddened at the hoisting of his own petard.

Sydney had been drawn to the neighborhood the moment she hit town.

Not so long ago, industrious welders, pipefitters, and electricians of all colors enjoyed steady work, at respectable pay, and a short commute to the base. Once their jobs vanished, they left a vapor trail, prompting the northeast side's housing market to spiral into oblivion. The area eventually regressed into the 'hood,' a pejorative moniker for a place with crappy housing surrounded by sagging storefronts, discount junk emporiums, and payday loan centers operating a half step ahead of usury. Nowadays, even cops stayed away from Fleet Landing after dark unless they rolled out at least five cars.

Sydney rounded back to Anson's odd offer. "Why don't you add Tipton Terrace to your holdings independent of others?"

"Hate to admit it, but I'm cash-strapped." Anson drummed his fingers on the file folder, then eyed the mayor. "These investors might require assistance though."

"Such as?" Wallace asked wearily.

"Ease your preservation requirements. Give them a little flexibility."

"What do they propose to erect in Tip's stead?"

Sydney shot to her feet. "Mr. Mayor, greenlighting any action that'll displace locals is a bad idea." She faced Anson. "Promise they won't gentrify the neighborhood by swapping historic residential buildings for pompous boutiques and trendy restaurants."

Lantana clenched her jaw. "Hart, are they suggesting mansions and retail ventures?"

"I'm simply brokering this deal," he said.

Wallace pinched the bridge of his nose. "This deal? Are there others in the offing?"

A passionate discussion about unabashed expansion versus historic preservation became a shouting match between Anson and Wallace. When Anson accused Wallace of overt bigotries, the mayor bored a hole into him with an implacable glare.

"Spare me the lecture," Wallace said. "You think the good people of Charleston have forgotten your family's storied past?"

Everyone pivoted toward Anson.

Wallace said, "Oh, they don't know about—"

"Stop." Anson waved his hands in surrender.

"Spill the beans, you two," Sydney said. "Lies become truth if perfidy doesn't find a light."

Wallace's nostrils flared. "What do you mean?"

"Perfidy? Treachery. Betrayal." Sydney tapped her pen on the notepad. "I believe the insinuation is you and your families are, or at least were, card-carrying members of the Ku Klux Klan."

Wallace shrugged. "I renounced the White Crusaders long ago. What about you, Hart?"

Anson's shoulders sagged. He leaned on fists resting atop the mayor's desk. Without anger, he said, "We've all done things we aren't proud of."

His response sounded more like a confirmation than denial. If Anson was a current or former member of the Klan, that cast a distorted filter on his generosity toward the predominantly Black neighborhood.

Lantana let out an exasperated "Hmpff" before dropping her own thick folder on the mayor's desk. "Since we've moved off-topic, I intend to sue the city on my brother's behalf. I'll be asking ten million dollars due to false imprisonment and I'm holding you, Mr. Mayor, personally liable."

"Outlandish," Wallace retorted. "Utterly without merit."

Coop turned to Sydney and whispered, "What's happening?"

"Her brother is my Innocence Network case. Remember? I mentioned Nate Sharpe needs your help." She pressed her palms together.

Wallace stabbed a finger at Coop. "You can't testify. I won't allow it." He curled his lips into a hideous grin. "Ms. Hardwick, you're out of your league. Besides, we have more urgent matters in the public interest to address than one Black man—" He caught himself and made a pretense of adjusting his tie. "Men of color, like your brother . . . fire is in their nature."

Sydney was shaken at witnessing his benevolent mask crack. "Pump the brakes, Mr. Mayor. You are way out of line."

Mayor Wallace deflated.

Lantana didn't let up. "That's the same bias you baked into Nate's first trial. Your prosecution led an all-white jury to give credence to flimsy circumstantial evidence and ignore reasonable doubt." She paused a beat before facing Coop. "Witness intimidation is a criminal offense, am I right?"

"Indeed," Coop said.

Wallace's face pinched. "My prosecution was zealous. Police found a book of matches in your brother's pocket. And he had a criminal history."

Lantana held up her hands. "Petty larceny and truancy. Nothing came close to what you accused him of."

Mayor Wallace rounded the desk and loomed beside her. "You've said your piece. I trust the court will bounce your frivolous lawsuit."

Lantana took a swing at Wallace.

Sydney lunged for her, but acted a second too late.

The mayor ducked, and Lantana's blow caught Anson square in the face.

Anson let out a shriek, and blood gushed from his nose.

Coop unpocketed a sterile compress for the mogul's oozing schnoz.

Sydney used the distraction to wedge a voice-activated recording device beside the cushion of Coop's chair.

Once Coop controlled Anson's minor injury, he jammed his hand in another pocket and removed a paper evidence bag, dumped the bloody tissues inside, then handed the waste to Sydney for disposal.

Coop said, "Mayor, the tension in this room is indicative of what's happening outside. I strongly recommend raising the threat level."

Wallace clenched his jaw. "Make it happen. Now, leave my office."

In the hallway, Coop signaled Lantana. "Helluva right cross."

Lantana shook her head. "I'm sorry I lost my cool."

Sydney said, "Well, I'm stunned to learn about Wallace and Anson's alleged ties to White Crusaders."

"Yeah, I better reexamine our partnership," Lantana said.

Sydney winked. "You and Anson aren't—"

"No siree. Strictly business to help improve Fleet Landing." Lantana slackened. "You know . . . In a weird way, I'm sort of glad Nate wasn't released yet."

Coop's eyebrows lifted. "How so?"

"I leased a nice house. A place to call his own once he's free." She paused. "The house I rented . . ."

"Yeah?"

"Address is 1389 Kinkaid." Lantana sighed. "You think this fire is an unpleasant coincidence or more bad luck for Nate? Because he's never caught a decent break his whole life."

Coop said, "That address is ground zero for today's fire. No way it's a coincidence. Plus, Wallace's attitude toward you really chaps my cheeks." He pounded a fist into his hand. "Ladies, sign me up to help Nate."

Sydney swelled with relief. "I'll tell his attorney we have a bona fide expert to testify at Nate's retrial."

19

Coop returned to the Moultrie Building at 9:50 p.m. following Mayor Wallace's meeting.

Haley kicked open the office door. Lamar trailed behind her and rested his backpack on the floor.

"Twink, you bothering the young man?" Coop asked.

"Lamar helped me with my homework," she said. "He's real smart about math stuff."

"Pack up. Mom is waiting for you at the hospital."

Haley shoved worksheets into her backpack and stormed from the office, listing slightly to starboard from the weight of her books.

"Sorry. She and I are—" Coop shrugged and tried to block her wounded expression from his mind. He'd stepped into another dad trap. "How about you? You and your old man see eye-to-eye?"

Lamar toed the floor. "It's only me and Mama. She works hard. Taught me to play baseball."

"Sounds like you have it made." Coop glanced at his jar of singed baseball cards on the desk, ready to change the topic. "What position do you play?"

"Second base."

"Any good?"

"Great glove and a silky swing." Lamar pointed at the scorched cards. "How 'bout you? Collector or a ballplayer?"

Coop rounded the desk and leaned against the corner. "Walk-on center fielder for the Gamecocks."

"Clemson offered me a full ride. Guess that makes us rivals."

"The pressure to earn an athletic scholarship . . . I can't imagine. Only thing left is for you to stay out of trouble." Coop let the words hang there.

Lamar frowned. "What's with those cards? Why are they burned?"

"My uncle gave 'em to me a long time ago. A boy in Greenville had been playing with matches. He died. These serve as a constant reminder." Coop bit his lip to drive away ripples of regret. "Rules save lives."

He lived by that simple credo. It covered every situation and didn't require amendment or refinement. Most importantly, it kept him alive.

Lamar grabbed his backpack. "Long day. I better head home."

"Let me walk out with you." Coop pointed at Lamar's pack. "You have everything?"

"This is all I brought." Lamar prepared to sling the backpack over his shoulder. Instead, he held it out. "Need to inspect it?"

"Nope." Coop regretted taking the swab of Lamar's backpack. His thoughts shifted to the many Black men who carried the weight of other people's suspicions and guilt. One day, they were going about their life. And the next, they found themselves pleading for it—lucky to survive. Coop said, "Thanks for helping my daughter. Hope she wasn't too much of a pest?"

"We worked on dividing fractions. Invert and multiply. That formula never changes no matter how much microtechnology is developed."

Coop and Lamar filed down the stairs to the second floor. Coop signed twenty business cards with a note in case police stopped any interns on their return home or back to campus. After all, he'd insisted on a city-wide curfew and didn't want his legion in trouble because of him. Coop handed the cards to Bosco, then jumped on a desk. "Hey, everyone. Grateful for the help. Need you back tomorrow, if your schedules permit. Check out with Captain Bosco." He hopped down and passed a card to Lamar. "Can you come after practice?"

Lamar hesitated. "You think the person who set today's fire is the same guy who did all the others?"

"Perhaps." Coop latched onto the opening and wondered if Lamar was ready to confess. "But I'll bet he didn't mean to burn whole blocks. Now he's jammed up, without a plan to surrender."

"And he'll be blamed for Tip's explosion, too?" Lamar asked.

Coop hunched his shoulders. "Being blamed and actually being responsible are two different things. My job is to sort it out. Like searching for common denominators."

"And you're the best, right?"

"You might say so. But I have a lot of resources at my disposal." He eyed Lamar. "You've seen what we're doing here. Who do you think should be our focus?"

"That's a no-brainer—Fleet Landing's badass gang called the 843Z."

•

When Coop returned to his office, he found Sydney at his desk.

She disconnected when she spotted him. "What's your impression of our mayor?"

"Never been kicked out of a meeting before," Coop said.

"I'm used to it." She spilled onto the couch. "Thanks for agreeing to help Nate. Did the former fire marshal leave any notes in a desk drawer?"

Coop shook his head. "I'll ask Dino to retrieve the case file from CPD's evidence warehouse. By the way, did you plant something in the mayor's office?"

"Did I?" Sydney checked her watch. "Wow, Cal and I need a ride to the TV station. I'm broadcasting in less than an hour."

"Bosco can drive." Coop studied her. If Sydney was feeling drained from recent events, she didn't show it. He wanted to say something kind to let her know he was there for her. "This is gonna sound stupid."

"A lot of that going around."

"How are you doing?"

Sydney didn't move. She didn't even exhale.

Coop said, "It's none of my—"

"You gonna catch the lugnut who torched my house?" she asked.

"Absolutely."

Sydney brought a hand to her face. "Time for me to fight fire with fire."

Her raw emotion ripped into his heart. He opted to lighten the moment. "Even for a reporter, that's a tactical error. Ask any fire-fighter here. They'll tell you the best way to fight a fire is with water."

She laughed. If only for an instant.

Haley returned, dragging her book bag. Her eyes darted between her dad and Sydney.

An unfamiliar combination of pride and uncertainty broke over Coop. "It'll be way past your bedtime by the time you get home."

"OMG, please don't say *bedtime* in front of real people." Haley coiled the tip of her hair around an index finger. "I'm almost twelve. Practically thirteen." She tilted her head and fluttered her eyelashes the way little girls did before giving their fathers palpi-tations. "Mombo says I can pierce my ears and use lip gloss when I'm thirteen."

Blood waned from Coop's head. Haley knew how to get under his skin with daughterly expertise. He didn't want another argument. And now wasn't the time for parental banalities. He closed his eyes and let the frustration pass. Especially since jewelry and makeup weren't in his wheelhouse. "Let's talk about that later," he said.

Haley offered Sydney a suspicious nod.

Coop asked, "Hey, Twink. Did you eat?"

"Ages ago. What about you?"

"I'm always hungry."

"Remember my rule," Haley said, dancing toward the door.

Coop slumped in his chair. "She hates me."

"Nah, she adores you," Sydney said. "But maybe you should cut her some slack."

"I regret torpedoing the kid. Even so, I won't normalize pouting."

"What's her rule?" Sydney asked.

"I'm totally strict on the job. My mantra is 'rules save lives.'"

"Yeah, I heard you the first and second times." Sydney wrapped a lock of hair around her finger, mirroring Haley. "Take it from me, I've learned the value of disregarding rules when toeing the line simply doesn't cut it."

"Anyway . . ." Coop spread his fingers over his mustache. "After I moved out, my daughter and her mother announced they'd become vegans. Lots of vegetables, fruits, nuts. Pretty strict, too. I need fish, eggs, meat. Only a few plants. And absolutely no seeds. I'm a guy, not a bird. I could be the veritable poster child for the beef and potato lobby. But Haley was emphatic. Her mantra became 'real men don't eat meat.'"

Sydney said, "That means stocking your pantry with legumes and couscous. And veggie burgers and hummus in the fridge whenever she stays."

Coop puffed his cheeks. "I first told her she'd eat what I served. Then I did some digging. Read books on the subject. Accepted a little razzing at first, though I couldn't find any flaws in her argument. The rate of diet-related diseases runs off the charts in fire departments."

"Donut jokes aside, cops are fat, too."

"Did you know firefighters are more likely to die from heart disease than fighting fires? Right then it hit me. So, I reduced my risk of cancer and a heart attack by trading my morning biscuit for a protein smoothie. Swapped the fried chicken sandwich at lunch for a black bean burger. But I can't bring myself to go full-on veg. I sneak a steak on occasion." He shook his head. "From the day that little girl was born, Haley turned my world upside down."

"True vegans also abstain from leather, silk, and cosmetics derived from animal products or animal testing," Sydney said. "Perhaps you caught a break on the lip gloss."

20

At 10:30 p.m., Lamar arrived at Tyrell's Kitchen on the corner of Nimitz and Halsey Streets, about three blocks from the big fire. The old-school eatery had earned panache among locals and tourists for serving fried chicken, gumbo, and other Southern classics. Ornamental wrought iron balconies and window grills crafted by famed local blacksmith Philip Simmons adorned the brick building.

Eager to snag leftovers from the grill, Lamar pushed open the door and stopped cold when he spotted Ice seated at the counter talking to Mama. If Ice had come to intimidate her, Lamar would have to act to protect the pack. Though if it came to any sort of tussle, he'd likely lose.

Ice stood and sneered at Lamar when he exited, marking his territory with an unspoken threat. Mama locked the front door behind the granite blockhead.

"Sorry I'm late," Lamar said. "You know that dude?"

Mama hunched her shoulders and moved into the kitchen. "Never seen him before. He was just making conversation."

Lamar exhaled with relief. She had simply been making nice with a new customer.

"We made food for the folks staying at the Tobacco Mill," Mama said. "I put together fifty peanut butter and banana sandwiches, and Tyrell did fifty meatloaf ones."

Tyrell spoke with a Gullah twang. "Got enough fried okra and potato chips to feed the cavalry." He shoved a cardboard box heaped with foil wrappers toward Lamar.

Mama said, "Word came that the Tobacco Mill owner opened the building for people to stay a couple of nights, until FEMA trailers come around." She hiked the strap of her purse over a shoulder. "Grab a box and help tote the food to Tyrell's Buick. Then, we'll stop for ice cream at Piggly Wiggly. If we leave now, we'll be home in time to check the late news. See if they caught the fool who set the big fire."

Lamar sighed. "What channel?"

"You know I'm partial to the pretty lady on Channel 7."

Lamar's face lit up. "I met her, Mama. She's working with Agent Bellamy and the task force."

Mama beamed. "Did I tell you how proud I am of you working there? Won't surprise me if you nail 'em."

•

Coop scanned the local TV channels. Every station opened with the day's obvious top story. Some sensational, some empathetic. He warmed when Sydney popped on screen. He hadn't stopped fantasizing about her. For all her bluster, Coop believed she harbored a fragility below her gorgeous veneer. Haley, who'd sprawled on the couch, shot up when she heard Sydney's voice.

"Investigators are piecing evidence and witness statements in an effort to determine a cause for the fire that destroyed numerous Fleet Landing homes and the explosion that nearly leveled Tipton Terrace. ATF Special Agent Cooper Bellamy wouldn't state for certain this deadly combination is the work of a serial arsonist plaguing the city the past several months."

The screen cut to Coop in a head shot, saying, "The entire area is an active crime scene."

Haley gaped. "It's you."

Sydney's face filled the screen again. "On a different subject, thousands of demonstrators have gathered in Marion Square to protest alleged police brutality. Similar marches have been staged across the South in a show of solidarity, galvanizing young people of color who claim they are devalued by systemic racism and state-sanctioned violence in their communities. Our police chief applauded the protestors' peaceful nature. For Action 7 News, I'm Sydney Quinn, reporting live."

"Do you like her?" Haley asked.

"She's a fine lady."

Oh, yeah. Sydney was a real pro.

She never mentioned the arsonist's manifesto, or that her own home had been torched, or that she'd sustained an injury from the riot. Moreover, she didn't divulge any confidential task force business, such as the two dead bangers at her house. Coop was glad he'd agreed to give her an interview.

After a commercial, the screen cut to another clip from Coop. "We're working hard to uncover the fire's origin and cause. And ultimately who is responsible."

The anchor said, "A fifty-thousand-dollar reward is being offered by Arson Stoppers for information leading to the arrest of anyone connected with the blaze."

Audio cut to Coop's voiceover. "The person or persons responsible for this heinous crime remain at large. Please call if you have any information leading to the apprehension of suspects."

Coop was also pleased the fire chief had secured reward money. Traditionally, a tip line lured lots of nut cases. Even so, money proved a positive motivator in tough cases.

"Sheesh, you're kinda like a TV star," Haley said.

"Glad you think so."

The grim scene of Tipton Terrace filled the screen.

Sydney said, "Residents of my troubled neighborhood are mourning the loss of two women, a man, and two children who died here. Victims' names are being withheld at this hour pending positive identification and family notification. Six others with serious burns were taken by helicopter to a clinic in Augusta, Georgia."

•

Following the broadcast, Coop and Haley loaded into his Jeep.

An assistant fire marshal had retrieved the vehicle from the alley earlier in the evening. He drove west on Calhoun and waded into the massive crowd at Marion Square. He skirted the congestion by looping south, snaking his way through the tony Radcliffborough neighborhood, eventually arriving at the Medical University of South Carolina.

MUSC was the Lowcountry's only Level One trauma center. Their sprawling campus encompassed more than eight blocks on the peninsula's west side near the Ashley River. Coop swung the Cherokee into a reserved spot at the Public Safety Building a half-block from University Hospital, then eased his daughter from the back seat.

The former Mrs. Bellamy met them near an information kiosk on the ground floor. Her rigid posture indicated she wasn't about to yield any ground. "We need to talk," Cassie said. "I'm working an extra shift to deal with injuries from the fire and riot. Please keep Haley until morning."

"Seems both our jobs force us to neglect our daughter," Coop said.

"Now isn't the time for your warped humor." She hugged Haley. "Finish your homework?"

"One of Dad's interns is a real genius. Taught me a shortcut to use with fractions."

"Sounds nice. Let's go upstairs so your dad can see his friend."

Haley demonstrated an unreasonable amount of energy skipping across the tiled atrium, tapping her sneakers, shifting with excitement. The elevator doors opened on the fifth-floor Surgical ICU.

Sydney was huddled with a knot of Action 7 reporters, editors, and producers. She offered Haley a warm smile, then divided her glance between Coop and his ex-wife. She extended a hand to the ex. "Sydney Quinn, Action 7 News. Coop is teaching me arson investigation."

"I'll bet," Cassie said dryly. "Excuse us." She guided Haley away.

Coop asked, "How's your cameraman?"

"He's in a bad way."

"Fingers crossed." Coop offered a reassuring nod, then jogged after the two Bellamy gals.

Cassie paused to let him catch up, then pointed to a corner room. "Paul is in there. A surgical team removed the bullet from his thigh. He suffered an adverse reaction to the anesthetic. Explains why he's in intensive care rather than the Med-Surg ward."

Coop flattened his mustache. "Will he be okay?"

"They've controlled the anaphylaxis. Should be fine in a few days."

"What a relief. Did you meet his wife and explain his situation?"

"She didn't need my assistance. She was a navy nurse with ER credentials. Interpreted the allergic reaction for me." Cassie peeled back the curtain. "It's too late for visitors, but I'll sneak you in. Haley, stay here. This'll only take a sec."

"Sure, Mombo." Haley slid down the wall and collapsed on the floor. She pulled her backpack to her knees and rested her head.

"Thanks, Twink." Coop braced himself and pushed through the glass door.

Paul's room was chock-full of medical machines monitoring every bodily function. The cardiac monitor's flickering LED lights cast an eerie glow throughout the place. Bags of fluids hung on an IV stand. Oxygen lines meandered behind the bed after wrapping both of Paul's ears and passing under his nose. So many cords, hoses, and lead lines twisted around the wounded battalion chief, Coop froze—afraid to step closer.

Cassie glided around the bed and gently nudged the patient's shoulder. Paul didn't respond.

"Cause for concern?" Coop whispered.

Cassie shook her head. "Sleeping like a firefighter after a twenty-four-hour shift."

Coop backed out the door, wanting to forget about the gurgling tubes and pressure bandages. "I couldn't do this every day."

"A hospital room scares you?" Cassie hiked an eyebrow. "But not a thousand-degree fire?"

Coop bent over, hands on knees, shaking his head. "My brave isn't built that way."

21

Sydney dabbed sleep from her eyes as cheery sunlight knifed through tilted slats covering the window in Reggie's ICU pod. She kneaded kinks in her neck and lower back. After she finished a cat-like stretching routine, she scooted the chair next to the bed and reached for her favorite cameraman's hand. A frosty shiver shot through her as though he'd just emerged from a polar plunge.

She clenched his icy hand. "I'm here, Reg. I won't leave you." Sydney had the overnight watch while his wife was home with the kids. "You're young and strong. You can fight this."

Last night, doctors had placed Reggie in a medically induced coma and swathed him in a cooling blanket they hoped would give his brain trauma time to heal without the body performing radical triage by shutting off blood flow to its damaged sections. Much of the medical jargon required interpretation, but the underlying message was clear—Reggie was in deep trouble.

A jumble of hoses and fluid bags hung on a pole beside the bed. One line led to Reggie's arm, carrying hydrating liquid, powerful sedatives, and antibiotics. A breathing tube was stuffed into his mouth. Another lonely wire connected a grotesque Frankenstein bolt lodged in his temple to a pressure-monitoring contraption. All the while, the super-saturated odor of institutional disinfectants marched around the room like a garish celebrity in a sterile parade.

Sydney drummed her fingers on a magazine, mesmerized by squiggly green lines and red blips pulsating on the cardiac monitor. Peaks and valleys indicated a normal sinus rhythm that convinced her the cameraman was winning his fight.

A mechanical ventilator purred and hissed in alternating succession. Beeps and whirs from a host of other machines prompted her to draw a sweater around her shoulders and gnaw the inside of her cheek.

Reggie lay motionless.

Then, without warning, his blood pressure cuff inflated. Sydney jumped and Reggie's body bucked. The red blip on his EKG flatlined and the ventilator began screeching a hideous alarm.

Sydney lunged for the emergency call button as additional machines joined the shrill chorus. Two nurses flew into the room. While Sydney watched in numb disbelief, one nurse rechecked Reggie's IV and airway, then administered emergency drugs.

The second nurse inventoried the blaring monitors. "I think this guy threw a clot. Begin chest compressions." She pulled the code cord.

Reggie's rib cartilage crunched beneath the clasped hands of the nurse performing CPR. The red line on his EKG went berserk. A crash team arrived seconds later, brushing Sydney from the room. She pressed her forehead against the glass partition and studied the choreographed chaos.

The lead physician in the rolling flutter of white coats stood out wearing pale blue scrubs. She lubed two defibrillator paddles before placing one near Reggie's clavicle and the other on his left side below his heart. "V-fib. On three." Her sturdy tone instilled order, moving everyone away from the bed, the patient, and the equipment before engaging the defibrillator. "One, I'm clear. Two, you're clear. Three, we're all clear."

A nanosecond later, the machine shot two hundred joules through Reggie's desperate body. Sydney glared at the EKG's red line, but it refused to return to normal. His heart muscle hadn't responded to the electrical prod. The thing was beating so erratically, it failed to move sufficient blood through his arteries. Without juice, Reggie's vital organs and brain were being deprived of oxygen.

Sydney figured his body was racing through its own unique protocols. Shedding one essential function after another. Since the brain was programmed to stay in business, it fought with ruthless determination to save the heart and lungs for last—before switching off in the deadly cascade.

The doctor repeated the process, upping the defibrillator's charge to three hundred joules in a valiant attempt to save Reggie's life. Sydney's chest tightened and she pleaded for his heart to beat on its own. She shifted her gaze to his face, confused by his stoic serenity. Perhaps he'd found peace despite an EKG red line as jagged as Utah mountain peaks. She dug her nails into her palms as the cardiac code team's resuscitation efforts continued.

Three hundred sixty joules.

Violent. Cruel. Undignified.

She wanted to rush into the room and restore order. But she had nothing to contribute. Unlike the doctors and nurses, with their knowledge, innovative technology, and advancements in emergency medicine.

Their role was important.

Elegant.

Though utterly useless.

•

Lamar kicked off a knot of sheets and stared at the ceiling.

In his dreams, he'd begun calculating a surefire strategy to take down Falcon. Now, wide awake, the ideas jumbled together, causing his stomach to seize. He dashed to the john. Kneeling in front of the porcelain bowl, he ran through it again.

One night last October, Falcon stopped him after he'd finished working as an equipment assistant for the local minor league team. The Charleston RiverDogs defeated the Columbia Fireflies, and Lamar stayed behind to collect autographs from four visiting players sure to be called up to the majors one day.

Falcon's offer had been too good, yet it wasn't the reason why Lamar said yes. Falcon's threat against Mama had sealed the deal.

Lamar wiped his mouth, then brushed away the taste of vomit. He popped two aspirin before returning to his room. He threw on a pair of jeans and a Clemson Tigers T-shirt.

Time to walk away. He'd fulfilled his part.

He reached under the mattress for the burner phone and sent Falcon a text before he lost his nerve: *Need to talk.*

A response came immediately: *No.*

Lamar slid down the wall. He grew lightheaded and contemplated Falcon's betrayal. Someone else had started multiple fires along Spruance, and set him up for the Tip explosion. Perspiration beaded on his face and arms. Soon, his T-shirt was drenched. He squeezed the phone, nearly crushing it in his grip.

His hands trembled as he typed the next message: *Why?*

Four anxious minutes passed before Falcon replied: *Can't be seen together.*

Lamar huffed, shoved the burner phone under his mattress, then stumbled into the living room. He surveyed the gloomy appliances, fake leather sofa, and plywood bookcase stuffed with mystery novels and math books. He moved over to the window and stared past a dumpster, across the rear alley to the circus of commuter traffic on the Crosstown Connector.

He started to pace the full length of the shabby front room while flipping through every channel on a forty-six-inch plasma to find news about the fire investigation. Channel 13 aired videos taken yesterday interspersed with a live feed from Tipton Terrace.

Lamar slumped on the sofa and imagined himself playing second base for the Atlanta Braves, hitting .350 as a rookie All-Star phenom. Then his thoughts swung back to reality. He was officially a hoodlum who no longer deserved to attend college or be a major league All-Star.

He flipped to Channel 7. Their crawl strip read: *Area schools cancelled today.*

He grabbed a soda from the fridge and a handful of chocolate chip cookies from a covered bin on the counter.

A few minutes later, Mama shuffled in and poured a cup of coffee. "I called Tyrell and asked if you might wash dishes since there's no school. Interested?"

"Sure, Mama." Lamar longed to tell her about his troubles. He wanted to come clean before the roof caved in. He needed her help. Her wisdom. Her courage. "Mama, I—"

She set the steaming cup on the counter.

Awkward and ashamed, Lamar couldn't bring himself to disappoint her. That'd come soon enough. He bit his lower lip. "After Tyrell's, I'll head to the fire office for more internship hours."

"So, you best get moving. I'll meet you at the restaurant." She latched the front door.

Lamar circled the kitchen, cruised through his bedroom, then returned to the living room and dropped onto the couch.

He skimmed a newspaper article about a retrial for the notorious train station arsonist. That was important to Lamar because, according to Falcon, Nathan Sharpe went to prison for a fire Mama's brother had set. Uncle Jamal had never been formally accused, mostly because he died in the fire. But he was the reason Mama changed her name to Gallivant.

Lamar hoped the name change stuck. Especially if the Innocence Network helped free the man from prison. His release would prompt police to come sniffing around for someone new to blame, like dead Uncle Jamal. And sniffing around would put Mama in an unfortunate spotlight.

Lamar never believed Uncle Jamal or Mama actually did what Falcon claimed they did. But he couldn't take any chances.

Since when had the truth protected people like them?

Lamar funneled the last of his soda and swept cookie crumbs off his lap. He folded the newspaper and tossed it on the table. "Aw, damn. The boots."

He changed into sneakers before grabbing a garbage bag from under the sink. He dumped bleach over the leather Timberlands before tossing them into the bag. He pressed his backpack into the bag, as well, then cinched the drawstrings. He slung the garbage bag over his shoulder like Santa Claus and headed outside.

A pair of slimeballs huddled across the alley, smoking weed.

"Lamar, need a toke?" one asked.

"Naw, man. I'm good."

"Lamar gonna play professional ball one day," the other guy said. "He don't use drugs. Ain't that right?"

"I'll mail you tickets when I get to the show." Lamar reached the dumpster but kept moving. He didn't want those two losers finding the boots he'd worn while setting all those fires.

Once he rounded the corner, he sprinted a few blocks until he located another dumpster. He buried the boots under heavy chunks of scrap drywall and tar paper, a brusque goodbye to practically everything tying him to the fires. His last hurdle would be erasing video of him wearing the boots that was part of the fire marshal's collection.

Lamar returned to his house and checked the burner phone under his mattress out of habit. An unexpected text from Falcon spelled out another target: *74 Lenwood Boulevard. Tonight*. He slumped on his bed, fired up his laptop, then typed in the address using Google Maps. The place was near the Battery and he'd never be able to beat the curfew or roadblocks.

Besides, he didn't want to. He'd completed the requisite ten jobs.

He typed the address in a reverse directory. The house belonged to Cora Rose Bishop. He entered her name into his browser and discovered she was the Bishop Tea Plantation's blue-haired matriarch. Lamar wondered what beef Falcon had with an old white lady.

He carefully texted a response: *Can't. Curfew.*

Falcon's terse reply came quickly: *Do it. OR ELSE.*

•

Sydney sprinted for the hospital elevator, holding her stomach as she ran.

An acerbic taste of blood smacked her tongue. She nearly bowled over Coop and Haley when she stormed off the elevator on the ground floor.

Coop cocked his head. "What's wrong?"

"Reggie . . . My cameraman—" Her voice cracked. "They tried. He never came back." Sydney tightened her jaw and reflexively moved it from side to side. "How's your guy?"

"I'm told he's doing fine." The cell phone attached to Coop's belt chirped. He thumbed the screen until he retrieved a text. "This is awkward."

"What is it?" Sydney growled.

"I'm needed in the autopsy suite. Haley's mom is still working, so she's mine today."

Sydney led them to the Forensic Autopsy Section of the hospital's Pathology Department. From experience, she knew that group specialized in medicolegal cases referred by South Carolina coroners. Pathologists also provided testimony in criminal cases.

Dino, CPD's top homicide detective, frowned when Coop and his daughter slipped off the elevator. His jaw dropped when Sydney followed. "This is a surprise. I only expected Coop."

"What can I say, I'm a pack animal."

Haley pointed at Dino. "He's wearing a gun."

"He's a cop," Sydney said. "What do you have for us?"

"Us?" Dino scoffed.

"The task force. Remember?" Coop said.

Dino forced an insincere smile.

"We'll enjoy a good laugh about this later," Sydney said. "But I'm tired. My house burned. And Reggie—" The words caught. "Reggie's gone."

"Aw, sorry, Ladybug," Dino said.

Coop located a chair and dragged it into the hallway for Haley. He turned to Dino. "She safe here?"

"Yup." Dino edged away, ensuring Haley was out of earshot. "The coroner asked MUSC to examine the two bangers found at Syd's yesterday evening." He glanced at his notepad. "They were shot with a medium-caliber weapon. Short range. Execution style. Both died before the car fire. No soot in their lungs. Yahoos were wearing utility uniforms. And the Dominion Energy van was boosted two days ago."

Coop said, "Makes sense those guys gained access to Tip's apartments by posing as gas company employees. That act goes a long way to validating my theory about the explosion."

Sydney asked, "The Italian restaurant job?"

"The what?" Dino said. "You two are speaking a foreign language."

Coop said, "The Tip blast most likely came from a massive gas build-up. Probably caused by those two guys fiddling with a whole mess of pilot lights."

"Are you officially labeling the explosion intentional?" Sydney asked.

Coop shook his head. "Long way from proving it. Need to rule out accidental causes." He turned to Dino. "Why did you buzz me?"

Dino pulled a plastic sleeve from his folder. "The forensic doc emptied the two yahoos' wallets and pockets before she prepared the bodies. Found a picture of—"

"A falcon," Sydney blurted.

Dino didn't respond.

"Am I right?"

"Ladybug, you stepped on my punch line."

"Sorry." She didn't mean it.

"Then ground it in with a heel," Dino said.

"We get it." Sydney's voice dripped with sarcasm.

Dino grudgingly offered the plastic sleeve containing a color photograph of a falcon in flight: thin tapered wings, hooked bill.

Sydney said, "Dead bodies bearing a kitschy representation of the guy claiming responsibility. Another weird twist in Falcon's never-ending saga."

"Cruel irony," Dino said.

Sydney tapped the photo of the raptor's outstretched talons clutching a rat. "This tells me the dead guys were snitches."

"Or the two guys were loose ends in an unrelated crime," Coop said. "And the photo was planted to misdirect my investigation. Maybe Falcon isn't even a part of yesterday's mess, even though he claimed credit?"

Sydney said, "He's being framed? Priceless."

"Kinda causes a headache, doesn't it? All the possibilities."

Sydney scrunched her nose. "If Falcon planted this photo, how could he ensure it would survive the fire?"

"Planted after the vehicle fire," Coop said. "Let's deliver this to the crime lab. See if they can pull any prints."

Sydney debated whether she'd underestimated the 843Z. Maybe Coop was right about their connection.

·

Sydney volunteered to drop Haley at the Moultrie Building en route to meeting Coop and Dino at the West Ashley crime lab.

"Since school is closed today, Sheila needs your help sorting evidence receipts. Sound like fun until your dad gets back?"

"I suppose," Haley said. "Your house burned down, right?"

Sydney suspected she was being tested and hoped to win the kid over. "Yes, it did."

"What's it like, losing everything?"

"Hasn't sunk in yet."

"My mom would freak if she lost a single pair of shoes."

"Me too," Sydney shuddered. "Thankfully, I kept my shoe stash at the TV station."

Haley seemed to work that over. "Do you love your job?"

"It's pretty cool being on TV. Lots of perks." Sydney shook off the dread of being targeted by Falcon. Definitely a wicked perk. "Why do you ask?"

They climbed the stairs to the third floor.

"We watched you on TV last night," Haley said. "I think my dad likes you."

"I'm flattered."

Haley curled ringlets of golden hair around a finger. "I also think Dad likes Lamar more than me."

Sydney shook her head. "Why do you say that?"

Haley paused. "I'm being dumb."

"Your secret's safe with me."

Haley hesitated. Then averted her gaze. "Mom says he wanted a boy. Instead, he's stuck with me."

Oh, goodness. What an awful thing to tell a child.

Trying to keep the shock from her face, Sydney said, "I'm a real good judge of people, and I'm certain your dad loves you very much."

"He has a funny way of showing it." Haley jutted her lower lip again. "He even told Lamar about those nasty baseball cards. Whenever I ask, he says it's none of my business."

"What did he tell Lamar?" Curiosity about the burned cards crossed her mind. Yet Sydney had never found an opening to ask about them.

"Dad said, a long time ago, a Greenville boy died from playing with matches. It's why he has so many rules that ruin my life."

22

Coop handed the falcon photo to one of the evidence technicians in the crime lab.

The tech removed it from the plastic sleeve with tweezers and attached the picture to clips dangling under a fume hood. Next, he sprayed both sides of the photo with ninhydrin, a chemical reagent commonly used to raise latent fingerprints. The solution reacted immediately with amino acids left behind by whoever had handled the photo. A darkish compound, called Ruhemann's Purple, formed around one full and at least three partial prints. The tech photographed the prints with a high-resolution camera for further examination by a print analyst.

Since ninhydrin damaged DNA, Coop had weighed the prospects of forfeiting potential genetic material recovery. Retrieval of latent prints seemed more fruitful to his investigation. And far more expedient than time-consuming and expensive genome testing. Every police lab had a permanent DNA backlog, and Coop didn't want anything to slow his work.

He surveyed the lab as the technician worked. Expensive scientific equipment covered glistening stainless-steel tables. However, a rancid odor from bacon sandwiches lingered.

"The average fingerprint is composed of at least one hundred fifty individual ridge characteristics," the print analyst said with the enthusiasm of a person delivering their own eulogy. "Characteristics are largely defined as arches, loops, and whorls."

"This isn't my first rodeo," Coop chided.

The analyst shrugged it off, retrieving the hi-res photos on his computer. He moved a cursor over each magnified image to differentiate as many unique characteristics as possible. On the full print, he marked twenty points of reference for comparison in the FBI's Automated Fingerprint Identification System or against any investigation samples. The analyst scanned the partial prints, finding fewer unique points. Nevertheless, he coded them for submission.

The print tech said, "State Law Enforcement Division requires a day to return probable matches. An AFIS run takes longer since they work through more than seventy million prints in their system."

Coop turned back to the lab tech. "What about the paper, the image, or the printing. Anything we can use?"

The tech examined the photo using a magnifier. "Standard stock. Hundred percent cotton fibers. Bright white. Available at any office supply or big box store."

Coop shrugged. "No help."

Next, the tech scanned the falcon photo and a few keystrokes later, an array of identical pictures filled his computer screen. "The image is cut-and-paste. Downloaded from the web."

"Even less help," Coop said dryly.

The tech enlarged the scan. "Wait. Here's something."

"What?" Coop squinted.

"Shadows in the sky here and here?" The tech pointed at the screen with a pencil. "Looks like an echo from the printer's memory. A ghost image."

"Explain?" Coop asked.

The evidence tech seemed eager to offer his educated analysis. "Most multifunction office machines store a digital image of every document they scan or copy. This one must've glitched during the print process, leaving a sort of double exposure. What we see here is most likely from the document printed immediately before this page. I'll enhance the ghost by removing bits and bytes forming the bird."

The tech typed, then the screen blinked. After refocusing many times in rapid succession, the tech's manipulations produced partial text from what appeared to be a personal memorandum.

Who knew success smelled like bacon, Coop thought.

He clapped his hands. "Nice going. Print the screenshot and send me a file copy, too."

The technician reached for the printer output. "I'll try to retrieve text from behind the bird's breast. Might tell us more."

Coop nodded. "Like who sent it and who was it addressed to? It'd be nice if we could read the memo too. Safeguard the original and the usual caveats apply. Only share this information with Captain Burton."

"This could be a fine example of Locard's Exchange Principle in the high-tech environment," the technician said with great satisfaction. "If this pans out, I'll write a paper for the forensics journal."

Coop was familiar with Locard. "His definitive theory of trace evidence."

"Exactly. This double exposure was unforeseen by the offender and, at a minimum, ought to determine the printer in question. Then you perform your detective magic and bring me a suspect whose fingerprints I can compare to the latents."

Coop was savoring the new lead when Sydney kicked open the lab door, holding two evidence pouches. Dino lagged behind, toting a dusty banker's box containing the train station fire's archived file.

Coop pointed at their collection. "I guess the warehouse search yielded treasures."

Dino dropped the box on a counter and scowled. "Syd pawed at boxes in several bins beside where I retrieved this one before I could stop her." He lofted a beefy hand for the lab techs. "Don't worry, fellas. She didn't break any seals. I double-checked. Except—"

"Case identification number 85-H115." Sydney's voice sounded an octave higher than normal. "I kept repeating 85-H115. And presto."

Dino shook his head. "She managed to unearth four unsealed boxes."

Sydney held two clear bags out for inspection. "Marked 85-H115.

These were stored in the wrong box."

The lab tech grimaced. "No way."

Dino sighed. "I ordered the evidence custodian to conduct a full inventory and reseal the open files. What a nightmare."

Coop grabbed the evidence bags, read the case number, then glared at Dino. Next, he inspected the bags. Signatures, dates, and unbroken seals. The chain of custody remained intact despite the apparent filing error.

"I repeat, a friggin' nightmare." Dino shook his head. "At least those pouches from Nathan Sharpe's first trial are unaltered. We can swear to that."

Coop turned to the tech. "Do you have a safe?"

"The captain does."

"Call her. I need these items examined and secured. Prints, DNA, the whole shebang. And fast, unless the department wants a giant lawsuit on their hands." His cell phone vibrated with a text. "Brody says Gang Intel identified the two dead bangers. Street names are Croc and Ray-Ray. We need to make notifications."

"Not familiar with those yahoos," Dino said. "But I'll drive."

•

After working the breakfast rush at Tyrell's, Lamar flew up the stairs to the Moultrie Building's second floor, where the interns hung out.

Area universities hadn't canceled classes, so he grinned when he spotted only two interns at work. That meant fewer human obstacles for him to dodge while erasing incriminating photos.

Lamar selected a terminal away from the pair of college chumps and opened the database file marked INTERN VIDEO. He quickly scrolled through source clips, debating how much to erase.

He opted against destroying any evidence that did not implicate him directly. And Lamar couldn't erase the damning clip Red would remember of him wearing the boots. He did delete several segments of him wearing the hoodie, then edited Red's clip. He enlarged the screen grab, which resulted in shaving off the frame's bottom third of the video—so the boots didn't show.

Next, he scanned a file marked KINKAID STILLS for any pictures of him at the scene. He located a couple and dumped those into the electronic trash, then emptied the electronic waste basket. "Ta-da," he whispered.

Lamar strolled over to one of the chumps. "Need any help?"

The chump flinched and jerked an earbud free. "Couldn't hear you."

"Anything good?"

"Sociology lecture. Kinda putting me to sleep. They bring food yet?"

Lamar shook his head, thankful he'd eaten a big breakfast at Tyrell's. He pointed to the terminal he'd claimed. "I'm over there if you need me."

The guy poked the earbud into place. "Shout when the pizza arrives."

Lamar trundled to his terminal and opened the video clips with highlight rings one more time. He played it through, satisfied no incriminating images of him lingered in the montage. He stretched his long arms with satisfaction, then remembered he needed to erase the same files from the master database.

But he couldn't access those secure files unless he got called back to the third floor.

Lamar changed the screen just as Knob entered the room.

"Yo, Lamar. Working on something important?" he asked.

"Always."

23

Coop hopped in the passenger seat after Dino eased his Kona Blue Mustang next to the sidewalk in front of the Crime Lab. They drove east for Fleet Landing.

"What's our plan?" Coop adjusted the radio and stopped on an oldies channel playing "Baby Love."

"Never pegged you as a Motown man."

"I keep telling you, I'm more than a pretty face."

Dino grinned. "Do me a favor, no singing. Diana is backed by her Supremes. She doesn't need you."

"Darn, and I was starting to stomach you," Coop said with fake outrage. "I thought maybe we were full-blown friends."

"If you say so." Dino slid a pair of sunglasses from his pocket and into position. "My intel says you have a daughter?"

"Mighty fine detective work, Lieutenant. Why are you asking?"

"Syd wanted me to remind you to call the kid. She says stay connected, even when you're in the field."

"I'll tell Haley you two are on board." Coop wove in a dose of sarcasm to hide his resentment at being told how to handle his daughter.

"I mean it. Call her. Tell her 'Hi.' Say you're thinking about her and care what she's doing. Ask what's on her mind."

Coop shook his head. "We don't say those things." Though he wished they did.

Engaging in a normal conversation with Haley sounded great. He was embarrassed about how badly he misread her feelings and knew he'd better start getting it right soon.

Dino said, "Look, I'm only the messenger. Let's get down on some real police work." He pulled a notecard from his pocket with

"1716 KINKAID" neatly printed and passed it to Coop. "This address is west of the fire. A snitch for the drug unit said this is where we'll find D-Jazz's aunt. The unit sat on the place overnight. But no sign of our guy. After we see if she's willing to give up her nephew, we'll work the two dead bangers' notifications."

The mutilated hulk of Tipton Terrace loomed on the skyline as they made their way up Nimitz Avenue. Rainbow Row gave way to sun-bleached blah. Broken streetlamps replaced copper carriage lanterns. Seersucker couture morphed into ill-fitting jeans and baggy jerseys.

"Tell me about Fleet Landing," Coop said.

"My first beat. Drug dealers and hustlers were easy picking in the neighborhood park. Lots of repeat customers. But I used to check on people who lived there rather than grab one collar after another. Morale and welfare became my priority."

"You ever live there?" Coop asked.

Dino hung a right into the Tipton Terrace parking lot. Mesh fence, topped with a strand of razor wire, circled the property. "This place was built in 1950 with one hundred fifty-six apartments. Back in the day, my dad worked for the Navy as an underwater welder. Lots of shipyard workers rented here because they were close to the base. Spent five years up there." He pointed at the building's crushed north end. "Apartment 406 before we moved to Sullivan's Island."

"Sullivan's Island? Sheesh, Dino, you come from money."

Dino threw his head back with a hearty laugh. "What else can I do to destroy your stereotypes today?"

Coop hesitated, hoping to avoid stepping in another smoldering pile.

"Messing with you. It's really not a race thing around here." Dino erased the whole thing with a hand swipe and pulled back onto Nimitz Avenue. "Doesn't matter whether you're a cop or a firefighter, the public only sees a badge. Never crosses their minds that folks in uniform are real people."

"Amen."

They motored west on Kinkaid past the wreckage of yesterday's fires. Coop eyed numbers tacked to porches, searching for their prime suspect's aunt's place. He pointed ahead at a three-story shithouse. "Gray one. On the right."

Cars were parked snug to the curb along the narrow street. They slow-cruised past 1716. Plastic toys littered the bare front yard. An azalea hedge blocked the porch. Scorch marks covered an empty shell's piazza to its left. Across the street, a flame-ravaged home tilted on its crooked frame. Other vacant ruins, with broken windows, graffiti tags, and overgrown weeds, served as a reminder how far the neighborhood lagged behind the rest of the affluent peninsula.

"We need backup?" Coop asked.

Dino flashed a crooked grin. "Don't you trust me?"

"Just checking."

A block ahead, Dino wedged the Mustang between a pair of beater cars. He unfolded as two tough guys materialized from behind a clapboard shack. They wore jeans, ball caps pulled low over their ears, and permanently pissed-off expressions.

Dino motioned the bangers over. He reached into his wallet and removed a pair of twenties, then ripped the bills in half. "This car better be here when I return. No scratches. All four tires and rims." Dino signaled the guy wearing a dozen bro-chains, including a large 843 medallion, and handed him half of the torn bills. Everything about the other guy read sharp angles. Jutting jaw, bony shoulders. Dino's glance darted between the two. "Deal?"

Bro-chain's toothy sneer showed off his gold incisor. "Y'all Five-O?"

"Fire department," Coop said without hesitation.

Bro-chain glared at the rice-white agent. "You're a day late."

"Never left. Thanks for watching the Mustang, fellas." Coop headed for 1716.

A few paces from the front door, Dino asked, "How do you fire guys slide by with sarcasm?"

Coop said, "I meet people on their worst day, armed with only a water cannon, and help them. Cops show up armed to the teeth and usually arrest someone. Or worse." He spun to face Dino. "Admit it, you wanted to be a firefighter when you were a kid."

Dino rubbed his chin. "Maybe so. But check me now—armed to the teeth."

Coop spotted a dark sedan on the cross street. Tall weeds and a massive crepe myrtle nearly obscured the car. Concealed was a better word. "We're being followed."

Dino didn't flinch. "Black Mercedes? Behind the tree?"

"Yup."

Dino knocked on the front door. "Been tailing us a few blocks. Super clumsy. I'll slip behind him and light him up if he's still with us when we're done here."

"In the meantime, remove the aviator shades. We look like a pair of stooges from *In the Heat of the Night*."

A woman, who'd stuffed herself into poorly fitting workout pants, cracked open the door until the security chain caught. "What do you want? My stories are on and you bothering me."

Dino stepped forward and jammed his foot in the doorway. "Mrs. Hines? Latisha Hines?"

The woman reared her head back and shouted, "Tisha, the po-po here for you." She melted into the ramshackle house.

A few moments later, a smaller woman, also wearing unflattering yoga pants, came to the door. "Yeah?" Her cheeks were swollen and her eyes puffy and red.

"I'm Lieutenant Bernadino and this is Special Agent Bellamy from ATF. May we come in?"

She fixed a hard stare. "You the one who shot my baby girl?"

"No ma'am," Dino said. "Though I'm sorry for your loss."

Coop imagined receiving a knock on the door from two officers and being told horrible news about a loved one. He knew from experience cops hoped they never came off as insincere.

She eyed them with a heaping helping of resentment.

Coop nudged Dino. "She can't remove the chain with your foot in the door, Lieutenant."

Dino stepped back, and the woman closed the door to lift the chain from its flimsy track. When she opened the door, Coop and Dino moved inside and discovered two more women slumped on a ragged couch. One pre-teen boy played a handheld video game. And a couple of toddlers in diapers crawled along the floor in the gloom of poverty. Light from a TV flickered across their dark faces.

"Anyone else here?" Dino asked.

The women shook their heads. Owl-eyed toddlers clung to the nearest human leg.

"Mind if I take a quick peek?" Dino prowled the space without waiting for a reply.

Coop distracted the women while Dino crisscrossed the living room, then disappeared upstairs to execute his search for D-Jazz or any other lurking problems. "Are those collards and ham hocks I'm smelling?"

A woman wearing a bathrobe grabbed a baby off the floor. "Does it remind y'all of home? When you were an itty-bitty baby down on the farm?" Her voice dripped hostility.

Typically, when a white law enforcement officer worked a non-white neighborhood, he could expect resistance. Hell, Coop often found himself downright stonewalled. This time, he hoped to defuse the situation to his advantage. "Reminds me of something my wife made. Except she left out the bacon." He smoothed his mustache. "Added red pepper flakes and grated parmesan. Who does that?"

"Bet she's no longer your Mrs., is she?"

Coop laughed. "I wanted bacon."

Dino returned to the living room without brandishing anyone

in cuffs. "Is there a place to talk, Mrs. Hines?"

"Call me Tisha. And the kitchen table's where I do my talking." She sidled to the rear of the house.

Three large pots filled with greens covered the stove. Bubbling chicken broth caused the lids to flap. Every so often, a pot belched and starchy broth oozed over the side.

Coop hooked a chair leg with his foot and pulled it away from the table. Dino plopped on a stool near the sink. The boy wandered in and dug an orange soda from the refrigerator.

"You two related?" Dino asked.

"He's all I have left," Tisha said.

"What about D-Jazz?" Coop asked.

"What about him?"

"Isn't he your nephew?"

"He's trouble." The boy's voice was fortified with defiance. "Tries to strut his stuff sitting down."

"How so?" Coop asked.

Tisha placed her hands on the table. A faint tremble in her bottom lip. "I'm single. Work nights. Can't keep my eye on them. Have to trust 'em. D'Angelo, he shoulda never been trusted. Needed a man around to set him straight." She held the boy's hand. "I worry about how I'm gonna keep D'Vonte from the 843Z all by myself."

"Tell me about D-Jazz," Coop said.

Tisha's eyes watered. "Blast from the Tip shook pictures right off the wall. Sounded like a bomb. Is D'Angelo behind the trouble?"

"It's what we're here to find out." Coop's voice softened. "What's he been up to since his release from prison?"

Tisha pushed D'Vonte away and narrowed her eyes. "D-Jazz brought that darn gun into my house when he came over a while back. I told him I wouldn't stand for it. Look, I know he's been bad. But he isn't capable of killing people. It's not in his nature."

Coop knew she'd probably lied. A forgivable untruth under the circumstances. "Where can we find D-Jazz?"

Tisha twisted a ring on her finger, and her face clouded. "He said he found a way to generate money. Move us out of Fleet Landing. Told me he knew who's behind the fires."

"Who?" Dino asked.

Coop tilted his head. "Did you find it the least bit curious Fleet Landing didn't have any fires the whole time D-Jazz was incarcerated? Then, they start burning major league right after he gets released. And when he goes back to jail for thirty days, the fires stop. Now, he's out again, and—"

"Are you telling me my nephew is the firebug?" She slumped. Tears trickled down her cheek. Then an idea seemed to flash, prompting new life. "What if I let y'all keep D-Jazz? Will cops pay me for killing my li'l Destiny?"

"Sorry, but you aren't in a position to bargain." Dino stood. "We're going to find D-Jazz with or without your help. And I really am sorry for your loss."

That stock phrase again, though Coop felt Dino's tone continued to reflect genuine sincerity.

Tisha smoothed her cheek. "Why didn't you cops use a Taser or rubber bullets on my baby girl? Mamas ain't supposed to outlive their children—even in the hood."

Dino sighed. "We used the same bullets she did."

Tisha sobbed. "She didn't mean to jump-start no war."

Coop didn't want to belabor the reality of a righteous shoot. "What can you tell us about a fella called Ice?"

Tisha mumbled a few indecipherable expletives. "Y'all go ahead and shoot him."

Earlier, Coop's ATF boss had provided additional information that bumped Ice, AKA Robert Moses, high on Coop's radar. Tisha surprised him by acknowledging the guy who'd purportedly muscled his way to number two in the 843Z. The mere mention of him had aroused a feral response in her.

Before they departed, Coop wanted to square matters with a

subtle, unmistakable shift in his voice. "My responsibility is to keep more fires from happening. Tell me about D-Jazz's money plan."

Tisha laughed at her nephew's apparent heady vision. "Real estate. No more gangsta for him."

"Any idea where he is?" Coop asked.

She frowned. "He don't come round anymore."

24

Sydney made good time en route to Lieber Correctional Institution in the small town of Ridgeville, less than an hour's drive from the TV station.

Rob Noble had convinced his client, Nathan Sharpe, to add her to his authorized visitors list. The prominent lawyer also finagled the warden into granting special permission for Sydney to meet Nate outside of the system's regularly scheduled visitation days. She knew any exception to the prison's strict regulations was indeed a major compensation.

Lieber was one of six high-security prisons in the state correctional system housing violent offenders. Gun turrets were positioned at every corner of the sprawling site, and the perimeter was surrounded by two rows of welded fencing made of heavy gauge stainless steel topped by several spirals of razor wire. A sunny patch of green yard was visible through the fencing.

Sydney checked in with correctional officers overseeing her visit. They'd be responsible for her protection while maintaining custody and control over Nate, the inmate, despite him having earned trustee status as a result of model behavior. In short, he wasn't really considered a threat.

By rule, she couldn't bring a camera or writing implements, though the warden and his security team authorized a few pages of notes. Once she cleared the metal detector, they escorted her through an institutional lobby into the spacious visitation room. She stored mental images of the sterile fixtures, stagnant odor of Lysol, and the facility's overwhelming beige-ness.

Sydney had met with dozens of offenders at the Law Enforcement Center's holding area and county jail. Yet, this was her first meeting with anyone confined in an honest-to-goodness prison.

Nate hitched into the room wearing government-issued orange pants and shirt. He stood tall and thin, with tight curls of jet-black hair showing no signs of age. He flashed a welcoming smile revealing crooked teeth. "Ms. Quinn, I presume?" He wrapped the words around a chuckle.

Sydney exhaled a long breath. "Sydney." She stuck out her hand. "May I call you Nate?"

"Sure. You helping my new lawyer?"

She bobbed her head. "I'm a reporter for Action 7 News in Charleston. I've read newspaper accounts of your first trial and watched whatever video I could lay my hands on. They left plenty of holes I'm hoping you can fill. But before we start, I'm sure Rob told you to avoid saying anything you wouldn't want repeated on TV." Despite seeking the truth, she didn't hold a lawyer-client privilege, and wasn't eager to derail Rob's case.

"I'm a big fan," Nate said. "Ask me anything."

She disregarded her prearranged sequence of questions in favor of tacking from an oblique direction. She looked Nate square in the eye. "Who did you lose that fateful day?"

Nate rubbed his forehead as he processed the question. Then he splayed his fingers on the table.

Sydney noticed his hands tremble. "Sorry, I didn't mean to—"

Nate made a small shake of his head. "After all these years, the questions are pretty standard. But no one, I repeat, no one has ever asked me that before."

She didn't know whether to feel satisfied by her line of inquiry or peeved at the countless others who'd come before her. A yawning silence passed, and she wasn't sure whether he intended to respond. She let him take his time.

Nate coughed into his elbow. "Jamal Price. My best friend never made it out." His voice became husky with sentiment. "I worked as a shoeshine boy. My stand was located on the concourse near a bunch of shops." He surveyed the room, then stoked a grin. "You know, I remember I was making about three bucks an hour back then. Usually doubled my haul with tips, plus free food from the girls running the café's speed line. Jamal worked at the newsstand selling papers and cigarettes. He kinda resented me for making more money, even though I shared my windfall with him. And the girls."

Sydney tuned into every nuance in his tone and expression. He, in turn, seemed to read her with probing, intelligent, kind eyes.

He said, "Had to be solid with my man, Jamal, because I was dating his sister. Didn't want it getting back to her I flirted with the waitresses." Another hint of a smile crossed Nate's face. "I came clean to Raney 'bout that years later. You know, she still comes 'round at least once a month."

Sydney rolled her lips inward, contemplating her next move. "Who do you think started the fire?"

"There you go again. Asking what no one else ever did." Nate brought a finger to his cheek. "Haven't given it any thought since …"

Sydney hated asking him to traipse through his memories. But she was anxious to hear a firsthand account. "Tell me about it, if possible."

She didn't expect him to recall minute details. But from her own harrowing experience, she knew the mind held onto a few vivid aspects. She let the quiet pass before resuming eye contact.

Nate paced a tight circle in the narrow space between the wall and the table. Eventually, he leaned against the beige cinderblocks. "It's pretty foggy." He rhythmically tapped his thumb against his thigh.

Sydney sensed his overwhelming rush of grief. She'd crashed headlong into history and found herself at a loss for the appropriate words to coax his story. She chose silence.

Nate began slowly, seeming to parse his reply before settling in. Sydney's breathing tripped when he recounted a whittled-down version of the most agonizing events. Moving people to safety. Gulping suffocating smoke. Trying to locate his pal, Jamal. Excruciating pain.

Cruel mental torture from hours of interrogation.

Sydney clasped her hands so tightly that her fingers lost color. Without grilling him, she asked, "Why did you go to the police station?"

"Thought I was helping. No reason to suspect otherwise. I knew I didn't do anything wrong, so why would cops get that kind of hairbrained idea?"

The more he explained, the more baffling his story became.

"And the confession?" she asked.

"Same old song. I'd have said anything to get out of there. Wanted to . . ." He shook his head. "Go home."

His words pierced her. Nate must've read Sydney's reaction because he reached over and patted her hand. This small gesture, like his sister Lantana's unexpected hug, helped her persevere.

"During the interview, I felt invincible. And stupid," Nate said in a low thrum. "One time, the police said I could go. You know, I was this close." He pinched his thumb and forefinger together, leaving no space.

Now, Sydney's anger ballooned. "Did the cops ever say you were officially under arrest?"

Nate scratched his chin. "I'd been there all night. With no food or water. I got tired. Real tired." His shoulders sagged, reliving the exhausting ordeal. "Mr. Noble says that's where the cops and my first lawyer messed up bad."

"I'm not a lawyer, so I'm learning with you. Even though you were treated badly, the only reason for your retrial is about technical fire matters. Rob has secured an ATF agent—an arson expert ready to testify on your behalf. Things look promising."

Nate deflated like a bald tire. "Lifers aren't allowed to raise their hopes. This one's a real long shot."

"What's it like in here?" Sydney hadn't meant to ask that prosaic question, yet Nate Sharpe touched her at a level beyond the current storyline. Shared trauma, perhaps. Or maybe his quiet nobility, his positivity in the face of unimaginable injustice. She doubted that in his place, she'd be so well-adjusted.

Nate responded without hesitation. "I am a property of the state." His expression signaled defiant dignity. "At first, being called *property* humbled me in ways I never imagined. Of course, there's also the stuff you see on TV. Like bone-crushing loneliness, fear of the unknown, lack of privacy. For those, you better adapt in order to survive. But the property label shakes your sense of humanity. I hope I can overcome that tag if I ever get out."

Sydney tried to imagine being told what to do, when to do it, and having to adhere to intractably ingrained schedules. No wonder ex-cons found life difficult on the outside.

Nate shook his head, then offered an impish grin. "And I can't wait to use real silverware."

Sydney joined Nate in congenial laughter. "Thank you for your candor."

"I'm grateful for your visit. Like I said, I'm a big fan." Nate hitched a thumb over his shoulder. "Better get back."

25

By the time Coop and Dino finished speaking with D-Jazz's aunt, the lurking Mercedes had vanished.

A light drizzle beaded on the Mustang. Dino rounded the car checking for damages before handing his half of the torn money to the tough guys guarding his prized automobile.

"Can either of you tell me anything about the fire?" Dino said.

"Which one?" Bro-chain asked. "Plenty to choose from."

"How about yesterday? Or the Tip explosion?"

The two glanced at each other and hooted.

Bro-chain sneered. "Y'all don't know 'bout that? D-Jazz fighting for control of his crew from Ice. We smack dab in a real turf war."

Coop said, "Which side are you fellas on?"

"Side payin' the most." Bro-chain stroked his face and attempted to furtively shake his head to a passing BMW with two young white guys in the front seat. Probably students from a local college hoping to score drugs. "Time to move, Five-O. You cuttin' into my biz."

Dino asked, "If I patted you down right now, what'll I find?"

"A hard-on and a tight ass."

Coop climbed into the Mustang. "No thanks."

"I gotta radio it in," Dino said.

Bro-chain said, "I thought we friendin'. I risked telling you stuff—like Ice the one who bombed the Tip."

Dino held up a pair of fresh twenties to sweeten the pot. "Where is D-Jazz cribbing these days?"

Bro-chain and his partner squared their shoulders and pretended to zip their mouths.

Then Bro pilfered the bills from Dino. "He at a ho house in Sangaree."

As they pulled away, Coop radioed Detective Tate with the possible location for D-Jazz. Along with the curious tidbit regarding Ice's connection to Tip's explosion. He surveyed the streets as Dino drove west on Knox. "Riding with you is a real lesson in geography."

"Charleston is a pretty great city despite a few sewer holes. Easy to move around, except for the darn one-ways. They'll make you crazy." Dino swung into the parking lot near a collection of non-descript, one-story brick buildings immune to the arsons hounding the rest of Fleet Landing. Paved walkways curved through live oaks. And a bright green lawn was crowded with playground equipment and kids unexpectedly home from school.

"Jeez, I hate making notifications," Coop said.

"Worst part of the job."

"You think Ice or D-Jazz killed the two guys found in the stolen van at Syd's place?"

"Let's find out." Dino checked another notecard for a unit number and pointed. "Six-B." He swiveled his head, evaluating the surroundings.

"Expecting trouble?" Coop asked.

Dino grinned and thumped the front door. "When I'm with you, I'm a good guy by association."

A light-skinned African American woman in a mint green bathrobe and matching fuzzy slippers eased open a peephole. "He ain't here."

"Is this where Ray-Ray lives?" Dino asked.

"What part of 'he ain't here' didn't you comprehend?" She flailed her hands to shoo Dino away.

Dino held his badge for inspection. "May we come in? I have some bad news."

She pulled open the door and shuddered. "What's he done this time?"

Dino entered first and repeated his routine of searching the premises. When he returned to the front room, Coop was seated in an oversized faux leather recliner across from the woman.

Coop motioned for Dino to sit. "Ray-Ray is her grandson. Works at Piggly Wiggly. Produce department."

Dino said, "Sounds like a swell job. You raise him?"

The woman nodded. "He turned out okay for being a crack baby. Born small. Tough first year. But he graduated high school." Her body tensed. "What's your bad news?"

"Any reason Ray-Ray would ride around in a Dominion Energy van?" Coop asked.

She pinched her face. "Am I talking too soft for you? He works at Piggly Wiggly."

Coop leaned forward. "Did he work there yesterday?"

She picked a magazine from the coffee table. "Day shift, every Monday through Friday. Left here early. About eight. Same as always." She shifted her gaze between Dino, the magazine, and Coop. She settled on Coop with a nervous glare. "Never checked your badge."

Coop reached for his wallet. "I'm working with the Charleston Fire Department."

Her nervousness evaporated, and she teetered on the edge of hysteria. "Oh, no. He died in that fire, didn't he? That's why he didn't come home." Her hands flew to her face, though she managed to summon enough strength to avoid becoming a sodden mess. After a beat, she grabbed the magazine, absently turning pages while holding back tears.

Dino said flatly, "Truth is, Ray-Ray and another man called Croc were shot. Anyone you'd like me to call to come stay with you?"

The weight of the news hit her, and she let go a full-on blubber. "Please leave."

Dino gave Coop a quick glare that read *stay in your seat.* "First, any idea why Ray-Ray was riding in a power company van if he was supposed to work the produce counter at a grocery store more than a mile away?"

"Maybe it had something to do with his other job." Her words sounded soft and uncertain.

"What other job?" Coop asked.

"He's learning plumbing and electrical."

"From who?"

"Rivertown Academy."

That information squared with Coop's notion the two local gangs, Rivertown Academy and the 843Z, were behind the fires to further their repair scam. "Talk to me about Robert Moses. He lived over on Kinkaid most of his life."

The woman quit sniffling at the mention of Ice. Her tears vanished, and she coiled her hands into fists. "Did he kill my Ray-Ray?"

Coop said, "We need to talk to him. Any idea where I can find him?"

She made an emphatic head shake.

Coop couldn't deny the visceral reaction the mere mention of Ice elicited. He asked, "What is it about Ice—"

"He stole my house. Been in my family three generations. He and the gang go about scaring people like me into selling. Else we get burned out. Now, I'm forced to live in the projects."

"Go on," Dino said.

"A few folks had their house burnt more than once. You gonna stop him?"

Coop eyed Dino, then her. "Is Ice the brains of the gang?"

"Oh, hell no. He's dumber than a sack of dirty socks. He's the muscle. Ice finds the guns too. Come to think of it, he's probably the one who shot Ray-Ray and Croc." She eyed Dino with exasperation. "By the way, nobody you need to warn about Croc."

"How did Ice steal your house?" Coop said.

The woman tossed the magazine on the coffee table and slid forward. "Ice, or someone else from the gang, comes knocking at the front door. They force their way inside and concoct a wild offer to buy. Say they're doing you a big favor. Being how the house is in the ghetto and worth nothing to nobody. 'Grab the money,' they say. 'Head to West Ashley.'"

"But?" Dino prodded.

"They only offer a few thousand dollars or so. Those who want to stay in Fleet Landing, tell the thugs to move along. If they do that, they can expect a fire in the near future. We became good at predicting the warning signs, and managed to watch out for each other. Took turns staying awake all night. Called 911 if anything burnt. Even snapped pictures of a young fellow lighting some newspapers on a front porch." She turned her glare to Coop. "Phoned the fire tip line, though nothing happened."

Coop leaned forward. "Remember when? Maybe have an address?"

"I can do better." She pulled a pen and a pad from her robe pocket and jotted a note for Coop. Then she went to the sideboard and retrieved a photo. She handed him the picture and softened her eyes. "That's a copy of the one we submitted. Now, what about my house?"

"What are you asking?"

"Ice never burned it. He just stole it." She paused to take a deep breath. "I've no right to ask, but I don't know where else to turn. Any chance it'll be mine again? I'm begging you."

Coop said earnestly, "I'll do my best."

Dino frowned but laid a business card on the coffee table. "Please call if you have any additional information."

She plucked the card from the table and dropped it in her pocket. "Even if you find Ice, there might be more trouble than you bargain for."

Coop rose to leave. "Oh? Why is that?"

"I hear the real brains is some kinda bigwig."

Coop's cell vibrated with a message from Detective Tate. "We're about to cross that bridge. Dorchester County SWAT apprehended D-Jazz."

26

Sydney loved hanging out at the TV station. But today was different. Reggie would never crack another joke about her overdependence on lip gloss. Eric was doing okay, though working with a new cameraman was like training a puppy.

She tossed her purse on her cluttered desk before quarantining herself in Editing Bay 5, where she focused on Fleet Landing. Prosperity petered out by the time upper King Street redevelopment reached the hood. Knox Street became the line of demarcation separating the haves from the withouts. The landscape became one of vacant or neglected buildings ripe for crime and fires despite their immediate proximity to the district.

Even on the old naval base where Sydney lived, many repair shops stood rusted and abandoned. Only a few small mom-and-pop outfits dared startups, reducing the hulking post-Cold War installation to a mere footnote. Thankfully, Hart Anson was managing a slow turnaround despite resistance from Mayor Wallace and the city council.

Shifting gears, she pinched her cheeks, then fixated on the surprise discovery of items recovered from the old train station scene, which were never processed or admitted into evidence. Such a finding seemed earth-shattering as a standalone, and fueled Sydney's hunch Nate had been framed. She swallowed a bitter gulp and marched to her cubicle, curious what role the mayor, née former prosecutor, had played in the apparent scheme.

Mandy plopped onto Sydney's recliner and tucked her legs. "I've finished charting Falcon's manifesto addresses you received in that email. So, let's talk Civil War. Specifically, 1861."

Sydney dropped into a chair. "My favorite year."

"Spoken like a damn Yankee." Mandy straightened her legs, reached under Sydney's desk, then pulled out a bottle of wine and a Diet Mountain Dew from the tiny refrigerator.

Anyone born and bred in a Union state earned the Yankee moniker. The modern South welcomed Yankees, but only for as long as they visited. A damn Yankee, like Sydney, overstayed their welcome and never returned home.

Mandy poured a glass of pinot for herself and handed the Dew to Sydney.

Sydney clinked glasses. "To 1861."

"Whoa, that was a horrible year for Charleston. And since the Holy City is where you call home, I suggest you pay attention." Mandy sipped her wine and rested the glass atop Sydney's desk. "April's bombardment of Fort Sumter launched the war."

"I remember learning that."

"Eight months later, on December 11th to be precise, a catastrophic fire devastated our fair city. Darned thing swept from one side of the peninsula to the other."

Sydney sat forward. "Holy sh—"

Mandy held up a palm. A few interns popped their heads over cubicle dividers.

Sydney's interest spiked. "Who set it?"

Mandy leaned forward in a conspiratorial manner. "Rumors of Yankee saboteurs abound. But the most popular conclusion blamed a slave rebellion for the arson. Retaliation for South Carolina's secession."

Sydney didn't want to quash her friend's enthusiasm, yet she needed clarity. "How does it relate to Falcon, our modern-day anarchist?"

Mandy swallowed another sip of wine. "Witnesses were amazed at the fire's speed. Every building between Market and Queen Streets was aflame. Then when hope seemed lost . . ." Mandy paused for dramatic effect. "It started to rain."

By now, every intern and a handful of assistant producers hovered around Sydney's cubby, glued to Mandy's history lesson.

Mandy returned the wine glass to the desktop. "Once the flames jumped Broad Street, the fire burned clear to the Ashley River. Despite wide-scale destruction, only five people died."

Sydney rubbed goose bumps from her arms. "Those coincidences are plain creepy. But it seems implausible Falcon knew in advance how many people might die in his fire and explosion. And you haven't told me anything about the manifesto addresses."

Mandy slapped her knee as though the connection was obvious. "Quit being dense. Every home on Tradd, Legare, Meeting, and Queen Streets—destroyed in the Great Fire. And those are the same addresses Falcon wants to burn."

Sydney digested the significance of the new information. "Terrible, yet it doesn't explain why Falcon is tormenting Fleet Landing as a prelude. Tell me, how did the neighborhood cope during the war?"

Mandy glanced at her notes. "Fleet Landing didn't exist back then. Locals called the area Clifford's Neck. A shipping magnate named Samuel Bishop owned the land, which consisted mostly of piers and waterfront operations."

Sydney recalled what Falcon had said during his threatening phone call. "The South shall rise again. This time in a different color."

"That's odd to say, even for you." Mandy unfolded a city map on Sydney's desk with the manifesto addresses highlighted. She pressed two fingers into the map. "I live on Legare. My great-great-grandfather built my house in 1880, probably using reconstruction money. Dammit, Syd. Falcon is coming after me."

Sydney threw an arm around her friend. "Falcon has been apprehended. Coop says the Dorchester County sheriff has D-Jazz booked and fingerprinted."

•

Coop returned to the Moultrie Building as the muddled sun began a steep glide over the yardarm. Twinkling streetlights silhouetted the city's ubiquitous palmetto trees against a cherry sky. He plopped at the office table with Haley while they snacked on veggie tacos, washing them down with coconut water.

Haley bubbled with excitement. "I watched Sydney this evening. Her job is way chill. Being on TV every day."

Coop clutched his chest. "Are you saying my job isn't cool?"

Haley smeared her lips with a paper napkin and frowned. "I'm not sure what you do?"

Coop bundled the pile of waxed wrappers and shoved them into the take-out bag, trying to hide his disappointment. His own daughter had no idea how he earned a living. "I investigate suspicious fires."

"You mean when bad guys burn a house on purpose?"

"Exactly."

Haley slumped in her chair. "Bor-ring."

He wished she would express the same enthusiasm for his career as she did for Sydney's. "I'm gonna show you one little thing I do at the fires I investigate." Coop placed his investigator's case on the table, then laid out technical gear: tools, casting kit, and a solid sample evidence canister. He asked Haley to secure a large sheet of newsprint using FIRE LINE DO NOT CROSS tape. Next, he dumped a small sample of soot and ash onto the paper.

"Ick," Haley groaned.

Coop handed Haley a pair of vinyl gloves and a mask, then slipped a dime into the debris while she busied herself donning the safety gear. "Let's sift for evidence."

Haley reached for the trowel and dug in. "What am I looking for?"

Coop placed the sifting screen over an empty tin. "Any goodies you think the lab techs should analyze. One day, the supervisor can show you the gadgets and equipment she uses to catch bad guys with stuff we collect."

Haley worked the soot over the sifting screen until she discovered the hidden dime. Coop passed her a pair of tongs, and she squealed with delight, sliding the coin into a resealable Kapak pouch. "Okay, Dad. Your job isn't so bad after all. But it's way less chill than being a TV star."

"Probably."

Haley squirmed in her seat and clenched the trowel with both hands as though something else bugged her.

"What's on your mind?" Coop asked.

"Why did you move away?"

The question knocked him off his axis.

She pooched her lips. "When you divorced Mombo, you left me too, Dad. What did I do wrong?"

Her mournful expression shattered his soul and he didn't know how to respond. Coop's throat tightened as he searched for the perfect words. Instead, he stammered, "I— We—"

If he truly welcomed a chance to soften their relationship, he knew he'd better dad-up. But how did you tell a kid—his own daughter, the person he adored more than anyone else on the planet—that her Mombo had been a jerk for shoving him out the door? Worse, Mombo couldn't be trusted.

Coop found his voice. "I never meant to hurt you. I wish I could explain it better . . . this tension between me and Mom—"

"What about it?"

"Simply put, it's between me and her. You did nothing wrong. I love you so much. And I miss you when we're apart."

He recalled the day she was born. He'd driven Cassie to the hospital and waited ten hours before the kid finally popped out—healthy. He'd never seen anyone so beautiful in his whole life. Eventually, she could say, 'Da-da.' Her arms spread wide, grinning ear-to-ear.

Life seemed simple then.

Now, Haley was eleven. Almost twelve. Nearly thirteen. And a chameleon.

One minute, the spitting image of her mom. The next, someone he didn't recognize.

At that moment, her expression read confused. Vulnerable.

Coop pulled Haley close and she tucked herself under his chin. He kissed the top of her head and flicked hair from her face. She smelled like warm honey. "I'm here for you. It's my favorite job."

"I'm sorry I take it out on you because—"

"You're scared I won't be around if you need me."

"A little."

Coop dried a single tear from her cheek. He didn't want the tender moment to end. "Scares me too, Twink."

"Why do you call me that?"

He hummed the lullaby, *Twinkle, Twinkle, Little Star.* "I used to sing you to sleep and it made you giggle."

She twirled a lock of hair on her finger before grabbing the jar of charred baseball cards. "Tell me about these."

"Maybe when you're older." Coop turned away mumbling words Haley couldn't understand. Just as well, they weren't meant for her. She'd made him uncomfortable again.

They'd reached a perfect opportunity to talk about his childhood friend and ease his painful memories. Yet his Greenville guilt, that's what he dubbed it, held him back.

Haley stood with hands on hips, mirroring Sydney. "Why do I have to wait?"

"Because I said so."

"It's lame—" She stopped, her eyes so full of hurt and hope.

"You're right." He swallowed hard. "A long time ago—"

"When you were a little boy?"

Coop nodded. "I made a huge mistake."

"I knew it."

He examined the jar. "These remind me—"

"You aren't perfect." She grabbed his hand, and the unexpectedness of her gentle gesture shook Coop's foundation. "But you'll always be my dad."

Coop scooped her into his arms and kissed her forehead again. "My Dad job is way more chill than being on TV."

Haley patted his shoulder. "Hold onto that dream. And, since you told me a secret, I'm gonna tell you one. Mombo is dating a doctor from her hospital. So, you have my permission to date Sydney."

Coop thumped his forehead with his palm. "Oh?"

Were his intentions regarding the reporter so obvious even Haley could sense them?

Then, his mind orbited to his ex-wife.

So, Cassie had fallen for somebody better than him—a doctor. Seemed like her speed. She'd hooked a guy with more money and a less dangerous job. One who came home every night. Perhaps she'd rub it in Coop's face one day.

He wanted to confront Haley. Ask for more sordid details to questions he didn't really want answered. But it wouldn't be fair to her.

Coop's biggest fault was that he worked too hard. Tried too hard to provide a good life for his family. He reasoned the split had been genuinely unfair to him.

How ironic—it almost sounded like the same argument Cassie made when she threw him out.

Time to move on, he thought.

"How's about I ask Sydney to dinner?" Coop winked. "Want to join us?"

"Dad, sometimes you're such a dweeb. You have to do that all by yourself."

"Special Agent Dweeb, if you please."

27

Satisfied he'd made a positive gain in the fractured relationship with his daughter, Coop propped his feet on the desk, rested the keyboard on his lap, then rubbed his face. Haley was curled on the couch, fast asleep. As he perused D-Jazz's arrest report, he learned deputies had discovered bomb-making materials in the banger's car, prompting the Dorchester County Sheriff to roll the bomb squad to clear the scene before towing the car to CPD's crime lab.

Huge chunks of evidence were mounting against Coop's prime suspect. If they could nab Ice, that might be all they needed to close the investigation.

Next, he pulled out his notebook to establish a timeline for the two catastrophes. A precise sequence would be useful in breaking or confirming suspect alibis, finding holes in witness or suspect accounts, and preserving a snapshot of known events for posterity. Coop used military time to avoid confusion.

Alarm time: 1015. Meaning the fire probably started a few minutes before someone called it in.

Arrival time: 1019. Four minutes for the fire department to arrive on-scene was a solid response.

Controlled time: 1502. Kinkaid was called earlier, but wrangling the Tip scene proved a real challenge for firefighters.

Last unit cleared time: 1833. In total, fire crews had been deployed at Kinkaid and Tipton Terrace for more than eight hours. Investigation teams worked past that hour.

"Charleston Fire Department," Coop mumbled. "They bust their ass to save yours."

Finally, he examined the intern's video mashup. They'd compiled a nice montage, yet nothing remarkable jumped out to the skilled investigator. On a lark, he scanned the server for deleted files and erased metadata. He restored expunged files into a new folder and came out of his chair when he opened a video showing an unidentified suspect in dark pants and a dark hooded sweatshirt pulled over his head and running away from the fire.

Coop played the segment again. No markings on the guy's clothing meant he had street sense. He played it once more, this time comparing the video with the grainy photo Ray-Ray's Nana had provided. He duplicated the deleted clip onto a flash drive and dashed to the task force conference room. Detective Tate stabbed his phone off when Coop handed him the flash drive and photo.

"Check these out, Brody. Any chance it's D-Jazz?" Coop asked.

Detective Tate examined the photo before cueing the video on his laptop. He projected the clip onto the large flat-screen. "Where'd you find these?"

"Recovered the video from an erased file cache and the photo came from a witness to a prior fire."

Detective Tate shouted at the officers around him. "What the hell, fellas? The boss finds evidence in the trash. I want an explanation."

An officer said, "Run it again."

The detective replayed the clip.

The officer jabbed the screen with his index finger. "I remember this. One of the interns, a film student, showed me how to use geometric overlays to showcase special features. This must be an early attempt to create highlight rings. Gotta be a dupe."

Coop shook his head.

"No way." The officer slid behind his laptop and exploded into action. He punished the keyboard for a few moments, followed by a lengthy period of awkward silence. He finally turned to Detective Tate. "He's right. Someone wiped this clip."

"Why? Who?" Detective Tate barked. "Heads are gonna roll cuz this looks incriminating."

"Lots of hands in the cookie jar." The officer typed more keystrokes. "No prob, that segment is still in our master. See, that's why we firewall all our original footage on another server."

Coop said, "Let's say the clip was intentionally deleted. Perhaps whoever did it is familiar with this person. An important piece of information, agreed?"

Detective Tate scowled. "You mean someone on our team may have intentionally purged evidence?"

"Pass it along to the people you trust," Coop said. "Enhance both images. Decide if it's the same guy. It's impossible to ignore this person at the fire. But if he moved west, it'd be easy to disappear in streets filled with college students and tourists. Any details you raise are bound to be valuable. Might break the open case."

Coop returned to his office and found Halcy bouncing on the balls of her feet while examining a copy of the falcon-and-rat photo that'd been removed from one of the dead bangers at Sydney's fire.

Haley fixated on the picture as though conjuring her own theory. "Is this important?"

"It's key to my working hypothesis."

"Falcons eat rodents," Haley said with authority. "So, falcons are higher on the food chain. What eats a falcon?"

"Let's find out." Coop propped his feet on the desk, rested the keyboard on his thighs, and opened an internet search engine. "Says here falcons are on top of the raptor pyramid, though humans are their greatest predators."

"I'll need to chew on those new deets before drawing any conclusions."

Coop burst out laughing. "Deets?"

"Details."

"Twink, this photo is just between you and me. Our secret. Okay?"

She agreed without protest.

As of that moment, examining crime scene evidence officially qualified as quality father-daughter time.

"Ready to leave?" he asked.

Before she answered, the door cracked opened and Sydney poked in. "Mind if I join you?"

"Sure." Haley winked. "Right, Dad?"

Coop gaped at Sydney, all showered and well-dressed. "We were heading out. Haley needs some shut-eye."

"Darn," Sydney said. "I have several questions."

"Come with us." Haley moved by Sydney's side. "Please."

Coop scratched his chin. "Fine by me. You can work at our place. Eat. Sleep. TV. Whatever you want."

Sydney brightened. "How can I resist?"

Coop's knees knocked and his toes went numb as he inhaled her luminous floral fragrance. Flowing hair spilled onto her shoulders. He wanted to perform handsprings, though his inner beast screamed, 'Hey, pal. This isn't a one-night-stand kind of gal.'

"C'mon, Dad. It's past my bedtime."

Coop slapped his thigh, then used a screechy falsetto. "Did you say bedtime? I'm so embarrassed. Oh, snap."

"Kind of an outdated expression," Sydney winked.

"Yeah, Daddy. Don't be weird."

He smooched Haley on the cheek. "I love you, too."

28

Coop leased a carriage house at 74½ Lenwood Boulevard for use while he headed the task force. The single-story, with white brick and black shutters, was called the Kitchen House because it once functioned as a service area behind the main residence. The primary mansion and his temporary abode were situated near White Point Gardens. The majestic, oak-tree-lined park was better known as the Battery, the place where locals maintained the Ashley and Cooper Rivers met to form the Atlantic Ocean.

On that night, scores of people snubbed the mayor's curfew and clogged the normally bucolic setting straight from a Conroy novel. Instead of viewing sailboats skimming the waters of Charleston Harbor, officers in riot gear illuminated them with megawatt spots. Similar scenes played out at other significant locales around the city, commanding additional security, such as Broad Street, Marion Square, and the College of Charleston.

Coop tucked his daughter into bed before joining Sydney in the living room. "Haley is zonked out." Knowing his kid slept nearby helped him avoid acting on his obvious attraction for the gorgeous reporter.

Sydney rested her purse on the floor and removed her shoes. "Dino told me you phoned her this afternoon."

Coop hid his embarrassment. "How'd you know she needed—"

"Eleven-year-old girls can be quite complicated. I was one once, so I recognize the trapdoors."

"And?"

Sydney sighed. "One day, you're Daddy's little girl. And the next, you're falling off your high heels, hoping he'll catch you."

Coop flipped his palms up. "Translation?"

"She's maturing. Dealing with hormones wreaking havoc with their own agenda, while also working through issues regarding your split." Sydney sank into the couch. "By the way, Cal and I met one of your neighbors just now when he dropped me off."

"Which one? Wait, let me guess." Coop held up a hand. "Bald guy across the street? He gave me the stink eye this morning."

Sydney shook her head. "Mrs. Cora Rose Bishop." She let each overarticulated word ooze with a honeysuckle drawl as though performing in a Tennessee Williams play.

"Ah, my landlady." Coop stretched his hands behind his head. "What's she doing at this hour?"

"Keeping an eye out for marauders."

"Seriously?" Coop grinned. "Someone out to pillage the estate?"

"She's worried Fleet Landing's bad element might work its way down here."

Coop raked at the stubble on his cheeks. "Thankfully, no gangs or Klan around these parts."

"You make it sound as though the Ku Klux Klan is extinct." Her honeysuckle evaporated. "I did a package on Klan recruiting in Goose Creek only a month ago. Flyers were spread over a neighborhood near the Naval Weapons Station. They tied leaflets in plastic bags weighted with rice, apparently for easy tossing during the drive-by. Police became involved because the White Crusaders violated a city ordinance banning distribution of handbills." She jumped to her feet and dashed to the dining room where she'd dumped her files.

"We done?" Coop called after her.

She returned carrying a thick folder overflowing with clippings and thumbed through the stack. "Here it is." She passed an article to Coop. "White Crusaders were the Klan's militant arm. Responsible for scores of church burnings and murders over the past hundred years."

"Is this the same group operating in Goose Creek?" Coop asked.

"If so, I'm sure Bureau agents are digging into their illegal guns and explosives."

Sydney hunched her shoulders. "Today's Crusaders advertise themselves as more of a nonviolent civil rights movement instead of a hate group."

"Sounds like a real stretch."

"Seems the modern Klan is prone to holding public demonstrations and are less secretive about their group's activities and membership."

"Working without the usual sheets and pointy hoods?" Coop asked.

"Those remain popular in other places. I guess their best traditions are worth preserving."

"Crusaders and 843Z? White nationalists versus Black separatists. That'd be a toxic crosstown rivalry." He waved the article. "What's your point?"

Sydney smacked her forehead with a palm. "Remember the exchange in the mayor's office between Anson and Wallace regarding their family histories? I confirmed Wallace renounced his affiliation with the White Crusaders, like he said. But Anson's Klan ties remain quite murky. Better add *alleged* ties so my legal department doesn't go apoplectic."

Coop was enchanted by Sydney. He sat upright when she transitioned the conversation to current suspects. He made his case for D-Jazz and Ice. Though, he was beginning to wonder whether either gangbanger could pull off such an audacious scheme.

Sydney went full tilt on blaming the White Crusaders, believing she'd latched onto something big.

Coop began to share her excitement. When he wasn't distracted by the reporter's verve and beauty, he managed to roll over productive points and counterpoints in her argument.

Sydney closed her case by arguing against D-Jazz and Ice, suggesting the fires seemed more personal than nuisance-oriented.

"And I think the White Crusaders were responsible for the train station fire, too."

"What was the racial mix of those killed at the Station?" Coop asked.

"Thirty Blacks and nine whites."

"Suggests Klan involvement is highly credible. You craft their motive?"

Sydney reclaimed the article from Coop and stuffed it into the folder. "Perhaps the Crusaders meant to kill a specific person. Or maybe they didn't care about the damage, hoping to kill as many Blacks as possible. After all, those diehards were a bona fide hate group back then."

"I find it hard to exonerate the Klan for any murders. But there's solid reason to conclude the train station fire-setter was Black."

Sydney straightened. "How do you know?"

"Captain Burton called with preliminary DNA results after conducting tests on the misplaced evidence you recovered this morning."

Sydney tossed the folder on the sofa. "I thought the crime lab needed weeks to run those kinds of tests."

"Rapid DNA analysis only takes a few hours. The captain drove up to Lieber prison and collected a buccal swab from Nate Sharpe. She compared it to the new evidence."

"He didn't mention it when I met with him. I sure hope I didn't uncover proof upholding Nate's conviction."

Coop shook his head. "Because DNA is the holy grail of forensic evidence, the genetic testing is bound to set him free. But don't spill the beans before we get a chance to enter the results into trial records."

Sydney growled through clenched teeth. "Does his attorney know? Rob had to agree to the swab, right?"

"Captain Burton sent the analysis to lawyers on both sides. She operates without a biased agenda."

"Boyd Wallace prosecuted Nate's first trial. Then he used the high-profile conviction to launch a political career. What if the verdict was the product of a massive smokescreen since the new-found evidence incriminates somebody else? Or worse, the real train station arsonist is the one who torched Nate's rental pad on Kinkaid, indelibly linking the two events." Sydney let out a reflexive whistle. "Might explain why yesterday's big fire was so different from the others."

"That's a lot to unpack," Coop said. "By your logic, Wallace should know who Falcon is if he didn't play fair the first time around."

She hated finger-pointing at Mayor Wallace, but she couldn't discount the discovery. "Sounds like something I should ask him on the record. His response could either bolster my conspiracy claim or clear him of any prosecutorial misdeeds. Though it doesn't reveal why Falcon would burn my house." Her voice tremored.

Coop wanted to comfort her but didn't want to sound like a sap. "I, uh—"

"Falcon must really want me off the hunt." Sydney glanced away, pulling in huge gulps of air. "Okay, back to the train station fire. You mentioned the perpetrator was Black. I suppose we can rule out all Crusaders. They don't allow Black members."

"The Klan in Colorado had at least one. A real quirk. But you're working the case like a seasoned pro. I suggest asking more questions."

"Like who benefits?"

"A surefire motive," Coop said.

"I mean, who benefits from the Kinkaid fire? And Tip's explosion?" Sydney jumped to her feet. "I see now why you focused the task force on D-Jazz. It makes sense because of his gang's repair scam. But does D-Jazz or Ice benefit enough to exact so much damage in their own hood? Even kill people?"

"I need to find out. Thankfully, I—" Coop's vibrating cell phone interrupted their conversation. He glanced at caller ID. "Dino, Syd's here. Let me put you on speaker." He punched a button on his phone and held it out.

"I'm at the crime lab," Dino said. "They lifted fingerprints from your Kinkaid rubble."

This time, Sydney waited for Dino to bask in his ta-da sunshine. He didn't pounce.

"So?" she asked with a hint of perturbance.

"Sent them off for comparison. We can expect a return in the morning if anything pops in SLED's system. AFIS takes a whole lot longer."

"Dino, your punch lines are a terrible disappointment," Sydney said.

"Hardy-har-har."

"You find Ice yet?" Coop asked.

"He's still in the wind. Maybe he was the punk in the Mercedes following us today. Out for now." Dino disconnected.

Sydney appeared confounded.

"Dino and I were loosely tailed while we made a death notification," Coop said.

"Nobody's ever tailed me."

Coop puckered his mouth. "A terrible reflection on the men in this town."

Sydney plopped on the couch. "What's next?"

"Go with the facts. Evidence never lies."

Sydney threw her hands in the air. "I'm tired of playing games with this pyro."

"This isn't a game," Coop said without sympathy. "For the criminals involved, it's straight-up business—avoid getting caught. I'm in the business of nailing them." He slammed his palm on the coffee table. "And for the last time, Falcon isn't a pyromaniac."

"What—"

"You've twice labeled the person involved in these fires a pyro. He's an arsonist. There's a difference."

"Mox-nix?"

"It's more than mere technicality. Stop blurring the distinction."

Sydney flagged her palms. "If you say so."

"For a pyromaniac, fire is an obsession. The offender gets excited or tense beforehand. And relieved or gratified afterward."

"And arsonists only want to set the world on fire." Sydney laughed at her own interpretation.

Coop winced. "Arsonists set fires with a criminal mindset. Vandalism. Revenge. Extremism. Profit. Or to conceal other crimes. Arson is the country's second-fastest-growing crime, and the US has the highest rate of arson in the world."

"Job security for you?" Sydney waved off the snark. "The hell with Falcon's *why*. I'd rather find out *who*." She shook her head. "Forget it. I'm a little upset."

"A little?"

Sydney's eyes hummed with electricity. Coop caught himself staring like a big lazy dog that'd dropped a toy at her feet. Waiting to be petted.

"Okay, a lot." She winked as though reading his mind.

"You're only human."

Sydney gathered her hair and retied it into a knot. "No one has ever accused me of that before."

"Sorry I went preachy on you."

"You are the foremost expert."

"Yeah, it says so on my business card."

Sydney asked, "What does your infallible gut tell you?"

"Time to raid the cupboards."

"If you only have kale crackers and quinoa cakes," Sydney frowned. "Then, no thanks."

"I hear you. I'm craving sweet and salty." Coop snapped his fingers. "Vinegar and onion chips. And chocolate candy bars."

"Add a Diet Dew, and you have a typical meal for me."

They moved into the kitchen, and Sydney opened a cabinet overflowing with crunchy goodness in every flavor. After grabbing an armload, they moved to the dining room. "Since you're weak, may I keep picking your brain?" she asked.

"Pick away."

"What compels a serial arsonist?"

"You sound like a reporter."

Sydney fluttered her eyelashes. "That's the second-nicest name you called me tonight."

Coop eyed Sydney. Her smile reached across the room. He liked the way her hair came undone and the way she talked. He admired how her brain worked and enjoyed their banter. His cheeks warmed.

"Here comes a knowledge bomb. The textbook version." Coop dropped into a chair, reflexively rested his feet atop another, then crammed his mouth with a handful of chips. He washed down the bite with a gulp of soda. "Serial arson is defined as three or more fires with a significant cooling-off period between each fire. The most common background for an arsonist is a troubled family life. Shrinks say fire-setting behavior is a symbolic expression of inner pain."

"A cry for help? Boo-hoo," Sydney teased.

"Yeah, I think shrinks check the mommy-issue box every time." Coop emptied the bag over his mouth, catching chip bits on an outstretched tongue, then mopped his lips with the back of his hand.

Sydney licked salt from her fingers before realizing Coop was studying her. "Hey, cut me some slack. My manners took the night off."

"Mine too." He yanked open another bag of chips. "I'd kill for a bowl of salsa. Maybe a foot-long."

Sydney fiddled with her wristband, seemingly more as an idle distraction than an attempt to read the time.

"Stay as long as you need," Coop said. "I enjoy the company."

"Will anyone from the task force think it's suspicious if I stick around?"

"What's suspicious is about 15 percent of all fires."

Sydney threw a candy bar, and it bounced off a lamp. "You're a walking encyclopedia."

"Careful, this isn't my stuff."

"I meant to hit you. A few more questions on background, okay?"

Coop's head snapped up and down. "First, let me ask for your read on someone."

Sydney nodded.

"The intern, Lamar. Did he seem off to you?"

"Maybe a little eager. Why? Any hunches?"

Coop shook his head and a twinge of regret galloped down his spine. He didn't want to mislead Sydney. He wanted to impress her. Sure, he had a hunch. Enough to swab the kid's backpack.

Sydney clapped her hands to gain his attention. "Tell me more about serial arsonists."

"You're interested in a profile, I suppose." Coop shook out his arms and legs. "Here goes. Arsonists carefully plan their targets in hopes of inflicting maximum damage. Like pyros, many jack off on the emergency response. Lights and sirens are powerful stimulants. But one big problem for the task force, most of Fleet Landing's fires were opportunistic. Suggesting the work of a prankster. And that profile doesn't fit with my gang suspects."

"Yesterday was no prank. People died." Sydney hung her head. "Reggie died."

"Here's a leap. What if the real train station arsonist targeted Nate because he knows the old verdict is about to be overturned, thereby connecting the two events."

"Really?" Sydney bonked her forehead with a palm. "Think I already served up that very notion."

Coop surrendered. "Let me start by saying, 'You might be right.'"

"Embarrassed I figured it out before you?"

"Hold the self-congratulatory applause. We're both missing something big."

Sydney drummed her lacquered nails on the table. "Boyd Wallace and Hart Anson are the proper age for having set the train station fire, but they're both white. D-Jazz and Ice are Black, yet they're too young. So where does that leave us? Square one?"

"As of now, I can't confirm or discard any prospects regarding the train station and serial fires relationship. But I do believe whoever is behind the newest wave of Fleet Landing fires is exceptionally dangerous and working without a script."

"You make it sound like throwing darts at bubbles."

Coop's cell phone vibrated. "Hey, Dino." He bobbed his head a few times. "On our way." He scooped keys from the table and clipped the cell onto his belt.

Sydney gathered her purse, then shot out after Coop. "Where are we headed?"

"Police headquarters."

"What about Haley?"

"Cora Rose offered to keep an eye on her. I'll call her from the car."

29

Sydney provided directions as Coop drove to the Law Enforcement Center, located across from RiverDogs Stadium in a refurbished section of Gadsden Green. Glossy police cruisers clotted the parking lot.

Coop nosed the Jeep under a lamp pole, then flashed his credentials for the cop on lot security detail. "How's it going out there?"

"Keeping patrols fresh," the officer said. "Don't want a repeat of Minneapolis."

Coop patted him on the shoulder.

"Stopping for chit-chat," Sydney whispered as they strode away. "Doesn't that violate your 'it's a felony to interfere with a firefighter' lecture?"

"Not really, because it's only a misdemeanor to interfere with a cop," Coop winked. "C'mon, Dino's waiting."

They collected visitor badges from the desk sergeant and moved through the foyer toward a bank of holding cells. Arrestees jeered at the newcomers.

"Mopes are pretty energetic for this hour," Coop said as they met Dino.

Dino led the trio past the tank. "We quit bringing in curfew violators once the house filled." He pushed open a door marked "Interrogation."

"What about the gang suspects?" Sydney asked.

"Got them segregated in south-side cells."

Coop plopped on a gray metal chair at a beat-up metal table with heavy metal rings welded on top. Dino spun another chair so the back faced the table and straddled the seat, elbows propped atop the backrest.

Sydney assessed the meeting's spartan accommodations. "I've had occasion to visit most of this city's underbelly. And I gotta say, this office is right down there with Tent City." She pretended to dust off a folding chair. "Correction. I have a source with an upholstered recliner under his tarp."

"I'm glad your peregrinations render you so worldly," Dino said. "This, however, is the best I can offer." He snapped his fingers. "Wait. May I pour you a Perrier, Ladybug?"

Sydney bunched her lips to one side. "Any chance you'll move this along?"

Dino turned to Coop. "Our canvass came up empty."

"Big surprise. The fire chief is sending more guys out tomorrow with an armload of free smoke alarms. I hope it opens doors."

Dino bobbed his head like a spring-loaded doll. "My best interrogator worked on a couple of fellas he has a relationship with."

"You mean confidential informants?" Sydney asked.

"I mean he had dealings with the yahoos before tonight." Dino rubbed his chin. "No trouble picking the ripest lollipop from the crowd. My guy leaned on that one pretty hard. He dimed-out D-Jazz as the 843Z ringleader without much persuasion."

Coop choked on a laugh. "Peregrinations. Yahoos. Lollipops. Your vocabulary range is astonishing."

"It's a cop thing. Gotta fit into the community I serve."

"Yeah, you're an urban chameleon. Let's focus." Sydney retrieved a pad and pen. "Didn't you already know D-Jazz ran the gang, even from prison?"

"But we never thought the 843Z could . . ." Dino jumped from his chair and edged to the door. He paused a second, then jerked it open. Satisfied no one was milling within earshot, he closed the door, then returned to his seat. "This is classified stuff, Ladybug. Absolutely no disclosure."

"You messing with me? Some sort of initiation?" Sydney glowered at Dino, who didn't budge. "Okay, I'll play along. Unless you plan on dropping me in the woods in my underwear."

Dino pointed toward the door. "My way. Or leave."

Sydney crossed her arms. "You know me. I'm a paragon of secrecy."

Dino gripped the chair back. "An undercover from the sheriff's gang unit infiltrated the 843Z."

"And?"

"The 843Z deal in drugs, guns, sex. The usual cash cows associated with organized crime."

Sydney threw her arms in the air. "I'd say the undercover learned the gang's obvious secrets in record time."

"Merely painting you a picture," Dino said with a hint of annoyance.

"Aw, you know I love art. That's so sweet." Sydney cleared her throat. "I've heard nothing newsy or confidential so far. So, I shouldn't have any trouble keeping my word."

Dino spun toward Coop. "Remember the two chuckleheads I paid to watch my car? They told us—"

"The thing about the thing."

Sydney thumped her fist on the table. "Drop the gobbledygook, fellas. Need I remind you, I'm on the team?"

"She's right," Dino said. "Sydney can be regarded as a trusted partner."

Coop didn't say a word. As she replayed the brief exchange, he did the unthinkable. He smoothed his mustache, his annoying habit when buying time or keeping secrets.

She jacked an accusatory finger at him. "I'm onto your little game. Spill it. It's late and I want to go home. Oh wait. I. Don't. Have. One."

Dino eyed Coop with a wide grin. "I told you she's a badass."

"Yeah, that's me." Sydney pushed back in her chair. "You can start by telling me about the two chuckleheads guarding your precious Mustang. What did you learn?"

Dino said, "Hostile takeover in the works."

Sydney cocked her head. "Someone out to overthrow

D-Jazz? Who?"

"Ice accused D-Jazz of going soft. Failing to seize all the illicit possibilities available in the hood."

"Who is Ice?" Sydney was peeved for letting the conversation run away.

Coop said, "The 843Z second in command. Hoping to become *numero uno*."

"Think he's connected to the two dead guys at my house?"

"Most likely." Dino uploaded photos from his cell phone's gallery. "I matched gang tattoos. First tat is D-Jazz. Next two are Ray-Ray and Croc."

Sydney scrolled back and forth as she compared the tattoos. "No rope." She tossed the phone on the table.

"Huh?" Dino snorted.

"They aren't the same. D-Jazz's 843Z tattoo doesn't have a rope snaking the anchor shank. Plus, the flukes are different."

"Gotta be a fluke you know what a fluke is." Coop scrolled the pictures. "Show me."

"Flukes are the pointy parts on the bottom."

Dino examined the photos with Coop. "She's right. D-Jazz's tat doesn't have a rope. But the two burnt guys do. And the points are different."

"No rope," Sydney repeated.

Coop said, "Heard you the first time. No need to rub it in."

"I'm badass, remember?" Sydney cemented the pieces. "Reggie noticed the difference when he eyed the girl firing at the crowd. Told me her ink didn't have a rope."

Dino said, "Could mean—"

"Falcon killed two kids who weren't even gangbangers."

"That means they were likely from Rivertown Academy." Coop paced in a loose circle. "Let's break it down. I can explain the serial fires by tying the 843Z to a torch-and-repair scam. Someone from the 843Z lights a nuisance fire at night so they don't get caught. The fire gets put out, by the homeowner or fire department, it doesn't matter. Fire, smoke, and water damage create the need for repairs by Rivertown Academy."

Sydney shook her head. "Hart Anson launched Rivertown with a goal of putting people to work, creating healthy communities, and increasing property values. Quality civic-minded stuff. That tells me they're fixing the damage Falcon inflicts without being part of the conspiracy."

Coop said, "Darn, you've thrown a wrench in my theory."

"You're welcome," Sydney said.

"She does that a lot." Dino choked on a laugh. "Hey, didn't Ray-Ray's nana tell us he was learning plumbing and electrical? That's consistent with Rivertown Academy's agenda and might explain why he and Croc were killed."

"How so?" Sydney asked.

"Maybe they witnessed something or were strong-armed into doing a bad thing for the 843Z. Like you said . . . Unwittingly involved in the larger scheme."

"Like blowing out pilot lights and causing Tip's explosion?" Sydney asked.

Coop bobbed his head. "They were wearing utility uniforms and driving a stolen gas company van."

Sydney iced over.

"What's wrong, Ladybug?" Dino reached for her trembling hand and gripped it tight in his big mitt. "I'll protect you."

She pulled her hand from his grasp and thumped a fist into her palm. "This is my fight."

"Asking for help isn't a sign of weakness," Coop said.

"Falcon destroyed my house." Her voice broke. "He killed those two kids. And five Tip residents."

Dino's cell phone chirped. "Text from Brody. He says D-Jazz wants to cooperate."

"Let me at him," Sydney growled.

30

S ydney, Coop, and Dino crammed into a room next to an interrogation booth. They were separated by a cinderblock wall with a large two-way mirror.

They watched Detective Tate press his face within inches of D-Jazz's. "Tell me about the 843Z connection to Rivertown Academy."

"Who are they?" D-Jazz said.

"You call that cooperation?" Sydney asked. "Better text your detective to adjust his line of questioning."

Detective Tate continued. "What about Ice?"

D-Jazz jutted his chin.

"You play a tough game," Detective Tate said. "But we both know you won't follow through with your threats."

"Not sure what you mean."

Detective Tate circled the table. "Where were you when your hood was burning?"

D-Jazz stared straight ahead. "Like I been sayin', I wasn't in the hood at that time."

"Word on the street says you're in charge of everything going down in Fleet Landing. I'm thinking you oughta be able to point a finger at the person who set all the fires and leveled the Tip." Detective Tate folded his arms across his barrel chest. "Tell me about Falcon, and I'll pretend to cut you a deal."

D-Jazz offered a toothy sneer. "Falcon? He's a homeless Jimmie sleepin' under the bridge."

Detective Tate pressed on. "What about Ice? You and he good pals?"

"No way," D-Jazz said.

"Then tell me why he blew up the Tip."

Dino said, "Here it comes."

"Followin' orders. Ice got his head so far up—"

"Say it," Sydney urged, as the three onlookers took a step toward the glass.

D-Jazz twisted his lips and tossed away a symbolic key.

Dino flipped off the audio. "Coop, I think it's fair to conclude your Rivertown lead is a dead end. On the other hand, D-Jazz put another dart in Ice's bull's-eye. I'll feel better when Ice is in custody alongside this yoyo."

Sydney rose to leave, happy she'd set the record straight on Rivertown. "Ice may have bombed the Tip, but I still believe the gang isn't the primary culprit behind the fires. White Crusaders seem more obvious."

"Proof?" Coop asked.

"D-Jazz said Ice was following orders. If you believe him, should mean neither of them is Falcon. Leaves me wanting to flush out more."

"C'mon, Ladybug," Dino snarled. "Wallace only appointed you to the task force to hold someone responsible if anything leaked out."

Sydney threw her hands in the air. "All I'm saying is, while you guys are processing evidence and conducting gang interrogations, I'll keep fact-checking. Now, I need to pee."

Coop moved to the door. "Meet you out front."

After Coop left, Dino spun Sydney by the shoulders. "Why are you hanging with the fire jockeys? This is police business."

"We've discussed this, Dino. It's my job. I observe and report."

"Well, my job is to protect and defend. And while I'm on the street protecting and defending, those fire guys are in their station houses eating and sleeping."

"I respect your work. But don't be petty, Dino."

Dino raked his fingers through his hair. "Look, I like Coop, but I think you can do better."

"What's that supposed to mean?"

"He's a firefighter, for goodness' sake."

•

Sydney walked with Coop through the LEC's parking lot, deep in thought about the White Crusaders and another plausible Falcon suspect. She wanted to return to the TV station to break down the new leads.

Coop's cell phone vibrated when they reached the Jeep. "What'd you forget, LT?" He clicked the speaker.

"Emergency services just received a distress call from the Anson house," Dino said. "Caller hung up before the operator got any details. Ninety South Battery, near Limehouse, if you're interested." He disconnected.

Coop powered south on Lockwood. Sydney told him to cut over once they reached South Battery. Blue and red lights from an ambulance, three cruisers, and a pair of unmarked police sedans strobed the street. Dino arrived less than a minute behind. He maneuvered his Mustang past Coop's vehicle and jumped the curb. Dino unfolded, then sprinted through the wrought iron front gate.

Sydney and Coop sauntered up the brick walkway toward the mansion, letting Dino enjoy the lead. Four columns adorned a two-story portico. A pair of stone lions rested atop brick pillars prowling stately landscaping which led to a secret rear garden. Every pine needle in the mulch bed rested in its assigned place.

Sydney examined the luxurious wicker furniture lining the porch. "We going inside or waiting for the smoke to clear?"

"A peculiar choice of words to ask a firefighter." Coop followed her gaze. "Nice place. I'll bet this represents serious money, huh?"

She nodded. "These are the SOBS."

Coop listened as Sydney explained Charleston's geographical factions. The Ansons, like others residing South of Broad, merited the catchy acronym 'SOBS'. They enjoyed the Holy City's largest homes, most charming vistas, and oldest money. The nouveau riche lived Slightly North of Broad and were grudgingly referred to as snobs by the sobs. And those with no money, the poorest of the poor—those were the unfortunate folks clustered in several compact blocks along the Cooper River in Fleet Landing. Apparently, they didn't even merit a catchy acronym.

"I worry Haley is gonna end up in a place like this." Coop hooked a thumb toward the mansion. "Her mom funded a trust for her."

"Not everyone with buckets of money is a double-barreled sob," Sydney said. "Mandy is loaded, and she's a peach."

An elderly man with steel-gray hair edged into view. "Excuse me. Any idea what's going on?"

Startled, Coop spun to face him. "And you are?"

He pointed at the house next door, an ornate Georgian. "Neighbor." He blinked. "Hey, you're Cora Rose's tenant. She and my honeybun go way back."

Sydney stepped forward and launched into reporter mode. "What can you tell us about the Ansons?"

The guy's nose was laced with capillaries like a road map. He ran his finger around his collar and swallowed so hard his Adam's apple bobbed a couple of times. He shot Coop a conspiratorial glance. "You won't repeat this to Cora Rose?"

"Strictly background," Coop said.

"She's a pistol, the Mrs." He cocked his head toward the house. "Mostly her money. Inherited from her father. He was a high-powered attorney who did criminal and tort work."

"Oh, yeah? Which side was he on?" Sydney asked.

"Pioneered mass-action lawsuits and built a fortune from high-risk cases against companies poisoning workers. Or those selling products that caused widespread health problems. He cared for the little people."

Coop grinned. "Billion-dollar settlements afforded his family a pretty extravagant lifestyle."

The neighbor cleared his throat. "Worst thing he ever did was team with Boyd Wallace on the train station fire case."

Sydney straightened at the mention of her passion project. She wanted to grill the man about the old trial. Coop shook his head.

"Sorry, I went off on a tangent," the neighbor said. "My wife says I can't hardly hold a decent conversation because I'm always going here, then . . . squirrel. Ha."

Coop clucked. "I'm taking her side."

"What else can you add about Mrs. Anson?" Sydney asked.

The neighbor adjusted his arms. "Mrs. Sunny Anson. Debutante. Fundraiser. First-rate ballbuster." He quickly covered his mouth. "Oops."

"I've said worse," Sydney said.

The neighbor continued. "She works with her husband, Hart. She's the smarty-pants in their company. Most certainly the influence peddler."

Two EMTs exited the house carrying medical bags.

Coop waved one over and badged him. "What happened?"

"Mrs. Anson claims she fell and hit her head. Refused further assistance."

"You believe her?"

"Why call 911 when the ER is only a few blocks away?" the EMT said.

"Maybe she's uninsured?" Sydney said drolly.

"She wants attention." The EMT pointed at the clutch of emergency and law enforcement response vehicles. "Treated the abrasions and told her to ice the eye. She'll have a shiner."

"Any chance her husband hit her?" Sydney asked.

"Someone did," the EMT said. "But that's not for me to speculate."

Dino filled the doorway and signaled Coop to come inside. "Mrs. Anson is in back. She asked for you."

"Me?"

"You learn anything from the EMTs?" Dino said.

"They think someone punched her," Sydney said.

Dino led Coop and Sydney through the house via a spacious central hallway. Oval drawing and living rooms flanked a grand staircase. They arrived at the tastefully appointed conservatory in the rear.

"Give me a shout if she says anything worthwhile," Dino said. "I'm gonna clear the call. Send the officers back on patrol."

"You sure she asked for me?" Coop said.

Dino threw his hands up. "I know. Who does that?"

31

Sydney nudged Coop's arm. "sobs have their own set of rules. Let me have the first crack." She didn't give him time to object and ambled over by way of an enormous telescope and well-stocked bookshelves. Reminiscent of other Battery mansions she'd visited, tranquility came in the form of soft colors, slow-turning ceiling fans, and warm sea breezes slipping through louvered shutters. A large fireplace covered one wall, and plenty of comfortable chairs were strewn around.

Mrs. Sunny Anson rested on a tufted divan beneath a tall bank of windows. She was clearly a woman of means. Expensive clothes. Pillowy lips. Perfect manicure.

Sydney pointed toward her puffy eye. "Did your husband do that?"

Sunny stared ahead with the vacant expression of a lost soul. Apparently, she was too well-bred to cause a scene. "Why do you ask?"

Sydney injected notes of concern. "This isn't the first time, is it?"

Sunny glanced away. "He can be awfully scary."

Sydney never figured Hart Anson for a domestic abuser. "Why stay?"

"He usually says he's sorry." Sunny spooned artificial resignation into vainglorious exasperation. "I've tried cajoling, flattery. Even threats."

Sydney couldn't comprehend the polluted logic of abused spouses and partners. Or understand why anyone allowed themselves to ride out the masquerade while braving recurring violence. But she knew better than to blame the victims. "Tell me about your father," she said, changing course without crippling the conversation.

"He was a great man," Sunny said flatly.

"Why did he assist the prosecution on the train station fire case?"

Sunny's gaze intensified. "After Mama and Hart's parents died in the fire, Daddy became terribly distraught. Working with the state to send their killer away helped ease his pain."

"Sorry, I didn't know."

Sunny fidgeted with long golden curls spilling off her shoulders. "Hart was a desperate nobody back then. I married him during the trial. He was studying prelaw at USC and offered to help Daddy with the mountain of paperwork. Hart dropped out a year later."

"Any chance they deliberately mishandled evidence?" Sydney let the insinuation hang in the air.

"I felt sorry for the convicted boy. He came from questionable breeding that spelled trouble from the get-go."

Sydney squeezed her hands. "Nate Sharpe was a sixteen-year-old shoeshine boy working at the train station. He assisted travelers who became disoriented from the smoke. Most hailed him a hero. Cops labeled Nate a delinquent because of a rap sheet filled with petty crimes. They dragged him to the police station on false pretenses and, after more than twelve hours of intense questioning, arrested him for arson. They amended the warrant to include murder after the death toll mounted."

Sunny wiped her cheek. "And now, that man is getting a new trial. Perhaps hoping to disparage the work of my daddy and Boyd Wallace."

"Nathan Sharpe deserves to play on a level field," Sydney said. "One where all the evidence is presented. The outcome of his new trial might surprise you."

"Little surprises me anymore."

"What about Hart? How will he react to an acquittal since he lost both parents in the fire?"

Sunny stared blankly. "He doesn't talk about it. They weren't close. The only thing they shared was their club."

"You mean the White Crusaders?" The question begged

elaboration, but Sunny didn't budge. Sydney filled the dead air. "I see."

"How could you? Daddy—" Sunny's eyes welled. Her emoting made for impressive theater, except for the complete lack of expression on the rest of her face. "Daddy believed Mama and Hart's father were having an affair. He didn't learn the awful truth until after she died."

Sydney waited for additional information.

"She loved Daddy deeply. Another reason he buried himself in his work. But nothing he did could bring back Mama."

·

Lamar opened his eyes before the alarm vibrated. He'd hardly slept, dreading the task ahead. He dressed in sweatpants and a dark T-shirt. Then slipped on sneakers, having spray-painted over the shoes' reflective stripes earlier while Mama was working at Tyrell's.

He snuck out of the house toting a brown paper bag containing a pickle jar swiped from the restaurant, a Zippo, and an old T-shirt. He'd siphon a pint of gas from a parked automobile before arriving at his target's address on Lenwood, about two miles away. Lamar jammed his hand into a front pants pocket and fingered the business card from Special Agent Bellamy. He wouldn't hesitate to use it if cops stopped him, though he hoped it wouldn't come to that. He had secrets to protect.

·

At the Anson house, Coop sat comfortably in a delicate armchair. Sunny beckoned him with an impatient sigh to rescue her from Sydney's inquisition. Sydney eased away, hovering within earshot.

Coop said, "Mrs. Anson—"

"Please, call me Sunny."

Coop noticed her nuanced play of facial features. The phony eyelash flicks. Coquettish lip pout. Even a slight tremble in her voice added to Sunny's performance. Though Coop continued to hone his interrogation skills, he'd acquired certain abilities, having been married for thirteen years. His ex-wife displayed the same coy confidence when trying too hard to bury something.

Sunny continued. "Investigating crimes seems a most unpleasant occupation."

Coop ignored her smokescreen. "Anything to add to the EMS report?"

Sunny's nose turned up as though she'd smelled something terrible. "I hoped you wouldn't prepare a formal report." She removed a crystal decanter from the bar cart, sloshed some liquid into a glass, and slugged a gulp.

Coop surmised this wasn't her first dose of self-medicating for the night. "I don't have any control over that." From the same thirteen-year experience, Coop knew alcohol never improved a bad situation—especially with domestic beefs. However, if brandy lowered Sunny's inhibitions, it could generate a solid-gold interview. He suppressed a smile. "Hey, tell me about the Tobacco Mill?"

Sunny's charm returned. "My favorite project. Previous developers abandoned renovations when the real estate market collapsed under the weight of the mortgage crisis. That's when Hart purchased the property for a song and rekindled the project. However, at every step—" She caught herself and her voice became husky with genuine emotion. "Boyd's suffocating restoration rules depleted our cash reserves."

"Why bite off such an elaborate project in a place like Fleet Landing?"

"To rejuvenate the tired neighborhood, of course," Sunny chirped with a flirtatious toss of her head. "We believe beautification and reuse of that iconic structure will create a domino effect, generating prosperity for the whole northeast side."

Coop caught sight of Sydney rolling her eyes. "Are the recent fires a setback or a boon for your business?" he asked.

"Death fits the neighborhood," Sunny said with a dismissive shrug. "Tell me, have there been any more fires tonight?"

Coop shook his head.

"What a relief." Sunny smoothed a strand of cool blonde hair from her forehead. "You should know the Tip was a hub for drug-infested criminal activity long before Fleet Landing's arsons became problematic. But we don't pander to those people."

Those people?

The hair on Coop's neck stood at attention. A period of stony silence lingered.

After a few moments, Coop glanced around and asked casually, "Where is Hart?"

Sunny dabbed her swollen eye. "He got mad when the police rousted him to go to the office."

Coop tilted his head in her direction, picking up where Sydney left off. "Did the Crusaders teach him that?"

"They are an important part of his life. He attends monthly meetings. You'd better leave now." Sunny brought an exaggerated hand to her face. Crocodile tears spread dark mascara tracks down her cheeks. "One last thing, Agent Bellamy. Don't cross Hart. He's quite a puissant figure in the community. And please, never tell him I mentioned anything about his business. He'll kill me."

•

Lamar struggled to adjust his vision in ever-changing light as spears of moonlight jabbed through high-scudding clouds without warning.

He managed to fill the pickle jar with siphoned gasoline from a sweet ride on Beaufain Street, but his mind kept bouncing to his target, Cora Rose Bishop. Also, he'd never set a fire south of Broad.

As Lamar prowled Tradd Street, a balding white man in a reflective vest caught him off guard and aimed a flashlight in his face. The vest was stenciled with "NEIGHBORHOOD WATCH" across the front.

Lamar froze for a five count.

"You're out late, young man," the guy said. "Live around here?"

"Making a Tyrell's delivery to a couple over on Gibbes. Want to check?" Lamar held out the brown sack, trusting that the fried chicken grease staining the bag quashed any gasoline odor. He willed the man to decline his offer to peek inside.

The guy shone his light onto the bag. He pursed his lips in and out, then tipped the light back on Lamar.

Neighborhood Watch didn't reveal whether he bought the concocted delivery story or not.

Lamar contemplated sweetening the tale, then quickly shot the idea down.

Keep it simple, he thought.

The man cast the beam onto the sidewalk. "You mean to tell me Tyrell's delivers? All this time, I've risked a ticket double-parking while I ran inside for carryout."

Fresh pangs of guilt washed over Lamar as he lowered the bag. He worried being deceitful was becoming too easy.

"Better run," the man said. "Nobody wants cold food."

Lamar sprinted away, then slowed to a jog once he rounded the corner out of sight from Neighborhood Watch. He threaded his way through parked cars lining the skinny street. Porch lights silhouetted the hulking trunks of Lenwood's palmetto trees.

Beyond the palmettos, Lamar glanced at his target—a massive house in the swanky Battery neighborhood. Palm fronds crackled in the breeze, and their familiar vibration provided odd comfort. He stood in the street staring at the mansion and its one-story carriage house. A *We Love Firefighters* banner hung between two live oaks.

Lamar tightened his grip on the brown bag. "No, no, no."

A block away, an SUV turned onto Lenwood. Headlights ping-ponged as the vehicle moved along the cobblestoned street. Lamar slid next to a brick column flanking a neighbor's driveway as high beams raked across his target's yard. He melted into the shadows when the car crept by.

Next, an iron gate cranked open at the corner house. The Explorer swung into the drive and through to the motor court behind the house. Two doors slammed, which activated a car alarm, which led to a barking dog.

Plantation shutters at an adjacent house wedged open seconds before a man stepped onto the porch. "Who's out there? I'm calling the police."

The open front door cast sheaves of light onto the street cutting near Lamar. He let the city swallow him, and his chest tightened. The night was about to spiral out of control and he hadn't set Falcon's fire yet.

Then, all at once, the car alarm stopped. The dog quit barking. And house lights flicked off. Lamar craned his neck and determined Porch Man had gone back inside. He closed his eyes, shutting out the entire world. In that moment he felt strong enough to break free from Falcon.

"I'm done," he whispered to himself. "I won't do this anymore."

Lamar made a quick scan and angled away. He spotted a dumpster overflowing with paint buckets and cardboard boxes at the house where the car alarm sounded. He lit the fuse and lobbed the pickle jar, firebombing the dumpster to dispose of his arson materials before disappearing into the night.

•

Coop spun his keys around a finger as he and Sydney departed the Anson house.

"Sunny pumped you," she said.

"Yup."

"She's lying, too."

"Yup," Coop repeated. "That creates problems."

The portable walkie attached to his belt squawked. "Engine 102, dumpster fire at 83 Lenwood. Cross-street, Tradd."

"That's your block," Sydney said anxiously.

They dashed to the Jeep. Coop cranked the engine, made a three-point turn, lurching across the curb, then drove west to Lenwood. When they neared, they spotted a small fire.

"Grab two cans from the back," Coop said.

"Cans of what?"

Coop skidded to a halt, then threw the Jeep into park. "Portable extinguishers."

Sydney dug around the back seat and found two red canisters. She handed one to Coop.

Coop broke the seal and tugged the pin on his extinguisher. "Pull, aim, squeeze, and sweep." He positioned the nozzle straight out and sprayed the fire with a jet of carbon dioxide to squelch the flames.

Sydney copied Coop and the fire was quickly abated.

Porch lights flickered as a siren from the approaching fire engine echoed.

Coop radioed the dispatcher. "Fire is out at Lenwood. Approach Code Two, lights only."

The dispatcher repeated instructions to the responding fire company, and within seconds, their siren muted. Beacons of red light glanced off houses and trees as the pumper neared. Coop flashed his badge for the captain riding shotgun.

Two crew members jumped from rear doors carrying Halligans. They raked debris in the dumpster, making sure the fire was completely out. One borrowed Sydney's portable extinguisher and doused a smoldering hunk of cardboard.

Cal edged up the sidewalk. "That you, Syd?"

"Hey, what brings you here?" she asked.

"Fell asleep in the car after I dropped you," Cal said. "Woke when I heard a dog bark. Then porch lights popped on and a car alarm sounded. I phoned 911 once I spotted the flames."

Sydney said, "Dogs, lights, alarms. A security triple play. Do you think this fire was intentional?"

"Without a doubt," Coop said. "See anything suspicious, Cal?"

Cal shook his head. "I thought the firebug is behind bars?"

"Me too," Coop said.

The captain climbed from the cab. "You live around here, Agent Bellamy?"

"A couple of houses down. Secure the scene while I retrieve my evidence kit." He dashed to the Jeep, then jerked his Pelican case from the rear. Returning to the dumpster, he snapped a few pictures. Next, he bagged and tagged pieces of cardboard and a chunk of broken glass reeking of gasoline.

"You arrived on scene so fast, the fire only had time to burn off the alcohol," the captain said. "No charring."

Coop recognized the hallmarks of a reluctant arson. And the irony of a dumpster fire amused him.

Falcon was either recruiting new fire-setters who didn't know what they were doing. Or he was expanding his playbook to sow confusion, stretch resources, or test department response time and tactics at an address forecasted in the manifesto.

Coop phoned the fire chief, advising her to deploy the department's ladder trucks to strategic locations South of Broad. Staging the big rigs amounted to something an admiral would do, moving aircraft carriers to political hot spots in an effort to deter aggression.

"Go ahead and call it," Coop said to the firefighters. "But my gut tells me to expect more tonight."

32

Sydney arrived at the TV station a little after 3 a.m. and tip-toed through the dimly lit newsroom. Blinking screen savers cast an eerie glow. A junior assistant producer sat alone in the sea of desks. His job was to cover the overnight network, AP, Reuters, and UPI feeds. Later, he'd scan morning papers for stories lending themselves to local TV coverage.

Sydney stared at the newsroom, the place she'd worked for the past seven years. It felt bigger than she was accustomed.

She offered the junior producer a weak wave, then pushed open the locker room door. A hollow pain wrenched her insides as she slid the security chain into place. Cold beads trickled down her spine, forcing her to chase goose bumps on her arms and legs like a game of Whac-A-Mole.

Sydney undressed and slipped into a lonely shower stall, her eyelids heavy from exhaustion. Warm water cascaded over aching muscles. She let out a groan while bending for her toes. She shook out her arms and rolled her shoulders. The past two days had been bizarre, even by her crazy standards.

She squeezed soap dregs from the bath wash bottle onto a loofah. While suds pooled at her feet, she replayed key events in her mind. Story tip from Rob. Kinkaid fire. Tip explosion. House gone.

Reggie. Gone forever. Her nadir.

For the past eleven years, he'd served as the optimistic yang to her harried yin. A true calming force in her tornado of a life. She missed him more than she dared confess. The soap bottle slipped from her grasp.

As she reached for it, her ears perked at a stray noise coming from the dressing area. A surge of fight-or-flight chemicals flooded her brain. She lost feeling in her arms and legs and became too afraid to call out.

Sydney managed to wrap herself in the shower curtain, wipe foamy lather from her eyes, then drop into a low stance. Knees bent. Back foot turned out forty-five degrees. Ready to attack or defend. But the slippery floor made it impossible to maintain her balance.

She lunged for a baseball bat leaning against a corner, edged into the changing area, and circled the locker room. Thankfully, the chain lock remained attached. She choked on a laugh, her imagination running amok. She figured her dad was to blame for causing her to mulishly reject Mandy's guest room offer, thereby putting her in that sticky situation. He'd instilled a lofty value of independence from day one.

"Look it up."

"Figure it out."

"Never rely on others for answers."

His lessons came with a steep price tag. She should be at Mandy's. Fully clothed. Asleep. Safe.

She returned the bat to the corner.

"Look at me. Badass reporter. Pretending to be tough."

Her mind veered off track.

What would Broadcaster Barbie do if someone had torched her dream house? Run home to Malibu Mommy? Use her titanium credit card for a suite at the Beverly Hills Hilton? Shack up with Ken?

Yeah. If Barbie went bad, she'd go all the way.

Atta girl.

Sydney unfurled from the shower curtain. Her anxiety and fear were replaced by a twinge of annoyance. From the moment Falcon had obliterated her home, the story swerved lanes from a straightforward bread and butter—film at six—to red meat and potatoes with sour cream and chives.

And Sydney hated chives.

She'd bumped heads with plenty of dipsticks in her career and never backed down. Falcon was simply another in a long line of wingnuts who underestimated her. He'd never appreciate how resilient she could be. In fact, Falcon didn't know squat about her.

She wasn't backing down. She was Scarlett O'Hara.

Scarlett never abandoned Tara.

Sydney chuckled, tickled at her penchant for movie references.

Fiddle-dee-dee, lugnut.

•

Sydney curled wet hair into a towel and slipped on a pair of CPD sweatpants and an ATF T-shirt.

With only one more change of clothes hanging in her locker, she opted to save it for on-camera interviews. Turning her back to the mirror, she rolled a sleeve to expose the dark purplish splotch surrounding a crusty gash. She floated her fingertips over the wound, knowing she could count on several more days of discoloration and pain. She applied a medicated bandage over the lesion, slid on a pair of tennis shoes, then plodded to her cubicle.

Sydney prepared to immerse herself in scads of Fleet Landing fire history. But first, she needed to address a nagging concern about the train station fire.

Sunny Anson had mentioned that her mother and both of Hart's parents had been fatalities. Sydney couldn't recall those specific details—and it'd become the third major revelation concerning that case. The first was the discovery of misplaced physical evidence at the police warehouse. The second, Coop's startling disclosure about DNA from those items.

Sydney opened the victim database on her computer and keyed in ANSON. She didn't find any matches. She rekeyed the name, blaming fuzzy vision or faulty typing. Same result. That prompted her to resort the entire file to ensure surnames were in alphabetic order.

The result—no victims named Anson.

On a hunch, she scrolled Charleston County's vital records and discovered Hart Anson Granger had legally changed his name to Hart Granger Anson a month before he married Sunny Celeste Manning. Sydney located Anson's birth certificate using the new information. He was born to William Hart Granger and Suzanne Dunne Granger.

She rebooted the database and located William H. Granger and Suzanne D. Granger of Charleston among the victims. She also spotted the entry for Sunny's mother, Elle C. Manning.

Satisfied that she'd cleared up that matter, Sydney shifted gears to sorting Cal's documents. He'd provided a year's worth of insurance claims for every fire in the 843 area code. Next, she arranged Mandy's property title information alongside the insurance claims. When she finished, she surveyed the mounds spread across her desktop. The familiar routine helped wrap her head around an enormous project.

Charting the janky fires seemed a solid next step.

Sydney pressed color-coded pins into a map. Each pin reflected various categories as defined by the fire department: structure, vehicle, outdoor, or storage. A sense of excitement surged as pins fell into geographically relevant position, confirming the obvious—Fleet Landing was the epicenter of a fire cluster. And the huge Kinkaid blaze represented a dramatic shift in *modus operandi*.

Sydney popped a Diet Mountain Dew and studied the board. Narrowing the parameters to Fleet Landing's fires only, she settled on three questions to explore.

Who owned the torched sites?

What was their insurance status?

And had owners made a repair claim?

Three hours later, Sydney tingled when she deciphered a complex mishmash lurking in the cracks—Hart Anson held deeds to seventy or so torched entities in Palmetto Quality Development's name, his business headquartered on Daniel Island. Even curiouser, he'd made other large-scale investments in Fleet Landing homes and apartment buildings hiding behind nondescript limited liability corporations. The LLCs proved to be a jumble of mailbox companies from Hilton Head, Atlanta, and Florence without a web presence or any indication they hired employees. In her mind, those were telltale indicators of shell corporations tied to offshore havens used for money laundering and tax evasion.

But her wackiest finding revealed the local Klan klavern of White Crusaders had purchased an assortment of properties before and after the fires. They also papered their holdings using layers of innocuous companies, apparently to conceal ownership in the predominantly Black neighborhood.

Sydney chucked her pen atop the piles. "I did not see that coming."

Next, she scoured Cal's insurance information and discovered the Anson and Klan properties were heavily insured, significantly above market value. Simply put, they'd both profited by overstating their losses, which translated to insurance fraud in any language.

Sydney rubbed her hands together. "Now, we're getting somewhere."

She began ruminating over the third element, repair status, buoyed by having thrown a proverbial wrench in Coop's theory about an alleged two-gang repair scam. Thus, it came as no surprise Anson had hired Rivertown Academy exclusively to complete his repairs. That squared, since he was their founder and chief backer.

Oddly, Klan-owned sites also relied on Rivertown to perform their repairs. Supporting a Fleet Landing nonprofit seemed a weird cause for White Crusaders to embrace, regardless of Anson's affiliation or influence with both groups.

Lastly, the privately owned properties, that was to say those not owned by Anson or the White Crusaders, had surprisingly opted against hiring the Academy. Sydney expected neighborhood residents to back their own. Instead, they'd uniformly chosen a fix-it company she'd never heard of called Holy Joe's.

Sydney came up dry trying to learn more about Joe's. They, too, didn't have any internet or social media presence, an unusual business model in a competitive market. She puffed her cheeks, dead-ended until she could ask Mandy to help crack the mystery.

33

By 6 a.m., local morning shows filled the bank of TV monitors on the wall near the senior producer's desk. Eyewitness 13's crawl strip strobed BREAKING NEWS. Sydney sidled over to read the eye-popping banner: GANG MEMBERS ARRESTED and TIPTON TERRACE SOLD. She used a remote control to increase the volume.

Their early anchor tossed a huge mane of wicked orange hair over her shoulder. "Sources close to the investigation confirmed as many as fifteen 843Z were arrested in connection with Monday's deadly fire in Fleet Landing, which also burned a pair of Freedman's homes. The latter buildings' loss is a setback for Mayor Wallace and other preservationists who sought to add them to the National Register of Historic Places.

"Our senior reporter, Julia Mayfair, also learned City Council approved the sale of Tipton Terrace to a private developer from Savannah in a closed-door session. Sources say council further intends to rezone and claim, via eminent domain, an additional quarter-mile stretch of private land adjacent to the Tip. Property values for the troubled area have already skyrocketed, ensuring owners of those parcels will earn a lot of money when the city moves forward on their bid.

"Next, researchers discover overeating leads to obesity. Find out if you're packing the right stuff in your kid's lunch box."

The newscast dissolved into a funeral home commercial.

The young assistant producer stood ramrod straight beside Sydney, scribbling notes. "Should I blurb it for Olivia?"

Sydney shook her head. "I'm certain our producer grasps the link between overeating and weight gain. And the rest is outdated."

"But they call it breaking news."

"What does that tell you about our competition's journalistic scruples?" Sydney leveraged the teachable moment. "Tell you what, I'll phone Julia Mayfair and find out what else she knows."

"Thanks. And I'm sorry to hear about Reggie. He taught me a lot about framing shots and selecting stand-up locations."

Sydney's heart sank. "Me too."

•

Lamar jerked awake when an incoming text from Falcon read: YOU BOTCHED LAST NIGHT. *Need U 2 eliminate Agent Bellamy.*

He scowled and sent his reply: *You're crazy. I don't kill people.*

Though Lamar was ready to tap out, he wished he hadn't dissed Falcon. He grabbed a fistful of sheet, jumped from the bed, then paced the four corners of his room until a response came: *Not what I meant. Buy some time. Derail his investigation.*

Lamar's stomach knotted, but he wasn't turning back. He texted: *No more. We had a deal. I did everything you asked.*

Falcon's reply was swift: *I own you. Mama's secrets go public if . . .*

Lamar shuddered at the implication. He was in over his head. He sat on the edge of the bed, rested his elbows on shaky knees, and wrestled with what to do next.

•

Rain pelted the task force conference room's windows. Coop diverted to his office and phoned his landlady.

Cora Rose answered on the fourth ring. "Bishop residence. May I help you?"

"Hope I didn't wake you," Coop said apologetically.

"Couldn't sleep after I collected Haley last night. I'm making sure nothing happens to your little girl. Care to speak with her?"

Coop eyed his watch. "She's up? That's incredible. I normally have to shake her a few times before she moves. Please, put her on."

"It's raining," Haley said. "Miss Rita is bound to cancel soccer practice."

"School is closed again. Mind spending the day with Cora Rose?"

Haley didn't answer right away.

"You listening to me?" Coop said.

"Can we watch a movie later?" Haley asked.

"Sounds great. Are you dressed? Eating breakfast?"

"Miss Bishop cooked shrimp and grits. Yummo delicious."

He smiled. Nothing vegan about shrimp. Nor the pound of butter Cora Rose most certainly added to her recipe. "Um, doesn't sound like your usual morning fare."

"I'm being polite. Besides, it's pretty good." She added extra syllables to each word. "You won't tell Mom?"

"Our secret. Please mind Cora Rose."

She paused. "Miss Bishop wants to talk to you."

"We'll be fine," Cora Rose said.

"Thanks for making breakfast. You hit a high note."

"Delighted to use the shrimp before they spoiled." She thanked him again for trusting her before disconnecting.

Detective Tate raced into Coop's office. "Captain Burton is on the horn with additional lab results."

Coop hurried to the conference room. "Captain, this is Coop. I'm here with the team."

"We lifted prints from a number of items, including last night's dumpster fire," Captain Burton said. "Unfortunately, no positive SLED hits."

"Send the prints to my boss. Ask him to expedite an AFIS run. Also, make sure Chanita Proctor gets a heads-up. Anything else?"

"Your ATF contacts helped us trace the threatening phone call your TV friend received."

Coop acknowledged the hoots and congratulatory high-fives from the investigators. "Go on."

"Big surprise, call came from a burner. But they managed to

triangulate cell towers where the call originated. Those results don't move the chains, though."

"Why?" Coop asked.

"The area includes seven downtown blocks," the captain said. "Lastly, GC-slash-mass spec analysis confirms a mixture of paraffins, cycloalkanes, and olefins consistent with unleaded gasoline from ground and soot samples in and around 1389 Kinkaid, 9125 Spruance, 7 North Hobson Avenue—Sydney Quinn's address—and the Lenwood dumpster." Papers ruffled on her end. "Furthermore, results are consistent with propane in the Tipton samples."

"Exactly what we expected. What else are you working on?"

"Techs are analyzing a printer Lieutenant Bernadino brought us."

"Thanks for the update." Coop disconnected, then faced his team. "Let me remind you how important it is for us to maintain absolute radio silence. Anything for me before I go?"

A firefighter raised his hand. "Fire investigation teams at the Tip say they are almost done examining gas lines on the northwest end. Rain is causing havoc."

"Sheila obtained hard shells for them. They'll be fine. Soggy and miserable, but safe."

Coop returned to his office and phoned Chief Sinclair, then Dino, relaying the key information received from the crime lab.

Once he finished briefing Dino, the cop swung into action. "Do you recall that weird sort of double exposure techs discovered behind the bird picture?"

"Yeah."

"I didn't want to say this in front of Sydney last night. It came from a memo addressed to Hart Anson. That gave us grounds to confiscate a printer from his private office."

"Captain Burton said you'd logged a device for analysis. Now I understand why she brought it to my attention. Can you be certain Anson sent the memo?"

"Still unclear, but techs continue fiddling with the resolution.

Want me to move on Hart Anson?"

Coop thought it over. "Not yet. We only get one chance at a first go-round with him."

Dino said, "Okay, I'll reign in my overachievers. By the way, someone tried to knock off D-Jazz."

"In jail? You telling me one of our suspects became a victim?"

"We relocated him to MUSC. Keeping him under wraps in an isolation room until we can sort out what happened."

Coop said, "I'll head over and squeeze him. Maybe he'll be more motivated following a brush with jailhouse foes. Sydney also got me thinking about the White Crusaders. On a lark, I'll collect prints from Wallace and Anson for evidence comparison. Without grounds for a warrant, I hope they voluntarily submit. And I promised her I'd work on my testimony for court. That fills my plate. Could use your help."

"I'm slammed too. Call Syd. Remind her she's on your task force."

Coop laughed. "And have her do what? You're the one hiding things from her."

"I know that'll bite me later, and I'll probably need shots," Dino said. "Here's an idea. Split the D-Jazz, Wallace, and Anson interviews with her. She's terrific at ferreting out the ferrets."

34

Sydney slumped onto the recliner in her work cubby and fell asleep.

Forty minutes later, Cal tapped her foot. His eyes bulged round as hubcaps as he stuck out his cell phone for examination.

"Hope you didn't wake me for another cat video," Sydney said.

Cal shook his head. "The first picture is from Kinkaid. The second, at the Tip. The third is from the old shipyard—your place. And number four . . ." He checked the phone. "Yeah, good ole number four. I took that one last night. Near Coop's. Right before the dumpster fire."

Sydney snapped her fingers and winked. "That reminds me. You displayed an alarming disregard for the mandatory curfew. That kind of behavior demonstrates real promise. I'll make a journalist out of you yet." She flitted through the four pictures, each of a black Mercedes, then returned Cal's phone. "I'm intrigued. And I hate coincidences."

"Wanted to show you before I turn these photos over to the task force."

Sydney bolted upright. "Oh no you don't. Not yet."

She believed neither the vaunted ATF, SLED, CPD, nor any other alphabet agency had evidence of what might be the same Mercedes at each most recent fire. She relished having a solid lead all to herself.

They moved to Mandy's cubicle and Sydney pointed at Cal's phone. "Any magic techno-thingies in your bag of tricks to enhance his photos?"

Mandy connected Cal's phone to her computer. "You have to ask?" She copied the four photos onto her hard drive, and a few keystrokes later, the computer started enhancing pixels—at the rate of glacial melt.

Sydney sighed. "How long?"

Mandy hunched her shoulders. "A little redefinition. A dash of amplification. Then presto, we read license plates. How about I use the time for a brain dump before you have to leave for the fire chief's press conference?"

"Good, because I have questions." Sydney pulled a comfy side chair from a neighboring cubicle for Cal. "For starters, did you know Anson changed his name after the train station fire?"

Mandy curled her legs. "Interesting, but a name change wouldn't fool anyone who knew him."

Olivia wandered by. "Why y'all huddled together?"

"Brainstorming," Sydney said. "Care to partake?"

Olivia leaned against the partition. "I'll give you one minute."

Something else nipped at Sydney. "Ever hear of Holy Joe's?"

"A Chuck-in-a-truck repair company," Cal said.

"You sure?" Olivia asked.

Cal rolled his eyes. "Spoken like a big sister who thinks I'm clueless."

"You two are adorable when you fight," Sydney said. "Go on, Cal."

"A client told me two Holy Joe's guys showed up unsolicited the day after his fire. Told him they could do the repair work cheaper and faster than any of the big-name companies. Sounded sketchy to my client, so he turned 'em down. Next day, two more dudes showed up. Goons with tattoos. Gold teeth. Big muscles."

"843Z?" Sydney asked.

Cal nodded. "I called dozens more clients who shared the same story. Said they were prepared to hire Rivertown Academy but were afraid of the consequences. I think the 843Z run Holy Joe's."

Olivia said, "Sounds like the gang stuck their dirty paws in some sort of skeevy repair situation."

Sydney tapped her lip with a finger. "More like extortion to go along with another insurance scam."

"Another?" Cal loosened his necktie. Citrusy flecks played off his brown suit.

Sydney explained what she knew about the White Crusaders' fraud—most importantly, exaggerated losses. Cal hadn't made the connection and argued in favor of telling the police. Sydney suggested he use the information to salvage his job before seeking any legal repercussions against the offenders.

Olivia swatted Cal on the back of his head. "Baby brother, sometimes—"

Cal faked a wince. "Ouch."

Olivia crossed her arms. "Frog's butt is watertight, if you know what I mean. Y'all should've anticipated this fraud escapade earlier. If so, you might've kept flies outside the screen door. If you know what I mean." She retreated to the altar.

Sydney almost never understood what Olivia meant when she offered her southern charm.

"C'mon, Syd," Mandy said. "Your job isn't to connect every dot. Just the spicy bits. Remember, you aren't a detective."

Sydney frowned. "The task force needs to link events and evidence if they want charges to stick. What if I finish the puzzle for them?"

"You mean for Dino? Or Coop?" Mandy asked coyly. "Which one of your hunky men are you trying to impress?"

"Furthest thing from my mind."

Mandy turned from her computer. "I hear what Cal is saying about 843Z gang involvement with Holy Joe's. But here's a wrinkle. Mayor Wallace endorsed Joe's as an official historical contractor a few months back. Licensed them to make repairs or renovate the city's most prized structures. That gives 'em genuine legitimacy."

Sydney huffed. "How did a gang-run, fly-by-night company become a blue-ribbon renovator? And why would anyone keep that accomplishment under the radar?"

She started to fuse Channel 13's breaking news, the serial fires and the Tip explosion, along with the repair scam with anonymous large-scale real estate purchases in Fleet Landing. The only possible conclusion—Falcon was the big kahuna connecting everything. And evidence of his fraud was a top-notch *get* she could leverage. Along with Cal's photos.

Mandy flung her hands to her face. "Oh, dear. Do you think the mayor is linked to the serial fires or 843Z?"

"If he is involved in the arson quagmire," Cal said, "this station has uncovered an epic scandal."

Sydney held a finger to her mouth. "Not ready for prime time yet."

"Why?" Mandy pleaded. "The public needs to know. You haven't forgotten what we do here?"

"So far, all we have is innuendo, not irrefutable proof. At Action News, we don't traffic in stupid."

Mandy pressed. "It's an exclusive. What good is being on the task force if you aren't allowed to bring a camera to the arrest party?"

"No party like an arrest party." Sydney glanced at Mandy's computer screen continuing to labor on Cal's photo enhancements.

"I'll keep digging." Sydney returned to her desk and phoned the person she suspected would have many answers about Rivertown Academy, the 843Z repair shakedown, and White Crusader's investments in Fleet Landing real estate—Councilwoman Lantana Hardwick. Sydney said, "Talk to me about the 843Z and Holy Joe's."

Lantana sighed. "One and the same bunch of thieves and thugs with an unlimited desire to inflict punishment on those who least deserve it."

"I'm guessing they don't share your sense of purpose in returning Fleet Landing to the mainstream."

Lantana blurted a laugh. "I think it's safe to say I'm taking lots of my constituents and council colleagues in a whole new direction—a historic course correction."

"What about Mayor Wallace?"

"Don't quote me, but he's one I'd like to skewer."

"Off the record. But I gotta ask why. He's done a lot of good for Fleet Landing."

"I can't see past him being the one who put my brother in prison."

Sydney eyed her notepad. "Any chance the White Crusaders are investing in Fleet Landing?"

"Oh, Syd. That'll be the day."

"I know, there goes the neighborhood." Sydney jotted Lantana's response. "Lastly, I'd like to spotlight Rivertown Academy."

"Talk with Hart. He risked a boatload of personal cachet to champion the Academy's efforts. Gotta run." Lantana disconnected.

Sydney drummed her fingers and made her own course correction. She phoned Anson to arrange a meet and discuss his bizarre association with both the Fleet Landing and train station fires. As well as his academy.

She heard Mandy's computer beep, signaling an end to Cal's photo enhancements. She dashed to Mandy's cubby and examined the screen. "Same license plate in all four views. I'll ask Dino to run it."

Cal leaned in. "Faces are a blur."

Mandy said, "Need to leave something for ATF and CPD's photo detectives to uncover."

"What's next?" Cal asked.

"A never-ending to-do list," Sydney said. "Press conference, interviews with family members of the deceased, follow-ups at the scenes—general broadcast requirements. Plus, Nate's retrial opens tomorrow."

"Ask for help," Mandy said.

"Have you met me?"

"Think of it as a group project."

Sydney steeled herself. "Why does everyone consider it a character flaw to fend for myself?"

Mandy puckered. "Because you're being selfish."

"I tried the *help* thing once. Didn't turn out so good."

Sydney crushed a notebook in her hands as she mentally replayed the whole mess. A giant Kiowa landed for an urgent ex-fil from an ambush that threatened to wipe out the entire company. Rotor blades *tha-whumped*, spraying sand everywhere.

"Helo. Now," Gunny barked.

Sydney's backpack snagged on a tangle of straps and harnesses. "Gunny, help."

His Ka-Bar glinted in the landing lights. He cut her free a split second before a sniper's round slammed into his neck. Gunny dropped like a sack of dirty laundry.

Crandall. Reed. Slater. Townsend. Walters.

The. Gunny. Effect.

Cal shook her arm. "Are you okay? You sorta zoned out."

She held onto the vision of Gunnery Sergeant Burt Walters' face. "I, uh . . . need to phone Julia Mayfair at Eyewitness 13." Sydney shook off ingrained pangs of guilt before moving to her cubicle and dialing the rival's station.

"Ha, I knew you'd call to congratulate me." Julia's nasal tone scratched like fingernails on a chalkboard.

"I actually wanted to offer my graphics guy," Sydney said.

"Because?"

"Breaking news is the only crawl strip your station uses. My guy can show you how to create something different for reporting old news."

Julia laughed. "You slay me, Syd. I think graphics is only a pretext to call little ole me. What's really on your mind?"

"Tell me about your source for the property story you ran this morning?"

"Are you referring to the Tip sale and eminent domain claim?"

"Yeah."

"I won't divulge my sources," Julia said.

"Cut the crap. You can't play the source card with me." Sydney elected to sweeten the pot. "I'll owe you."

"Next time, lead with the brass goodies. Okay, here it goes. My anchor, Lorna Maxwell, claims the city was going to rezone the Tip before it burned. It'd clear the way for selling or leasing property and displacing low-income residents squatting on prime real estate. Yesterday evening, when I approached her for additional information about that story, she recanted. Said her source isn't legit. I told her I'd tell the station manager she'd fabricated the story, even if it cost Maxwell her career. She tossed around a few obscenities, then the bitch threatened me." Julia came up for air. "Reminds me of when we schmooze. But you know something, Syd? She didn't scare me, either."

Julia's recap had tried walking Sydney in circles, never expecting to reveal anything important to a competitor. But she'd confirmed, in a roundabout fashion, Anson and his White Crusader cronies were indeed taking steps to plunder the city. And someone on the city council might be complicit.

The obvious next step was to speak with Mayor Wallace and find where he stood.

35

Coop angled the Cherokee between a tree and a red zone in the MUSC Public Safety lot. He rode the elevator to the hospital's top floor and strode directly to the room at the corridor's end. Stickers covered the door, declaring multiple infectious disease dangers. Coop showed his credentials to the cop guarding the arrestee, then donned a gown, mask, shoe covers, and gloves prior to entering the room.

D'Angelo Hines, AKA D-Jazz, lounged atop the bed, suggesting either he didn't comprehend the precarious position he'd landed in or he didn't care. He wore jeans and an oversized jersey resembling every other banger on the street.

Coop was anxious to challenge the local kingpin. He wanted confirmation the 843Z were responsible for the serial fires and whether Ice was on the hook for the Tip explosion. Lastly, he eagerly needed D-Jazz to identify Falcon.

Coop fired the first volley. "What, no jailhouse orange jammies for you?"

D-Jazz gave Coop the once over. "Who want to know?"

"Coop Bellamy, ATF." He held out his badge with a gloved hand.

D-Jazz sneered at the agent's outfit. "You look like an idiot wearin' all that."

Coop pulled two chairs around and flicked off the TV. He patted the back of a chair. "Since you aren't sick, let's talk."

D-Jazz gimped from the bed.

Coop eyed his shuffle. "Almost forgot, you nearly found yourself deleted."

"Damn straight. One of them Lowcountry Disciple dudes from Walterboro was in my cell. Dumbass cops shoulda never mixed the gangs."

Coop surveyed the guy from head to toe. The banger stood maybe five-seven. Hollow eyes and cheeks. An impressive gold earring pierced his left lobe, and tats covered his neck like a scarf. His pencil mustache from the prison booking photo had been replaced by a pointed goatee. The old mugshot had also framed his hair in a tight 'fro with arrows shaved into the sides. At present, D-Jazz's hair was longer and straighter. Coop wondered why the guy didn't bulge with prison muscle like typical repeat offenders who enjoyed weight-lifting privileges at the state's expense.

D-Jazz folded his arms across his chest and dropped into the chair across from Coop. "Let's get this party poppin.'"

Coop said, "Heard a lot about you. Started me thinking—"

"You spend time thinkin' 'bout me? I'm flattered." D-Jazz projected infuriating confidence. "Why am I here?"

"Protective custody."

"For real? That's dope."

"Someone from your crew fingered you as the 843Z leader."

"Nah, not me."

"And accused you of setting the fires," Coop stated.

"I'm good at settin' fires."

"What about having sex with prostitutes?"

"What can I say, I'm good at sex, too."

Coop grinned, giving the scumbag credit for his little show of bravado. "Hey, what's your beef with Ice?"

"He tryin' to move in on my territory."

"Rumor is, Ice won the takeover battle."

D-Jazz made an almost imperceptible shift in body language.

That fraction of a second was all Coop needed to read the guy. "Why are you burning Fleet Landing?"

D-Jazz waved his hands, pleading his case. "No. No. No. Fleet Landing is my hood."

"Then who's burning it up and why would you let that happen?"

The banger jumped to his feet. The chair spilled backwards and he windmilled his arms to maintain his balance. Coop caught D-Jazz by the elbow to hold him upright until he reset the chair. D-Jazz clutched his side.

Coop pressed on. "What about Croc and Ray-Ray?"

D-Jazz threw his head back and laughed. "Those two numbnuts. What did they say about me?"

Coop balled his hand as though he held a gun. "They aren't talking anymore."

"Naw." D-Jazz brushed Coop's hand. "Who killed 'em?"

"You tell me. After all, it's your hood." Coop sat back and crossed his arms.

Long pauses tended to punctuate complex interrogations. Coop used the time to study D-Jazz for signs of deception, then took up bouncing a pencil off its eraser end. The move was meant to hypnotize and annoy the hell out of the person being questioned with maddening repetition.

Coop broke the silence. "If Ice gained control, it'd end your role as head of the 843Z empire."

D-Jazz smoothed his goatee. "S'pose he did. What of it?"

"I'll bet he didn't want you around when you sprung from prison. Going back to jail must've been all he needed to cut you out."

D-Jazz crossed his arms, mirroring Coop.

Coop returned the conversation to the two dead teens found in the boosted utility van at Sydney's. "What's the deal with Dominion Energy uniforms? Part of your shakedown?"

D-Jazz blinked several times as he thought it over. Excessive blinking was a giveaway. The last question had struck paydirt. "Lawyer."

"You ask for one now, and I'm out of here. Cops will send you back to lockup, then revoke your parole." Coop resumed bouncing the pencil and D-Jazz became mesmerized. "A genius like you should be able to reckon your associates sold you out to save their asses." The pencil jumped from table to hand with synchronized tedium. "You have a bounty on your head. I know you'll give in eventually, but …" Coop slammed the pencil on the table. "Patience isn't one of my virtues."

Now it was up to D-Jazz to choose how he wanted to play his hand. His eyes widened, making it clear he feared reprisal if he had to return to lockup. Rather, he was the kind of guy who preferred the comforts of protective custody at MUSC. "You wanna deal? Okay. Ice killed them two numb nuts. What do I get in return?"

Coop liked what he heard. "Are you waiving your right to an attorney?"

"For now. I made reservations for one later, if I need."

"Tell me about Falcon," Coop said.

"What you want to know?"

"Are you Falcon?"

D-Jazz curled his lip. "Nah."

"Who is he? Ice?"

"You must be trippin'."

Coop sat forward. "Do you work for Falcon?"

"Still trippin'. I ain't no snitch."

"Your cousin used a weapon my ATF crew tracked to Ice. We linked Destiny's MAC 10 to other crimes. Did you tell her to shoot at firefighters?"

"I wasn't there."

Coop pressed him into an alibi. "Where were you during the fire and explosion?"

"A Summerville bro hit my numbers. Asked me to meet him. Nobody there when I arrived, so I went to the ho house in Sangaree. Humpin' my brains out 'til cops pounded through the door."

Another slip. Coop knew drone footage and facial recognition software had nailed D-Jazz at the scene. His location had also been corroborated by data collected from his phone's GPS tracking system. Lies were mounting in the prosecution's favor.

Coop said, "I have a theory—"

"Spill it." D-Jazz cocked his head, running out of steam.

"You knew in advance Falcon planned to set fire to a house on Kinkaid."

D-Jazz cast his glance around the room and said nothing. Coop imagined the banger was weighing his options. Calculating the angles. Maybe even trying to think of a new play.

Coop continued. "So, you coaxed your cousin into taking Ice's gun to the fire. Maybe told her to shoot a first responder, hoping she'd start a riot—"

"No way."

"I'll bet you never imagined police would kill her—"

"Stop." D-Jazz recoiled and made a rude gesture.

"You can blame Ice for her death."

D-Jazz blinked. "Got it figured out, huh?"

"I'll send a cop in to take your statement. Then, we'll work on your deal." Coop mentally crossed D-Jazz off his list of Falcon candidates. He felt certain the gang leader hadn't orchestrated the arson conspiracy.

Coop slapped his hands on his thighs before standing. He took one last flyer, hoping to link D-Jazz to the Tip disaster. "Where'd you learn to build bombs using cell phones? Because I gotta tell you, it's real risky. More likely, those two boneheads you hired didn't follow instructions. Let out the gas in too many first-floor apartments. Am I right?"

D-Jazz fixed his gaze on the blank TV. "Lawyer."

Coop stepped to the door, knowing he'd eventually get what he needed to nail Ice for Tip's explosion and subsequent fatalities. Along with numerous lesser offenses. When the time was right, D-Jazz would deliver more of his fellow conspirators to save his hide.

36

Lamar arrived at the Moultrie Building following another morning stint washing dishes at Tyrell's. He hadn't given any thought to derailing the investigation or sidetracking Agent Bellamy on Falcon's behalf. He hoped something brilliant materialized soon, for Mama's sake.

He chanced heading to the third floor. A firefighter he recognized let him in and Lamar went straight to the cubicle where he'd worked on Monday. When he rounded the partition, he spotted a granite block sitting in his chair. "Uh, sorry," Lamar stuttered.

The guy swallowed Lamar with a bone-crushing handshake. "Detective Tate told me some kid did a bang-up job collating fire data. You him?"

Lamar's fingers numbed, and he jerked his hand away. "I did stuff for the detective, sure." He shook out his hand and surveyed crime scene photos from various arsons pinned to the wall. Some were fires he'd set. "What's all this?"

"I'm working a project for Agent Coop. Want to help?"

Lamar played it cool. "Need me to pin more photos?"

Detective Tate strutted over. "Cory, you meet Lamar? This is the kid I told you about."

Lamar rubbed his right hand.

The detective grinned. "Lose feeling in your fingers when Cory squeezed?"

"Like a frickin' vise grip." Lamar liked these guys and wished the circumstances were different.

Detective Tate clapped Cory on the back. "Cory drives a fire truck and hooks hoses to standpipes. His crew tells me he doesn't even use a wrench to open fire plugs. Bring Lamar up to speed. Let's see if you can eliminate or add any fires to our list." For Lamar, the detective said, "The usual caveats apply. We clear?"

"Crystal," Lamar said.

The detective withdrew to the conference room.

Lamar turned to Cory. "Tell me what you need."

"Our prime suspect is a dude who has landed in and out of custody." Cory reached for a notebook and flipped a few pages. "Need to search the database and identify fires he could've committed when he was out. That'd be the opportunity leg of the criminal triangle."

"Incarceration as an alibi? That's whack." Lamar knew the task force wanted to pin as many fires as possible on D-Jazz. "I'll sort by date. Simple enough."

Cory held up his hands. "Good, cuz these fingers weren't built for keyboarding."

"Bet you can't text none, either." Lamar glanced around the cubicle. "Where you want me to work?"

Cory patted the monitor. "Right here."

Lamar dropped into the chair. "Need your code to open the files."

Cory scrunched his face, then typed his password, backspacing three times from fat-finger errors.

Lamar's insides cartwheeled. Cory's access had admitted him to the master database and secure files. Exactly the access he needed. He bit his lip, then opened the suspicious fire database and commenced organizing entries using an application from a drop-down menu. He ran the cursor over the column headers for sort criteria, then clicked his mouse into action.

Cory whistled. "Slick as snot."

"What's the date your guy was first out of circulation?"

Cory paged through the notebook. "April 14th. Five years ago."

Lamar scrolled the list until he found the first event following April 14th. "I was in junior high. When did D-Jazz get released?" He chanced using the banger's alias.

"March 28th. Last year."

Lamar highlighted inclusive dates and provided an inventory of fires jamming D-Jazz after his release. Based on those data, Lamar concluded Falcon had been burning the hood long before hiring him. Time to test his own theory. "If this guy is so powerful, could he run his crew from inside prison?"

"Great question," Cory said. "We'll ask a cop."

"Any food downstairs?"

"I suppose."

"Want some?" Lamar asked.

"Nah, I'm only doing proteins." Cory flexed his massive biceps. "You need lean meats to gain meaningful girth. You should try it."

"I play second base. Bulk will mess up my double-play jam."

Detective Tate stuck his head out the door. "Cory, you finish the list?"

He nudged Lamar. "Saving it to the server so you can use it in the bunker."

Lamar clicked his mouse. "Done."

"Quick question, Detective," Cory said. "Any chance D-Jazz was involved with the fires even while in custody?"

The detective nodded. "He didn't have to light a match to play his part in an ongoing conspiracy. Let's see what you have first and go from there."

They both ducked inside the conference room, leaving Lamar alone at the computer.

He glanced around before pouncing into action. First, he opened the "SUSPECTS" folder and searched for his own name. Much to his relief, he wasn't listed. The task force was primarily focused on 843Z members with ties to D-Jazz.

Next, he opened the folder labeled "WARRANTS." D-Jazz scored another big win. His file contained search and arrest warrants from Charleston's police and sheriff's departments, along with a matching pair of federal warrants from ATF. Lamar let out a long, low whistle.

The task force had it bad for D'Angelo Hines.

Time to erase incriminating pictures from the primary database.

Lamar clicked the mouse to locate the video and photo master directories. He scanned more than two dozen folders before he found "KINKAID & TIP MASTERS." He hurriedly erased his most damning photos and clips. Then he closed the open portals.

Lamar leaned back. Relieved. No, appalled at his illicit activity.

He quickly restored what he'd deleted, then clicked off as Cory stepped into the cubicle. The screen showed the Charleston Fire Department logo leaping from corner to corner.

"Glad you logged off," Cory said. "Forgot to remind you."

"What's next?" Lamar asked.

"Detective Tate says they need you downstairs."

Lamar stuck his hand out. "Thanks, man." He pulled his hand away as Cory reached for it, then swiped the side of his head. "Gotcha."

He hopped down the stairs to join his old group.

Lamar eyed fresh buckets of chicken and helped himself to three crispy legs.

Red elbowed Lamar in the ribs. "I'm a breast man, myself."

"Excuse me?" Lamar said.

He pointed at the plate. "Chicken. I prefer breast meat."

White meat for the white dude. Figured.

"I like breasts, too," Lamar said. "But legs are easier to eat without utensils." He cleaned his face with a paper towel and jammed another leg into his mouth.

"You suppose there's any correlation between the piece of chicken we choose and the women we date?" Red asked.

Perhaps another time, another place. Might make for an interesting conversation.

But Lamar had a part to play. "Why you gotta sound so weird? It's only food."

"Or is it?" Red pushed the glasses on his nose. "What would Dr.

Freud say?"

"He'd say, 'Eat the damn chicken so the other kids don't smack the crap out of you.'"

"Ah, regression." Red crossed his arms and placed a finger to his lips as though in deep contemplation. "Or is it repression?"

"More akin to projection. Or sublimation, displacement, denial? Or are these words we both memorized?" Lamar mirrored Red's pose. "Perhaps because ze psych midterm exam is next? No?" Lamar's fake German accent created an unexpected bonus.

"You nailed it." Red reached for a thigh and gobbled a big bite.

Lamar laughed so hard, he spilled his plate.

"What?" Red asked.

"You went for the dark meat, dude. Ole Sigmund would have a field day."

"I'm all about the bass—"

"Stop singing." Lamar fished for his wallet. "Ten bucks if you quit right now."

Captain Bosco arrived. "You two about finished? Need you back on video detail."

Red offered a mock salute. "Aye, aye, Capitan."

Lamar dug the burner phone from his pocket. "I'll send Mama a text to let her know I'm sticking 'round."

"Sure, kid," Bosco said.

Lamar reluctantly typed a brief update for Falcon, then hit send.

·

Sydney met Coop at a hotel coffee shop near City Hall before the fire chief's press conference.

He pushed out a chair with his foot, then propped an elbow on the table and rested his chin on his knuckles. An idiotic grin spread across his face. "Hey, D-Jazz almost got himself killed last night."

"Must mean something," Sydney said.

Coop hesitated. "Any chance you'll help me with a little

surreptitious evidence collection?"

"Love to, except—"

"Thought you'd jump at the chance."

"I'm tied up."

"Didn't know you were into that." Coop cocked his head, amused at his own joke. He seemed to sense his attempt at levity had crashed like a boat on jagged rocks, so he dove into Very Special Agent mode. "I'm pulling rank. Need you to chat up Wallace and find a sneaky way to collect his fingerprints."

Sydney cocked her head. "What do you mean?"

"You know, the way PIs do it on TV. Gather something with his prints, DNA, or both. Be creative because I don't have a warrant."

She already had Wallace on her interview list. But secretly jumped for joy at the *assignment*. With Dino, she often resorted to inserting herself into cases without permission. But she wasn't going to let Coop off without more effort on his part. "I'm always down with stretching a few regulations like warrantless evidence collection. But what about your strict adherence to pesky legal matters?"

"I never compromise when it comes to rules. This is as close to tight-roping as I'm willing to tread." Coop's tone contained an unforeseen dose of irritation. "While you're at it, measure Wallace's reaction to D-Jazz's death."

Sydney's voice echoed his annoyance. "You said it was only an attempt."

"It's okay to hold back the truth."

"Pro tip." Sydney smiled. "Rules will destroy you."

The waiter placed plates heaped with breakfast burritos and fried potatoes. The aroma made Sydney's stomach growl. She peeled off her cardigan and dug in, eventually breaking the silence teeming between them. "Been rehashing your theory. I think you are right about the 843Z repair scam. Ever heard of Holy Joe's?"

"Grunge band?"

"Good one." She sawed off a hunk of burrito and dragged it

through a dollop of salsa.

Coop's cell phone chirped with an incoming text. He glanced at it, then said, "Jot this down: *Won't approve COO at TM or OT without clear title at KI.* What do you make of it?"

Sydney glanced at her pad. "Reasonably cryptic. Might even win an award for spy craft. Can you break the code?"

"coo is undoubtedly certificate of occupancy," Coop said.

"TM must be—"

"Tobacco Mill," they said simultaneously.

Coop laughed. "OT and KI, any ideas?"

Sydney fell quiet for several seconds. "Got it. Ocean Terminal and Kiawah Island. What's the point of this exercise?"

Coop bent forward to speak. "Not for public release. What's it called? Deep background."

"I thought our relationship went beyond a mutual lack of trust. After all, you just ordered me to skirt evidentiary laws."

"I tend to work solo, so keeping things to myself comes second nature." Coop stared at the ceiling. "Remember the falcon photo the coroner found on one of the dead kids? Lab techs finished mining a personal memo ghosted within the picture caused by a printer glitch. What I had you write down is the crux of the note."

"Dammit, you buried the lede," Sydney said. "So, this memo … Who are the correspondents?"

"Hart Anson and—"

"Mayor Wallace," she finished for him.

Coop rocked back in his chair. "Badass intuition and smarts. Does me no good to keep you out of the loop."

"I guess that confirms Anson is up to no good."

"I thought you liked him."

Sydney pooched her bottom lip. "I'm recalibrating. Anson is squarely behind the Tobacco Mill project. And a brand-new Ocean Terminal is atop his wish list. He hopes to increase the number of cruise liners that disembark here, despite Wallace's standard objections."

"I'll bet Tipton Terrace makes the perfect location for a new terminal."

Sydney nodded. "Anson probably dreams of creating a swank waterfront complex—hotels, shopping, dining. The thing would complement the retail mix he built at the Tobacco Mill. What about *clear title at KP*?"

"Sounds to me like Anson is buying Wallace," Coop said.

"Payola? I hope not. But I'll ask him." She dabbed her mouth with a napkin, a whole lot little miffed about Coop keeping secrets. Then, she eyed the notebook containing Cal and Mandy's research—her own secrets. Time for a truce. "What if I can prove Holy Joe's is the key to your repair scam?"

"I'm listening."

"Cal calls them a Chuck-in-a-truck bunch, but they are an 843Z offshoot." She handed over Cal's insurance fraud confirmation. "Given elite status by the mayor you just accused of being on Anson's payroll. Does that make your toes curl?"

The shock on Coop's face told her he hadn't made that connection. "The former fire marshal investigated over fifty fires fitting the shakedown profile without finding any type of pattern. You uncovered something profoundly worse in only a few days. Unbelievable."

"Pshaw, throwing back the curtain on dipsticks and lugnuts is my thing." She glanced downward, and let a moment pass before resuming eye contact. "Something else you should know." She handed Coop copies of the Mercedes photos. "Cal took these at the four most recent fires. The car belongs to Anson's company, Palmetto Development."

Coop shot forward. "And you kept these from me? I should cite you for rotten sportsmanship."

She feigned regret. "One of my bad habits. I tend to work my leads before blurting them out."

Coop's expression relaxed. "Touché."

Sydney forked a mouthful of potatoes. "One more thing."

Coop's voice croaked with a smidge of excitement. "Sheesh, what's left?"

"My team discovered both Anson and the White Crusaders are hell-bent on buying distressed properties in Fleet Landing using anonymous shell corporations. I think it's intended to conceal obvious conflicts associated with their endeavor." Sydney gave her orange juice a fierce swizzle with the straw. "But here's what I don't understand. What's the return for the 843Z?"

"What do you mean?"

"Appears they're working with Anson, but he winds up pilfering valuable waterfront property. That tells me the 843Z are literally losing ground. Being driven from their hood. For what?"

"Money." Coop seemed to mull over her onslaught of valuable new information. "My guess is the gang tired of torching one house at a time and decided to cash in big time. They incinerated whole blocks of Kinkaid and Spruance this week for a whopping payday."

"So, that confirms Anson is Falcon, the wizard spearheading a greedy land grab. Makes sense he'd need Wallace's connivance. It'd be the fastest way to the Ocean Terminal's finish line. Anson may have offered to build a new school as a consolation. Maybe even a public housing project to replace what he and the 843Z destroyed."

They shared a moment of reflection.

Coop pushed away his plate. "What about the vacant port authority property adjacent to the Tip?"

"City acquired it from the state about a year ago," Sydney said. "That's probably when Anson hatched his plan. He's coveted that plot of land for years. Now, through a combination of eminent domain rip-offs, extortion thefts, and underhanded purchases—he stands to bank zillions. At least it explains setting fire to Nate's rental house."

"How so?" Coop asked.

"Lantana likely mentioned to Anson about her brother's potential acquittal. Along with the address she rented. It's one of his deeded properties."

"Whoa." Coop held up a hand. "Anson's motivation for torching Nate's rental pad could likely be retaliation for the fire that killed both parents. But burning 1389 Kinkaid specifically? He'd be insane to draw a line straight to himself."

"Enough to arrest him?" Sydney asked.

Coop shook his head. "If Anson is responsible for an intentional blaze at 1389 Kinkaid, and that led to scorching much of Kinkaid and Spruance, we'd have him on multiple Class A felonies. But I'm not there yet."

"Let me recap." Sydney slugged the last of her juice. "We believe Ice is responsible for the Tip explosion and D-Jazz is linked directly to the serial fires through his gang's role in the insurance scam. But Hart Anson orchestrated everything. He's Falcon. The 843Z are merely cut-outs doing his dirty work."

Coop said, "I'll have Dino put a tail on Anson."

"You gotta capture him before he reloads for the final confrontation. Because Mandy's house is on his manifesto hit list. So is Cora Rose's estate."

Coop stood. "Time to prepare for a whirlwind of arrests. Whatever comes from this fiasco will scar the city as much as the fires."

Sydney was gutted by a realization. If Anson's plan was successful, it would change the face of Fleet Landing by replacing modest homes with upscale retail and commercial. Thereby driving out hard-working and predominantly Black residents.

The hum of a vacuum jolted her back to the present. "What's next?"

Coop said, "I'm going to interview Anson before he realizes we're coming after him."

Sydney wanted to be the one who scored Anson's confession. Instead, she pounced on the next best thing. "I'll talk with someone at the White Crusaders."

"Will you collect Wallace's prints?" Coop asked.

Sydney nodded, though she was disappointed to possess information about his possible collusion and alleged payola from Anson.

Coop pulled her into an uncharacteristic embrace. "No more secrets. Agreed?"

Sydney's arms froze before mechanically returning his hug, uncertain whether she should demonstrate any signs of affection. Yet, she longed to feel safe and hoped she hadn't misread the moment, allowing herself to melt into his arms.

After a trice, she gathered her purse and resilience. "Anything else?"

"Don't screw up."

Sydney pushed through the exit. When she looked back over her shoulder, she spotted Coop dropping extra money on the table for the wait staff.

37

The fire chief's press conference lasted less than twenty minutes, during which time Sydney and Coop exchanged a barrage of texts hypothesizing about Anson and Wallace. She also composed a brief email for *jalewis@palmettodevelopment.com*, an address she'd found on Anson's Palmetto's website.

Sydney asked him or her to call about leasing opportunities in the "future" Ocean Terminal. She provided the number to a disposable cell phone to mask her identity. If this Lewis person did call, Sydney would pretend to represent a client seeking commercial retail space in the heretofore unapproved and unbuilt terminal. If Palmetto was already leasing space, Anson's company was committing more fraud since the city still owned most of the probable site.

On one hand, Sydney found something amusing about a coalition between white nationalists, a Black street gang, and a real estate mogul. Except for a series of felonies like fraud, extortion, and murder, the burgeoning partnership might have redefined urban renewal policy.

On the other hand, Sydney was loath to believe she'd been wrong about both Anson and Wallace's character. But evidence was accumulating. She also couldn't overlook the possibility the former solicitor, Wallace, might have buried evidence against Nate to propel his political career. Once in office, temptation to accept graft could've been overwhelming or merely the status quo. Similarly, Anson projected a munificent posture as community ambassador. Yet, one or both were involved in an epic public hoodwink.

After the presser, Sydney passed Coop on the sidewalk in front of City Hall. She flicked the side of her nose, resembling the signature gesture in *The Sting*. Their plan was afoot.

Mayor Wallace hadn't attended the press conference, so Sydney drove to his private residence on Daniel Island. She came off the interstate when she spotted the concrete gargoyles roosting atop the Island's welcome sign. Home to Charleston's toniest neighborhoods, it featured an exclusive enclave of boutique shopping, premier golf courses, colossal neo-plantation homes, and a bevy of private schools. In short, Daniel Island was a place where money bought more than just exclusivity.

Wallace and his wife lived in a modest townhome overlooking Ralston Creek. A retirement mansion on Kiawah Island, his suspected inducement for guiding approval of Anson's two pet projects—the Tobacco Mill and Ocean Terminal—would be a giant leap forward for the long-time public servant.

She parked under a spreading oak, then knocked on the front door. "Sydney Quinn, Action 7 News." She passed her card to the housekeeper, a woman of rather dull plumage. "I'm here to see the mayor."

"I don't care if you're Erin Burnett." She shook a dust wand at Sydney. "Mr. Wallace is in the study."

Sydney slung her purse over a shoulder. "Where?"

She pointed toward the staircase. "Sugar, this house only has six rooms. And you're probably a smart gal."

Sydney ascended to the second floor and discovered Wallace sitting behind a desk in the first room on the right. His carved mahogany number belonged in a more ornate setting than a converted bedroom in a cookie-cutter townhouse.

Wallace pointed at the television. "I see you didn't waste any time violating the public trust, Miss Quinn."

Eyewitness 13 continued running its crawl strip regarding the Tip sale to a Savannah developer. The developer was likely shilling for Anson, masking his purchase of the coveted property.

Sydney sat on a worn leather sofa near the desk. She removed a notepad and pen from her purse. "Mister Mayor, I work for Action

7. Content airing on other channels isn't my responsibility." She tapped the pen on her pad, pausing for effect. "Is it true?"

"What?"

"Did you accept Anson's offer and sell the Tip?"

Wallace rubbed his eyes. "It's been a long night."

"For me too." Sydney ached in places she didn't know could hurt.

"Phoning council members, department chiefs, influential civic leaders." The mayor held out papers as if to prove his point. "Stemming the tide of violence and threats to our fair city."

"Yet, another intentional blaze occurred near the Battery last night. Despite the arrest of many gang members allegedly responsible for Fleet Landing's fires."

He sank in his chair, visibly older and smaller in an instant.

She pressed forward. "Did you approve City Council's actions for rezoning Tipton Terrace? Perhaps Hart Anson leveraged undue influence?" She hoped to provide a chance for him to defend the ghost memo between him and Anson that seemed to reveal alleged corruption and malfeasance.

"Nothing is final. I maintain my opposition to the Tip sale."

Sydney questioned whether his pro-preservation stance was a calculated act. Did he have outstretched hands like other dirty officials?

She launched another big question. "Mr. Mayor, what's your official position regarding the White Crusaders?"

"From what perspective?"

She'd expected him to trot out a boilerplate condemnation, no matter what side he'd landed on. "From the perspective of membership."

Wallace spent the next ten minutes discussing his generational family ties to the Klan's White Crusaders with veiled pride. Neither distancing himself from the organization's horrific history nor panning their role in the city's shameful periods. Perhaps his sympathies for the group were still deep-seated despite overt repudiation.

Sydney asked, "Do you regret your membership in the KKK? I thought it's your only common ground with Hart Anson."

"My record of fair and impartial governance speaks for itself. I'll let Hart address his own actions."

Unfortunately, the mayor's fairness and impartiality were being thrust under the microscope.

Sydney was operating in full-on reporter mode. "How about the people jailed for curfew violations?"

"I've directed the release of those in custody."

"Peaceful rallies are scheduled this weekend throughout the Lowcountry. Have you ordered police to monitor those events?"

Wallace shook his head. "I'm planning to attend a vigil at the Tobacco Mill. Police won't be needed."

"What about Nathan Sharpe?"

A wave of his hand seemed intended to be dismissive, yet it ended with a sharp flourish which spoke more of anger. "His case is an old dog with fleas."

"Except for the thirty-nine victims."

Wallace tossed his pen on the desk. "I served justice as the solicitor for that matter."

Sydney shook her head. "You let the real killer go free by burying evidence. I'm saddened you failed the people you swore to serve. And as a result of your continued silence and reticence to acknowledge shortcomings in your prosecution, you are continuing to protect that person. Time to come clean."

Wallace balled his hands into fists. "The conviction was legitimate. I assure you."

Sydney leaned closer, undaunted. "What about intimidating witnesses as Lantana Hardwick suggested?"

Mayor Wallace ran his finger around his collar, then shifted in his chair. He seemed to be calculating a response for what Sydney considered an untenable position. "I resent the implication that some may draw from retrying one of my notable cases. The evidence against the Sharpe boy was undeniable. He set the fire that killed friends of mine. Good people."

Sydney realized the mayor only resented the aspersions she'd cast regarding his prowess as an attorney. He seemed most concerned with preserving that legacy. "Those good people—" Sydney tapped her notepad. "Klan members as well?"

"Are you saying, by virtue of membership in what was a completely legal organization, they deserved to be burned alive? How enlightened of you." His lips turned upward in a smirk. "Anyway, why are you so fascinated with a defunct organization?"

Sydney willed herself to avoid pointing an accusatory finger; instead, she hoped to expose Crusader secrets. "They aren't defunct. The local chapter of White Crusaders leases offices on King Street. Prime real estate three blocks from City Hall. And, I have proof they are aggressively acquiring property in Fleet Landing. My guess is they are taking advantage of damage from the fires." Sydney had raised her voice. Now she dialed it back. "Moreover, recently recovered evidence will buttress Nate Sharpe's claim of innocence. He will be exonerated. Admit it, you withheld evidence and your persecution of him was wrong."

"I think you mean prosecution," Mayor Wallace muttered. "And I never buried evidence or suborned perjury in any trial I prosecuted. That's slander."

"Not if it's true. Who is Falcon?"

"I'm quite certain it's a bird."

Sydney ignored his derisive chuckle. "Let's talk Kiawah Island."

"Ah, dear Kittiwah, as George Gershwin called it in *Porgy and Bess*."

Sydney tapped her pen on the spiral rings of her pad. "What are you naming your lavish island estate?"

Wallace's eyes narrowed. "An island estate? Unlikely."

Sydney gambled as though stepping out on a sturdy limb. "Oh? I spoke with an interior decorator at Three Rivers Design. Said your wife arranged window treatments and other home décor for your new residence. On Kiawah."

He folded his hands in his lap. "And what if we plan to move after I leave office? Are you branding it a crime for a humble city employee to save one's salary or fashion wise investments? Thereby affording a Kiawah property?"

She debated whether to confront him with evidence that he would be accused of trading favors for a KI mansion and opted against it, honoring Coop's deep background agreement. She shifted her thoughts to collecting Wallace's fingerprints or DNA.

"Next subject," Wallace said. "You seem eager to wave broad brushstrokes across a range of issues."

"Tourism," Sydney blurted. "The lifeblood of our city continues to skyrocket. Thanks, in part to detours you approved that allow tourists to breeze along the fringes of Fleet Landing, unaware police have essentially fenced in residents like livestock."

Wallace stiffened. "Hold on. I respect every member of our community. Our racial diversity adds to the rich—"

"Please don't say mosaic."

"Would you prefer color wheel? Medley? Montage? Charleston is the most cohesive ensemble. Anywhere."

Sydney winked. "Until Monday."

"An anomaly. One-off." Mayor Wallace attempted to dismiss the deadly calamity with a shrug. "It is what it is."

Sydney imagined Reggie's face behind his camera and wanted to rip into Wallace. Any jury would understand. Instead, she returned to Channel 13's bold allegations, hoping to link Wallace with Anson. "You mentioned earlier, one of my network's competitors reported City Council had approved Tipton Terrace's rezoning and sale. They also suggested council plans to annex neighboring houses and adjacent land via eminent domain. I suppose that means you'll let the city sell the old port authority yard as well. All three measures would allow Anson to attain the acreage he needs for his Ocean

Terminal venture."

Wallace grimaced. "His OT remains a pipe dream."

OT. He used the same abbreviation as in the ghost memo. *Ka-ching.*

Sydney pressed on. "Will you accept credit for the eventual hotels, shops, and dining Anson builds in Tip's place?"

"Credit? Sufficient compensation comes from maintaining and advocating responsible growth and development for the city I love." He stood and tugged the bottom of his suit coat. "Anson is a businessman. As are several council members. We have the owner of a used car dealership, a funeral home director, and other entrepreneurs. It's inconceivable any used their position to favorably enhance personal holdings."

"You're kidding. A real estate promoter is capitalizing on the neighborhood's fires to fleece real estate for personal gain. And he surely compensated others along the way. What's happening in Fleet Landing stinks like yesterday's catch. Left outside. In the hot sun."

Wallace's responses and demeanor left Sydney feeling certain he was either complicit or co-opted in Anson's cold-blooded land grab. Along with their White Crusader pals who were simultaneously benefiting.

Wallace said, "If Hart Anson or any members of the White Crusaders decide to substantially invest in my city, so be it. As long as they do it legally, without prejudice, and add to Charleston's appeal." He moved to his bookshelf. "Abandoned buildings are crime magnets. My goal is to seek reputable developers or responsible homeowners for renovating historic architecture. Besides, according to the former fire marshal, a homeless person caused the fires."

The neighborhood's vast number of vacant homes and dilapidated structures did offer prime targets for the arsonist. Since preservation proved a binary choice for purists like Wallace, his strict rules had created difficulties for those hoping to demolish buildings.

Else they'd endure sky-high repair costs. So, the wounded structures sat. And bad things happened.

Sydney said, "We're leaning in another direction and have made a number of promising arrests."

"We?" He scratched his head. "Oh, right. You and the task force."

"What if I told you the task force can prove Hart Anson is Falcon—the mastermind behind the fires?"

"Nothing would surprise me."

Sydney tucked her pad and pen inside her purse, then handed a business card to him.

Mayor Wallace examined the card and returned it, as she expected. "I know where to reach you. My housekeeper can show you out."

Sydney pinched the card in a corner where he hadn't touched and dropped it into her purse.

Mission accomplished.

38

Coop's official investigation had been underway for nearly forty-eight hours.

He looked forward to interviewing Hart Anson, the guy Sydney fingered as the most likely person behind the Fleet Landing fires and extortion. When Coop learned Anson had stayed behind at City Hall following the press conference, Coop marched directly to the mayor's office and entered unannounced. "Mr. Anson, I have a few questions."

Anson stopped rearranging photos on the credenza behind the impressive mayoral desk and spun on his heel. "Uh, Mr.—"

"Agent." Coop enjoyed correcting him. "Coop Bellamy, ATF."

Anson chomped his teeth. "Sure, Agent Bellamy."

Coop surveyed the palatial office. He remembered the framed oil-on-canvas paintings and photos of Mayor Wallace shaking hands with celebrities. But he recoiled when his gaze skimmed the outstretched talons of a stuffed falcon, beak slightly open, about to bite. The ugly creature hadn't been part of the stately décor on Monday.

Anson came around the desk and reached for the stuffed bird. "Isn't she's a beauty? Though I wish she'd been presented with outstretched wings. Sadly, a careless hunter shot one off." He turned the bird to show a patchwork of feathers.

"I feel bad for the bird, but the taxidermist did a fine job." Coop only supposed, since he didn't know the difference between a good or bad presentation.

"Thank you."

"You did the stuffing?"

"The correct term is mounting. I tanned and mounted the specimen as a gift for Boyd."

"Hobby?"

"More of a passion. My collection is rather large."

Coop didn't recollect any stuffed birds in Anson's conservatory. Maybe Sunny made him keep them in the garage. "Why falcons?"

"Raptors are powerful, fast-flying, magnificent creatures." Anson's voice trilled with enthusiasm. "Pesticide poisoning virtually eradicated the peregrine in this area. But they've enjoyed a remarkable comeback, thanks in part to our Awendaw Avian Conservancy."

"Where did this bird come from?" Coop asked.

"Left for dead near Stono Ferry by the bastard who shot her."

"Are you concerned our serial arsonist calls himself Falcon?" Coop plunked in the chair he'd used Monday night. He motioned for Anson to enjoy the upholstered chair behind the huge desk.

Anson, some five inches taller than Wallace, banged his knees on the desk's edge as he tried to roll under. "An unfortunate coincidence."

Coop pounced. "I hear police removed a printer from your office last night."

"Forced me out of bed." Anson nudged himself away from the desk, tugging at the cuffs of his monogrammed shirt. He probably wanted Coop to notice his expensive garb. "I intend to pursue the indignity with Chief Givens."

Go ahead, Coop thought. The police chief would ignore Anson's complaint. Much like Coop intended to do. "Where exactly was the printer located?"

"This sounds like an interrogation."

Coop flagged his hands in front. "Unintended. I only want a clear picture." He hiked a foot across his leg. Cotton threads from the hospital's hazmat suit speckled his dark tactical pants. Lint drove him crazy, so he plucked a few threads. "The printer was in your office, correct?"

"Sure, sure."

"And you were the only person with access? I mean, the printer is yours. The one you privately use?"

Anson attempted to move under the desk and banged his knees again. He uncoiled himself from the chair and sat next to Coop. "Why so much interest in my personal printer?"

Coop disregarded the question. "Where we you when you first learned about Monday's fire?"

"My office." A bubble of irritation seemed to wash over Anson. "What is this? Am I a suspect?"

"I'm inquisitive." Coop eased around to face Anson. "What time did you arrive?"

"You want me to provide an alibi? Easy peasy. I arrived before eight after stopping at Daniel Island Café for a bagel and coffee. I even purchased a newspaper. Wearing boxers or briefs—don't remember." He ran his finger around his collar. "C'mon, Agent Bellamy. You can't be serious. Next, you'll accuse me of setting the fires." He let out a good laugh punctuated by a smoker's cough.

"Did you?" Coop asked.

Anson cleared his throat. "Did I what?"

"Do the torching yourself or hire someone to light the fires?"

This time, Anson's high-pitched chortle strained Coop's hearing. "Utter nonsense."

"Are you familiar with D'Angelo Hines or Robert Moses?"

The question hung there while Anson sipped an iced tea. "I'm bad with names. In what context might I be acquainted with them?"

"Persons of interest. Rather, primary suspects in the rash of fires and Tip's explosion. How about D-Jazz and Ice?"

Anson swirled ice cubes in his glass. "More names."

"Gang members."

"I work with many area gang members. My community policing initiatives, welfare to work, and so forth place me in direct contact with a rather unsavory element."

"Do you work with D-Jazz and Ice? On your initiatives? Or are they business acquaintances, perhaps?"

"Possibly. Those people rarely use their given names." Anson poured a packet of sugar into the tea. "Chief Givens told me the 843Z sought credit for the fire and explosion. Retaliation for police killing the teenager."

Coop shook his head. "His logic is wrong."

"How so? I generally find the police chief quite astute."

"Timeline is off. The Kinkaid fire was rolling hot before cops killed the girl. And Tip's explosion came after the shooting. That'd be exceptional reaction time, even for the supremely organized 843Z." Coop sipped from a water bottle he'd brought with him. "By the way, D-Jazz was killed last night. In jail." A blatant lie, but Coop was hoping to provoke a reaction.

"Police brutality? A lot of that going around."

"Nope, assaulted by another arrestee."

Anson grimaced. "Maybe he had it coming."

Coop made a mental note. "You're in real estate. Correct?"

"I dabble. My development company is more of a brokerage. I bring commercial clients together."

"My research indicates you own many properties throughout the Lowcountry. How many of those are in Fleet Landing?"

Anson tapped a finger on his upper lip, then hunched his shoulders.

"What about the reported Tip's rezoning?" Coop flipped through his notepad. "You're behind that, right? I mean, you set the fires. Acquired the surrounding property using shell corporations. Even partnered with White Crusaders, right?"

"I'm involved with many projects. Property is merely a commodity."

Coop expected a different response. Even though Anson didn't possess the proper incentive to reply forthrightly, he hadn't denied the claims either. Coop uncrossed his leg and placed both feet on the floor. "Is it true you are acquiring the Tip, adjacent houses, and port authority yard for your Ocean Terminal project?"

"Perhaps . . ." Anson fumbled.

"What if I told you the task force received a tip suggesting you are part of a vast criminal conspiracy. Insurance fraud. Arson. Murder."

Anson raised his voice. "Wait—"

"We recovered additional fatalities from another fire."

Anson's jaw slackened. "Who are they?"

Coop flipped the script. "How's the Kiawah real estate market?"

Anson slowed to respond. "Mixed."

Safe answer. Coop had him tangled in the ropes.

"Ever hear of Magnolia Investment Group?" Coop asked.

Anson's poker face cracked. "No."

"How about Peachtree Properties or Atlantic Realty?"

Anson shook his head. "Tell me about the two men you found at the fire."

Coop ignored the request. "Those are three shell companies you used to conceal your identity for the purchase of multiple Fleet Landing properties. Then you burned them over the past seven months. Not to mention the properties Palmetto bought next to Tipton Terrace. You'll collect a fortune when the city buys you out. And still wind up with the land for development."

"Is that so?" Anson seemed to regain his footing, yet his facial features strained.

"Where were you early this morning, between three and four?"

"I told you, I let police into my office."

"Ah, the printer. Any idea why they confiscated it?" Coop loved asking questions when he knew the answer.

"None whatsoever."

Coop didn't believe him. "Afterward . . . You go back home?" He rubbed a finger across his cheek to lead Anson.

"Ah, Sunny's black eye?" Anson chortled. "You think I gave it to her?"

Coop clasped his hands on his lap. "How long have you been beating your wife, Mr. Anson?"

"Hey, now. You have it wrong." He stabbed a finger in Coop's direction. "Sunny might have given herself the shiner."

Coop rolled his eyes. "That's irrational."

"You married?"

Coop shook his head.

"Then don't judge." Anson strolled to the intercom located on the desk. His voice crunched like gravel. "Gina, anyone waiting for me?"

"Nope," came a curt reply.

Coop was on the move. "The defense subpoenaed me for Nathan Sharpe."

Anson hesitated. "Can't place the name. You can attest to my weakness in that area."

"Nate was convicted of setting fire to the Charleston train station decades ago. I'm surprised you don't remember. You worked on his prosecution with Wallace and your father-in-law. Not to mention, he was the young man found guilty of killing both your parents."

Anson turned away.

Coop said, "The new defense attorney is confident—"

Anson held up a flippant hand. "I have little desire to rehash the past."

"Who do you suppose set the train station fire?"

"Nathan Sharpe."

"Why?"

"Those people have a propensity for fire."

"Those people? Black men?" Coop noted this was the same twisted argument Wallace had used. Was this the common mindset of white supremacists? He leaned forward. "Then you think Falcon is a Black man?"

"Of course."

"The fires worked in your favor, though."

"If you say so."

Coop rested back and located Sydney's recorder alongside the cushion with his fingertips. He made a pretense of picking more lint from his pant leg. He hated letting Anson peddle hate and the audio tape would bury him. The situation called for another change of direction as he pocketed the digital recorder. "Has Chief Sinclair finalized your COO at the Tobacco Mill?"

"I defer to her to determine when the building is safe for occupants."

"Mayor Wallace originally opposed the TM project, didn't he? How'd you convince him to change their mind?" Coop purposely used the abbreviations from the ghost memo.

"City Council grasped the economic ramifications of revitalization and TM expansion." Anson boxed himself in. "Wallace encouraged the board to do the right thing."

"Any council member ever, let's say, straddle the line?"

"You mean incentives? Payola? Graft?" Anson grinned. "Ask Wallace how he managed to stay in office so long."

Coop allowed Anson the opportunity to enjoy a false sense of accomplishment. Though he was curious why Anson seemed eager to push the mayor into oncoming traffic. He said, "Before I go, do you happen to have a business card? Maybe with an email address."

Anson removed a card from his wallet.

Coop pinched the corner. "Thanks again for your time."

As he neared the door, Anson called after him. "You never told me about the two dead Black kids?"

Coop leaned against the door jamb and pasted on a wry grin. "When they come for you. And they will come—"

"Who?" Anson swallowed hard.

"Whether it's the police or 843Z thugs—and you better hope the cops arrive first." Coop shoved his hands into his pockets. "I want you to remember this meeting. Because this was your last chance to set the record straight. See, I never mentioned any specific details about the individuals killed on Monday around the Tip."

"You're crazy, Bellamy." Anson aimed a finger. "An arrogant sonovabitch, huh? You aren't supposed to feel comfortable enough in this office to proffer accusations. Now, you have a real problem on your hands."

"Such as?"

"I know you are friends with the fire chief. But if you fail here, it's more than a bad mark on a personnel report. This is your task force. That means it's your mess."

"I won't be the one ducking and covering when the ground shifts," Coop said. "As my daughter would say, 'That's so last week.'"

"Are you trying to sabotage your career?" Anson dried spittle from his chin with the back of his hand. "And for your daughter's sake . . . There's no place for you or any member of your family to hide. We aren't about to tolerate your bullshit here."

Coop moved directly in front of Anson and planted his hands on his hips. "Are you threatening me? Because it sounded like a threat."

Anson blinked and backed off. He circled the desk, plopped in the chair, then levered his feet atop the pull-out slide. "I understand the federal government provides excellent health care. You'd better test your hearing." He pressed a button on the phone, and a uniformed cop materialized at the door. "Officer, please escort Agent Bellamy to the nearest exit."

The cop held out a directional arm. "This way, sir." He pulled the door closed as they departed the office. In the hallway, the officer said, "I caught every word, if you need me to swear out a complaint."

"Thanks, but keep your nose clean. I got this."

•

When Coop arrived at his Jeep, his cell phone vibrated with a text from Sydney recapping her visit with Wallace. He knew she could hold her own on the investigative front. And he loved working with team players. This professional partnership was the real deal. Perhaps a different sort of partnership should be explored.

His reply read: *We're gaining traction. Gird yourself for possible new threats.*

As if on cue, his cell phone vibrated with a blocked Caller ID. Coop suspected the call was from Falcon. No worries. CPD, SLED, and ATF were monitoring his phone with trap and trace technologies. They could obtain the caller's number and location by triangulating cell towers pinging the call.

He answered on the fourth ring. "Bellamy."

"You and the reporter are goners." The caller disconnected.

If Falcon, presumably Anson, wanted to come after him, let him try. Coop would never take a knee because of lame threats.

39

Sydney eased her Thunderbird into a spot and threw the car into park. The White Crusaders' regional office on King Street was located in the heart of the entertainment district. She pondered her play.

Things were tumbling into position, providing a clearer picture of a plausible motive for a vast criminal enterprise she helped uncover. The indirect evidence she'd amassed would be gravy once the task force corralled a definitive confession or overwhelming physical evidence.

Sydney pushed through an unmarked door and was immediately astounded by Crusaders' office décor. No swastikas. No posters of villain leaders. No "WHITES ONLY" signs. Instead, the place consisted of standard office fare—desks, credenzas, file cabinets. Cheap oil paintings served as wall art. She eyed three white women preparing another round of promotional leaflets. A radio blared a Hot 40 single from Kelly Clarkson instead of an Aryan national anthem.

"May I help you?" one of the ladies asked with a tone as sweet as afternoon tea.

The others dropped their leaflets and rice-filled weights. They swapped glances, too dumbfounded to speak, easily making her as a TV reporter.

Sydney rested an elbow on the long counter. "Is the boss around? Someone in charge?" She pushed her card across the counter. It generated its own quiet statement of authority.

"You lost?" a husky man's voice growled behind her.

Sydney turned toward a bulldozer wearing khakis and a lemon-yellow polo shirt. The guy projected energy despite being imprisoned in a sagging body.

"Are you the Grand Poohbah or whatever the leader of this cult is called?" Poking the giant seemed an odd opening gambit. Especially since she'd come to elicit information. She figured on dialing it back once she'd established herself.

"Cult?" Bulldozer asked.

Sydney extended another business card for his review. "I expect full and docile cooperation. We clear?"

"Sure. Come into my office." Bulldozer held the door. A small desk fan churned humid office air.

Sydney edged inside. "Where do you keep the cross-burning pictures? My colleagues are never going to believe your decorator chose Renoir reproductions over the train station fire."

Bulldozer eyed Sydney with interest, perhaps unsure about her intentions. "Wasn't us. Besides, that fire came and went years ago."

"Want to come clean on any other unsolved crimes or fires where the statute of limitations has expired?"

"In exchange for what?"

"A clear conscience?"

"What a laugh." Bulldozer's strafing glare made holes. "Besides, you're trying to trick me. South Carolina doesn't have a limitations statute."

"Seems plausible you'd know the law," Sydney said.

"Let me ask you something. Did cops actually kill a Black girl during the riot?"

Sydney nodded.

"One more down," Bulldozer said.

Sydney understood he was trying to goad her and refused to bite. Instead, now seemed like a good time to build rapport. "Sorry you feel that way. I feel"—she thumped her chest—"right here, for those on your team killed during the train station fire. I came here hoping we could work together. You and I, we have a shared cause."

"Shared cause? With a TV reporter?" He uttered the words slowly, each syllable earning his full attention. "Go on."

"Nathan Sharpe, the guy dragooned into prison for the train station fire, was granted a retrial. A new verdict is expected soon."

"I told you, we don't have a dog in that hunt."

"You do, in a way. See, I ran into a guy over on Calhoun."

"With your car?" Bulldozer hooted at his own joke.

Sydney didn't skip a beat. "He told me the Crusaders took credit for Monday's fire and explosion. Maybe even had a hand in a number of other Fleet Landing's fires." A good lie was a giant part of her staging. "Didn't expect your group to be the bitter-end type."

A sly grin marched across Bulldozer's face.

"Help me clear your faction," Sydney said.

"How?"

She'd cast the last of her chum overboard. Time to hook the shark. "Tell me about the Grangers?"

Bulldozer sat back and folded his arms across his massive chest. "It's not a secret William Granger was a third-generation Crusader."

"Long lineage," Sydney said. "I'm guessing Hart was a lock for legacy admission?"

"Hart isn't a Crusader," Bulldozer scoffed. "He's never been welcome here."

"How come?"

"Not our kind."

"How did old man Granger feel when your elite group black-balled his only son?"

"He understood. See, we had to remove William from our rolls, too." Bulldozer leaned forward and rested his palms on the desk. "Banished because of indiscretions."

"Wow, I didn't know the Crusaders demanded such strict moral conduct," Sydney snorted. "Can you be more specific?"

"William was a notorious philanderer. It became a problem when my predecessors learned he ventured . . . across the tracks, as they used to say. Tainted everything about the family." Bulldozer feigned embarrassment, then quickly morphed into a touch of anger. "The fires . . . They are a call to action."

A shiver whizzed up and down Sydney's spine like a rogue elevator. "How so?"

"When your clothes are dirty, you wash them. When your pipes are clogged, you snake 'em out. Fires get rid of lowlifes and filth contaminating our city."

"And Crusaders buy the spoils?"

"What do you mean?"

Sydney jotted a note on her pad. "You may have denied Hart Anson access to your clubhouse, but he and your group have purchased over one hundred houses, apartment buildings, or empty lots in Fleet Landing. And you are both heavily insured, too."

"Meaning?" Bulldozer sneered.

"Insurance fraud. Torching or conspiring to burn your own holdings . . . Driving folks from their homes . . . Those are serious felonies."

"Air it, and we'll sue you and your network."

Sydney pocketed her notepad and rose to leave. "Thank you for confirming my information."

She departed the Crusaders' office surprised at her discoveries. Most importantly, she'd learned Anson was not, nor had he ever been a White Crusader. Despite a significant glitch in the simmering plot, he remained her prime target in the obvious land grab conspiracy.

40

Tyrell's Kitchen overflowed with lunch diners.

The owner signaled a waiter to bring Sydney into the kitchen. "My best customer never waits," Tyrell hummed.

A cook leaned over a stainless-steel counter piled with Styrofoam boxes and foil-wrapped food. "Y'all been here or come here?"

Here sounded like *hee-ya* to Sydney. Nevertheless, she understood the question of whether she was a native Charlestonian or a newcomer.

"A *comeya*," Sydney said.

"Your Gullah is getting better," Tyrell said. "You need to meet with the Geechees over on Wadmalaw. Find a Geechee woman who teach you to weave sweetgrass baskets."

The cook smiled. "The comeya know 'bout them baskets alright."

The other cooks laughed, and Tyrell placed a plate with meatloaf and cornbread in front of Sydney.

She sucked in the aroma before waving at the countertop. "What's with the boxes?"

"Feeding my people at the shelter," Tyrell said. "Anson is letting folks stay for free at the Tobacco Mill 'til it opens for real."

In light of what she'd learned about Anson, his public *philanthropy* made her skin crawl. "Any word on the street how the Kinkaid fire started?"

Tyrell finished tying string around the stacks. "Ain't nothing been said 'bout it."

She inhaled the food. "Your finger is usually on the pulse."

The cook stepped forward and rested an elbow on the counter near Sydney. "In the projects, people never see nothing. They never hear nothing. And they sure never talk to reporters. If they know what's best."

Tyrell shot the cook a fiery glare. The cook dried his hands on his apron and returned to the fryer.

Sydney plopped twenty bucks on the counter and grabbed her purse. "The meatloaf is terrific, gentlemen."

Tyrell held the screen door, offering a full view of the restaurant's back alley, ripe with the stench of raw fish guts. "Can't stop you from going to the shelter. Best if you bring food." He handed her the stack of boxed lunches and returned inside.

Sydney toted the food to her car.

A woman slid from behind the restaurant with a cigarette pressed between her lips. "You the TV lady?"

Being approached by strangers was a common occupational hazard. People watched her on TV and thought they knew her. "Sydney Quinn, Action 7 News."

"I'm Lorraine Gallivant." She blew out a curl of smoke. "Overheard Tyrell. You're taking those to the Tobacco Mill."

"On his behalf."

"My son works for the Arson Task Force. Maybe you know him."

"Oh, a firefighter or cop?"

Lorraine shook her head. "Intern. He's in high school. Only a few months shy of graduation. Wants to be an engineer or architect one day."

"What's his name?" Sydney asked.

"Lamar. Tall and skinny. But handsome." She gave Sydney a nod of pride.

"I met him. Nice guy."

Lorraine stubbed out her cigarette and studied the ground near her shoes. "Learned you're helping Nate. Nathan Sharpe."

"I'm working on the periphery."

"I had a brother. A few years older than me. He was killed in the fire."

Sydney prepared for an onslaught of resentment from the woman.

It didn't come.

Instead, Lorraine's eyes moistened. "My brother and Nate were best friends. Nate and I, we sort of dated."

Sydney realized Lorraine was the woman who still visited Nate every month. Raney, he'd called her. "How do you feel about his probable release?"

"Quite happy if they let him go. Trouble is . . ."

Sydney placed Tyrell's food into the trunk.

Lorraine dabbed swollen eyes. "Unsure how Lamar is gonna take it. Trouble with trouble . . ."

"Nate is Lamar's father, isn't he, Raney?" Sydney spoke softly without missing a beat. "Conjugal visits, perhaps?"

Lorraine wiped her eyelids. "How did you—"

"Does Lamar even know?"

"Neither one of them knows about the other."

Sydney drew a breath. "I suspect you aren't asking my advice, but seventeen years is a long time to keep something hush-hush that may soon come out and bite you in the butt. Secrets and comfort rarely coexist."

Lorraine's face tightened into a stoic mask. "I have an even bigger problem and hope you'll help me."

"Go on."

"See, I own a house on Spruance, west of the big fire. A while back, the gang offered me money to leave Fleet Landing after we had a small fire at our place. I told 'em no." Lorraine pushed her lips to one side. "D-Jazz told me his crew planned to fix the damage, making me obligated to sell to him. Else, he'd burn me out for good. The choice was easy, even though he never paid me a fair price. Then I double-crossed him. I kept his money and didn't move."

"That's a big problem. I'm betting you are quite fortunate the house is still standing."

Lorraine toed the ground. "My neighbors think I'm not square with the insurance company since I took their money for repairs too. I can't let anything jeopardize Lamar's scholarship. What should I do?"

"I happen to have a friend in the insurance business who knows Fleet Landing. I'm happy to refer him." Sydney jotted Cal Hampton's name and number on a slip of paper. As she handed it to Lorraine, the burner cell vibrated in her purse. "Excuse me. I'd better answer this."

Sydney dug out the phone. "Hello."

"This is Joyce Lewis at Palmetto Quality Development. You sent an email asking about retail space in the Ocean Terminal we're developing in Charleston."

"Thanks for calling. I represent an overseas investor interested in . . ." Sydney swirled her free hand while she calculated. "Eighty thousand square feet. Maybe more."

Lorraine slid Cal's number into an apron pocket and smiled curiously.

"Oh my, this is a fabulous opportunity for your client to step in on the ground floor, so to speak. We are also expanding the project to include an additional eight acres for retail and commercial space to complement the extraordinary mixed-use development previously designed."

"How far along in construction are you? My client wants input on both interior and exterior designs, if possible."

"We're scheduled to break ground in three weeks with a targeted soft opening in about two years."

"Fabulous," Sydney cooed.

Joyce continued, "We only recently acquired the additional property we eagerly sought. Permits are ready and we're all systems go to initiate site work. Let me send you the name of our architect for liaising regarding your preferred space choices. I'd love it if we could make it happen today. What's your schedule?"

Anson and his Palmetto firm were moving ahead faster than Sydney expected despite not owning the Tip, or old port authority property, or the other private houses pending eminent domain liquidation claims. But, according to Joyce, architecture plans had been completed and were ready to launch. That told her the Savannah shill must've been paid off. Excavators stacked at the ready.

In Sydney's mind, it proved Anson's involvement in the conspiracy to hijack Fleet Landing for personal gain. Furthermore, she figured existing permits meant the conspiracy spread among several city departments.

Sydney asked, "How late are you in the office?"

"Until five, Eastern."

"Joyce, we are making this happen."

•

Lamar broke from his internship duties and hopped an Uber ride to Daniel Island.

Falcon's latest threat aimed at Mama was the last straw. Lamar was tired of being scared and ashamed. He wanted out. No more fires. He vowed to take matters into his own hands despite Falcon's grip on dead Uncle Jamal's secret, Mama's insurance fraud, and his own fire-setting.

Lamar asked the driver to drop him a block away from the strip mall Falcon's business shared with a sandwich place and a dry cleaner. The Uber ride swung away, leaving him wishing he'd cultivated a better tactical plan to confront Falcon.

As he neared the Palmetto Quality Development office, Lamar spotted Ice opening the Mercedes's rear door. A fat man spilled out on the passenger side, lugging a heavy briefcase, probably heaped with cash. Two additional tough guys escorted Fatso inside.

Lamar had witnessed dozens of transactions involving payoffs or kickbacks, and he knew another Falcon con was underway.

Ice surveyed the street. He eyed Lamar, then waved him over. "Are you crazy?" His voice intensified with menacing urgency. "Why are you here?"

Lamar's stomach knotted. "Subway," he said tentatively.

Ice stepped closer. "What?"

Lamar could feel Ice preparing to dismember his limbs. He pointed at the sandwich shop. "Fire guys sent me here on a lunch run."

Ice's face pinched in anger. "Collect your food and leave." He seemed as potent as enriched uranium. "Falcon is inside meeting with a banker. Your kind of trouble isn't needed 'round here."

41

Sydney drove to the Tobacco Mill situated on the northeast edge of bruised and battered Fleet Landing. The five-story industrial fortress had endured its own rollercoaster run of lopsided fortunes, beginning as a cotton mill following the Civil War. Three decades later, a Havana tobacco company bought the place, and hand-crafted cigars and cigarettes on-site for the next eighty years. Afterward, the building proceeded to host a variety of enterprises, including a university, bookstore, and shoe repair shop, before developers sought to create a swanky residential and retail complex at the landmark location cornering Nimitz and Fletcher Avenues.

When the real estate market crashed in 2008, funding withered for the seventy-five-million-dollar project. Palmetto Quality Development purchased the property at auction nine years later for a fraction of its potential value. Palmetto's refurbishment plans called for the brick façade to remain while the building received new windows, a new roof, and a revised floor plan to create fifty luxury condominiums that'd sell from seven hundred thousand dollars to over three million bucks each.

Sydney waved to the children playing near the rear parking lot's garden of dumpsters. Inside, her pumps clanked on the concrete. At the center of the long hallway, she listened for a full minute, tracing sounds of laughter and music to an elevator shaft. Two-by-four wood planks crisscrossed the opening. She bent awkwardly over the temporary barricade as though kissing the Blarney Stone.

"Anybody home?" Her voice echoed in the hollow tunnel.

The laughter stopped and Julia Mayfair, from Channel 13, breezed in on a wave of lilac perfume. "You aren't the first one here, Syd."

"You never cease to disgust me. Isn't there a kitten in a tree your station needs to cover?"

Julia turned on her heel. "Follow me. I'll introduce you to a few indigents. I mean . . . victims." She climbed the stairs, stopping on each step to rearrange her long mane of bottle-blonde hair.

A sea of dark-skinned bodies lined every hallway in the vertical maze. Julia stopped on the fourth floor. Sydney acknowledged the people lounging in provisional beds or leaning against stunning mahogany banisters.

"You slumming?" a slight woman asked, poking her head up from a paperback.

Sydney held out the Styrofoam containers. "Sydney Quinn, Action 7 News. The food is from Tyrell's."

"You buy it? A bribe or something?"

"Bet you feel sorry for us, same as Blondie," said another woman pointing at Julia.

"I'm only a courier," Sydney said. "Tyrell asked me to drop off meatloaf and cornbread."

The first women signaled a handful of kids to distribute the boxed lunches. "What you want, TV lady? An interview?"

"Sure. What's your name?" Sydney asked.

"Mazie Tibwin." Her overarticulated drawl oozed indignation.

"Tibwin?" Sydney jotted the name in her notebook.

"Yeah, Tibwin. Of the upper west side Tibwins. Problems?" Mazie ground an unlit cigarette butt into the floor with her sandal.

"Syd didn't mean any harm," Julia said, backing away.

"You vouching for her?" Mazie asked.

Julia nodded. "Even though we're from different stations, she's good people."

Mazie circled her hand overhead. "Kum . . . ba . . . ya."

"Your interview technique better be charming," Julia whispered.

The corners of Sydney's mouth edged up and she shifted her

weight. "Mazie. May I call you Mazie?"

"If you want."

"Everything okay? Need anything?"

"Hell no, we ain't okay. We squatting in a darn warehouse. We need food, clothing, shelter. Maslow's basics."

Sydney placed her hands on her hips. "Okay, cut the routine. Who are you really?"

She ditched the drawl. "Mazie Tibwin—"

"Upper west side, blah, blah." A glint of recognition crossed Sydney's face. "Wait, you're a lawyer with the Innocence Network. Did Rob Noble send you?"

"Gotcha." Mazie grinned. "I'm here to assist with any legal issues I find."

"What do you have so far?"

Mazie ticked off her agenda. "Fire department's slow progress solving the arsons. A shameful lack of water pressure to fight the fires. Systematic relocation of our people. Shall I go on?"

Julia thrust her fist in the air. "Right on, Sister."

Mazie shook her head. Waved an arm across the ocean of refugees. "The fire. The explosion. The homeless situation. It's about basic civil rights. You want a piece of the action?"

Sydney considered their plight. "You bet. By the way, how'd you get in? Did Hart Anson provide keys?"

A few residents hissed at the mere mention of Anson. She once presumed he led the hood with compassion. Now she understood those handouts came at a steep price. Sydney wondered if they knew he was behind the fires all along, but never came forward.

A man with a soul patch on his bottom lip trundled over. "Both my parents and an aunt died in the train station fire. Mazie says the guy in prison didn't do it. Said you were helping find who actually killed them."

"And she'll help us, too," Mazie said. "She's a reporter. It's her thing."

Sydney's cell phone vibrated before she could respond. Her producer's name appeared on the screen. "Excuse me for a sec."

Olivia shrieked, "A man called to say he's coming after you and Agent Bellamy. Oh, Syd, I can't lose another person. What would it say about my leadership?"

"Write down exactly what the caller said," Sydney said calmly. "Then phone Coop and tell him. He's on top of this." She disconnected and smoothed her hair.

Mazie cocked her head. "Problems in TV land?"

"Always crazy in our business. Where'd we leave off?"

Mazie held Sydney's hand. "I've been here for hours. That gave me plenty of time to check out the features. Let me show you something crazy stupid."

They climbed the stairs to the top floor, then entered the center unit.

"This is one of the penthouses," Mazie said. "*Très* chic."

"Hubba-hubba," Julia added.

Craftsmen had finished transforming the fifth floor into elegant suites. Fifteen-foot ceilings, thirty-inch exterior walls, and gorgeous heart pine plank floors.

"And the stupid part?" Sydney asked.

"Keep looking. It'll come to you."

Sydney and Julia scanned the luxury condo's cabinets, paneling, elaborate trim package, and tinted windows.

Julia peeked inside a closet door. "Are other units on this floor open?"

"Oh, honey," Mazie said. "They're open now."

Julia wandered into the hallway and returned a minute later. "I figured it out. Builders shortchanged this unit."

"Huh?" Sydney asked.

Julia spread her arms. "This interior wall is too thick. I stepped off the distance from the hallway to the windows in a couple of condos. This one is at least three feet smaller." She patted above the light switch at the door and noticed a hollow thud. "It's pretty dumb to substitute square footage for wall thickness."

Mazie, Sydney, and Julia began thumping the wall.

"Maybe they had to run conduit or vent stuff," Sydney said.

"Only in this one?" Mazie eyed a small basket of construction debris near the door and dug in.

"What are you after?" Sydney asked.

"Anything with a blade. I want to open the wall."

"Please don't," Sydney said.

Mazie waved her off. "No worries. My dad is a drywall contractor."

Julia pulled a pocketknife from her purse. "Here, use this."

Sydney gave a wave of mild disapproval.

"Hey, don't judge," Julia said. "I work in some unpleasant areas."

Mazie pushed the blade into the sheetrock, chewing open a length. She completed cuts along the top, bottom, and other side, then pried off the chunk near the baseboard. Inside the wall, five-gallon paint buckets were stacked at least three high. "Hallelujah," Mazie said.

Sydney and Julia each pulled a container from the wall and wrenched open the lids. Neat bricks of hundred-dollar bills, some shrink-wrapped in green plastic, filled the buckets.

Sydney snapped photos with her cell phone. "Shove them back. Mazie, find some drywall goop."

•

Lamar signaled his second Uber driver to drop him under a bank's awning across the street from the Moultrie Building. He wanted to kick himself for acting cowardly with Ice. He sensed a flush of embarrassment as though he were thrashing in the deep end. No lifeguard on duty.

His disposable cell phone buzzed with a text from Falcon. Surely, Ice had relayed news of his attempted confrontation, and Falcon was prepared to retaliate. The message read: *Reminder. Get Agent Bellamy. URGENT.*

Lamar knew he'd never survive a showdown with Falcon, ATF, or the fire department. He toed a loose brick in the decorative sidewalk, and an idea materialized. He thumbed his cell phone and listened to a recorded message:

"You've reached Arson Stoppers. You aren't required to leave a name or callback number, but you cannot receive a cash reward unless your tip leads to an arrest and conviction, and we can verify your identity. If you want to speak with an operator, please press one, then wait on the line. Your call will be handled in the order received. If you want to leave a recorded message, please press two. Thank you for calling Arson Stoppers."

Lamar disconnected, unable to bring himself to dime out Falcon. He riffled through his wallet for business cards he'd collected working with the task force and found the one he wanted. He keyed the number, then squeezed his lips.

The phone rang twice before she answered.

"Sydney Quinn."

Lamar's head flooded with several options to plead for help. They each sounded pathetic. He mumbled, "I know who burned your house."

Sydney said nothing.

Lamar panicked. "Channel 7, right?"

"Who is this?" Her voice sounded tentative.

Lamar imagined she was fishing. Checking for background noises. Accent. Speech pattern. Anything to trap him. He should've disconnected.

But he didn't.

"Ice lit you up. Probably killed those two in the van. Because he's a tool."

"Please spell your name," Sydney said.

He could tell she was luring him. Lamar wanted to blurt everything. Tell her he'd set the Kinkaid fire. Hell, he'd set ten fires. He was the Fleet Landing arsonist. The most wanted person in

Charleston. Perhaps if he told her, she'd assist him and Mama.

Instead, he said, "Do the math. Ice and Anson are tight. You shake 'em down, you get Falcon." He disconnected and tossed the phone into his bag as though it might bite.

After a moment, he removed the phone. Burner phones were supposedly untraceable, but Lamar wasn't taking any chances.

He pried the back off the cell and removed the battery. He located the SD card and flicked it out. Then Lamar clipped every wire and smashed every circuit before tossing the broken bits into the trash. He discarded the battery and data card into different bins before returning to his internship duties.

42

Sydney allowed Julia to join her at Palmetto Quality Development to confront Anson about the money they'd found in the Tobacco Mill's wall. She also recorded that recent anonymous phone call that told her Anson knew Ice, and the banger was in deep. She parked near a black Mercedes and checked the plate number against Cal's fire scene photos. It matched.

"Nice ride," Julia said.

"The GLE 450 SUV. Three-point-oh liter inline six turbo with EQ boost. Three-hundred-sixty-two horses. Alloy block and head. Twenty-two-point-five-gallon fuel capacity. Four-wheel independent double wishbone suspension. Nineteen-inch five-spoke wheels. Heated and cooled seats. Around sixty-five thousand bucks MSRP." Sydney pocketed Cal's photos. "Once we're inside, follow my lead."

"Didn't know you were such a gearhead, but okey doke. Should I be scared?"

Sydney yanked open the front door, and a bell signaled their arrival. "Probably. Don't let it show."

A Black woman wearing a pricey Elie Tahari suit forced a thin smile, as though the two newswomen were intruding. "May I help you?"

"We're here for Hart Anson."

"Is he expecting you?" Her tone bordered on impolite.

Anson stepped into the narrow hallway. He darted his attention between Miss Office Essential and Sydney, attempting to read the situation.

Sydney seized control. "Good to see you again, Mr. Anson. This is Julia Mayfair, my associate from Eyewitness 13."

"Diana, be a dear and tell my wife TV people are here. May I offer you ladies a drink?" Before either answered, "Please bring three sweet teas and a sparkling water for Sunny. My wife is a fifth-generation Charlestonian. Even so, she doesn't abide sweet tea."

Sydney was a Diet Mountain Dew gal and hated sweet tea, too. Her dislike was easily explained; she was a Yankee. "To each their own."

Anson motioned for Sydney and Julia to sit on the tufted Chesterfield couch in his office. He sat opposite in a club chair upholstered in a herringbone-patterned fabric. Julia paged open a photo album from the coffee table, quickly slammed the cover closed, then placed it back on the table. Color drained from her face.

"What?" Sydney opened the album and gagged. Graphic color photos of birds in various stages of dissection, replete with guts and goo, filled the album.

Anson laughed. "Those pictures aren't for the squeamish. My apologies. Taxidermy is a hobby of mine."

Taxidermy? The book looked more like an illustrated primer for a serial killer.

The well-dressed office gal arrived with a tray of beverages that she placed on the coffee table near the photo album. When she eyed the book, she scrunched her nose and turned to Sydney, shaking her head. Solid advice, but a fraction too late.

Sydney reached for an ice-filled crystal glass and poured the sparkling water intended for Mrs. Sunny Anson. "We're interested in learning more about the good work you're doing in Fleet Landing."

"Where do I start?" Anson asked.

"Rivertown Academy."

"Very well." Anson sipped an iced tea. "I'm certain you both are keenly aware city officials neglected the neighborhood for too many years. I wanted to help without simply throwing money at their problems. Instead, I chose to incentivize long-term solutions. So, I approached Lantana Hardwick with the Academy idea. She jumped on board. Without Lantana's endorsement, we'd still be in a holding pattern." Anson sipped his iced tea. "Did you know her mother used to work for my family long before either of us was born."

Sydney said, "As I understand it, you buy abandoned properties. The Academy teaches building trades to neighborhood residents. They refurbish those houses. Then you lease or sell them without profit." She leaned her head to one side. "An impressive business model."

"Lantana is the inspiration. Pure genius."

"How many properties do you own in the neighborhood?" Sydney asked.

"A few. Practically giving them away helps me a repay a debt of gratitude."

"Would it surprise you to learn you own more than one hundred places?"

Julia gasped.

Sydney continued to press. "Of course, they aren't all in your name, *per se*. Some are titled to straw companies you run. I suppose for tax purposes. Maybe something regarding your non-profit."

Her statements hung there while Anson continued to sip tea. The implication was clear.

Sydney pressed forward. "But you aren't the only one making inscrutable investments in Fleet Landing. The White Crusaders are snapping up properties almost as fast as you."

Julia scribbled notes, attempting to keep pace with Sydney's alarming revelations.

"News to me," Anson said.

"Funny, I thought you were a member." Sydney wanted to determine whether he'd perpetuate the tidy lie. "Which raises the question, are you a partner in their holdings or competition?"

"Which is it?" Julia brightened as she seemed to bond disparate pieces together. "Complicit or rival?"

Anson lowered his glass to the table. "I . . . uh. We . . ."

"Let me help you," Sydney said. "The more I learn, I keep asking myself *why*."

Julia chimed in. "Why make such a huge investment in a run-down neighborhood without any hope of reaping a profit?"

Her pal was smarter than Sydney had given her credit for.

Sydney prowled the room as she offered her view on the land grab scheme with big brushstrokes. "Way I see it, your grand plan is to sweep up Fleet Landing's residential and commercial properties. Restore and flip a few here and there to cement your philanthropic image. But you have a serious problem."

Anson inched forward in his chair. "Go on."

"Deep pockets. At first, you only claimed discarded properties. Those abandoned due to foreclosure or damaged by neglect or fire. Working with Mayor Wallace, you paid very little for the privilege." Sydney removed a spreadsheet from her purse and flattened it on the coffee table. The print was too small to read from a distance, even though the color-coded columns and rows told a remarkable story—if you owned the decoder ring. "Then your name leaked as an investor. Not a stretch, since you openly back Rivertown Academy."

"Deep pockets," Julia repeated. "After the supply of abandoned properties dwindled, you needed your hands on more. But home-owners demanded full compensation. I'm guessing your generosity frayed like a worn rubber band."

"You two are rather imaginative," Anson said.

Sidney didn't miss a beat. "Enter the White Crusaders. "They serve two purposes. First, they buy property for you using anony-mous companies you are fronting."

Julia added, "Thereby shielding your involvement and saving you money. What's their other contribution, Syd?"

Sydney plopped on the sofa next to Julia and reached for a lighter lying beside an ashtray. She sparked the flame and drew in Anson and Julia like gypsy moths.

Julia stuttered. "You mean? He? They? The fires?"

Sydney tapped the spreadsheet with her finger. "A solicitor will find this compelling."

Anson cocked his head. "What about the 843Z? I thought they were responsible for the fires."

"Yeah, why did cops arrest those gang members?" Julia asked.

Sydney tapped the spreadsheet again. "Funny you mention the 843Z. How much did you pay them to also set fires in Fleet Landing?"

Sunny Anson entered the room and shuddered when she spotted Sydney. She absently rubbed her head.

Anson stood for introductions, outwardly relieved by the interruption. "Ladies, my wife, Sunny."

"Pleasure." Sydney reached for Sunny's hand and let her choose whether Anson discovered they had met after he'd battered her.

Sunny wore a crisp, white Stella McCartney, single button jacket and skirt. Makeup deftly concealed her black eye. "Forgive me for not greeting you when you arrived." She cast an air of saccharin and refinement.

"The ladies are spinning a yarn about our business," Anson said.

"Oh?" Sunny said. "That isn't my area of expertise."

"What is your area?" Sydney asked. "Of expertise, that is."

"This feels like a grilling," Sunny said. "Rather than an interview with a pair of third-rate TV reporters."

Julia dug her nails into the expensive upholstery.

Sydney's blood heated, and she turned to Anson. "I tracked several large payments from you to the 843Z."

Anson smirked. "Did you?"

Sunny removed a compact from her purse. For her, nose powdering proved an art form. "Go on, tell them. They obviously figured things out."

Anson shot Sunny a pitiless glare. "Okay, I gave money to the 843Z. For protection so they wouldn't firebomb my properties. They run the hood and collect a cut of everything happening there."

Sydney wasn't buying his explanation. "Paying the 843Z for

protection is tantamount to sanctioning racketeering and extortion."

"Merely the cost of doing business."

"They didn't shield you very well. Did they?" Sydney tapped a finger on her lips. "What about the White Crusaders?"

"What about them?"

"Their properties burned too. And they made aggressive insurance claims."

Sunny said, "Maybe they torched themselves."

"Or Ice did it," Sydney said. "I received a tip that he and Hart are tight."

Anson didn't flinch, and Sydney considered this a dead end. Whatever else he knew or connections he'd made weren't going to be revealed during this meeting.

Sydney asked, "What kind of car do you drive?"

"None of your business," Sunny said.

Anson ignored his wife. "Cadillac Escalade or Mercedes GLE 450. Why?"

"Cars confuse me," Sydney said. "But they both sound expensive. Don't you think it's dangerous driving pricey wheels in the hood?"

Julia offered Sydney an incurious, tight-lipped stare.

Sydney went on. "I drive domestic. Like me, off the rack." She sipped her water, holding Anson's gaze. "Know anything about the two dead guys at my place? I think someone in the gang killed them."

"I feel responsible," Anson said.

"Why?"

"I asked them . . . No, begged 'em to join Rivertown. I figure, a guy who looks as white as me, doing some good in the hood. It'd be a nice thing."

Sydney knew he'd revised his story since meeting with Coop. Apparently, Anson never imagined they'd compare notes. She made a quick decision to avoid challenging him about the wall money. She and Julia had photos, which were good enough for the time being.

Gotcha, Falcon. And Ice too.

43

Coop and Sydney rendezvoused at the West Ashley Crime Lab in the midst of another downpour. People scurried between cars. Umbrellas open. Heads down. Proud azaleas lined the walk leading to the front door.

Sydney laughed as an evidence tech extracted a card with Anson's prints from Coop's pocket. She pointed to her purse, and the tech retrieved her business card with Mayor Wallace's prints. "Like minds."

The tech zipped each card into clear evidence pouches before Coop and Sydney exited.

"How'd everything go with the White Crusaders?" Coop asked as they strolled the hallway.

"The guy coughed up big news—Hart isn't a member. Never has been. Unwelcome for some misstep his father made."

Coop nodded, then wanted to address an important thing that'd been bothering him. "Hey, about last night."

"What about it?"

"I detected a little spark. What if I hadn't driven you back to the TV station?"

Sydney fluttered her fingers. "Why Agent Bellamy, were you trying to seduce me?"

"Any chance? Unless you and Dino are a thing."

"What gave you that crazy idea?"

"He keeps tabs on you."

"Same way a dopey brother does. He's bailed me out more than once. Like Reggie—" Sydney swallowed hard. "Reggie showed me a way in with the police department when we first came to town. That's how I met Dino. And I've been the gum on his shoes ever since."

"Not my place—"

"Besides, your game plan contains a major flaw. She's about eleven."

Coop grinned. "Haley admires you. She adopted a few of your signature moves."

"Oh, yeah? Smart kid." She leaned over and kissed him on the cheek. "Let's finish this case, then see where we land."

"Forgot to mention, I received the call. Falcon said we were goners."

"Anson called my producer, too," Sydney said. "In my line of work, threats are an important lead."

Coop's cell phone vibrated. He glanced at the display and frowned. "It's Cassie."

"No worries. Meet you outside." Sydney headed for the door.

Coop hoisted a leg onto a bench and leaned an elbow on his knee. "Finish your shift?"

"Be a dear and keep Haley one more night." Cassie didn't phrase it as a question.

"Because?" He knew she wasn't working extra shifts. She wanted to canoodle with her hoity-toity doctor pal and didn't want Haley around. Didn't matter. Coop cherished all the time he could muster with his daughter. He wouldn't fight his ex-wife.

Cassie said, "This is your chance to erase the missed birthday parties. Countless nights filled with bad dreams and rumbling tummies." Dramatic pause. "The Christmas Pageant."

Cassie broke out the pageant debacle whenever she felt cornered.

"I've quit beating myself every time you recap my past failures." Coop debated whether to force her to beg. He swung for the fence. "I'll keep Haley for the weekend. Pick her up Sunday evening."

"Fabulous." Cassie disconnected without further discussion.

Coop pocketed the phone and joined Sydney outside. "This has been a long day. What's next?"

"I need food and sleep. I can get both at my station." She yawned.

"Were you able to find everything you need to prepare for Nate's testimony tomorrow?"

Coop bobbed his head. "Glad you had success with the Crusaders. And Hart Anson is such a smug bastard." He mocked Anson's supercilious vibe. "*Easy peasy*. What's that about?"

Sydney clenched a fist, and fingernails cut into her palm. "What did you say?"

"Anson's a jerk."

"No. *Easy peasy*. That's exactly what the manifesto caller said."

Coop's jaw dropped. "I'll phone Dino." The detective answered on the first ring. Coop punched the speaker.

Sydney shrieked. "We have proof. Put Anson in your crosshairs."

"Ladybug, you can't parachute in and order me around."

"I'm telling you, Anson is the manifesto caller. He also phoned Coop and my station with another threat."

"Three calls? So naturally you jumped . . . Rather, pole-vaulted over common sense—"

"C'mon, I know about OT, TM, and KI. The initials add up to an illegal land grab. He's the guy."

Coop said, "Look, Dino. Send Brody to Anson's office to execute a search warrant for his cell phone before the guy flees your jurisdiction."

"Messing with you guys," Dino said. "Already going after him."

Coop disconnected. "Is Dino always this obstinate?"

Sydney laughed. "Obstinate? Nah. Sometimes he's a real horse's patoot."

44

A dreary marine layer hung over the harbor, paralleling Coop's disposition.

Overnight, he and Dino spent hours haggling with the county solicitor over specific charges to file against Anson. They encountered even more trouble agreeing on charges to bring against Anson's alleged gang partners for the fires and explosion. In the end, no one on the prosecutor's team wanted to go after Mayor Wallace or address his alleged role in the land grab conspiracy until they'd reviewed and digested Sydney's financial evidence.

After drafting the charges, finding a judge who'd sign the summons for Anson's arrest became the next hurdle. Finally, at 5:34 a.m., Coop assigned Detective Brody Tate, along with twenty officers from CPD and the Charleston County Sheriff's Office, to apprehend Anson, confident they'd be able to collar Falcon, AKA Hart Anson, at his home.

For his part, Dino tasked the Department of Motor Vehicles to identify automobiles, trucks, boats—anything requiring registration belonging to Anson, Palmetto Quality Development, Atlantic Realty, or Magnolia Investment. He also asked the Georgia State Patrol to search Peachtree Property vehicle records. Once the South Carolina DMV results came back, Dino issued a BOLO for law enforcement in every county sandwiching I-95 to be on the lookout for those vehicles.

Chief Sinclair had repositioned her department's ladder trucks along the Great Fire's path for the past two nights. The move left other areas vulnerable to a slow tactical response. But Coop and CFD's Assistant Chief for Operations had worked out a plan with neighboring fire departments. They'd executed mutual aid agreements and ensured the city avoided lapses in coverage. Placing the big rigs out in the open had served as a solid deterrent. No fires in Fleet Landing or anywhere else on the peninsula since the dumpster fire. Coop phoned the chief to suggest rolling them back to their respective stations.

Coop rammed his key into the lock on Cora Rose's carriage house and instinctively searched for the family cat, though the orange tabby had never lived there. Dead tired, he crumpled onto a kitchen stool and replayed images from his life.

He once had a loving wife and daughter he tucked in almost every night. He'd been a classic suburban husband with a mortgage and damned picket fence. He enjoyed mowing the lawn for Haley to chip golf balls. Loved washing the family car, soap bubbles frothing from a bucket. Now, he was a hot-shit arson investigator living alone in a one-bedroom condo near Lake Norman and driving a company-issued vehicle.

On the upside, he sported a big crush on a smoking-hot TV reporter.

Coop funneled the last of his coffee, then set his "BEST DAD EVER" mug on the counter. He glanced at his watch: 7:30 a.m. He was due in court in a few hours. That gave him more than enough time to ship Haley off to school and peek at his notes one last time before taking the stand on Nathan Sharpe's behalf.

Coop called out, "Let's go, Twink."

Haley danced into the kitchen and vaulted into his arms.

Coop hugged her so hard he worried he'd snap her in half. Once she let go, he escorted her to the front door, stuck his key into the deadbolt, and clicked the lock. On the porch, he eyed his daughter. "Where's your backpack?"

"Oops." Haley curled a wisp of golden-colored hair around her index finger.

"No problem. People will wait for the world's best arson

investigator. However, your homeroom teacher is bound to be less forgiving." He jammed his key into the lock.

His landlady emerged on her long piazza facing the carriage house. "Yoo-hoo, Agent Bellamy. Do you have a sec?"

Coop blew out a jet of air. "Nope," he whispered to himself. Then, he spun on a heel and waltzed over.

Cora Rose opened the screen door. "I won't keep you. Thought you'd like to know, they've canceled school again."

Haley returned with her backpack. "No school? Perfect. I'm getting used to the time off."

Cora Rose continued. "Haley can stay with me if you want."

"Such a nice offer. And I do need your help." Coop turned to Haley. "You mind?"

"I'd love to spend the day with Miss Bishop." Haley pushed past her father. "May I play your piano?"

Coop took the hint. "I can't compete with a baby grand."

"Haley and I had a fine time playing piano and sitting on the joggling board yesterday."

Sydney motored into the driveway, then mounted the stairs onto the porch.

Cora Rose waved everyone inside. "Let me ring for something to eat."

"We don't want to be a bother," Coop said.

"I'm grateful for the company. This big house is so lonely. Pimento sandwiches?"

Haley scrunched her nose.

"My daughter is a vegetarian. She'd love to try your pimento."

Haley glared at him. "I'll play on the porch until the food is ready."

"I'll follow you out." Coop's voice sounded stern enough to make his point.

•

After Coop and Haley exited, Sydney said, "This is such a lovely house. In your family long?"

Cora Rose replied, "We've resided on this parcel since 1837. Rebuilt in 1868 after it burnt during the Great Fire. I come from a long line of shippers and tea farmers. My husband had a hand in imports-exports using the shipping line my great grandfather founded." She sighed. "We enjoyed many fabulous years in this house."

"History is more vibrant when it comes from a real person."

"Thank you." Cora Rose rang a small bell and her housekeeper responded. She placed the breakfast order and suggested service in the sunroom.

When the housekeeper backed away, Sydney said, "Tell me more about your life in Charleston."

Cora Rose's eyes twinkled. "Oh, where to begin . . ." She sat forward and folded her hands on her lap. Prim. Proper. Sydney mirrored Cora Rose as she extolled the virtues of life among the palmettos.

The Duchess of Broad Street, Cora Rose Bishop, was the Battery's undisputed matriarch. A glittering social scene had centered on her mansion for nearly five decades. Guest lists included Charleston's best, along with famous southern artists, musicians, writers, and politicos from the national capital region.

"My husband died in 1997. That's when my big caviar days ended. Everything was big back then. We SOBS found ourselves weak with privilege and little appetite for changing the way we carried on our business."

"Any issues of race?" Sydney asked.

"Sugar, times were different. We used to rule the world. Or at least try to."

"Meaning?"

"Everyone had a place. But with each passing year, those lines blurred. I suppose my people acted poorly. But at least we were upfront about our bigotry. Unlike you Yankees who closet fear and resentment under a veil of equality. In the South, the only thing separating us from them is money and fine breeding." Cora Rose refilled her sweet tea. "Peaceful protests. How quintessentially American." Her mind seemed to wander.

When Coop returned, Cora Rose turned to him. "I imagine you've made your family quite proud."

"Except my daughter." Coop squirmed. "She's at an age—"

"They never outgrow that age," Cora Rose said. "Think of it this way: she'll always be your child. You'll always have the chance to turn it around. If not today, perhaps tomorrow."

Coop stood taller.

"Thank you for your candor, Mrs. Bishop," Sydney said.

She sipped tea, then dabbed her lips. "Please, call me Cora Rose."

Sydney lowered her voice. "May I ask a favor?"

"You may ask, dear. Whether I'll grant your wish remains a mystery."

Sydney blushed. "Tell me about the train station fire."

Cora Rose sat back. "I never traveled by rail. But as I recall, the big fire came on the heels of many smaller fires. Similar to what Fleet Landing's poor are experiencing now."

"The convicted man isn't the real fire-setter," Sydney said. "I'm hoping to discover who is to blame."

Cora Rose folded her hands across her lap again. "I always believed the Crusaders were involved somehow. It resembled their line of work. Intimidating the coloreds."

"And Boyd Wallace earned his bones prosecuting the case," Coop said. "You think the Crusaders held influence over him?"

"Through the years, Boyd courted favor from all sides of the tracks," Cora Rose said.

"What about Hart Anson?"

"The Ansons are simply wretched people. Nevertheless, they enjoy a fine address." Cora Rose dabbed her lips with her kerchief again. "Hart and Boyd were hoodlums. Pure and simple. Same as their fathers before them. Though Hart hated his father. And his mother ignored him."

"Breakfast is served," the housekeeper announced, and handed a telephone to Cora Rose. "You have a call, ma'am."

Cora Rose tilted her head. "We'll meet in the sunroom."

Moments later, Cora Rose smiled when she returned and everyone had been seated. "Agent Bellamy, I made an unexpected appointment for later this afternoon. May we fashion an alternate plan for Haley during that time frame?"

"I'll send one of my guys if I'm still in court. I'm lucky to entrust her to your care."

45

Coop's Jeep climbed the curb next to Sydney as she lingered outside the Municipal Court Building near RiverDog Stadium and the Law Enforcement Center. Coop and Dino spilled from the Cherokee.

She glowered at Dino. "What are you doing here?"

"Moral support for you and my pal, Coop."

She volleyed her glance between the two. "Don't ruin this for me. I have a lot invested in Nate's acquittal."

"Your big story for tonight?" Dino asked.

"I'm disappointed you think my involvement is single-minded. I'm far more complex."

"Complex barely scratches the surface with you, Ladybug."

"What about Hart Anson?" Sydney asked. "Your guys nab him?"

Dino shook his head.

Coop frowned. "Problems?"

"He slipped his tail," Dino said. "Nothing to worry about. We'll find him."

Sydney's new camera guy strolled over and handed her a stick microphone. Eric mounted the camera onto a tripod. "Ready for your tags."

She licked her lips, tucked a lock of hair behind one ear, and signaled Coop. "Agent Bellamy, as a renowned arson expert, was Nathan Sharpe railroaded during his original trial?"

Coop scanned his case notes a final time, then slid the folder under his arm. He'd memorized key witness statements implicating Nate, scoured police photos supporting the accusations, and analyzed expert testimony, which had sealed the man's fate. The original defense attorney and solicitor had created a real legal mess, though bogus statements from the purported fire expert galled Coop the most. But those were the '80s. Since then, experts had debunked every prior certainty associated with fire analysis.

This time around, he'd provide competent scientific and technical testimony to convince the jury they should renounce Nate's wrongful conviction for Charleston's deadly train station arson.

Coop winked at Sydney before responding to her question. "My review of trial transcripts suggests the first jury based their findings on false beliefs and spurious techniques as compared to modern science-based fire investigation." He pushed the camera aside, then waited until Eric turned it off. "Railroaded? Oh, yeah. But it's off the record. Air it, and I'm out of a job." Coop straightened a button on his suit coat and casually flicked a piece of lint from his sleeve.

Dino propped a foot on a neighboring bench and wiped an imaginary smudge from his shiny oxford. Sydney got whiplash bouncing her glance between the two, then rolled her eyes. "Quit preening." She signaled Eric to record. "On a different topic, how close are you to nailing the person responsible for the rash of fires plaguing Fleet Landing and terrifying residents?"

Coop stared directly into the camera. "Ms. Quinn, based upon your work with convicted train station arsonist Nathan Sharpe, you can attest how difficult an arson crime is to prove. Since the Fleet Landing Task Force's work is ongoing, all I'll say is it won't surprise me to discover more than one person is involved. Precisely why I'm continuing to ask residents to report any suspicious activity. A tip from the community will help solve these fires."

Sydney made a slicing motion across her throat for Eric to stop recording. "Well, I hope that adequately informs and confuses, as we planned."

With the arson investigation rounding the home stretch, Coop opted to make his move. As Dino and Eric headed for the courthouse stairs, he fell back into step beside Sydney. "Dinner tonight?"

"You bet. Meet you inside. I'm waiting here for Nate."

•

Fifteen minutes later, Sydney chucked a half-eaten pimento sandwich when a patrol car came to a stop behind Coop's Jeep. A sturdy sheriff's deputy sporting Ray-Bans gripped the belly chains manacled around Nate's torso, pulled him from the back seat, then elbowed his way through the crowded courthouse hallway. Sydney scurried ahead and opened the door to their assigned holding room on the second floor. Rob Noble was seated inside.

Deputy Sunglasses removed Nate's restraints. "He's all yours, counselor."

Nate rubbed his skinny wrists. Sydney forced herself to exhale and waited in the hall while he slipped out of his orange outfit and into a blue blazer and pants. When Nate opened the door, she skated to a chair, then slid a bag with a chicken salad sandwich, pretzels, and a soda to him.

Nate tore into the sandwich and slugged the Diet Mountain Dew in a couple of gulps before examining the can. He contorted his face. "You drink this? Contains enough caffeine to wake the dead." He shook his head as he emptied the pretzel bag.

"Lots of long days and nights at the TV station. My producer likes me better when I'm stoked." Sydney eyed Rob. "Sorry I missed the prosecution's opening yesterday. Why didn't you call?"

"We enjoyed an unexpected docket move." Rob glanced up from his legal pad. "The shift underscored the other side wouldn't take long to present their case. I knew you were busy, so Nate and I handled it by ourselves."

"Any surprises?"

"The prosecution offered convincing proof the fire was the key factor in the deaths of the thirty-nine victims."

"Yikes. That's a real shocker."

Rob's buoyant expression indicated his team was ahead on the scoreboard and understood her tone was meant to mock the other side. "The prosecution failed, however, to offer any proof Nate was the person responsible for the deadly fire. And none of their evidence gave him a motive. In short, the solicitor raised nothing new, nor could she resurrect the same level of bias that buried Nate in his first trial. Common sense alone should help him prevail. Today, it's our turn to drive in runs."

Sydney tamped down the excited inflection in her voice. "We only need one expert, our ATF agent, right?"

Rob extended his index and pinky fingers in a downward manner. The lawyer either expected to call two witnesses or he wanted Sydney to throw a sinker. "Nate, these two guys will be the linchpins in your case."

"You sure lynchin' is the right expression?" Nate's voice cracked.

Sydney offered an energetic smile. "Who else are you questioning besides Coop?"

The lawyer scrolled through his legal pad. "Sit back, Syd. My turn at bat will astound."

Deputy Sunglasses pushed open the door before Sydney could protest.

•

Only a trickle of spectators gathered in the courtroom. Not the eruption of renewed local interest Sydney expected. The commodious space featured many striking details, including mahogany wainscot, elaborate window surrounds, and a two-hundred-year-old, hand-carved oak panel mounted near the judge's bench.

Sydney parked directly behind the defendant's table. Cal Hampton and Lorraine Gallivant arrived moments later, and Sydney patted seats next to her. Lantana Hardwick slid in as the bailiff stirred to life.

"All rise. The Court of South Carolina's Ninth Judicial Circuit, Criminal Division, is back in session. The Honorable Jerome P. Hughes presiding."

The bulbous-nosed jurist blew through the door from his

chambers, pushing soft gray curls off his forehead. "You may be seated." Judge Hughes settled in at the bench flanked by the American and South Carolina flags. He began shuffling a mountain of folders atop his perch, evenly distributing the collection into smaller piles. "Mr. Noble, call your first witness."

"Thank you, Your Honor. Defense calls Cooper Bellamy." Rob moved to a lectern located between the prosecution and defense tables as Coop took an oath to tell the truth. "Please give your name, occupation, and a summary of your professional qualifications."

Coop folded his hands and prepared to recite his bona fides, including his expertise in both fire and arson investigations. "Cooper Bellamy. I'm a Special Agent with the Bureau of Alcohol, Tobacco, Firearms, and Explosives, Charlotte Field Division. I've served with the Bureau for a year. I also served seven years with the Greenville Fire Department and four years as the Chief Arson Investigator for the South Carolina State Law Enforcement Division. I hold bachelor's and master's degrees in fire science; certificates from the National Fire Protection Association, International Association of Arson Investigators, National Fire Chiefs Council . . ."

The solicitor, an African American woman wearing a fabulous Givenchy suit, rose. "The People acknowledge Agent Bellamy's reputation and stipulate as to his expertise as a qualified arson investigator."

Rob flashed a polite smile. "Agent Bellamy, please describe your review of the State's evidence against Mr. Sharpe."

Coop focused on the jury. "I examined fire investigation notes, photographs, and witness statements. And recently, I examined two pieces of newly recovered physical evidence, with associated forensic analyses by the Charleston Police Crime Lab."

"Anything else?" Rob asked.

Coop glanced toward the judge. "I understand no other evidentiary materials remain from the fire."

This time, the solicitor stood like a wobbling prizefighter and grabbed the table to steady herself. "The People stipulate as to the limited availability of physical evidence. Litigants in civil trials against a manufacturer consumed large samples of ceiling materials in the early 1990s."

"What about the alleged new evidence?" the judge asked.

"Clerical error, Your Honor," the solicitor said dismissively.

Rob sported a broad grin for judge and jury. "Your expert conclusions, Agent Bellamy."

"Modern fire investigation is an amalgam of science and technology, combined with lots of experience. The fundamental goal of any investigator is to determine a fire's origin and cause. In my opinion, the investigator who testified at Mr. Sharpe's first trial grievously misinterpreted incendiary evidence."

"Incendiary? Please explain," Rob prodded.

"The best way to evaluate whether a fire is incendiary is to test for the presence of flammable or combustible liquid accelerants in fire debris. The most important decisions for an investigator are determining what to collect and where to collect it. I discovered the investigators collected little of relevance. Yet, despite their glaring errors, let me be clear. I have no doubt the fire at the Charleston train station was deliberately set, notwithstanding the so-called facts presented at Mr. Sharpe's first trial. Rather, each point raised by the chief investigator as evidence of an incendiary has been uniformly denounced as bogus by quantitative research and professional analyses."

"Such as?" Rob coaxed.

"Crazed glass, V-shaped burn patterns, multiple points of origin, and so forth. These items were often cited as telltale facts of arson back in the day. We now have proof they represented a mere collection of myths and personal beliefs instead of competent forensic investigation."

"Tell the Court exactly what you mean."

Coop walked through a scientific overview behind each

phenomenon. He spoke in an even tone and provided instructive, easy-to-understand examples. When he finished, he reeled toward the jury. "In short, every element the original investigator pointed to as arson was plain wrong. Mr. Sharpe was convicted with junk science."

Lorraine rested a hand on Nate's shoulder and squeezed. He patted her hand, then laced his fingers in his lap. Nate focused his gaze on Coop with keen anticipation.

Sydney spent time studying the six jurors, confident Rob was prepared to further plumb the depths of Coop's expertise. Though she didn't possess a lot of jury knowledge, it didn't require a trained eye to know they viewed the handsome ATF agent with equal parts fascination and skepticism. She easily spotted four jurors ready to take Nate's side versus two who required further convincing.

Rob pounced. "Agent Bellamy, you say the evidence against Mr. Sharpe was wrongly labeled as arson, yet you state the fire was deliberately set. Which is it?"

Juror Number 5 bent forward, rested his forearms on the handrail, mouth slightly agape. Even the four who seemed keen to support Nate bobbed their heads, wanting to resolve this apparent conflict.

"Objection, Mr. Noble is arguing with his own witness," the solicitor said without conviction.

"Sustained."

"Let me rephrase," Rob said. "What led to your professional opinion the fire was intentional?"

"Based upon eyewitness accounts and photographic evidence, a fire appeared to have been deliberately set inside a janitorial closet. A balloon or similar synthetic device, filled with gasoline or a comparable accelerant, was placed near a fuse directly on the closet floor. Based upon photos of ash and residue, I concluded the fuse was a bundle of cigarettes and a book of matches fastened together. The offender lit one or more cigarettes. Then placed the fuse in the vicinity of the accelerant, allowing the offender an opportunity to discreetly leave the area. This served as a crude, though effective, delayed ignition source."

Sydney quit taking notes and slipped the pad into her purse. She and the jurors followed Coop with rapt attention. Lorraine squeezed her hands so tight, she had to wring them out every few minutes.

Coop's testimony soared and he revved his baritone into high gear. "The cigarettes smoldered, eventually setting the matches on fire. The matches flamed, ultimately igniting the accelerant, which in turn caused the small closet to become fully engulfed. From there, the fire quickly spread across ceiling tiles into the adjoining smoking lounge and retail shops. This scenario is further supported by witness statements. Flaming ceiling debris dropped to the floor and shelves, igniting more combustibles. Thus explaining what investigators erroneously labeled as multiple points of origin. Excessive smoke, heat, toxic fumes, and flames caused panic in the crowded station." Coop paused, seeming to measure his words. "In the ensuing terror, eight people were trampled to their deaths."

Rob allowed everyone a chance to absorb the atrocity. "Please remind the jurors the cause of death for the other thirty-one souls that terrible day."

Coop blew out a breath. "As you learned yesterday, the coroner concluded each died from smoke inhalation."

"What else did those thirty-one have in common?"

"Ironically, those thirty-one bodies were found in the smoking lounge."

Two jurors gasped.

"Why didn't they try to escape?" Rob asked.

"The lounge door had been jammed from the outside." Coop shook his head. "They were trapped. No way out."

Juror Number 5 slumped back. Others who'd sided with Nate earlier now sneered at him. Nate sat motionless. This time, Sydney rested a hand on his shoulder.

Rob moved to the jury box and leaned against the rail. "Was this evidence substantiated at Mr. Sharpe's first trial?"

"The first solicitor suggested Mr. Sharpe, described in the transcripts as a frail teenage boy, somehow physically restrained the door," Coop said. "Though how he was alleged to have accomplished this Herculean feat was never made clear. And no witness ever placed Mr. Sharpe around the janitor's closet prior to the fire."

The solicitor softly demurred. "Objection."

Rob whirled in her direction. "On what grounds?"

"Mr. Noble, please allow the Court to inquire." The judge's thundering voice echoed throughout the cavernous courtroom. He glared at both attorneys for a beat. "On what grounds?"

The solicitor hesitated. "Facts not in evidence."

"Precisely, Your Honor," Rob said. "Agent Bellamy stated he recently examined new physical evidence that had been collected from the fire scene. Those items were suppressed . . ." He leaned forward. "Correction. Unavailable at the first trial. An alleged clerical error." Rob's manner was sharp as moldy cheddar.

The judge banged his gavel. "Mr. Noble—"

"And this solicitor also chooses to ignore that physical evidence." Rob finally came up for air.

The judge glowered. "Mr. Noble, when this Court bangs his gavel, lawyers are supposed to quit talking." He smoothed his chin. "Am I making myself clear?"

"Yes, Your Honor," Rob said, arms folded.

The judge continued. "Counselor, why should the Court allow this line of questioning? Are you alleging prosecutorial misconduct?"

Rob shook his head. "My esteemed opposing counsel has been dealt an appallingly bad hand. But I reserve the right to address the first solicitor's conduct another time." He smiled toward the jury. "Your Honor, may we receive a ruling on the objection?"

"Overruled." The judge shook a fist at the cowering solicitor. "Defense may introduce these new items into evidence if you choose."

"Thank you." Rob placed two evidence pouches on the witness box ledge. "Agent Bellamy, please describe for the Court Defense Exhibits A and B."

Coop studied the bags. "Exhibit A is an empty Marlboro package that was found tucked inside Exhibit B. Between the Marlboro's outer paper wrapper and foil insert, a wad of used chewing gum was recovered."

"And Exhibit B?" Rob asked.

"Exhibit B is a metal wedge with a hollow core generally used to hold open a stubborn door. You push it under with the toe of your shoe. We also discovered new documents and photos showing both exhibits lodged beneath the smoking lounge door."

Jurors gasped. Two brought hands to their open mouths.

"Go on," Rob said.

"The cigarette package, the chewing gum, and the doorstop were examined for trace evidence."

"Objection," the solicitor charged. This time, her voice held a hint of defiance. "Your Honor, Special Agent Bellamy possesses many degrees and talents, but the People assert he isn't best qualified to interpret forensic evidence gleaned from testing these items. If Defense wants the Court to hear testimony on this matter, please compel them to provide another expert."

Sydney tapped her finger on her lips. A second expert. Rob had calculated that strategic requirement on Nate's behalf.

"May it please the Court," Rob offered. "Madam Solicitor is correct. I withdraw the question. Nothing further for this witness."

The solicitor absently waved her arm. "No questions."

46

Rain clouds swirled overhead as Lamar held the door to his tiny house for Haley. A warm wind blew through the open kitchen window, sweeping a curtain over the table. He was flabbergasted Cora Rose had allowed him to take her, though relieved he didn't need to rough up the old lady or the little girl.

Lamar hoped grabbing Haley would be enough to derail Coop's testimony as Falcon had directed. And ensure the 843Z kept their mitts off Mama while Lamar fine-tuned a plan to leave Falcon for good.

Haley placed a hand on her hip. "Who lives here?"

The question surprised Lamar by its directness. "Me and Mama."

Mama's design flair was on full display in the front room. Most prominent were pictures of Lamar at various ages wearing grass-stained baseball uniforms, kneeling beside trophies taller than him.

"It's honest." Haley cleared her throat. "Unlike Mombo's phony-baloney friends. She's a doctor, and they get paid way too much money."

"Money is nice." Half-moons of sweat under his armpits testified to rising humidity.

"But my mom thinks she's important, cutting up people. My dad actually saves people from burning buildings and car crashes. You ever wanna be a firefighter?"

The question caught Lamar off guard. "Uh, no. I'm gonna be an engineer. Or maybe a professional baseball player." He scratched his neck. "Most likely an engineer."

"On a train?"

Lamar shook his head. "Electrical or structural. I want to design power grids, or buildings and bridges."

"Way cool. I bet you played with Legos as a kid."

"For real. You hungry?"

"I ate at Cora's. Pimento sandwiches." She scrunched her nose. "Broke a few of my mom's rules."

"My mom has rules, too."

"Like what?"

"Stay in school. Finish my homework. Stuff like that. What are your rules?"

"Clean my room. Hang my dress." Haley pursed her lips. "My dad makes way too many rules. It's why he and I argue. He means well. But I'm a butterfly. I can't be bound to Earth by his strict rules. I'll suffocate." She flopped on the sofa, clutching her chest. "But I made one rule my dad totally hates."

"Yeah?" Lamar grinned. "What?"

"Real men don't eat meat."

Lamar laughed. "Wanna bet?" He handed Haley a stack of DVDs. "Our cable's out." He fibbed, but he didn't want her watching the news. "I'm changing my shirt. This one is soaked."

He fished a new burner phone from his pocket and sent Falcon a text: *Took Agent Bellamy's kid. She's at my house.*

•

Sydney assessed the growing contingent of courtroom onlookers buzzing with excitement regarding the defense's scintillating morning session. The jury fixated on the defense attorney in anticipation of what was to come next. Dark clouds swirled outside. A single clap of thunder ushered in a torrent of raindrops.

The judge eyed the storm buffeting his courtroom windows. "Call your next witness, Mr. Noble."

"Defense calls Draymond Bernadino."

Sydney smiled as her cop friend entered through the rear door, sauntered to the witness box, then introduced himself to the Court.

She shook a fist in his direction.

Rob rested both hands on the lectern. "Lieutenant Bernadino, were you present when the police department's crime lab examined the cigarette pack and chewing gum, along with the metal door wedge, Defense Exhibits A and B?"

"No," Dino said flatly.

"Wait a minute," Judge Hughes said. "Any objection by the People as to the ability of this witness to provide evidentiary testimony?"

The solicitor pulled herself from her seat. "After consultation with the police department, we determined Captain Burton, CPD's Crime Lab supervisor, is unavailable. In the interest of the Court's time and patience, the People stipulate as to Lieutenant Bernadino's limited expertise."

The judge frowned, his bushy eyebrows snapping together. "Go ahead, Mr. Noble."

"Tell us about the exhibits," Rob urged.

"Captain Burton found the chewing gum stuck between layers of the cigarette package," Dino said. "She extracted the gum and submitted it for rapid DNA testing. The captain also lifted a latent fingerprint from the inside foil, and thumb and forefinger prints from the doorstop."

"Was DNA testing conducted on either the gum or cigarettes prior to the first trial?"

"No. Genetic fingerprinting was in its infancy and commercially unavailable." Dino sat back and hooked his right foot atop the other knee. "Besides, these items were only recently recovered. Misfiled in another case box."

Rob allowed a wee smile. "What were the results of the identification tests?"

"Smudged prints. AFIS, the FBI's Automated Fingerprint Identification System, couldn't identify anyone, including Mr. Sharpe. But the lab analyzed DNA from saliva on the chewed gum and epithelial cells from one smudged print. DNA can degrade over time depending on the environment it's stored in. In this case, both had been preserved by soot."

"Remind us the significance of DNA classification."

Sydney suspected the jury had more than an inkling of its importance. Even so, Rob had asked Dino to spell it out.

Dino said, "Every person's genome is composed of unique patterns of alleles and short tandem repeats at specified locations called loci. I know that sounds complex, so here's the lay version. Technicians are able to scientifically compare two samples of genetic material, such as blood, sperm, sweat, urine. Or in this case—saliva and skin residue. From their analysis, they can determine whether the samples are statistically likely to come from the same person."

Rob nodded sagely. Nodding was proven body language for conveying trust and assurance to the jury. "Tell us the results of the lab's DNA testing."

"The saliva and epithelials matched each other—meaning they came from the same person. And both were a partial match to the defendant."

Nate jumped to his feet. "But I didn't light the fire. My lawyer settin' me up."

The judge hammered his gavel. "Restrain your client, Mr. Noble. Or a deputy will do it for you."

"Make him quit." Nate wielded toward Sydney, Lorraine, and Lantana. "Please stop him. I didn't set the fire. I didn't kill those people. You trust me, right?"

The judge's slamming gavel muffled Nate's heated pleas. "Deputy," Judge Hughes shouted as the stack of folders cascaded to the floor.

Sydney sidled over to Rob while the deputy cuffed Nate to the table, and the bailiff scurried to retrieve the judge's papers. "You sure about Dino's testimony?"

"Oh, this is happening." Rob spun back to the judge. "Begging the Court's indulgence, we apologize for the outburst. My client isn't amused with the tack I'm taking. If I may ask a few more questions of this witness, I can clarify this matter to my client's satisfaction."

"The Court is even less charmed." The judge eyed the solicitor.

She shook her head. Defeated. "No objection."

"Proceed, Mr. Noble. But arrive at your point. Quickly."

"Lieutenant Bernadino," Rob said, "you stated DNA is a partial match to the defendant. Please elaborate?"

"DNA testing indicated a strong resemblance, though not an exact match to Mr. Sharpe. Captain Burton determined the match can be defined as familial. That is to say, a close biological relative's genetic profile."

"Such as a parent, child, or sibling?"

Dino nodded. "Mr. Sharpe does have one known sibling. A sister, Lantana Hardwick."

"No," Nate cried. "Not Lanny."

The judge shot a contemptuous glare at the defense table.

Rob pivoted toward Nate and patted the air with his palms. "Did Ms. Hardwick provide her DNA for comparison?"

"She volunteered a sample. Her genetic markers are also a familial match to the recovered evidence." Dino cocked his head. "But her sample wasn't necessary."

"Why?" Rob asked.

"Captain Burton determined the DNA came from a male. That is to say, the defendant's brother or half brother."

Lorraine moaned. Lantana's hands flew to her face. Nate slumped forward. Sydney eyed the jury; each member appeared riveted to Dino's unfolding testimony.

Rob said, "And?"

"Mr. Sharpe doesn't have any brothers or half brothers we could find using official birth records. That means someone else, a man not known to us, is biologically related to Mr. Sharpe and Ms. Hardwick."

"And what else does this exculpatory evidence suggest?" Rob asked.

"Objection," the solicitor said. "The jury can determine whether this is exculpatory."

"Sustained."

Rob slammed his hand on the lectern. "Detective, you've stated DNA from the State's only physical evidence tying my client to the crime of arson, and arson being the proximate cause of death for thirty-nine people, is scientifically proven to come from a man other than my client."

Dino said, "It's clear from the physical evidence examined by Charleston Police Department's Crime Lab, Mr. Nathan Sharpe is not the person responsible for the train station fire nor the eventual deaths of those people."

Rob threw his hands in the air. "Defense rests."

Sydney allowed herself a huge sigh of relief as the state's case against Nathan Sharpe completely unraveled.

47

Lamar slipped from the front room to change clothes while Haley watched *The Vampire Diaries*, a supernatural series about a teenage girl who loses both parents in an automobile crash, then inexplicably falls in love with an ancient vampire. He hated mythology stories with a muddled storyline. And guys his age never watched chick flicks. As he reached for his phone to check for Falcon's reply, the house shook.

Haley let out a high-pitched scream. "Lamar, help me."

Lamar rushed into the living room so fast, he defied the laws of physics.

The front door dangled on one hinge. Wood shards from the splintered jamb peppered the room. A gangbanger dressed like Black Rambo, with a P220 handgun aimed directly at Lamar's chest, blocked the doorway. A second banger pinned Haley to the floor. She was sprawled face down with a bandana tied across her mouth. The guy placed his knee in the center of her back, then zipped a plastic cable around her wrists. She cried out. Followed by a muffled whimper.

Lamar flagged his trembling hands. "Don't go borrowing trouble. Do you have any idea who this kid belongs to?"

Rambo sneered and punched Lamar's face so hard, it broke his nose.

Lamar staggered and fell. His confused gaze darted between the two 843Z intruders. Dizzy with surprise, he couldn't focus.

Rambo fired his gun and a bullet creased Lamar's shoulder, causing a jolt as though he'd stuck a wet finger in a live socket.

Lamar clutched his arm. "You came for her? Why?"

"You even care?" Rambo asked.

A bitter truth forced itself on Lamar. His hopes for a peaceful showdown with Falcon had fizzled. Instead, Falcon sent guys to get him.

"Leave her alone," Lamar said. "She's just a kid. Won't say nothing to nobody." His voice tightened as he fixated on the barrel of Rambo's smoking pistol. He lunged away before a second shot shattered the window behind him.

"Willing to risk it?" Rambo sneered.

Haley squirmed and fought while the banger who'd zip-tied her jerked her upright. She lashed out, kicking his knee. The man dropped to the floor.

Lamar lay helpless as Rambo slapped Haley. The guy without the pistol regained his footing, tossed Haley over his shoulder, then the three fled the tiny house.

Lamar squeezed his arm. A strange weight crushed his chest, as though he'd deserted Haley. Failed to protect her. He needed to contact Agent Bellamy and tell him the gang stole his daughter. Then Lamar would hunt down Falcon without chickening out.

He stumbled to his feet and staggered outside. Lamar's breathing grew hoarse with rage. He fumbled the phone—his fingers weren't working right. The phone slipped from his hand.

An old woman who lived next door rushed to him. "Oh, child."

"Call the fire department," Lamar said.

Captain Larry Bosco shouted as he crested the porch with a long stride. "That won't be necessary."

Detective Tate assumed a tactical shooter's crouch and knifed into Lamar's house.

"They're gone," Lamar said, but the detective ignored him.

Bosco radioed dispatch using his walkie-talkie. "Shots fired at my location. One vic—male. Single GSW." The Deputy Fire Marshal holstered his radio and turned his attention to Lamar.

Rocked by the timely arrival of two task force members, Lamar said, "How did you know—"

"You needed our help?" Detective Tate said as he returned to the porch. "Call it cop intuition." He twisted Lamar's hands behind his back and snapped handcuffs on the teen's wrists. "You have the right to remain silent."

Lamar grimaced. "They stole Haley."

•

The jury spent little more than an hour in deliberation, during which time the downpour subsided. Once the foreperson announced the not-guilty verdict, Sydney moved outside with Coop and Dino.

"Coop, you still owe me a bourbon." Dino flicked his cell phone. "Let me check with Brody on Anson's apprehension, then we'll celebrate."

Sydney hugged Coop and Dino. "Tuck your phones away. I need reaction soundbites before you run off." She motioned for Eric to record. "For nearly forty years, Nathan Sharpe was a state prisoner, convicted of arson and thirty-nine counts of murder stemming from a fire at the Charleston train station. This afternoon, Nate is a free man, thanks to the Innocence Network and compelling testimony from two unlikely sources." She made a slicing motion across her throat. "Dino, you ready?" She tugged his sleeve. "Rolling, three, two, one. I'm with Detective Lieutenant Draymond Bernadino, who provided persuasive testimony on Nate's behalf. Lieutenant, is it unusual for police to side with the accused at trial?"

Dino scratched his chin, then pasted on a sardonic smile. "The city pays me to throw bad guys in jail. And keep them there. Nate Sharpe isn't a bad guy."

Sydney nudged Dino aside. "Coop, you're next."

"You must feel pretty good," Coop said as the camera operator pushed closer.

"I'm grateful. Nate steadfastly maintained his innocence." She motioned Eric to resume filming. "In your professional opinion, did the jury reach the right decision?"

"Advances in modern fire forensics and the introduction of new physical evidence helped persuade this jury," Coop said. "Especially compared to the largely circumstantial case presented at the first trial—a textbook example of injustice."

As Sydney prepared another question, Coop's vibrating phone intervened. "Go ahead. Take it," she said.

•

Coop answered with a hint of annoyance. "Captain, I'm in the middle of something."

Captain Burton sounded pitchy with excitement. "I left a half dozen messages."

"I've been in court testifying. No cell phones allowed. What do you have?"

"A DNA and fingerprint match."

"To what?"

Captain Burton said, "The massacre. Hart Anson is the train station arsonist."

"Holy crap," Coop said. "What clinched it?"

"The bloody tissue."

"Tissue?" Coop wrinkled his face, then snapped his fingers. "Anson's nosebleed when Lantana punched him at City Hall. How did you wind up with it?"

"Your TV friend asked me to run the sample," Captain Burton said. "Didn't need a warrant since it wasn't custodial evidence. I matched the blood DNA with touch DNA off the business card you gave my tech. Then tied it to the old evidence."

"Radio silence, Captain. I'll give Brody the news." Coop disconnected.

As if on cue, an unmarked cruiser skidded to the curb. Detective Tate lunged from the driver's seat.

"You nab Anson?" Coop asked.

"He's still in the wind," Detective Tate said. "But your SLED buddy called. Agent Proctor matched prints our lab couldn't from the glass shards you found at Kinkaid's fire scene."

"Anson?" Sydney asked.

Captain Bosco bolted from the car. "Lamar Gallivant."

"The sketchy kid?" Sydney asked.

Bosco held out a hand, indicating more news. "The Crime Lab also processed the swab Coop gave them from the kid's backpack."

"What?" Sydney shrieked. "You swabbed his backpack?"

"And?" Coop ignored her.

"Consistent with ignitable materials used in Kinkaid and other fires," Bosco said.

Sydney gasped. "Did you arrest him?"

"He was working at the Moultrie Building with other interns all morning," Bosco said gravely. "Left for lunch before we received the results."

Coop scrutinized the two men, who seemed anxious to provide additional details. "What else. Go on. Blurt it out."

"Haley's missing," Bosco said. "I drove over to Cora Rose's like you asked me. But she told me someone from the office had already come for your daughter. I asked if she remembered a name or what the guy looked like. She provided a description of Lamar. He took her without permission."

"Cora Rose is blameless. And Haley knows Lamar, so she wouldn't object." Coop rehashed the situation out loud, though the news landed like a mule kick. He closed his eyes, engulfed with pain. His biggest fear had come to fruition. He wasn't around when she'd needed him. Coop sank to the steps and dropped his head between his knees. "Did Lamar hurt her?"

"We snagged him at his house," Detective Tate said. "He'd been shot. Told us two goons snatched Haley from him."

"Goons? Who—"

"843Z. I issued an Amber Alert. Then uniforms drove Lamar to the hospital. Read him his rights. He's only seventeen, so I need to locate a parent before I drop him in the box."

"I'm Lamar's mother," Lorraine Gallivant said, emerging from the courthouse with Cal and Lantana. "Did you say someone shot my son?"

Sydney moved to her side. "You'd better go to the hospital."

Coop tossed his keys to Bosco. "You accompany Ms. Gallivant. I'll ride with Lieutenant Bernadino and Detective Tate."

"I want to help find Haley," Sydney said.

"Me too," Cal said.

Coop jumped in the car. "Move Nate and Lantana to safety. Anson is going to come after him now that their ancestry has been disclosed to the whole world."

•

Sydney dashed into the courthouse to find Nate and Rob Noble.

Nate said, "Both of you promised my release from the Iron Bar Hotel. I'm grateful beyond words."

Rob said, "Your sister and I will work on collecting you a fat check from the city for wrongful imprisonment."

"That'd be right nice. She had a heap of confidence in my release."

Rob grabbed his arm. "Please don't try settling any old scores. Leave everything to me."

"My heart holds little anger toward Wallace for putting me away." Nate tilted his head. "No time for bitterness. Only catching up. I never had no father and my mother died while I was in prison. Only me and my sister all these years. Now, there's a brother we don't know." Nate slowly exhaled. "I suppose Lantana and I need to locate him, best we can. Even though he's the one who set the fire." His voice trailed off. "And let me spend more than half my life locked away."

Sydney grasped Nate by the shoulders. "I know who your half brother is."

<h1 style="text-align:center">48</h1>

reen plaid sheets curtained off MUSC's eight emergency treatment bays. Four patrol cops fronted the first bay as Coop and Dino slid in. Lamar jumped to his feet, even though he was cuffed to a chair. He wore jeans and a blood-soaked T-shirt. One eye was swollen shut and his split lower lip was caked with blood. The kid was probably more nervous than he'd ever admit.

"Sit down," Coop snapped.

"They want me for the fires," Lamar said.

Coop rubbed his chin. "Cops cast a dim view regarding serial arson."

Lamar slumped. "Find Haley?"

Coop eyed the intern and guessed the kid wanted to tell his story, too tired to lie anymore. Or maybe Lamar couldn't figure out how to fix his mess. Coop debated whether to help knit Lamar's life back together. "Police have corralled D-Jazz, Anson, and you. First one who talks, walks."

"I'm listening."

"I might be in a position to help you. Maybe offer some advice." Coop shook his head. "Problem is, I don't care about you." A big. Fat. Fib. He'd grown fond of Lamar and reasoned the young man didn't want to set fires. But he got jammed up, somehow.

Lamar poised to speak but squirmed away. He impatiently tugged at his fingers, cracking each knuckle.

Coop stabbed his finger in the middle of Lamar's chest. "Why did you kidnap Haley?"

"Falcon made me. I had to do it to protect Mama." He spoke with the tone of a teenager's ragged insolence. "Tried to protect Haley, too."

Coop didn't want to travel this road. "Then why did the gang kidnap her from you?"

"No idea, I swear." His voice filled with conviction.

Lorraine Gallivant stepped into the space and gasped. "Oh, my. Lamar, you are a landslide of bad news." She eyed Coop and Dino with a disapproving scowl. "This interview is over."

Dino motioned for Coop to leave, and they waded through the ER. "We need to tighten the screws on D-Jazz. But I won't allow you to confront him. Goes against every regulation. And common sense."

Coop faced Dino, ready to bring the heat.

Dino waggled a finger. "You're working this like a father rather than a competent law enforcement professional. We gotta play it by the book."

"Which book? The one I've been a stickler for my whole career? The one that says bad guys won't steal my kid?" Coop punched the elevator button for the top floor. "So, tell me, what good is the book if I'm the only one heeding it? Let me at D-Jazz, and I'll ensure he feels obligated to tell me where Haley is."

Dino shook his head with emphasis. "This one's mine. You sort of lost it with Lamar."

"You're kidding?" Coop sneered as the doors opened. "Someone snatched my kid to warn me off. It won't work."

"I'm talking as your friend. We go back a long way."

"Yeah? What? About four days."

"Thick and thin." Dino thumped his chest. "C'mon, do yourself a favor. Don't cross a line you can't walk back from."

Coop shook his head and hooked a thumb at D-Jazz's door. "What an idiot. Taking Haley only makes me stronger. And super pissed off."

"I'll squeeze D-Jazz. We own this dude. The lollipops and shit-birds always talk."

"She's my daughter. I'm supposed to protect her. It's my job. And my job comes first. Ask anyone." Coop rested a hand on Dino's shoulder. "Wait out here, pal. Even if I've gotta bend a few rules, I'm doing this."

Dino showed his palms. "Tell Internal Affairs I put up a helluva fight."

Coop kicked open the door to the isolation room.

His stomach knotted, knowing he needed to lean on D-Jazz and squeeze information from him as quickly as possible. He surveyed the banger's tattoos with displeasure, then cocked his head at the TV. "Turn it off."

D-Jazz thumbed the remote, and the room fell silent. Ever the tough guy, he tried to inflate his ego by folding his arms across his chest, seemingly indifferent to his jeopardy. "Now what?"

"Give me what I need, or I'll ensure corrections officers toss you in gen pop and tag you with the snitch label for good measure. Your enemies will crawl over you like beetles on a pile of shit." Though weak-kneed, Coop erased the track of Haley screaming for help playing in his head and focused on the task. "The game you're playing is rigged. You're never gonna win. But things can go easier if you cooperate." Coop sprawled in a chair and reaffixed his glare on D-Jazz with radiating intensity.

A staring contest ensued.

Whoever blinked first would find themselves behind the rest of the way. Coop waited for the pressure to build on D-Jazz. It didn't take long.

The gang leader limped over.

Coop continued. "You tried to cement your power over Falcon without success. Now, I'm doing what you couldn't. Putting Falcon out of business." This line of questioning sucked valuable time. But if Coop could get D-Jazz talking, he could sift through his lies and determine where the gang was holding his daughter. "You want to help me bust Falcon? Maybe save Fleet Landing." Joining forces with a felonious banger went against every instinct, but D-Jazz was

Coop's best lead. In fact, he was all Coop had right now.

D-Jazz worked his chin from side to side before plastering on a stupid grin. "What do I need to do?"

Coop pressed forward with both hands flat on the table. "First, let's clear up some irregularities with your previous statements."

D-Jazz's smile faltered. "I ain't never lied to you."

"Try again. You lied about where you were when your cousin, Destiny, shot the battalion chief." Coop parked a photo of the black Mercedes on the table.

D-Jazz blinked rapidly and made a huge mistake pushing the photo away. "That's Ice's ride."

"Well then, case closed." Coop rocked back on his chair's hind legs and knew he'd hit his mark. "But there's the matter of those darn fires." He pretended to study his mental notes before laying it out. Half educated guess, half firm evidence to back his play. "Did Ice hire Lamar to torch Fleet Landing? Or was that your idea?"

"Lamar? Lamar who? You playin' me?" D-Jazz arranged a handful of pencils as though laying kindling for a campfire. "And I told you I was out of town humpin' when Kinkaid burnt up."

"Another lie. SLED confirmed you were in Fleet Landing when that fire started." Coop lowered his voice to become more menacing. "I have indisputable evidence tying Lamar to the Kinkaid blaze and a bunch of other fires in the hood. But he didn't kill those two Rivertown teens and dump 'em at Ms. Quinn's." He flattened his mustache. "And that was damn stupid risky—what you did at the Tip."

"Tell me."

"First, natural gas needs time to build."

"I don't even barbecue."

Coop continued in a professorial manner. "Before it'll explode, a precise concentration of gas or vapor has to combine with air. Once an ignition source is introduced—*kapooph*. You're lucky the whole building didn't crash on your head."

D-Jazz fidgeted with his hands. "I said it wasn't me."

"An explosion? Naw, not Lamar's style. Ice is your man with the guns, right?"

"Sure, I threw some action his way." The words tumbled out before D-Jazz caught himself. "But shooting dudes and blowing up stuff? You're accusing me of something I didn't do."

A fleeting mental picture of Haley in the morgue caused the hair on the back of Coop's neck to stand at attention. "I learned Falcon acquired the Tip through some fast and loose political she-nanigans. Anson doesn't need you to burn out residents anymore. No more insurance scams. No more cheating little old ladies out of their houses."

D-Jazz mumbled a handful of obscenities, then leaned forward in defeat. "Anson planned the shakedown. We only did minor repair work."

"Sure. And Ice killed Ray-Ray and Croc. And Lamar set the fires. While Anson swiped the property." Coop shook his head and rose to leave. "You weren't in charge after all. You're simply a loser. With nothing to offer. A pretender."

"Un-uh."

"A wannabe."

D-Jazz huffed. "No way—"

"A fraud." Coop sneered. A rush of blood throbbed at his temples.

"Shut up," D-Jazz shouted.

"If you aren't the fuck-up I think you are—" Coop slammed his fist on the table. "Tell me how you knew when to toss a lighter to blow the Tip?"

"Ice gave them two fools cells while I . . ." D-Jazz was jamming a finger at Coop when it seemed to dawn on him: he'd incriminated Ice and admitted being part of the explosion conspiracy.

D-Jazz had broken the inexorable code of the street.

Coop throttled back. "Criminals say the dumbest stuff. Cell phones, huh? Synchronized by using a group calling program, I'll bet. That's a darn good way to create a simultaneous ignition source." He tapped his temple with two fingers. "Pretty solid plan. Now I understand why your crew wanted to bail on you and run with Ice."

D-Jazz's nostrils flared and he thumped his chest. "843Z be my gang. I formed it. They listen to me. I'm the only dude in charge. I'm bossing even from prison. The 843Z can't score nothing without my say-so."

Dino was right—the shitbirds always talked.

Coop's insides seethed from a controlled burn, ready to flashover. He had the gangbanger on the ropes. Time for the big score. He rocked forward and slammed his fist on the table again. "Where's Haley?"

D-Jazz turned away with a fathomless glare.

Coop rounded the table, shoved D-Jazz onto his seat, then pressed his full weight against the banger's torso, pinning him to the table. D-Jazz flailed his arms and tugged at Coop's hands, gripping his head like a bowling ball. "Your goons took my daughter."

"Anson took her. He's the one calling the shots." His words slurred.

Coop jerked D-Jazz up against the wall and growled through gritted teeth. "Where?"

The banger froze with indecision.

"Anson never tell me jack." He pointed to his bandages. "Tried to have me killed."

Dino opened the door and waved Coop into the hallway.

Coop shook his head. "Two more minutes with this scrotebag."

"Brody brought someone who'll get him to spill," Dino said. "And keep you out of trouble."

Coop dropped D-Jazz, then moved into the hall as Detective Tate rounded the corner escorting Latisha Hines, D-Jazz's aunt.

Dino said, "She knows what we need."

Coop sighed and caught the door before it closed. He wedged a wad of papers to prop it open.

"Why are you here?" D-Jazz asked.

"Agent Bellamy says someone shanked you," Latisha said. "Where's his little girl?"

"I can't—"

"Where is she? No need for you to protect Anson any longer." Latisha's voice broke. "Destiny, my baby, is dead. And Anson tried to kill you, too. I know you haven't done the right thing often enough to be any good at it. But try."

"I'd tell you if I knew," D-Jazz said.

Latisha bit her lip. "Let's be clear, it was Anson all the way? The extortion, the fires, the kidnapping?"

"Anson behind everything. Probably ready to flee the country."

49

By 3 p.m., nearly everyone in Coop's orbit was keenly aware four hours had passed since the 843Z gang nabbed Haley. He'd avoided telling Cassie about Haley's disappearance and dreaded the call he needed to make to his ex-wife, even though she deserved a chance to scream at him for failing their little girl.

Sydney, Cal, and Nate rode to Palmetto Quality Development in search of Coop's daughter, even though every law enforcement department in the tri-county area enjoyed a giant head start. Sydney scanned the parking lot, hoping to find either Hart Anson, who continued to elude capture, or the dark Mercedes from Cal's photos. She never expected to encounter Sunny Anson.

"Where's Hart?" Sydney asked.

Sunny jutted her chin forward. "What concern is it of yours?"

"Are you aware of the bombshells dropped at Nate Sharpe's trial this afternoon?"

Sunny eyed the three with suspicion.

Cal said, "We understand why your husband despised his father. Seems Daddy catted around."

Sunny offered a phony little laugh. "Old news."

Sydney said, "Let me spell it out another way. Court evidence revealed Hart is Nate's half brother." She angled her head in his direction.

Sunny fumbled her purse and wobbled on skinny legs. Nate reached for the purse and handed it back. Her face tightened. "Are you the one who set fire to the train station?"

"Jury acquitted me," Nate said. "Like they shoulda done the first time."

Sunny clutched her bag to her chest, lips curled upward in a snarl.

"That fire killed my mama."

"And thirty-eight others," Nate said. "One was my best friend. I am truly sorry for your loss. But it wasn't me."

"Then who?"

Sydney patted Nate's arm. "Bombshell number one, Hart is Nate's half brother. Bombshell number two, Hart was responsible for the fire. He killed your mother and both Grangers."

Sunny's knees buckled and she tumbled to the pavement. Cal and Nate reached for her and gently lifted her to her feet. She tugged her arms free from the two Black men.

Sydney broke through her façade. "More old news, right?"

Sunny smoothed her skirt, hands trembling. "My husband swore his innocence. I trusted him."

"Your shrink's gonna have a field day with that," Sydney said. "But we're here on an even more pressing matter."

Sunny barked a laugh. "More pressing than learning my husband is a murderer?"

Cal said, "His felonies keep adding up. Murder, insurance fraud, extortion, and aggravated arson, for starters."

"You're both going down," Sydney said. "Hart, for what he did. And you, for not stopping him."

"How interesting," Sunny said. "One cannot stop what one doesn't know about."

Cal said, "He kidnapped Agent Bellamy's daughter. Any idea where he's hiding her?"

Sunny wobbled again but caught herself using the door handle. Her gaze shifted between the three accusers. "You don't believe I'm responsible for taking the girl?"

Sydney squeezed out her words. "This has been hard on all of us, so I need you to pay attention. We're certain Hart is the notorious Falcon, a serial arsonist who burned my house and half of Fleet Landing."

Sunny gasped.

"More, Falcon promised another massive fire. Perhaps endangering Haley. Please. If you have any decency . . ."

Sunny shook her head and turned away.

Cal blurted, "He also shot two teens or had them shot."

Sydney moved forward. "What's the true nature of his business with Boyd Wallace and the 843Z? And tell us about your company's sketchy acquisition of Tipton Terrace."

"Boyd Wallace is a good man. I'm certain he's not involved in anything illegal that Hart has conjured." Sunny threw up her hands. "I'd help if I could. But as I told you, I'm unfamiliar with his side of the business. Hart keeps it to himself. He—" Her shoulders straightened, and when she spoke again, she'd recovered her old coolness. "Do you have any proof of these allegations? Physical evidence? Papers? Recordings of any sort?"

Sydney dug in her purse for the phone and played an edited snippet from the vile conversation between Anson and Coop recorded in the mayor's office. "I don't craft baseless allegations. The White Crusaders have a long track record of burning churches. Your father. Hart's father. Even Mayor Wallace. They were torches bent on destroying the ethnic parts of the city. Back then, same as now."

Sunny's tears left a trail of mascara cascading down her cheeks. "I swear—"

Sydney was relentless. "You told me your father helped Wallace with Nate's prosecution. Why did they blame Nathan Sharpe?"

Sunny mumbled something unintelligible before her gaze met Nate. "It was Hart's profoundly stupid idea. I suppose he needed to pin the fire on someone other than himself. He chose which boy to accuse and molded the evidence and witnesses to fit his narrative."

"How could you stay with him? That fire killed your mother. Hart killed your mother. Your complicity speaks volumes."

Sunny lolled her head. "I learned about his involvement much later. Hart didn't know my mama would be there. He was only after the Grangers. After he tried to join the Crusaders, that's when he

found out his father had fooled around with the house help—"
She glanced at Nate. "Your mama. Until then, Hart could never
comprehend why his own mother ignored him. Come to find out,
she wasn't his real mother; he was half Black." Her breath caught.
"We were respectable people. The stigma of bad blood gnawed at
him. From the moment he learned about his ethnicity, he plotted
his revenge on the Grangers."

"A man of many secrets," Sydney said.

"You have no idea."

"And now his goons have kidnapped a little girl. Where would
they take her?"

Sunny shook her head. "All I know is, Hart is a coward. He'll
take the coward's way out."

As if on cue, Sydney's phone vibrated with a text from her producer: *Located Anson's car on the bridge. Think he jumped. Eric meeting
you there for live remote.*

Sickened by Sunny, Sydney spun away, pushing her phone into
her purse with unnecessary force. "Never mind."

•

Sydney, Cal, and Nate raced crosstown to the Ravenel Bridge.
Coast Guard Station Charleston's search and rescue teams con-
verged quickly since they were located less than a mile from the
apparent jump site. Guardian boats cordoned off the Cooper River,
the port of Charleston's thriving shipping channel, and conducted
parallel search patterns around the gleaming diamond span on the
Charleston side. A pair of orange-and-white Coast Guard helos
hovered overhead, prepared to launch swift water rescue swimmers
to join the search for Hart Anson.

Dino stood near Anson's Cadillac.

Sydney tapped him on the shoulder. "Any luck finding Anson's
body? Or Haley?"

Dino shook his head.

"Where's Coop?"

Dino pointed toward the CPD command van parked behind the Escalade.

Sydney pressed her way past the uniformed patrol and found Coop leaning against the van. He'd changed from his suit to tactical gear—black cargo pants and ATF polo.

"How are you?" she asked.

He didn't respond. Stone-cold silence.

The hush dragged on for an awkward minute while Sydney tried to come up with something sparkling and reassuring to say.

Instead, Coop crossed his arms and his eyes flared. "This is your fault. I would've been with Haley if you hadn't involved me in Nate's trial." His face reddened and his distress seemed to increase tenfold. "I knew you were bad for us."

Too startled to protest, Sydney understood the source of his anger. Rocked by her own tornado of fear, she bit her lip and turned to walk away.

"Wait, wait." Only the sincere remorse in Coop's voice stopped her. "I didn't mean it. Just . . . Need someone to blame besides myself. You should know . . . Haley . . . She wasn't in the Escalade. No hairs or fibers. Diddly."

The roar from helos circling overhead nearly drowned him out.

Sydney squeezed her hands together, then pointed at an evidence pouch in his hand. "What did you find?"

His dour expression telegraphed bad news. "Anson left a note and a receipt for thirty-two gallons of gasoline he charged less than an hour ago. This car only has a quarter of a tank. So, where's the gas?"

Sydney felt relieved Coop was talking and didn't flat-out order her to get lost. "What does the note say?"

He passed the evidence pouch containing Anson's purported suicide note. Shaky handwriting gave the note an air of legitimacy. "Crime Lab is reviewing the writing to determine authenticity." He raked his fingers through his hair and gave her a nod. "Be smart when you go on the air. This is an exclusive."

Sydney scanned the note.

Anson's rambling text showed no remorse for the fires. Said he felt motivated by deep-seated hatred of Black people and wanted to 'open a race war to rile whites so much, they will finally eliminate the Blacks.' Most startling, he stated Tipton Terrace's explosion was a 'preview of things to come.'

Coop waved a portable gas chromatograph wand around the Escalade's trunk. Results popped positive for gasoline.

Sydney asked, "Any chance Anson planted an explosive device somewhere in town, then drove here to jump? His wife labeled him a coward."

"Possibly," Coop said. "But this scene is staged, merely for show. Cops are examining video from bridge cameras."

"Text me if something solid evolves."

Sydney sprinted to a clutch of Coast Guard officers and spent several minutes gathering information for her report, then hurried to her mark located near the Action 7 News van. She clung to the bridge's handrail, awaiting her cue. In her earpiece, Action 7's anchor said, "We interrupt our regular broadcast for breaking news. Let's go live to Sydney Quinn."

She waited for Eric's red light, then launched into her segment. "Police and Coast Guard rescue units are searching the Cooper River for local businessman Hart G. Anson after his Cadillac Escalade was found abandoned on the bridge, driver's door open, car running, with a haunting suicide note on the passenger's seat."

She tucked a lock of wind-blown hair behind her ear. "In a bizarre confluence of events, the Arson Task Force sought to apprehend Anson for the 1985 train station fire that killed thirty-nine people. ATF Special Agent Cooper Bellamy indicated Anson is also wanted for his part in the cruel and calculated epidemic of arsons plaguing Fleet Landing.

"However, when police prepared to serve a summons, Anson had disappeared. A statewide search for him and his fleet of vehicles led police to the abandoned vehicle found here on the Ravenel Bridge, where Anson has apparently jumped two hundred and twenty-five feet into the Cooper River."

"Sydney, has anyone ever survived the jump?" the anchor asked.

She held up one finger. "Since the bridge opened in 2006, twenty-one people have leapt to their deaths. However, I spoke to a Coast Guard officer involved in today's search who said his divers have devised an aggressive search pattern based on real-time tidal data hoping to find their second living jumper. Sydney Quinn, Action 7 News."

•

Fifteen minutes later, Sydney had assembled enough information for another breaking news segment. Coop and Dino continued scouring grainy video footage recorded from cameras at both ends of the bridge. And the tri-county law enforcement community remained on high vigilance, tracking every sighting of Haley received via the Amber Alert. Cal briefed Nate about Anson's more recent crime spree and had driven him to the hospital to meet with Lorraine and Lamar.

Sydney awaited her cue from Eric. "The Coast Guard continues to search for Hart Anson, the mixed-race son of legendary segregationist William Granger and his family's African American housekeeper. His parentage was secreted until being uncovered during the retrial of Nathan Sharpe, the man wrongly accused as the train station arsonist. According to a source close to Anson, this apparently haunted him and motivated a decades-long alleged criminal conspiracy. If found alive, Anson may also be charged with federal hate crimes stemming from racist rhetoric."

"Roll VO1," Olivia said in Sydney's earpiece.

The studio engineer played Sydney's captured audio with a huge banner that read *anonymous source* and *unsubstantiated conversation.*

"Cue Sydney," Olivia said as the audio recording concluded.

Sydney composed her thoughts before proceeding, prepared to relay additional information garnered from her Coast Guard sources. Such as learning bodies drifted in a predictable grid, away from the bridge, in the tidal current's direction. But the public had just heard Anson traffic in racism, which required context. "At long last, undeniable proof this local businessman engages in an astonishing level of ignorance."

Following her special broadcast, Sydney reconsidered Coop's notion regarding the staged suicide scene. If Anson hadn't jumped, then she figured exactly where he and his goons would take Haley—the Tobacco Mill.

The narcissistic prick would never leave behind all that cash crammed between the studs in a penthouse loft.

50

Sydney double-timed her way across town through brutal rush-hour traffic.

Anson was on the hook for thirty-nine counts of murder stemming from the 1985 train station. And when successfully prosecuted for Monday's malice, he'd tally at least seven or eight additional counts of capital murder for the Kinkaid/Tip horror. He could even add additional counts if he did anything heinous today.

She skidded to a stop a half block from the Tobacco Mill and dashed to the building's rear. The Mercedes she'd etched in her mind from Cal's photos was parked behind a row of dumpsters overflowing with construction debris caused by a trio of chutes snaking from the upper floors. The vehicle's interior reeked of gasoline, spelling trouble for the people inside. She phoned Coop, kicking herself for withholding information about Hart's multimillion-dollar stash.

He didn't answer. Coop was ducking her.

Nevertheless, she sent Coop and Dino a text about the Mercedes. Then phoned 911. Haley was likely being held captive alongside Mazie and other displaced residents.

Sydney examined the rear entry for signs of trip wires from a possible Claymore directional mine, as she'd learned from marines during the time she was an embedded reporter. She hadn't expected any, yet was thankful none were present. Gravel crunched behind her and she spun into a low attack position.

Nate and Cal jumped back with their hands out in front of their bodies.

"We came to help," Nate said.

"Why aren't you with Lorraine and Lamar?"

"Raney told me about Lamar. I didn't want to meet my son for the first time while he was in custody. Told her I'd help you first. Then catch up, once our boy is out of lockup."

Cal pointed at the Mercedes. "Ice's ride?"

Sydney nodded. "We need to find Haley and free everyone before he and Anson torch this place."

"Anson?" Cal said. "He didn't jump?"

"Unlikely," Sydney said.

Nate's eyes darkened with pain from old memories. "And he's gonna torch the people inside? You got a plan to stop him?"

Before Sydney could answer, Cal dashed to the dumpsters and repositioned a trash chute on the ground. Nate and Sydney helped free the remaining chutes.

"Why are we doing this?" Sydney asked.

"For sliding out," Cal said.

"Will they hold people?"

"Works in the movies."

Sydney lifted onto her tiptoes and reached into a dumpster for a length of rope. Without warning, bullets ricocheted off the bin. She broke left and took cover behind another metal container. From there, she traced the gunfire to the top floor as more shots splatted the ground with dull, wet thuds.

Cal scrambled around and dove by her side.

"Nate?" Sydney shouted, then popped back down.

"I'm hit," he groaned.

Crandall. Reed. Slater. Townsend. Walters. "Go away," Sydney whispered to herself and redirected her concentration by rubbing her hands together.

Cal cowered tight to the bin. His body quaked.

Sydney rested a hand on his shoulder. "C'mon, show me more of your deathmatch triple whammy xyz stuff until the cavalry comes." Saying it for him bolstered her confidence, too.

Cal clenched his jaw. "We aren't gonna stay hiding here, right?"

Sydney shook her head. "I believe Haley is inside. But first, I need to move Nate from the line of fire."

Cal nodded, his video gamer courage mounting. "Gotta admit, getting shot at for real is very scary."

"You can say that again."

"Very scary."

Sydney winked. "How fast are you?"

"Huh?"

"I need you to sprint to the door. Fast as possible. Zigzag." She motioned with her hand. "I'll pull Nate behind here while you draw fire."

"Draw fire?" Cal's voice shot up a couple of octaves.

"I'll tend to Nate's injuries, then join you inside." Sydney bobbed her head ensuring he agreed with the plan. "I already checked the door for booby traps. We're clear."

"Booby traps?"

"I read somewhere attitude is the only difference between an ordeal or an adventure. Positive attitude, Cal. Let's roll."

•

Back on the bridge, surveillance footage confirmed Anson hadn't jumped as Coop suspected. An accomplice in a dark-colored sedan tailed him onto the bridge. Coop wagered the getaway car was Ice's Mercedes from Cal's photos, with Haley slumped in the back seat.

Various traffic cameras tracked the sedan through Mount Pleasant until they lost coverage. Local cops and state police were scouring surface roads and the interstate, on the lookout for the luxury auto, hoping to hem Anson in. The search was complicated and expensive.

Radios crackled. "This is USCG Rescue One. We located a vehicle matching your BOLO at the Tobacco Mill."

The radio on Coop's belt squawked. "Towers 102, 202, Battalion 103, Engines 109, 106, 108, and 201, respond to 1200 Nimitz. Rescue 115, reports of shots fired. ATF One, report to same."

Coop and Dino sped to the Tobacco Mill as emergency service dispatchers continued to roll out police and fire units, plus specialized teams from both departments. Amid the backdrop of towering church steeples, cobblestone streets, and willowy palm fronds, Charleston's police and fire departments were facing a formidable hostage crisis, including the daughter of a federal agent.

He gripped the dash for support before pulling the cell from his pocket to phone his ex-wife. "The gang I'm tailing took our daughter. She's been missing for a while now." Coop clenched his jaw, bracing for Cassie's fury.

"What? How could you not tell me sooner?" Her voice quaked with anger and fear.

"I was following a lead. I thought I could handle it." Coop's regret weighed heavy in his tone. "I didn't want to worry you until I was sure—"

"Sure about what? That you'd solved your case before finding our daughter? You are always putting your job first. That's your top priority. Right?"

"I wanted to find her. Get her back." The weight of his failure pressed down on him. He disconnected and hung his head.

When Coop caught his breath, he spotted three unanswered calls from Sydney that he'd ignored. Then he read her text about the Mercedes and realized how stupid and childlike his behavior had been. And might have cost him precious minutes in rescuing Haley. The combination of calling Cassie and ignoring Sydney felt like he'd been dangled by his ankles above a cruise ship's churning propellers in choppy seas.

Coop's official fire investigation had been underway for over fifty-three hours. Haley had been missing for the last five.

•

Sydney and Cal assumed a runner's crouch alongside the dumpster.

"On three." She held up her index finger. Added her middle

finger. Then threw her arm out like a sailor launching airplanes from the carrier's deck.

They bolted from their positions.

Cal cut back and forth in a lopsided pattern.

Sydney broke over to Nate, who was splayed in long grass. He'd caught a high-velocity round in the arm and was bleeding profusely. Thankfully, the sniper had quit firing, though Sydney's fear of dying had long evaporated. Unblanched by Nate's appalling wound, she grabbed hold of his ankles and dragged him behind the trash container, hoping she didn't cause any more damage. She ripped off the tail of her blouse and pressed into Nate's hemorrhaging bullet hole while she phoned an emergency dispatcher. "Nate, I need you to be strong."

"Doing my best," he said.

"I'll stay with you until the ambulance comes."

"No." He clawed the blouse bandage from her and pressed it into his wound. "Go save Haley and the others. I promise I won't pass out."

"You sure?"

Nate offered a feeble wink.

Sydney returned the gesture. "I'll find Lorraine after we finish here. We'll meet you at the hospital." She sprinted for the Tobacco Mill's rear door.

Cal pressed against the building, pale and panting. "How's Nate? Is he—"

"Waiting on EMS. Let's go castrate the dipstick who shot him." She yanked open the metal door, surveyed the wide hallway, then signaled toward the south elevator. "We'll climb the shaft to access each floor."

Cal sighed. "Stands to reason Anson didn't install working elevators. There's no way the jackass will get a million bucks for these units."

"Let's debate the housing market later." Sydney nosed into the shaft. Sounds of children's wracking sobs echoed. Sydney jerked Cal's pant leg when he reached for the ladder. "Let's move folks out the side entrance to behind the building with the big smokestack. Oughta provide sufficient cover until the fire department comes."

Once they arrived on the second floor, Cal swung a leg, then pulled Sydney off the ladder. They eased down the hallway, hugging the wall. At the midway point, audible whimpering pierced a sheet of drywall hastily screwed over a door jamb.

Cal removed a knife from his pocket and plunged it into the sheetrock, slicing an opening large enough to claw with his hand. He jerked the drywall and tore a chunk away. People screamed.

Sydney *shushed* them with a hand to her mouth while Cal ripped away enough to allow more than fifty people to funnel out.

Cal grabbed a woman by the elbow. "Go outside and head toward the big smokestack." He hooked a thumb over his shoulder. "Run behind the building and stay there."

A man wearing a Carolina Panthers jersey signaled Sydney. "There's two of them. Told us the doors were wired with explosives. Said they'd blow the place up if we tried to escape."

"Anson and Ice. Where are they?" she asked.

He pointed up. "Are they the ones shooting at you?"

"Yeah." Sydney's eyes narrowed. "Move everyone behind the smokestack. They are planning to set this building on fire."

Emergency sirens *whoop-whooped* in the distance.

She continued. "Tell the cops exactly what you told me. Let everyone know Sydney and Cal are inside, too."

"Sydney and Cal. I won't forget."

"Hey, did they have a little girl with them?" Sydney asked. "Name's Haley."

"Plenty of little girls," the man sighed.

She signaled for him to leave while dashing back to the elevator shaft.

"Why did Anson come here?" Cal asked as they climbed.

"Because he stashed millions in cash on the fifth floor."

•

In the Tobacco Mill's parking lot, Coop checked on the ambulance before it departed for MUSC with Nate onboard. He learned Sydney and Cal had gone inside searching for Haley. Coop huddled over building schematics with the police department's SWAT commander as tactical planning options and questions ping-ponged in his head. What did Anson seek as his endgame, suicide-by-cop? Or was he creating a diversion for another escape? Where was Haley?

Coop reasoned Anson had come here to make a statement like he'd declared in the planted "suicide" note. He said, "Anson wants to kill more people. How many in there?"

"Could be up to a hundred-fifty squatters," the SWAT boss said.

"Prepare for every contingency."

"This is a local police matter, Agent Bellamy. We know what we're doing. We have negotiators. Special weapons. Let us handle this."

Coop shook his head. "Gotta rely on the fire department. Their Rapid Intervention Teams can go inside with infrared cameras to scan the entire building. They'll mark where people are before you breach. Ladder trucks can also drop firefighters and SWAT on the roof. Establish rappel lines for swift entry."

The SWAT commander bobbed his head toward a battalion chief. "Do what he said. And drop extra padding underneath the lines."

51

Sydney and Cal freed hostages from the Tobacco Mill's third and fourth floors before climbing to the top. To their amazement, they spotted Anson and Ice moving the money-filled paint buckets across the hall, perhaps shoving the cash down the waste chutes.

The stench of gasoline permeated the hallway.

"Dammit, he's gonna light this place up," Sydney whispered. "Need to find Haley. You go left. I'll go right. Good luck."

She crept into the first penthouse, methodically opening every closet and cupboard, hoping to locate Coop's daughter. Satisfied the girl wasn't in that condo, she worked her way to the next one in line. Cal emerged from across the hall at about the same time and shook his head.

They continued moving up the hallway without success until they arrived next to where the bad guys were shuttling the loot. Cal dashed across the hall to join Sydney. They hunkered near a window facing the street, glanced out, and spotted the law enforcement and rescue contingent assembled below.

She eased the cell from her pocket and hit speed dial for Coop. He didn't answer. "We need to check the units on the west side," she whispered.

Cal moved to the door. "Afraid you'd say something stupid like that."

"If she isn't there, then we've narrowed the search to the center penthouse, where the pros will rescue her. We have to wait until both lugnuts go for another load, then sprint past."

Cal nodded approval. "Good thing they don't know we're here."

In the next instant, the door crashed open.

Expensive mahogany splintered as bullets slammed into the window trim near Sydney's head. Several rounds struck glass and the giant panes shattered.

"Run, Cal." Sydney uncoiled and sprang toward Ice, ignoring his gun. She threw the banger off balance and his head snapped sideways while Cal escaped.

•

Cal hurdled feet first into a trash chute. He ricocheted off the sides of the nylon slide, skidding five floors before crashing to the ground atop a mound of cash spilling from overturned paint buckets. A half dozen recently released hostages helped him to his feet.

"I told you to hide behind the smokestack," Cal shouted as he massaged an aching right knee. "This place might explode." He followed their gaze to the pile of loot. "Okay, grab a fistful. Then run."

Cal limped around the building and located Coop at the command post.

Coop pointed at the shattered windows. "What happened up there?"

Cal bent over with his hands resting on sore knees. "They have her."

"Haley?"

Cal gulped air. "Anson. Ice. Sydney. Top floor."

"What about Haley?" Coop asked impatiently.

Cal shook his head. "We didn't find her yet. She's likely on five. That's where they shot at us." He held up two fingers. "The second time."

"Jeezus," Coop said.

"We sent all the hostages from the first four floors behind the stacks." Cal pointed toward the old utility building. "Didn't finish searching five before Ice shot at Syd. I bolted for the chutes." He continued talking fast while sucking short, shallow breaths. "Nate needs an ambulance."

"ems has him headed to musc."

"Send cops out back. Mercedes is there. Along with the cash."

"Cash?" Coop asked incredulously.

"Anson buried lots of money in the walls," Cal said. "Sydney tried to tell you. But you dissed her."

•

Sydney skittered to a stop as Ice leveled the pistol's barrel at her head. She knew he hadn't expected the bull rush, but now she'd lost her advantage. He bound her wrists and ankles with zip ties, then duct-taped her mouth and dragged Sydney into the center penthouse condo, where he tossed her next to Haley. The little girl lay on the bare floor, similarly bound.

"We need to leave," Anson said.

Ice pointed at the remaining buckets jammed between the studs. "What about the rest of the dough?"

"Leave it." Anson lit the fuse on a Molotov cocktail and tossed it into the gasoline-soaked hallway. "Lock and load. It's gonna be hot out there."

•

Coop was the first to spot smoke billowing from broken windows on the fifth floor's northeast end, adding to the urgency of rescuing his daughter. And find Sydney and anyone else trapped inside. Thankfully, the fire department had dropped lines at nearby hydrants.

Chief Sinclair elbowed the swat commander. "It's a fire situation now. Lay it out for me."

Coop flattened his mustache with his fingers. "Priorities are: rescue the hostages, apprehend Anson and any other suspects, and extinguish the fire."

"I agree," the fire chief said. "But we work them in concert. I want bunker gear for at least ten police officers." She spun to Dino. "Do your guys know how to use scbas?"

"Police teams are good to go," Dino said. "We use breathing apparatus for riot duty. But please teach us how to find our way out of the smoke."

"Simple," Coop said. "Follow the hose."

Chief Sinclair folded her arms. "Alright, I want four police search teams. Three RIT teams. Position the aerials, two each on the east and west sides. Assistant Chief Lowry is the Incident Commander. Battalion 3 will assist." She thumped Dino on the chest. "I want a clear four-block perimeter. No people, no cars, no rioters, no lookie-loos."

"What about me, Chief?" Coop squeezed his walkie so tight, he thought he'd break it.

"Stay here."

Coop Frisbeed a pile of blueprints across the command tent.

She held up her hand. "That's an order."

Coop rubbed his eye with a knuckle. "Your fire marshals told me they are afraid of losing people in there. Tall ceilings trap heat. Crappy visibility. Too many impediments to snag lines. Difficult for a rescue. Or survival."

"We'll find her," Chief Sinclair said confidently.

•

With her hands bound in front, Sydney easily ripped the duct tape from her face after Anson and Ice bolted from the condo. "Please don't scream," she whispered and gently removed the tape across Haley's mouth.

Sydney found a shard of glass on the floor and cut the plastic zip ties from her ankles, then freed Haley's wrists and ankles.

Haley sliced the plastic around Sydney's wrists. "Is Daddy here?"

Sydney moved to the door and cracked it open. Thick, black smoke filled the entire hallway, along with searing heat. She slammed the door closed. "I hope he's searching for you right now."

•

Coop paced between the command post's computer monitors with the nervous anxiety of a tweaker looking for a fix.

He'd modeled *cool* his entire career. Perpetual calm. Levelheaded. Steel nerves.

But this situation was different.

He tried to wrap his head around what was happening. Had the 843Z actually taken his daughter? Yes, he was certain his precious Haley was inside. Along with Sydney.

Dead? Alive? He wanted to bet on the latter, yet negative thoughts pummeled him from every direction. The result—a mixture of anticipation and brittle fear. Those two were stranded in a burning building, waiting on a firefighter to rescue them. Waiting for him to rescue them.

Coop flinched when a cop dropped his radio.

Yeah, this fire was very different.

This time, he had everything to lose.

Smoke continued to swell from broken windows as firefighters opened nozzles onto the blaze. Coop prayed every professional did their job, risking life and limb to save those trapped inside. He'd saved countless strangers despite infernos raging around him.

But this time was different.

This time, Haley needed saving from choking smoke and unbearable heat. His angelic daughter. His top priority. His whole world. She had every reason to expect he'd rescue her.

Instead, he brooded on the sidelines. As ordered. Playing the role of good little soldier.

He resumed pacing at monotonous lengths, unable to stop himself. Kinetic energy. Wound tight.

Time slipped away.

His judgment was off, and he doubted every decision he'd ever made.

Second-guessing was new to him and it strangled his energy.

Rules saved lives. And orders were the most sacrosanct of rules. Violating an order went against every fiber of Coop's being.

But what the hell was he doing—waiting for permission to save his own kid? No parent should ever be put in that position.

Coop wanted to kick himself for feeling stupid and ashamed. Screw it.

Bitter heat filled his cheeks as he poised to commit occupational hara-kiri.

He grabbed a helmet and covered the ground to the burning building's west side in long, angry strides.

Ignoring the chief would scuttle his career.

It didn't matter. Haley needed him. Now.

His mind ran free, grasping details he'd missed earlier when his narrow focus had blocked the important information he needed to process. Coop donned bunker gear as he climbed the stairwell, passing rescue teams tugging fire lines. In the smoky fourth-floor hallway, he chased a pair of shadows, locking on two men moving toward an open window.

Ice pivoted and squared in front of Coop.

From this angle, the gangbanger appeared thick, with shoulders spreading wider than a boulder. He also had a broken face, as if he were used to mixing it up with others who'd landed a flurry of punches over the years. Despite an imposing physique, Ice's SIG forced Coop into something crazy—even dumber than disobeying the chief.

Coop rushed forward, spurred by an inexplicable chemical reaction inside him.

Ice squeezed the trigger. Sound from an empty magazine changed the odds in Coop's favor. Coop slammed into Ice with his whole body. The gangster crashed backward and banged off the wall onto his butt. He burst off the floor, then barreled into Coop.

Coop landed hard on his left shoulder with a sickening crunch. He staggered to his feet, woozy and in pain. A pounding pulse in his ears drowned out all sound. Coop knew he only had one last gasp in this dogfight and it had to make Ice pay.

As Ice neared the window, he took his eyes off Coop for a split second. That was all Coop needed.

Coop balled his right fist and belted the gangster with all the strength he could muster. Ice's jaw jacked, and his head snapped sideways. Coop shoved him out the window into a waste chute, feeling a little disappointed he hadn't inflicted more damage.

From the corner of his eye, Coop spotted Anson bolting across the hallway. Coop dragged himself forward, clutching his throbbing left shoulder. Not exactly what could be defined as hot pursuit. But he eventually cornered Anson cowering against the wall, hands up.

Coop's insides boiled. "I'm about to ruin your day. Where's my daughter?"

Anson affixed a smarmy smile and lurched for Coop, flattening him faster than a guy sporting a blubber-filled waistline should. Flat tire—that's what the meatheads called it.

Ordinarily, Coop would've been quicker and more agile. But he was nursing a possible broken collarbone and concussion.

No time to split hairs. The fat real estate developer was never gonna get the better of him.

Coop twisted away and scrambled to his feet, even more wobbly than when Ice had dropped him. Anson came at him again. This time, Coop raised his knee and caught him in the crotch. Anson crashed to his knees and let out a high-pitched squeal.

Coop dove atop Anson and raised his fist in the air, ready to drive into the mogul. "Where's Haley?"

Anson pushed Coop away. "I don't have her." He windmilled his arms, meekly glancing a few blows off Coop. Then he clambered onto Coop's back and managed to get an arm around Coop's neck in a chokehold. Anson's breath was hot against Coop's neck. He arched and lifted Coop off the ground.

Coop wriggled his feet back under him, then thrust backward.

Both men rammed into the wall. Coop's body crushed into Anson's chest, and when the mogul's grip loosened, he spun, then punched Anson so hard and fast his hands blurred. He landed several good blows in Anson's solar plexus.

Air blasted from Anson's lungs. Then Coop swung a wicked right hook into Anson's ribs—the kind meant to break bones. Anson toppled like a bowling pin.

Anger and despair burbled inside Coop as he grabbed Anson's hair, then ripped at his eyes and ears. He smashed the guy's face into the floor. Twice. Blood shot from Anson's nose. Snot and spit flung everywhere.

Coop jerked Anson upright, gripping the guy's shirt in his powerful good hand. He slammed Anson against the window frame, then pressed his forearm across Anson's throat. "Where's my daughter?"

Anson yelped. Bucking. Writhing.

Coop drove a fist into the pit of Anson's abdomen, doubling him over again. A right uppercut from a liquid underhand straightened Anson back out. "Where is she?" Anger roiled into a scream, and his voice grew hoarse. "Where's Haley?"

Anson made a tough-guy face, which was probably hard to do while he was spitting blood. Coop wondered how either of them found any strength to keep going.

Coop reared back to deliver a punishing knockout blow: a cross to the jaw.

But an explosive concussion pitched both men out the broken window. They jettisoned onto an outstretched aerial pumper's articulated boom.

Coop lay flat on his back, staring at clouds and gulping breaths when a desperate realization sank in. All he could think about was finding his daughter in the fire-bombed disaster. He twisted to his feet and spotted Anson dangling from the boom's basket by one hand.

Coop catapulted into the basket and grabbed Anson's arm. The man's wriggling caused his weakened grip to slacken. "For the last time, where's Haley? Tell me, or I'll let your sorry ass fall."

Blood oozed from Anson's mouth. He snorted like a mad dog, slinging snot everywhere. Barely clinging to the basket, Coop clenched his massive hands around Anson's wrist.

Anson's eyes moistened.

Pity? Fear? It didn't matter. Coop wanted to drop the scumbag.

"On five." Anson's voice sounded tremulous, though the ringing in Coop's ears could've affected his interpretation. Then Anson's lips curled into a hideous grin. "The explosion probably killed her."

Coop went numb. "Bye-bye, asshole. Booyah." He broke eye contact and let go of Anson's wrist.

No regrets.

No remorse for dropping the creep who'd snatched his kid.

Anson shrieked as he lost his grasp on the basket, unaware firefighters had rigged a net below him. Plus, the ladder had been winding inward, making his fall less than ten feet.

Coop spotted Detective Tate slam an elbow into Anson's chest, wrestle him into a pair of handcuffs, then dump him next to the already-restrained Ice.

Coop yelled to the ladder operator, "Back to the top."

The telescopic boom on the aerial fire truck ratcheted upward amid a flurry of cash. Singed hundred-dollar bills, remnants of Anson's ill-gotten gains, fluttered free from the building's obliterated north end.

Coop made entry through the west side and radioed Chief Sinclair. "Brody took both scumbags into custody. How bad is it inside?"

"I have two rapid intervention teams working the scene," the chief said.

"Did they find Haley and Sydney?"

52

The whole building juddered from the explosion, triggering the fifth floor's collapse. Sydney and Haley plummeted to the fourth floor.

Sydney came to rest on her side. Her torso and arms were smashed tight against spikes of exposed rebar, which narrowly missed impaling her. She wriggled her fingers and toes to make sure they had feeling. All essential body parts seemed in working order. Even so, she felt scared, lost, and perplexed—the *dim sum* platter of humiliation.

She adjusted her eyes to slashes of light leaking through the dust and rubble. "Haley? Where are you?"

Haley groaned. "Over here."

Sydney managed to lever onto her knees, knocking her head on whatever fractured building materials spanned overhead. "Are you hurt? Bleeding?" She crawled toward the sound of Haley's voice, feeling ahead for jagged and painful obstructions. When she neared Haley, Sydney managed to yank a wooden column from atop the little girl's arm before the debris pile could shift and snap a frail limb.

Haley whimpered. "I twisted my ankle when we crash-landed."

Her sob hit Sydney like a gut punch.

Sydney bowed her head as her mind spooled to Nate and Cal, before hunkering down to action. She examined the girl and found nothing out of place. Luckily, a V-shaped collapse pattern had trapped them in a small, habitable void alongside a sturdy exterior wall.

Fire burned around them and the heat intensified.

Sydney groped around, reluctant to disturb the large beams keeping fifth-floor remnants from crushing them. Then an idea sparked.

She gingerly pulled a slat of decorative barn wood from the rubble. Next, she tore a length of material from her blouse, tied the flap of fabric to the stick, then wedged it through a slit in the exterior wall.

"What are you doing?" Haley asked.

"Making a flag so the rescue teams can find us." Sydney fished her cell phone from her pocket. "I'm glad we cut the zip ties off. At least our hands are free—"

The debris pile quaked and a wooden beam teetered. Then a slab of concrete slid off the pile and smashed onto Sydney's left side, pinning her to the floor.

Haley shrieked.

Sydney knew her ribs were cracked. They might even be splintered, causing a variety of dodgy internal problems. "Find my phone. Call your dad. Tell him . . . Hurry." Her vision dimmed at the edges and it hurt to speak.

Hurry, Coop, she thought.

•

Haley patted the floor around Sydney until she located the cell phone. She poked in her dad's number and waited for him to answer.

One ring. Two. Then her father's voice came over the line. She swallowed hard to keep from bursting into tears.

"Syd?"

Daddy sounded frantic.

"Where are you?" he asked.

"Daddy," Haley sobbed.

"Twink? Is that you? Oh, thank goodness."

Haley thought she heard a hitch in his voice, but Daddy never cried. Not ever.

He asked, "You with Syd, Twink?"

"She's hurt, Daddy. I'm scared. We need you bad." Haley punched the speaker button and held the cell for Sydney.

"Was on . . . Fifth floor . . . Collapsed . . ." Sydney wheezed.

"Explosion . . . Trapped . . ."

"Any idea where?" Daddy asked.

"Side facing . . . river. Stuck flag . . . Wall hole. Light blue."

"Stay put." Then he disconnected.

Haley shoved the phone in her pocket so she didn't lose it if they tumbled around again. Sydney grimaced like Jimmy Nolan had when he broke his arm on the jungle gym during recess. His shirt and jeans had been covered in blood, and she'd seen a bone sticking right out of his arm.

Haley couldn't see any blood on Sydney, even though she looked like she was hurting really bad.

She was afraid to touch anything. "What can I do to help?"

Sydney made a face like it even hurt to smile. She repeated the same thing Daddy had told her. "Stay . . . put."

Where am I supposed to go? Grownups can be such dumb dweebs, Haley thought.

•

Coop radioed the fire chief with a request for exterior personnel to search for the small piece of blue fabric on a stick marking Sydney and Haley's location, presumably near the fourth floor. He worked his way to the south stairwell and joined Station 15's Rapid Intervention Team.

Radios crackled. "Spotted the blue strip. East side."

Smoke distorted the situation as Coop and the RIT picked their way through a giant pile of splintered timbers and twisted rebar.

Coop signaled the RIT captain. "We sure this floor is stable?"

The captain shook his head. "What choice do we have."

A huge mass of fallen timbers and broken concrete blocked the hallway.

Coop said, "Captain, put one of your men on the FLIR, one on the K12, another on the Sawzall. I'll use a Halligan. You rig the Stokes for transport and alert EMS about an injured adult female. Possible broken bones, internal bleeding, collapsed lung."

The captain moved his team into position. His engineman operated the FLIR, a forward-looking infrared camera used to detect thermal images, such as people. A pair of firefighters prepared the K12 and a Sawzall, cordless reciprocating saws capable of cutting through wood and rebar, and began attacking the tangled debris. Coop grabbed the forged steel Halligan tool, a combination fork and adz, and probed the debris heap, scraping away loose impediments. Coop also took responsibility for shoring the team's larger holes with timbers he confiscated from the hall.

They made slow, tedious progress coring and shoring newly created voids. The strenuous work rapidly depleted oxygen in their air packs, and they changed cans several times.

Radios chirped with an update. Firefighting teams had cleared the building to ensure nobody else but Sydney and Haley were trapped inside. "Fires are out. Two aerials positioned at blue flag."

"Roger. ATF One out." Coop tapped Syd's number on his cell phone.

His daughter answered on the second ring. "I can hear the chain saws getting closer, Daddy."

"I'm coming for you, Twink."

The RIT crew removed the last massive concrete slab between them and the stranded pair.

Coop pressed a palm to his heart and grinned at Haley through mangled rebar as jagged as a row of shark's teeth. She reached for Coop through the opening, and he gently tugged her into his arms. Though every body part strained, he couldn't feel it. Haley's rescue served as the best painkiller.

Maybe it took a moment like the one he'd found himself in. A golden opportunity to make everything right.

Coop said her name with a voice shaky and clogged with emotion. "Haley." He kissed his daughter. His dearest Haley.

•

Sydney felt a rush of happiness as she watched Coop envelope Haley with his large mitts. A hint of triumph played on his face, and he didn't let go, despite other firefighters attempting to pry her away. Every girl wanted hugs like those, no matter what their age. She knew, for a fact, you never outgrew a father's warm embrace.

Eventually, one firefighter managed to slip an oxygen mask over Haley's face, and Coop kissed her forehead. Another firefighter scooped her and headed downstairs.

Sydney wanted desperately to learn the status of Nate's gunshot wound. But she couldn't form the words to ask. And what about Cal? Had he injured himself diving out the window into the trash chute? Was he alive?

•

Coop reached through the opening and handed Sydney a mask attached by a long tube to an oxygen canister propped near his feet. He surveyed her precarious situation, then glanced heavenward and blew out a pent-up breath. He stared at her until he was certain she understood the danger they were in. "Fine mess you've gotten yourself into. Ready to leave?"

"Didn't teach . . . extri . . . cation . . . in J-school . . ." Sydney groaned, then sucked a gulp of air from the mask.

Coop's voice singsonged with wonky laughter. "No worries. I promise to get you out."

The crew managed to quickly widen the hole.

Coop signaled the captain with a suggestion on how to remove Sydney once he hoisted the rubble pinning her. They nodded in agreement.

Coop puffed himself up and wedged the Halligan under the concrete slab, then levered the bar with a ferocious surge. The slab didn't budge. His feeble left shoulder quivered from blinding pain.

He rubbed his eyes. They stung from sweat and tears. He shook out his good arm and wished he'd spent more time in the gym. Seemed like the only thing his back-in-the-day firefighting muscles were good for these days was prying shingles or breaking glass.

Coop gritted his teeth. "C'mon, I got this."

He sucked a huge gulp, then threw all his weight onto the Halligan and hoped to hell the steel bar didn't snap. As if that was possible.

The slab barely lifted.

Just enough for the captain to shinny Sydney free.

Coop let the concrete block drop and released the Halligan. He locked eyes with Sydney, then made a tiny fist pump. "I told you; lifesaving is kind of my thing."

"Now you're . . . showing . . . off," Sydney said. "By the way . . . dinner plans?"

He let out a slow grin, then helped ease her across the spiked rebar and into the Stokes basket.

Once they emerged outside, he bent over, hands on knees. He yanked off his mask and drew in fresh notes of jasmine-perfumed air. He gave Sydney a wink when paramedics ruled out a collapsed lung.

She fixated on him with those warm emerald eyes. A charge of electricity passed between them.

Sydney forced a weak smile. "Always more . . . Fragrant . . . After the rain."

53

Coop rested a weary elbow on the podium festooned with microphones and digital recorders from the mass of reporters who represented TV networks and newspapers up and down the East Coast.

Scarcely two hours following the successful extrication of Sydney, Haley, and nine firefighters and cops from the collapsed Tobacco Mill, the area in front of Charleston's Law Enforcement Center was abuzz with updates on the explosion. Money in the walls. Arrests. Reporters were also eager to learn about Nate and Cal's situation. The bullet had been successfully removed from Nate's arm. And Cal had been treated for minor abrasions and sprains from his plummet down the waste chute.

Haley kissed her mother's cheek and moved to her dad's side. She gripped his hand as megawatt lights bathed their bruised and tired bodies.

A warm sensation washed over Coop and he feared he might squeeze Haley's tiny hand too tightly. "I love you, Twink," he whispered.

"Ditto," Haley said.

Coop knew she meant it. He returned his attention to the media and fielded his final question.

A reporter from the *Post and Courier* asked, "Please describe the equipment used to free everyone."

"We got lucky," Coop said. "Haley and Sydney were trapped near an exterior window. The others were tangled in bent rebar and pinned under thick wood beams, metal studs, and cinderblock. RIT personnel used the K12, a great rebar cutter. And Sawzalls for cutting everything else. The Halligan bar is the best tool for

333

forcible entry and prying. And they used a variety of shoring materials to stabilize rickety spaces during the rescue." He rubbed his forehead. "Thank you for coming. This remains an open criminal investigation."

Chief Sinclair moved to the podium as Coop retreated inside with his daughter and ex-wife.

Sydney stood alongside Cal near the interrogation rooms. "Dino stalled as long as possible waiting for you."

"You ready for this?" Coop asked.

She placed a hand over her cracked ribs. "Taking down corrupt dirtbags—that's my thing."

Haley enveloped Coop. "Daddy, you came for me. Like you promised." She didn't let go or try to push away. "I'm sorry I gave you a hard time about your job."

Coop brimmed with pride. Was this the same kid who had enjoyed berating him time and again? Now, she nibbled his cheek with out-of-control kisses like a newborn bird, while professing he was the world's greatest father.

He said, "I'm so happy you're safe. I was scared—"

Haley laid a finger on his lips. "What about Lamar? He's in big trouble, right? Any chance you can fix it for him?"

"I don't know."

"Remember, he did try to protect me."

Coop eyed Cassie. Despite Haley finally taking a ride aboard the Coop bandwagon, his ex-wife would never be his cheerleader. "I promised Haley a humongous wedge of chocolate cake for being so brave. How about you take her to Kaminsky's while I finish here?"

Haley pooched her lips and twirled a curl of hair around her finger. "With ice cream, Mombo?"

•

Following the presser and mandatory examination by paramedics, Coop and Sydney were anxious to huddle with Dino in the observation room adjoining Anson's interrogation box. Multiple cameras and microphones were positioned to capture both suspect and interrogator from various angles.

After the scumbag had signed the necessary paperwork, Anson told Detective Tate he would waive his rights to counsel and to remain silent.

Coop stiffened, soaking up every word as he glared at the man who'd nearly killed his baby girl.

Dino drew himself toward the agitated ATF agent. "You wait here. I'll score the confession."

"I'm good to go," Coop said with a sizzle, hoping Dino would back off.

"If you go in there hot, the judge will hammer us."

Coop squeezed his good hand until his knuckles cracked.

Dino blew out a gush of air. "Great. Then I'm here for nothing. But if Anson walks because of your bull . . ."

Coop pushed open the door to the box and strutted to the table. He collapsed in the chair across from Anson and forced a smile. His face conveyed kindness that disguised his anger. "You've been busy."

Anson ran a finger around his collar. "Are you appealing to my *dark* side?"

Coop ignored the man's irritating ritual.

"What about Boyd?" Anson asked.

"What about him?"

"Tell me how you think he ties in."

Coop cocked his head and opted to jab his quarry's ego for an incriminating response. "Evidence suggests he was the big kahuna. You took orders from him."

Anson jumped up and growled. "I thought you were smarter. I don't work for Wallace. He works for me." Spittle oozed from his puffy mouth like a mangy dog. "It was my idea to acquire waterfront property by going scorched earth. I've been pulling Wallace's strings ever since . . ."

Coop clasped his hands behind his head. *Shitbirds and lollipops.*

Anson swabbed his mouth and plunked onto the chair. "Nicely played."

In this battle of wills, Anson had come unarmed.

Coop nodded sagely. "Scorched earth. Like Sherman's March to the Sea?"

"Everyone remembers the general had a little fire problem." Anson smirked, then leaned forward on his elbows. "See, Wallace only pretended to side with pro-preservationists. He played his part, collecting millions along the way. And he claimed credit for renovation successes after reluctantly agreeing to demolish damaged properties when nobody would okay the restoration. But he's a clichéd politician." Anson poked a finger in Coop's direction. "You should know he lit fires as a boy. Typical White Crusader all the way."

Coop imagined the scene. Boys playing with matches.

He erased the noise by focusing on his immediate task. "Tell me how things went down?"

"Between the White Crusaders and 843Z, we were reshaping this city," Anson said. "I brought the gang onboard for the dirty work."

"Your wife says you're a dangerous man. And you always get your way."

"Did she? That's rich coming from her."

"She also told one of my associates, Wallace, never knew you framed Nathan Sharpe back in the day. Makes me think you're lying about the mayor now."

"Oh? You gonna believe everything Sunny says?"

"She'll make a great witness against you—"

"She can't testify—spousal immunity."

"Then, how about this." Coop folded his arms. "My bureau combed through Wallace's financials with a high-powered magnifier. The guy is clean—never took so much as a gratis cup-a-joe." Coop let that sink in. He felt confident Sydney would enjoy vindicating the mayor—whom she'd supported through this whole debacle. Coop had one last piece of the riddle to nail down. "Who hired Lamar?"

"Ask D-Jazz. Not everything he did was copacetic."

"D-Jazz told me Falcon. That's you. Right?"

Anson stared at his hands. "If you say so."

"I need you to say it. Makes it legal."

Slowly, Anson raised his eyes to hold Coop's gaze. "You'll have to ask my attorney."

•

Coop met Sydney and Dino in the hallway separating Anson and Lamar's interrogation rooms.

"Something isn't right," Coop said.

Dino frowned. "Any actionable specifics?"

Coop stroked his mustache. "Send Anson's wife in. Keep an eye on them. I have a few more questions for Lamar."

Sydney said, "Let me join you. No need for you to intimidate the kid anymore."

"Ladybug, don't tell me you feel bad for that punk," Dino said.

She flipped a lock of hair over her shoulder. "C'mon, you both know my specialty is aggravating you guys. Besides, if there's more to his story, I'd like to hear it."

Dino winked. "Interfering must give you great satisfaction."

"Let me have this one. I need a win."

Coop nodded and pressed open the door.

Lamar was resting his head on folded arms cuffed to the table and still wearing a bloody T-shirt.

Sydney knocked her fist on the table. "A few more questions."

Lamar rubbed his nose and eyed her. "I did a dumb thing." A plaintive sob clogged his throat.

"Why?" she asked.

"Falcon came at me with cash. I doubted the money was clean.

But I didn't care. Said I only had to do a few favors every now and then. Sounded harmless—"

"Harmless favors? Are you kidding?" Sydney smacked a palm on the table. "Haven't you ever seen *The Godfather*?"

Coop glared at Lamar, trying to gauge his level of fear.

Off the charts.

Coop rested a hand on Lamar's arm. A small-gesture interrogation protocol defined as a wrong move, yet he felt it was the right play in this situation. "Police are gonna run you through the wringer—"

"I deserve it," Lamar said without a single flash of bravado.

"Probably, but you have rights." Coop turned to Lorraine. "Such as having your mom here because you are a minor."

Lamar didn't respond. He seemed to measure the crafty ATF agent.

Coop said, "Your prints are on a piece of glass I found at 1389 Kinkaid. It's all the solicitor needs to put you away."

In fact, the solicitor needed a whole lot more than a single piece of physical evidence to convict.

Coop pressed on. "Neighbors also caught you on video at the Kinkaid fire—despite you trying to erase an official task force file. That's evidence tampering. And a home security camera caught you at the dumpster fire on Lenwood." Coop opted to bombard Lamar with a combination of best guess, yet unsubstantiated claims. "So, I gotta ask, did you start the Kinkaid fire and kill those people?"

He caught himself, regretting the compound question. Dino was probably doubled over behind the glass for the boneheaded interrogation mistake.

Coop needed to rephrase so a good attorney didn't pick Lamar's confession apart. "We have you on multiple counts of arson."

"Except the Tip, I didn't do it," Lamar pleaded.

Sydney eyed Lorraine and mouthed *lawyer*.

Coop said, "Do the math, kid. You're the common denominator."

"Enough," Lorraine said. "I want to call an attorney for my son.

Lamar, no more talking, you hear."

Lamar shook his head. "What if I can solve a fire that's off your radar?"

Coop considered the offer. "You want to deal? With your mother's permission, I'll give you two minutes to prove you know something I don't." He was betting Lamar wouldn't take the fall for Falcon if he could find a way out. And if the kid cooperated, it'd go a long way to benefit his position.

Lamar turned to Sydney. "Remember when the mansion burned at Kiawah last year. Killed them two richie-rich businessmen from Georgia?"

Sydney said, "The final outcome was ruled accidental. Gas line rupture, I think."

"No way," Lamar said. "Falcon lit the fuse. Made me watch."

Coop keyed his cell phone and sent Bosco a text to research the Kiawah fire. "Tell me how you hooked up with Falcon?"

•

Lamar had been keeping score, and for the first time, he figured he'd pulled ahead of Falcon—a greedy scoundrel who destroyed everyone like an Ebola carrier. He prepared to hand Falcon over on the proverbial platter.

"Falcon told me Uncle Jamal lit the train station fire. And Mama committed insurance fraud. I agreed to set ten fires to protect her from jail." Lamar glanced at Mama, who couldn't hide her shock.

"Insurance fraud? That's why you did all this?" Coop asked with a disapproving scowl.

Lamar reached for his stomach as if his guts might literally spill out if he didn't hold them. "Falcon told me Mama accepted money she wasn't entitled to for our burnt house."

Lorraine reached for her son's hand. "Falcon played you, child."

Sydney said, "D-Jazz paid her as a part of his intimidation scam. He wanted her off the block before she ratted him out. He's the crook, not her. And now there's proof Hart Anson is the train station arsonist, not your Uncle Jamal. You should've come to me. I'd have set you straight."

Lamar hung his head. "I wanted to . . . I was the one who called you about Ice."

Coop's phone vibrated with Bosco's response. "The kid's right. St. John's Fire Department suspected arson at the Kiawah fire. But they didn't have evidence to support their hunch." He turned toward Lamar. "You have a high price to pay for your crimes. But the prosecutor might deal if you will confirm who Falcon is."

Lamar had hoped to feel exhilarated upon confessing. Instead, he was overcome by embarrassment and exhaustion. Agent Bellamy's threatening face. Sydney's accusatory glare. And Mama's shame.

He dipped his shoulders.

Mama wrung a tissue between her fingers. "Please, Lamar. Help yourself."

Lamar fidgeted as he worked up the nerve.

Sydney signaled a uniformed cop to uncuff Lamar from the table. "Here's an idea."

She escorted Lamar to the observation room across the hall and tossed him a lifeline. "Go ahead; Anson can't see you. Finger him for the record."

Lamar turned to Sydney. "Falcon is in that room alright. But I never once said Falcon is a dude."

54

Sydney and Coop waltzed into Anson's interrogation box, barely able to contain their excitement.

Hart stared into space, absently drumming his fingers on the metal table. Sunny chucked a nail file into her purse and tucked the purse under an arm. She seemed as clean and polished as the barrel of a gun, and equally deadly.

Sydney leaned against the wall opposite Sunny and clapped her hands. Applause caromed off the tiny room's cinderblock walls. "End of the road, Falcon."

Sunny froze.

The uniformed cop grabbed Hart by the arm and yanked him from the chair.

Sydney asked, "Why in the world did you marry such a scumbag, Sunny?"

"I swear I didn't know Hart—"

"Was the train station fire-setter? Or Falcon?" Sydney paused for dramatic effect. "At least you're batting five hundred."

"What's that supposed to mean?"

Sydney fixed her stare. "I think you know."

Sunny's gaze shifted toward Hart.

"Don't say anything," Hart implored. "They can't make you."

Sydney said, "We have all the corroboration we need, Mrs. Anson. Or should I call you Falcon?"

After a beat, a wry smile crossed Sunny's face. "Lamar? Bless his heart."

Hart shot a glower between Sunny and Sydney before his mouth puckered in confusion. Then, he spoke in a voice flooded with rage and wonder. "All this time I thought you were just an ignorant bitch."

After the cop hustled Hart away, Sunny said, "At times, I didn't know how I could ever maintain a sufficient reservoir of iciness toward him. I hated him from the instant I discovered his bad blood." She set her jaw but probably knew better than to scowl so the lines around her mouth and eyes didn't crease. She removed a compact from her purse and powdered her nose. "He's never been worthy of me. I'll never erase his stench."

"Interesting relationship," Sydney said.

Sunny tried to wither the reporter with a sideways glare. "I've suffered a rough couple of years."

"Why didn't you file for divorce?"

Sunny said nothing.

Sydney had a dozen questions to ask but couldn't decide where to start. "My heart goes out to you. You endured a lot of crap."

Sunny sat tight-lipped. Miserable. Desperate.

"What else can you tell us?" Sydney asked.

After a stony silence, Sunny said, "Such as?"

"So far, you haven't denied anything."

Sunny scrutinized Sydney with malicious ardor, then twisted an earring. She had an irritating habit of drawing attention to the expensive diamond studs. Her tell wasn't necessary. Astronauts on the space station could attest to their sparkle. She said, "My story is a good lie because I repeat it so often." She grinned at her apparent haughty candor, then pawed through her purse and pulled out a pack of cigarettes. "They all set fires. Hart set fires with Boyd. Boyd set fires for Hart's dad. Burning crosses. Lighting up churches. The whole thing was only a game to them. Until Hart discovered his daddy's dirty secret." She lit a cigarette, drew a long drag of nicotine, then studied the reporter through exhaled smoke. "For generations, white men from the big house have strayed into the housekeeper's room at night. Plenty of children came from those unions. Segregationist by day, philanderer by night."

Sydney wanted to nail down her confession but knew better

than to offer words or lead her. Sunny had to tell the story with her own details.

A smoke ring floated overhead. "When I learned Hart was responsible for the train station fire, I pressed him for details. In a drunken stupor, he told me about his father's affair. I decided right then I'd never have kids with a bad-blooded scoundrel. He wasn't about to stick me with a nappy-headed rug rat while he went off to prison. But as the years went by, we were convinced he'd gotten away with it. Nobody came for him. Then you went digging into the old fire. You said Nathan Sharpe received a raw deal and had science on his side. It meant vindication for him. And most certainly a conviction, along with dreadful gossip, for Hart."

"You had it comfortable," Sydney said. "Why didn't you run away once I closed in?"

Sunny rolled the cigarette between her fingers. "I know every cobblestoned street, hedge-lined avenue, and dark alley in Charleston's five square miles. In the highbrow enclaves, pastel antebellum homes are shaded from the raucous summer sun by majestic oaks. Even the seedier sections are permeated with uplifting notes of camelia and magnolia. Yet beyond the crinkle of swaying palmettos and sublime bursts of pink and white oleanders rest the ugly reminders of life's tender mercies. An earthquake. A nasty hurricane. And a deadly mass shooting."

Sydney allowed Sunny her soliloquy. Coop gave Sydney a supportive wink.

Sunny was unrelenting. "My life's work became burning the city's bad spots and erecting great buildings in their places. The first blaze destroyed a cemetery garden that had occupied the same stretch of land for more than one hundred seventy years. A simple garden. The one place in town where colors mingled without concern." Sunny drew another long drag on her cigarette. "I can vividly recall each spring when the plot sprouted flowers and bushy shrubs atop weathered graves of slaves and their descendants. Perennial flora represented an unwavering optimism I never valued. Like so many Gullah folk tales I endured as a child. Steeped in convoluted metaphors, I rarely understood what those people were talking about. Though, on rare occasion, a heavy truth spun me off-kilter." She paused. "Nevertheless, I enjoy my history with a side of buried secrets. What about you?"

Sydney opened her arms and encouraged Sunny to continue.

"A couple of gang members caught Hart setting a fire one night about a year ago. They wanted a piece of the action, else they'd tell the police. He was supposed to erase them, but Hart is as greedy as he is stupid. He thought he'd create a way to earn more money and implicate the gang if anything surfaced. Then, word on the street spread fast. Falcon was taking credit for the fires. Hart believed D-Jazz was Falcon. D-Jazz thought Ice and Falcon were one and the same." Sunny blew out a ring of smoke and cackled. "The astonishment on Hart's face just now—priceless. He never knew I'd outsmarted him. I'm Falcon." She spoke with convincing fervor. Viciously pleased with her performance.

"So, you framed Hart?" Coop asked.

"Daddy was an honorable man to the bitter end. I swear he never knew Hart killed Mama or withheld evidence from Boyd Wallace that'd exonerate Nathan Sharpe. Knowing either of those things would've destroyed him." Sunny took another drag. "I'm not a monster. That's a better description for Hart because he killed my mama and besmirched my daddy's reputation. I simply needed to atone for my biggest mistake, marrying that awful man. Recently, I learned he canoodled with one of his own kind—" Sunny threw her head back and laughed. "That bad-blooded idiot is fodder for a Tennessee Williams tale. Sleeping with his own half-sister."

"Never happened," Sydney said. "I know because I spoke to Lantana. What do you know about the cash at the Tobacco Mill?"

"Hart siphoned that money. My money." Sunny ground out her cigarette with the heel of her designer boot. She shook her head. "I suffered his mixed race. But I will never tolerate a thief. He's nothing but a two-timing hustler hoping to climb over me. To build a name for himself." She lit another cigarette and blew a cloud of smoke. "No one uses Sunny Manning. No one."

55

Coop fumbled his tie tack.

Haley slipped the Maltese Cross from his hand and pinned it in place. "Hurry, Daddy. We're late."

Coop checked his watch. "Sydney said she'd pick us up at 5:30. It's 5:45. She's late, not us."

"Where do you think she's taking us?"

Coop grinned as the doorbell rang. "Said something about hot dogs and cracker jacks."

Haley flung open the front door. "RiverDogs."

Sydney's face brimmed with apology. Coop guessed it was due to her frenzied schedule until she removed his jar of singed baseball cards from a brown bag.

He frowned. "Where'd you—"

"Haley told me your story, so I sent these to a lab."

Coop stiffened. "Why?"

"It's what I do. I'm curious that way."

"I never—"

"Anyhow, the lab didn't find any evidence of ignitables." Sydney placed the jar on the coffee table and met his gaze. "I also researched a 1992 fire in Greenville. Scoured reports. Even phoned the city's old fire marshal. He's retired now but to my good fortune, he'd retained notes about the fire." Sydney recited facts obviously from memory. "A grocery store stood abandoned for over a year before the blaze. Investigators initially ruled it as an arson, maybe caused by kids playing with matches since they located a dead boy in the fruit cellar." She tilted her head to one side. "But you know the details."

Coop eyed the jar suspiciously. He'd never wanted the cards

analyzed. Afraid lab techs would discover his best friend, Rick, had doused the store with gasoline and set the place on fire—like he'd promised. And Rick died from that stupid juvenile prank because Coop hadn't stopped him.

Sydney continued. "The old fire marshal and you have a lot in common."

"He's my uncle. Mom named me after him." Coop retrieved the jar. "He told me he found Rick clutching these cards."

"There's more." Sydney's voice buzzed with excitement. "Your uncle, a consummate professional, considered the fire curious enough to build a full-size replica and recreate the specific conditions. He also interviewed more than thirty-seven people before reaching his expert conclusion."

Coop braced for it.

"Origin and cause. That's what you do, right?" Sydney didn't wait for a response. "Your uncle determined an electrical short in the coffee pot a squatter had used was the primary cause. Your young friend died from smoke inhalation instead of setting a fire. You might've discovered those details years ago. Though your Uncle Cooper told me you've never once asked about it."

Coop gulped. "Every time I stumble down memory lane, I hit a pothole and veer off course. I've tried to repay the world for Rick's death by sticking to the rules. Being a good firefighter and a solid investigator. Disobeying the chief's order at the Tobacco Mill . . ." He forcibly exhaled. "Hardest thing I've ever done."

"What's your penance?" Sydney asked.

"She says I owe her big." He shook his head and grinned. "Told me to think about the vacant fire marshal job in her department."

Haley beamed. "I'll come live with you, Daddy."

Coop scooped his daughter into his arms. "At least those findings about the Greenville fire are a relief. Your investigative ability is astonishing, Syd. You'd make a darned good cop."

"What? And forego my glamorous TV life? You're out of your

mind." She met his gaze. "At last, you can forgive yourself."

"Pot? Kettle?"

"Yeah, I can be—" Sydney scrunched her lips. "Sort of broken."

Coop rejected the notion she was the least bit breakable. "You don't have to pretend to be perfect."

She kissed his cheek. "Good thing. Perfection wears off."

Haley exchanged glances between her dad and Sydney. "Are we going to the baseball game? And if so, why does Daddy need to wear a tie?"

"Because he's throwing out the first pitch," Sydney said.

Haley squealed. "I'm going to eat three hot dogs."

Coop shook his head. "What about—"

"Oh, Daddy. No rules tonight."

"Whatever you say, Twink." Coop refused to jerk his daughter around anymore now that they were back on track. He cemented the new life lesson: confident rules were malleable on occasion. He turned to Sydney. "I think we work pretty well together. Even though you kept a lot from me." He waggled an accusatory finger.

"Name one thing," Sydney protested.

"Anson's bloody tissue. His money in the walls at the Tobacco Mill. The baseball card analysis."

"I said one thing," Sydney grinned. "Besides, it all worked out."

"In the future—"

"We have a future?"

"Of course." Coop fixed a wide smile, sharing Sydney's optimism. "At least, I hope."

He'd been too quick to blame her when Haley went missing and knew he needed to wrap his head around all of his shortcomings before he deserved sustained attention from a woman like her.

Sydney threw her arms around him and Haley. "C'mon, we're late.

They piled into her Thunderbird and detoured to Fleet Landing.

"Spoke with the judge today," Sydney said. "She told me Lantana and Nate can file a claim against the Ansons' fortune."

"How much is the city forking over for Nate's false imprisonment?" Coop asked.

"Wallace brokered the deal to pay him eighteen million dollars. Nate told me he's splitting it with Lantana and Lorraine. Wallace even apologized to them. Said he never realized Hart lit the fires. And he confirmed that he didn't know Hart withheld evidence in Nate's first trial. Lastly, Wallace added that he never sent the ghost memo to Anson."

Coop whistled long and low. "You believe him?"

Sydney nodded. "Nate agreed to forgo civil action against the former prosecutor. You know, I have a weak spot for Wallace. I believe he outgrew the bigotry that'd consumed him as a young man and truly renounced the White Crusaders. And he didn't suspect Anson of his myriad felonious misdeeds. He seems genuinely devastated by his prosecutorial errors and blamed it on a reprehensible lack of ability."

Coop smiled at Sydney, who smoldered with her own hidden strength. "I'm glad City Council voted Lantana in as the new mayor."

"What about Lamar?" Haley asked.

"Rob Noble is working a deal to keep him out of jail," Sydney said. "He's lucky he didn't hurt or kill anyone with his fires. Since he helped your dad, he might receive probation, perform community service, pay restitution."

Sydney pulled into a parking lot at the Knox Street projects. Ray-Ray's Nana met them on the sidewalk.

Coop reached into his pocket and removed a set of keys. "I promised I'd return your house. I'm glad I could keep that promise."

"Oh, my heavens," Nana said. "It's a miracle."

Sydney added, "And no more fires in Fleet Landing."

"What about you? Mr. Coop said the nasty bunch burned your house too."

"I'm fortunate to have plenty of friends who have offered me a place until I find something," Sydney said.

"Hope you stay in Fleet Landing. Kind of nice having someone like you integrate the hood." Nana threw her head back with a hearty laugh and dangled the keys. "Now I have a room for you too."

Coop passed Nana an envelope. "This should help you settle back in."

Nana's eyes widened, then she burst into tears when she spotted the check for fifty thousand dollars in reward money from the Arson Tip Line.

"Thank you for your vigilance," Coop said. "Your photo was invaluable in putting an end to Falcon's war on Fleet Landing."

Sydney threw her arms around Nana. "Would you like to join us? It's Rob Noble Night at RiverDog Stadium."

"No kidding," Nana said. "Who's Rob Noble?"

Sydney doubled over. "My pal, Rob, was the team's greatest catcher. But the guy couldn't hit a slider."

"Oh, that Rob Noble." Nana fanned herself with the envelope. "What's a slider?"

ACKNOWLEDGMENTS

Writing a novel is a turbulent journey filled with twists, turns, and unexpected joyous revelations, much like the mystery stories we love. Crafting this book would simply not have been possible without the support of many wonderful people.

First and foremost, I want to thank the brave women and men of the Charleston Fire Department, and specialists in the Fire Marshal Division, headed by Battalion Chief Michael Julazadeh, for their unwavering patience during this project. They are a boundless source of suggestions, and any technical errors or omissions herein are mine alone. They kept me going even when the plot seemed to unravel, and their reassurances became the foundation upon which this story is built.

To the reporters and producers at WCIV ABC News 4 in Charleston (past and present), I am indebted to your professionalism, advice, and humor in cultivating the quintessential TV newsroom. Also, hats off to the staff writers and editors of Charleston's *Post & Courier* who took me under their wing and not only taught me about journalism and ethics but relentlessly suggested I alter the employment medium for one of my main characters from broadcast—to the real world of print.

A heartfelt thank you to my content editor, Beth (Jaden) Terrell, whose keen eye and insightful feedback helped shape this story into what it is today. She managed to elicit more from me than I dreamed to write. Your dedication and expertise are invaluable. To Hannah, Emily, and the entire team from Books Forward and Books Fluent for bringing things all together. Special thanks to my resident chemist, Fred MacDonnell, PhD, for his expert advice and suggestions. And my talented voice actors, Paul Schmidt and Daryl Mayfield, who gave verve to these characters in audio format.

I am also deeply grateful to several law enforcement professionals, including Missy Ortiz, Patty Pletcher, and Rick Mahan, who generously shared their time and expertise, providing me with the knowledge and authenticity needed to develop realistic investigative scenes. I hope to capture more from your stories and anecdotes in future endeavors. And when I sought additional legitimacy, I looked no further than Lee Lofland's Writer's Police Academy and the amazing talent he amasses and annually shares with writers of all breeds. Those collective insights were instrumental in bringing this mystery to life. Furthermore, I appreciate Clay Stafford and his Killer Nashville conference for immeasurable encouragement and leadership.

Throughout this process, I was amazed at how collegial the writing community could be toward debut authors. I'd like to raise a toast to Robert Crais, Karin Slaughter, Jeffery Deaver, Janet Evanovich, Hank Phillippi Ryan, and James O. Born, whose award-winning and best-selling writing prowess is exceeded by their kindness. You may not remember me, but your simple acts of goodwill made indelible impressions on this fledgling writer.

A very special thanks to my closest groups—Linda, my family, and Michigan friends (shoutout to Jon and Ellen Thompson for all the right reasons); The *Nation*; and my Delaware contingent—for their camaraderie, food, and constructive criticism. Your honest (and often painful) critiques were offset by ringing enthusiasm in redefining the twists and turns of this tale. You always helped me see the story from new perspectives and made it stronger. And to Lara Falardeau (clickedbylara.com) for the author photo.

Lastly, to my readers, thank you for embarking on this journey with me. Your love for mystery and suspense is what drives me to write. I hope this story keeps you guessing until the very end.

9 781953 865878